Ron —

To the worst
we love!

Ken May 2011

Manifest West

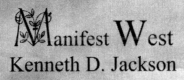

Manifest West
Kenneth D. Jackson

Treble Heart Books Publishing
Sierra Vista, Arizona

WhoooDoo Mysteries
A division of
Treble Heart Books
1284 Overlook Dr.
Sierra Vista, AZ 85635-5512
http://www.trebleheartbooks.com
Printed and Published in the U.S.A.
First Edition

ISBN: 978-1-936127-06-1   1-936127-06-7

Library of Congress Information

LCCN: 2009935584

Acknowledgements

The day after Christmas 2006, I drove home to Western Colorado to visit my ailing parents. I took my manuscript with me. For the next week we got together every afternoon in their bedroom where I read a few more chapters to them. One or the other invariably dozed off, but it never mattered to me. I kept reading until I got to the end.

Two months later my father suffered a hemorrhagic stroke. He died the next month.

The following year my mother had a stroke of her own. She survived, but suffered significant cognitive loss.

I don't come in contact with death and dementia on a daily basis, but I've dealt with a substantial amount of each over my 34 years practicing medicine. With my own parents it was a caustic reminder of my own mortality. I love the life they prepared me for. For the remainder of it I will cherish the opportunity I had to share with them the book I spent thirty years writing.

The greater part of *Manifest West* takes place on the Fort Apache Indian Reservation in Arizona. I spent the first five years of my career there amongst the White Mountain Apaches. They enriched my life by sharing their fascinating lives and fabulous homeland with me.

I would like to thank my publisher, Lee Emory, for having the faith to take a risk on an unknown writer. I am in her debt forever.

The same can be said of my editor Barbara Warren. I learned more from her in two months than I had in twenty years of reading "how to" books about writing a novel.

The following is an incomplete list of those who played a significant role in helping me bring *Manifest West* to life. Samuel Baseler, my ninth grade teacher who taught me all the English skills I'd ever need. The late Geneva Parker, my Apache nurse, who invited me into her world and gave me an intimate view of her people. Claudine Randazzo, Leigh Bennett, and Penny O'Hair for their editorial input. Chris Purslow, for introducing me to Claudine. Carl Shelton for his literary insights. Judith March for her faith. Tim and Joan Mueller for their enthusiasm. My brother Steve for his love. My step-daughter, Molly Johnson, for coming back into my life. Kevin Morgan, for being such a good friend. Judy Ehlers for being Judy. Karen Gutler, a wonderful human being whose kindness and support carried me along the way. Phyllis Shaw, Stacy McDaniel, Debra McComis, Sandi Terry, Dinah Moran, Catherine Timm, and all the others in my office who helped make my life in medicine so much more meaningful. A hundred or more of my patients who had the patience to put up with years of lame excuses of how I had yet to finish the book.

That leaves my dear friends, Doreen and Dick MacDonald, without whom *Manifest West* would have died an unpublished death. It was their encouragement and devotion to the project and to me that kept me from giving up. The two of them took on the task of studying the market, sending out innumerable queries, and traveling back and forth across the country in search of a fit for the book. With my daytime job I had neither time nor desire to do any of that. Their input into the content of the book was invaluable. I will always look upon *Manifest West* as a joint effort of the three of us.

Kenneth D. Jackson
Summer 2009
Kingman, Arizona

MANIFEST WEST is dedicated to my loving children, Jamie and Melissa, both kind and gentle citizens of this world.

Manifest West

A novel by
Dr. Kenneth D. Jackson

Prologue

The dead boy's body bounced up and down over the cantle of the saddle. Matted strands of blond hair fluttered out from under the Indian blanket in which he was wrapped. An untied shoestring snapped and darted about as burst after burst of wind jerked at the leather straps keeping the boy tied to the saddle. One gust stretched the straps taut, pulling the body up off the rump of the horse and holding it momentarily tethered in the air.

A shaft of sunlight pierced the cloud cover and spotlighted Bronco Dazen astride his horse, warming his weathered face and highlighting the flecks of gray in his long black hair. In a moment the light was gone, extinguished by the storm stalking him. From the top of the embankment he stared down at the rust colored creek rushing beneath him. It ran shallow and clear most of the year but for the past six weeks the daily monsoon rains had hammered the Mogollon Rim, flooding the canyons to the south.

The mare had fought him ever since he'd lashed the body of the dead boy to the back of the saddle. She showed no interest in carrying either of them across the mess roiling below. She crow hopped back and forth. He popped the reins and swore at her in Apache. She tossed her head and reared. He kicked her in the ribs and drove her down the embankment and into the swollen stream. To keep from being swept away she redirected herself diagonally against the force of the current. She lunged across the creek and up the opposite side leaving behind a trail of divots the Tribal Police would have no trouble following.

Dazen paused at the top of the slope to make sure the dead boy was still secured to the saddle. Looking back across the creek he could see the coyote that had been shadowing them since midmorning. He pulled his rifle and hoisted it above his head. When the coyote saw the gun it dipped its tail and skittered away.

He turned west and pushed farther into Indian Country. Passing through a pristine stand of ponderosa he picked up a game trail that led him across a rock outcrop and down into an amphitheater. The floor of the natural arena was a quarter of a mile across. Far above it a collection of Mogollon dwellings clung to the cracks in the cliff.

Dazen forced the mare down the chute leading to the arena. She slid sideways before rasping to a stop on the edges of her metal shoes. After again checking the boy he directed the mare toward the lone pine tree at the far end of the amphitheater. The floor was a series of sandstone shelves and the crunch of her shoes echoed about the walls as she ground her way through drift after drift of busted rock.

Watching from the ancient ruins in the upper recesses of the red rock cliffs were the ghosts. The Mogollon were the original inhabitants of the region. They'd left the ghosts behind to watch over things when a decades-long drought had driven them to abandon their holdings and disperse deeper into the Southwest. The ghosts were engrossed with the dead white boy the horse and rider were carting across their land.

Before Dazen could reach the far side of the amphitheater the storm caught up with him. It poured in from the east and fired off a thunderbolt that split the top of the pine tree he had just passed beneath. The lightning flashed down the trunk and shredded the limbs on one side before grounding out in a cloud of ozone. A blast of wind took hold of the splintered limbs and flung them at him as he kicked his horse into a gallop.

A driving rain chased him up a spring-fed canyon to a cluster of ground level ruins plastered into an alcove. He found shelter in the doorway of an ancient three-story dwelling. At his feet lay a metate and a mano, stone kitchenware left behind by a colony of thirteenth century corn grinders. He looked inside. Nobody was home. No one had been for the past 700 years. Through a hole at the top of the decaying façade the light filtered in and illuminated a carpet of antediluvian dust. The carpet was sprinkled with polychromatic potsherds, the fragmented remains of a vanished race.

Dazen untied the dead boy from the back of the horse and crawled with him through the narrow opening in the dwelling. He unwrapped the blanket and curled up in the dust with his arms around him. He could feel his heart pounding, as if it were trying to pump life back into the body of the boy for whose death he felt responsible.

At first light he awoke to the sound of water trickling over rock. The sound was coming from a spring bubbling out of the base of the canyon wall. After filling his canteen he pulled his rifle from the scabbard and gathered up the boy. He carried him to the other end of the ruins where he came upon a large circular pit. Centuries of falling debris had taken out its ground level roof and left it chock-full of rock and mortar. The subterranean structure was a kiva, the religious and ceremonial meeting place for the Mogollon. It was also the site most sacred to Dazen.

He excavated a channel that ran east to west. Using the water from his canteen he washed the acrid smell out of the boy's hair. He rearranged his shredded clothes and tied tight the strings of his Converse tennis shoes. After wrapping the boy back up in the blanket Dazen laid his body in the kiva with his head facing east toward the land of the dead. He covered the grave, then sprinkled the site with a handful of the sacred pollen he poured from the buckskin pouch he carried on his belt.

He took up his rifle and shouldered it towards the rising sun. Before he could squeeze off the shot that would send the boy on his way the coyote darted out from the underbrush and took off down the streambed. Out of habit Dazen drew the animal into his sights. He held it there for a second before raising his rifle to the horizon and pulling the trigger. The blast rocketed down the canyon. As the echoes fused and faded into the red rock walls he wished the boy's spirit a safe journey home.

One

Backed all the way to the fire exit, the occupied gurneys crowded the ER corridor like airplanes on the tarmac. Dr. Michael Ganson threaded through them trying not to think how many more patients he'd have to find a place for by morning. The exit alarm hadn't worked for weeks. Although he was yet to have a single patient disappear, it wouldn't have surprised him to open up the back door and find a number of them rolling around on their gurneys in the parking lot.

The never-ending nights of fluorescent glare, suffocating heat and non-stop noise were enough to drive anyone nuts. Ganson had gotten into the habit of stepping out back for a few minutes whenever he could. There was nothing there except the sweltering heat radiating from the asphalt and the smell of rotting vegetables drifting across the alley from the China Cafe's dumpster but it gave him a break from the insanity inside. Most of the patients he treated were wards of the county welfare system. He had nothing against the indigent but it was all he could do to tell himself their sufferings weren't their fault and they weren't purposely showing up to make his life miserable.

Ganson's medical school's mission statement had been "to educate and train physicians to render quality care with compassion." The last four months of residency had rendered that statement irrelevant. He continued to do all he could to care for his patients but somewhere along the way he'd begun to believe it was of little matter. Those who died were going to do so in spite of his efforts. Those who survived would be back. The voice inside him kept telling him that wasn't the way things were supposed to be but he no longer listened to it.

Halfway down the hall Ganson stopped in front of the room reserved for psychiatric consultations. The door was ajar. Coming from within was a refrain of howling chants and metallic thumps. The racket had been reverberating through the hospital for over an hour and Ganson had received orders from upstairs to do something about it. He stuck his head through the door and found the young Indian woman sitting on the edge of a worn-out couch. With her arms raised above her head, her straight black hair swished to and fro as she swayed back and forth. When she saw Ganson she stopped and stared at him over the raised ridges of her Athapaskan cheeks.

Dr. Luther Shock was sitting beside her. The psychiatrist had a metal trashcan wedged upside-down between his legs and he was banging on it with a rubber reflex hammer. His body was bent forward and his head was bobbing to the beat. He didn't notice Ganson until the Indian woman stopped chanting and sagged back into the couch. When Shock looked up, his face was flushed red and the sweat was dribbling from his goatee like lacquer from a paintbrush.

"Can I help you?" the psychiatrist asked.

Ganson didn't answer for a moment as he wondered which of the two performers was most in need of therapy. "I'm sorry to interrupt but I need to have a few words with you."

"Can't it wait?" Shock asked.

"This will only take a minute," Ganson replied.

Shock whispered something to the woman as he dropped the rubber hammer into the pocket of the corduroy jacket he was wearing. He followed Ganson through the gurneys and into an unoccupied exam room. "What do you want?" he asked after Ganson closed the door.

"I'm truly sorry," Ganson said, "but for the sake of everyone in this place I was wondering if you'd consider wrapping things up for the night."

"You can't be serious," Shock said.

"It's been a long shift."

"It's going to be a lot longer if I'm not allowed to give my patient the care she deserves."

"Dr Shock, I don't mean to be insensitive to her needs or disrespectful of your methods but the noise the two of you are generating is driving the rest of us crazy. Even the patients are complaining."

"Would you rather my patient revert to the way she was before I got here?"

"I'd rather you either commit her or send her back out to wherever she came from."

"You do your job and let me do mine," Shock said as he walked out of the room.

"You could at least keep the door closed," Ganson suggested as he followed the psychiatrist down the hall.

"It's hot in there."

"Have you thought about taking off your jacket?"

Shock gave him a half wave but didn't answer as he disappeared into the consultation room. He reappeared a second later and took off toward the back exit. When Ganson looked inside the room and saw the Indian woman was no longer there he followed Shock out into the parking lot to help search for her.

"Are you happy now?" the psychiatrist asked Ganson after they were unable to find her anywhere on the grounds.

"Happy about what?" Ganson asked.

"About what happened to my patient."

"What are you talking about?"

"If you hadn't interrupted us she wouldn't have felt the need to run off."

"You're kidding, right?"

"Absolutely not."

"Whatever," Ganson said as they both reentered the hospital through the back exit.

"Who is your superior?" Shock asked.

"My chief resident is Dr. Helen Cassidy."

"I should have known," Shock said.

"Here's something else you should know," Ganson said. "Dr. Cassidy came down here about an hour ago. She got in my face and demanded I call security on you. It seems your drum work was rumbling through the ventilation ducts and into her operating suite. She told me to tell you the noise was distracting her and she was going to hold you personally responsible if anything went wrong with her cases."

"That bitch is crazy!" Shock yelled out as he turned and stomped toward the main entrance to the ER.

"Doctor," Ganson called after him, "would you like to be notified if your patient comes back in tonight?"

The psychiatrist stopped and turned back around. "I doubt she'll ever come back to this hospital again."

"I've seen her here before. I'm sure I'll see her again."

Ganson watched Shock walk out the same double doors the Indian woman had come through earlier that night. The Tucson police had found her in the middle of Miracle Mile looking like she'd had a seizure. In route to the hospital she woke up and started wailing. They brought her to the ER where she crawled into a corner and wailed even louder. Nurse Karen Hannigan wanted to fill her full of IV Valium. Before Ganson could get around to giving the order Shock showed up. He'd come to the hospital to consult on another patient and happened to hear the woman carrying on as he was passing through.

She'd come in the same way the previous month. Ganson remembered her not so much for her wailing as for the designer clothes and silver jewelry she was wearing. During her previous visit she'd settled down on her own before submissively leaving the ER in the company of an older white man wearing a western suit and a string tie.

In spite of how he'd responded to Shock, Ganson was upset at having lost the woman out the back door. He knew she wouldn't have gotten far if the alarm had been working but he felt responsible for everything that went on during his shift.

He stood at the sink and splashed his boyish face with water. After running his fingers through his collar-length brown hair he walked over to the nursing station where he stretched his near six-foot frame across the counter. He closed his eyes and concentrated on the sounds of the chirping monitors and wheezing ventilators. He'd listened to them nightly for the past four months. For some reason the noise they made gave him a feeling of security.

At three in the morning two policemen patrolling the park found the Indian woman passed out in the men's bathroom. She was lying face down on the concrete, blowing bubbles in a puddle of toilet water. The policemen scooped her up and whisked her across the street to the hospital. By the time they dragged her through the double doors and laid her out on the table she'd stopped breathing. Her native face was as white as the drugs she'd overdosed. Her hands were as blue as the Guess jeans she was wearing. She had the empty look of one whose soul had abandoned its body to board a celestial escape pod bound for a more peaceful place.

At Ganson's disposal were the wonders of western medicine. They included a cardiac defibrillator, a respiratory ventilator and a cart full of life support medications. None of them would be of any use if he couldn't quickly establish an airway for his patient. He grabbed the bag and mask hanging on the wall, elevated the woman's jaw and sealed the device over her face. He squeezed the oval shaped rubber bag but the air inside it went nowhere. He squeezed it harder. This time he blew out the seal he'd created between the mask and the woman's mouth and nose. He repositioned her head and tried again but he still couldn't force any air into her lungs.

He had no idea how long it had been since she'd drawn her last full breath but knew she was close to never drawing another. He jerked open the top drawer of the crash cart, grabbed a laryngoscope and snapped the curved blade of the scope into position. The tiny light at the tip flickered but stayed on. He positioned himself at the head of the table, leaned over and slid the blade into her mouth. He used it to push her tongue out of the way and advanced it down her throat until he could see her vocal cords. Like the rest of her they lay silent and still. He took the endotracheal tube Nurse Hannigan handed him and threaded it along the curvature of the metal blade and through the cords. Careful not to advance the plastic tube too deep he connected the bag to the other end and gave it another squeeze. This time the air rushed down the tube, expanding her chest. After allowing her lungs time to recoil and drive that breath back out he compressed the bag and delivered another.

Ganson had two interns working with him that night. While one watched over the rest of the patients in the ER the other took over the resuscitation of the Indian woman. Ganson ripped the silver button covers from her bile splattered silk shirt and dropped his stethoscope on her braless chest. He could hear the air blowing through her lungs. After making sure she had a pulse he drew up an amp of Narcan and flushed it down the endotracheal tube. The Narcan was a narcotic antagonist used to counteract the lethal effect of the drugs her pinpoint pupils told him she'd taken. By squirting it down the tube he could get it through her lungs and into her brain without having to wait for an IV.

The woman's main problem was that the drugs she'd ingested had overrun her brain and broken into her brainstem. Buried deep within the central nervous system, the brainstem was responsible for keeping her vital systems up and running. The longer it remained under attack, the less likely her chances of surviving. Her chest continued to rise and fall with each assisted breath but she looked lifeless. Her tattooed eyelids weren't fluttering. Her pale lips weren't quivering. Her ring-laden fingers weren't twitching.

Ganson delivered a second dose of Narcan through the IV Hannigan started. He chased it with an amp of glucose. The woman didn't wake up but her pulse and blood pressure stabilized. He connected the ET tube to the ventilator and adjusted the settings before slipping a nasogastric tube through her nose and down into her stomach. He then drew four vials of blood out of her radial artery. While compressing the puncture site with a piece of gauze he listened to the somewhat reassuring sound of her cardiac monitor.

The months of stress-filled nights and sleep-deprived days had drained the joy from Ganson's heart, yet he continued to be amazed by the hearts of his patients. Some couldn't endure much but others refused to give up. Even as the organ systems around them were failing, their physiologic pacemakers continued to fire impulse after impulse at their embattled ventricles, urging them to keep contracting. He'd seen blips of activity register on the EKG monitor long after the code had been called and the patient pronounced dead. He'd once watched the heart of a dying newborn send out its agonal electrical impulses for over an hour.

As Ganson looked over his patient he noted all her jewelry. She was wearing multiple earrings in each ear, multiple bracelets on each wrist and a ring on every finger. A turquoise beaded choker encircled her neck. A tattoo of a war lance with a feathered shaft ran diagonally across the width of her abdomen. The tip of the lance lay just below her heart and the shaft looked as if it were balanced against her bellybutton. Beneath the lance her stomach crowded her designer jeans.

Hannigan pulled off the jeans, which along with the black lace panties were soaked. She inserted a Foley catheter into the woman's bladder while Ganson examined her tattooed abdomen. He thought he could feel a mass but wasn't sure.

"Would you mind sniffing those panties?" he asked Hannigan, who had finished with the Foley and was in the process of dropping the woman's wet clothes into a plastic bag.

"Be my guest," she said as she brought the bag over to him.

He pulled the panties out of the bag. After taking a whiff he tried to hand them to Hannigan. "Tell me what you smell," he said.

"No thanks," she replied.

Ganson dropped them back in the bag and again ran his hand across the woman's belly. "They smell salty, like amniotic fluid."

"She's pregnant?" she asked.

"Let's give a listen," he answered. "Whatever happened to that new Doppler we had around here?"

"It disappeared when the OBs pulled out."

"What kind of hospital is this," Ganson said, more to himself than to Hannigan. "Didn't anyone in administration take into account the possibility that we might still have to treat a pregnant patient in this hospital from time to time?"

"How about this?" Hannigan asked as she handed him an arterial Doppler she found in the bottom drawer of the crash cart.

He stuck the stethoscope part of the Doppler in his ears and covered the tip of the probe with KY gel. He placed the probe against the woman's belly but heard nothing. Pushing the probe deeper he heard the flow of blood. He counted seventeen beats in ten seconds. That calculated out to one hundred and two beats per minute, the same rate as the one registering on the woman's cardiac monitor.

"Do you hear a baby in there?" Hannigan asked in a

voice loud enough for him to hear over the pulsating sounds coming through his earpieces.

Ganson shook his head no as he continued to listen. He was pretty sure the swish he was hearing was the sound of blood pushing through a placenta. The rate would be the same as the mother's. The rate of a healthy baby's heart would be considerably faster. He listened all across the woman's abdomen. The only other thing he could hear was static. It was as if he were trying to tune in a radio station that was no longer on the air.

He set down the Doppler and phoned the ICU at the Medical Center. He told the on-call resident he'd be sending him a woman who was comatose from a drug overdose. He advised him the patient would need an OB-GYN consult for evaluation of a possible fetal demise.

Ganson looked at the clock and made note of the time. Depending on whatever else was going on in the city that night it could take anywhere from ten minutes to two hours to get an ambulance. The less critical patients had been lying in the hallway half the night waiting for one. As his comatose patient lay in wait of hers, Ganson studied the results of her blood gases. He adjusted the settings on the ventilator the respiratory therapist had wheeled in and placed a drape across the woman's legs.

He was toweling the gel off her belly when he felt what he

thought was a tap. He pressed the tips of his fingers deep into her skin but didn't feel it again. He picked up the Doppler, stuck the earpieces back in his ears and reapplied the probe. There was again only static. He pushed deeper and listened longer. Just as he was about to give up and turn it off he picked up a cadence of muffled beats. At 60 per minute the beats were like a distress signal from a sinking ship.

Ganson grabbed a glove, lubricated it with KY and did a pelvic exam. He inserted his index and middle fingers into the woman's vagina and through her partially dilated cervix but felt nothing. He was getting ready to withdraw them when something brushed across his fingertips. It was the miniature hand of a baby. He had no way of knowing if the baby was old enough to survive outside its mother but judging from its heart rate it was going to die if it stayed inside her much longer. After instructing Hannigan to radio an emergency plea for an ambulance he grabbed the house phone and dialed the OR. Seven rings later circulating nurse Sylvia Estrada answered.

"Can I help you?" she asked.

"This is Dr. Ganson. I need to speak with Dr. Cassidy right away."

"I'm sorry, Dr. Ganson, but she is in the middle of a case. Can I take a message?"

"This can't wait, Sylvia. Will you please take the phone to her?"

"You know how she is, Dr. Ganson. If I go in there she's going to start cursing me and—"

"Sylvia," Ganson interrupted.

"Yes."

"What case is she on?"

"The ruptured appendix you sent us."

"Who's with her?"

"A third year resident and two medical students."

"Who's the resident?"

"Dr. Watts."

"Sylvia, I have an emergency down here and I need you to take the phone and put it up to Dr. Cassidy's ear. She won't even have to break scrub." There was silence on the other end of the line. "Sylvia, are you there?"

"I'm sorry, Doctor Ganson, but Dr. Helen has told me never to interrupt her during a case. I did it once and she cursed me out and told me it didn't matter who wanted to talk to her during surgery. She said there was only one of her and she could only take care of one emergency at a time."

"Didn't that make you feel better?" Ganson asked.

"That she can only take care of one emergency at a time?" Sylvia asked in a surprised voice.

"No, that there is only one of her."

A burst of laughter came from the other end of the line. "If you can hold on for a minute I'll see what I can do."

"Thank you, Sylvia. I'd come up there and face her myself but I can't leave here right now."

Through the phone Ganson heard Sylvia enter the OR suite and tell Cassidy about the call. He next heard Cassidy spew out a flood of profanity, consisting mostly of different verb forms of the word fuck. To Sylvia's credit she persisted until Cassidy finally let her put the phone up to her ear.

"Let me guess," Helen Cassidy said. "You've called to give me an update on that lunatic, Luther Shock."

"I'm so sorry to interrupt you, Helen, but I have a woman down here who has overdosed. She's comatose. She's also pregnant and leaking amniotic fluid. The baby's heart rate is down in the—"

"Wait a minute," Cassidy interrupted. "Why are you telling me this?"

"I'm telling you this because I believe this baby is about to die."

"What do you expect me to do?"

"The woman is already intubated. I can get everything set up for you or Watts to run down here and do a stat C-section."

"Are you fucking insane?" she shrieked. "There hasn't been a baby delivered in this hospital for months and there's not going to be one delivered here tonight. Quit wasting my time and get that fucking druggie out of here on the next ambulance."

"Helen, if you'd just come down here you could set up and have the baby out in less than five—" Before he could finish he heard Cassidy yelling at Sylvia to get the fucking phone out of her face. After that it went dead.

The ETA of the ambulance was twenty minutes. It would take at least another twenty to get the woman across town to the Medical Center. While Ganson was adding up the time it would take the obstetrician to decide if he wanted to risk an operation the picture flashing through his mind was that of a newborn baby being delivered to the pathology lab floating face down in a bucket of formaldehyde.

"Karen, I'd like you to put together a surgery tray."

"You're not getting ready to do what I think you're getting ready to do, are you?" Hannigan asked.

"No," he answered. "After I get everything set up I'm going to call Cassidy back. I'm hoping she'll agree to at least let Watts come down here."

"And how do you plan on talking her into doing that?"

"By appealing to her sense of compassion."

"She doesn't have any," Hannigan said as she started dropping sterile instruments on the makeshift surgery tray. "Is there anything else you'd like?"

"How about someone to take care of the baby?" he asked.

"That would be good," she answered. "There's got to be a pediatrician in house. How about an anesthesiologist?"

"The only one in the hospital is in the OR," Ganson said gazing down at his comatose patient. "This woman looks to be in a deep enough sleep not to need any anesthesia." He dialed Sylvia and again asked to speak to Cassidy. He heard the circulating nurse put her hand over the receiver but heard nothing else until she came back on the line.

"She's refusing the phone."

"How about Dr. Watts?" he asked.

"I'm so sorry, Dr. Ganson," Sylvia answered. "I'm not going to repeat what Dr. Helen said to me but I can assure you neither one of those doctors is going to speak with you right now."

Ganson thanked her for trying before slamming down the receiver. He grabbed the Doppler and listened to the baby's heart rate. It had dropped below fifty beats a minute. "I give up," he said. "Let's get this stuff out of the way and get this woman ready for transport."

Karen Hannigan stared down at the woman's chest, which was rising and falling in response to the bellows in the ventilator. "I feel bad I wanted to give her Valium earlier," she said. "I know she shouldn't have done this to herself but nobody's baby deserves to die an uncontested death."

Ganson moved the surgery tray out of the way so he wouldn't be influenced by the seductive sterility of the stainless steel instruments.

Other than lancing a boil or excising a sebaceous cyst the closest he'd come to doing an operation was as a first assist. As he leaned against the table waiting for the ambulance the voice inside him told him to pick up the scalpel and do the case himself. It pointed out how well he knew the anatomy and how easy the operation would be to perform.

Ganson could feel the sweat soaking through his scrubs. It gave off the pungent scent he'd smelled in surgeons struggling in the OR to salvage cases they'd screwed up. The Mexican farm hand who'd worked for his family had once told him how a horse could smell fear in a man. Ganson was certain that was the scent pouring out of his armpits. He knew if he operated on the woman he'd be killing his career. It wouldn't matter whether he saved anyone or not.

He stepped back from the table and placed the Doppler back on the crash cart. A moment later the pediatrician rolled into the room with a newborn isolette and a suitcase full of resuscitation equipment.

"Sorry I didn't get down quicker," the pediatrician apologized. "It's been a while since we've had a birth in this hospital. I had to do some scrambling to find all the stuff but it will just take me a few seconds to get set up.

"Thanks for coming," Ganson said, "but you don't need to unpack."

"Why not?" the pediatrician asked.

"We're going to transfer the mother to the Medical Center."

"Is the baby okay?"

"Not really."

"Is it still alive?"

"Last time I listened it was."

"What are we waiting for?"

"I can't get anyone to come down here and do the case."

"Why not?"

"Dr. Cassidy insists that since it's an obstetrical case it needs to be done by an obstetrician at the Medical Center."

"She knows it's an emergency?"

"Life and death."

"And she still instructed you to ship the woman out?"

"She was quite adamant about it."

"That's a shame," the pediatrician said. "Isn't there anyone else here that can do this?"

The voice inside Ganson screamed at him to save the baby. He splashed the woman's belly with Betadine antiseptic, put on a pair of sterile size 7 1/2 gloves and picked up a scalpel. Without hesitating he buried the knife blade right below the woman's bellybutton and dragged it down toward her pubic bone. The woman jackknifed up off the table and took a bite out of the ET tube. The tubing disconnected from the ventilator and slapped Ganson across the face. The scalpel flew out of his hand. It careened off the table and did a 360 on its way to the floor, where it stuck in the tile like an arrow.

The woman tried to cry out but all she could do was blow air out the disconnected end of the ET tube. She pawed at the tube with both hands. Before she was able to pull it out she let out a gasp and collapsed back onto the table in cardiac arrest. Ganson had to decide whether to stop the operation and code the mother or continue on and deliver the baby. He grabbed a second scalpel off the tray and split the layer of fascia that covered the woman's abdominal muscles. Hannigan helped hold things out of the way while he spread the muscles and cut into the woman's belly. Filling the lower half of the abdominal cavity was the uterus. He made a stab through the lower segment of it and used his index fingers to tear an opening through the muscle. He wedged his hand inside and grabbed hold of a pair of bony little legs. He pulled the baby girl out like he was pulling a bullfrog out of the backwaters of the San Pedro River. No bigger than a bullfrog, she came out purple and limp. After clamping and cutting the cord Ganson handed the newborn baby to the pediatrician, who resuscitated her right in the room before leaving with her on the ambulance to the Medical Center.

It took Ganson two minutes to get the baby delivered. For those two minutes the mother lay dying on the table. He pulled the defibrillator paddles off the crash cart and positioned them on her chest. He hit the switch to charge them. After telling everyone to stand clear he pushed the buttons that sent 360 joules of electricity through her lifeless body. The current arced through her heart but failed to shock it out of ventricular fibrillation. While Hannigan pushed an amp of epinephrine Ganson recharged the paddles. He was getting ready to discharge them a second time when Helen Cassidy and her two medical students burst into the room.

"What the fuck do you think you're doing?" she screamed as she rushed forward and grabbed Ganson by the front of his shirt.

"Helen," he responded in an even voice, "you need to let go of me and stand clear."

"If you don't put down those paddles and back away from this table I'm going to call security."

"Helen," he said with his thumbs positioned over the buttons, "I'm going to count to three. Unless you feel up to taking this current I suggest you back off. One."

"You are fucking insane."

"Two."

"Let go of those—"

"Three," he said as he dropped the paddles. He ripped Cassidy's hands from his shirt and shoved her out of the way. He reapplied the paddles. Before he could discharge them Cassidy made another run at him with her arms flailing. She would have crashed right into him if he hadn't reached out and stiff-armed her in the chest. The air went out of her with a groan. She buckled and stumbled backwards into the arms of the medical students, who half dragged, half carried her out of the room.

When Ganson delivered the second shock the woman converted to a normal sinus rhythm, but her heart was soon back in fibrillation. Over the next hour he pushed a dozen different drugs and delivered a dozen more shocks. He could never get her heart going again. When he finally called the code he asked everyone to leave. He covered the woman's body with a clean sheet and tried to straighten up the room.

The table was covered with blood. So was the floor beneath it. Surgical instruments lay everywhere. Ganson's feet crunched over the splintered glass from a broken IV bottle as he moved about the room picking up the instruments. The scalpel he'd dropped was still stuck in the floor at the head of the table, standing like a marker to a grave. The condition of the room reflected the fact that a life and death struggle had taken place. To someone outside the medical profession it would have been difficult to determine whether those involved had been trying to save the woman or kill her.

When Ganson walked out of the room a hospital security officer and two police officers were waiting to escort him off the property. With staff and patients looking on, the officers followed him through the double doors and across the parking lot to his truck. The sun was already up by the time he pulled into the driveway to his apartment. After making sure his cat had enough food and water for the day he curled up on the couch and wept.

Two

G anson entered the marble floored lobby to the Office of Medical Education and introduced himself to the receptionist, an attractive blond who was wearing way too much makeup. She told him the doctor was running late and asked if he'd like a cup of coffee. He declined and took a chair at the other end of the lobby.

While the receptionist fussed with her nails he gazed at the picture on the wall, a gold framed portrait of Dr. Frederick Nix, the man Ganson had been summoned to see. Nix served the dual role of Chief of Psychiatry and Director of the Medical Center's Continuing Education Program. Ganson had just come from a contentious meeting with Dr. Alexander Murphy, the Chief of the Department of Surgery, and he wasn't looking forward to another one with Nix.

It had been ten years since the last one. Ganson had never forgotten it. Nix had been Chairman of the Medical School Admissions Committee and Ganson had been a senior in college interviewing for a slot in the coming year's class. On a sunny Saturday in December Ganson met with Nix at the psychiatrist's office, a dreary place with drawn window shades, a black leather couch and half a dozen busts of Sigmund Freud stationed about the room.

Nix went on the attack before Ganson had a chance to get settled, wanting to know why he'd "cleaned up" for the interview. It took Ganson several seconds to figure out Nix was referring to the fact the picture on his admission packet showed him with shoulder length hair he was no longer wearing.

On the advice of his undergraduate advisor Ganson had cut his hair to fit the conservative image the school was noted for seeking in its applicants. Even though he was certain Nix already knew that, he couldn't bring himself to concede the point. Instead he offered that he'd gotten tired of wearing his hair so long. He sat there hoping to do better with Nix's next question. To his dismay the psychiatrist asked him the same question again. Ganson responded by mumbling something about taking responsibility for his appearance.

When Nix asked him the very same question a third time Ganson made the mistake of asking the psychiatrist why they were wasting so much time on such a meaningless point. Nix came up out of his chair like someone had shoved a Sigmund Freud bust up his ass. He didn't sit back down until after he'd informed Ganson that he was the one conducting the interview and that he would be the only one asking the questions.

Nix next went after the essay Ganson had written on why he wanted to become a doctor. Everyone applying to medical school was required to write one. Ganson figured his was about the same as every other one Nix had looked at that week. They were all full of the kind of altruistic bullshit a twenty-one year old would write about his desire to serve mankind by caring for the sick and needy.

It wasn't that Ganson didn't believe in the nobility of that cause but it wasn't that cause that had drawn him to seek a career in medicine. Like everyone else he was there competing to ascend to the top of the academic food chain. Kindness, compassion and a sense of service were all integral to the practice of medicine, but for most medical school applicants these were nothing more than feelings feigned to impress the admissions committee.

Nix spent the next hour ripping into Ganson. He asked him questions about subjects such as abortion and the right to die. He made sarcastic remarks about some of Ganson's answers while straight out laughing at others. Ganson did what he could to salvage the interview and convince Nix of his worthiness as a medical school candidate. Nix seemed far more interested in picking a fight than in learning anything about the way Ganson thought or felt. When the interview came to its merciful end Nix asked him if he felt shattered. Ganson had no answer for him.

He received his letter of rejection three days later. After finishing college he enrolled in the Peace Corps but never let go of his dream of becoming a physician. He reapplied to medical school two years later. Fortunately for him, Nix was no longer associated with the Admissions Committee. Ganson breezed through his interview and received a letter of acceptance the following week. Getting into medical school had taken the sting out of his earlier rejection but he had never forgotten how Nix had treated him.

Ganson turned away from Nix's portrait and closed his eyes. He pictured himself lying half submerged in the silt at the bottom of an icy pond. He could look up and see life swimming about in the waters above him but he had neither the desire nor the energy to join it. He dozed off and didn't wake up until the receptionist touched him on the shoulder and told him Dr. Nix was ready to meet with him.

"Where's your attorney?" Nix asked as he motioned for Ganson to take a seat.

"I didn't bring him," Ganson bluffed. He hadn't even consulted a lawyer.

"The last thing I said in the letter I sent you was that it would be in your best interest to have legal counsel here today."

Ganson nodded but didn't respond.

"Son, I'd like to know what you thought gave you the right to try to destroy the reputation of our residency program."

"I don't know what you mean, sir," Ganson said.

"You know exactly what I mean."

"I'm afraid I don't."

"Are you trying to tell me that stunt you pulled in the ER wasn't cooked up in advance?"

"What are you talking about?"

"What I'm talking about is that I believe your feelings of inadequacy and inferiority drove you to show everyone what kind of a hero you could be. That's why you did what you did at County."

"That's crazy," Ganson said.

"Then tell me what you were thinking," Nix said.

"It all happened so fast I didn't have time to think about anything," Ganson retaliated.

"Dr. Murphy informed me that you were the one who set up the surgical tray."

"I had no idea I was going to do the surgery myself until I picked up the scalpel."

"When you try to defend yourself in court I guess you can claim you acted on instinct and intuition." Nix paused to take a sip of coffee from a cup with a picture of Sigmund Freud on it. "Why did you come here?" he asked.

"Because you sent me a registered letter."

"Don't get smart with me, son."

"I'm sorry, sir. I guess I don't understand what you're trying to ask me."

"Why did you leave the program the first time?" Nix asked.

"I wasn't sure what I wanted to do," Ganson admitted.

"Was the work too hard for you?"

"It wasn't what I expected."

"Why did you come back?"

"One of the reasons I left was that my father was ill. After he died I decided to give surgery another try."

"Give surgery another try," Nix repeated, not bothering to comment on the passing of Ganson's father. "According to Dr. Murphy your credentials for succeeding were marginal at best."

"If Dr. Murphy had such a negative read on me why did he reaccept me?"

"I believe that decision was based on the recommendation of Dr. Helen Cassidy."

Ganson couldn't imagine Cassidy recommending him for anything. They had once been close but that had been years ago. "I'd be interested in hearing her version of what went on that night."

Nix picked up the newspaper lying underneath Ganson's file. "This is the version you should be more interested in hearing."

The day after Ganson's patient Angela Miller died the front-page headline had read "Woman Wakes Up During Surgery."

Along with a picture of Ganson there was a lengthy article detailing a number of doctors in the state who were or had been in trouble with the Board of Medical Examiners. The board, or BOMEX as it was called, was responsible for hunting down and punishing all the apostate physicians in the state. The investigative reporter who had written the story ended it with a sarcastic suggestion that if Arizonans were ready to accept the substandard care of such poorly trained physicians the state could solve its physician shortage by training and certifying doctors through correspondence courses.

"And there's this gentleman," Nix said as he opened the newspaper to a full-page ad he held up and showed to Ganson. "Do you know him?"

The ad showed a man sitting atop a spotted horse. He looked like a younger version of the Marlboro man; only he didn't have a cigarette hanging out of his mouth. He was wearing a cowboy hat with matching slicker and had a self-assured look about him. The caption at the top read "David Dunbar, Malpractice Specialist, The New Sheriff in Town." At the bottom was a 1-800 number followed by the guarantee of a free consultation.

"Should I know him?" Ganson asked.

"If you don't, you will," Nix answered. "He's a malpractice lawyer who has made millions suing the doctors in this state. He's already contacted the County Hospital for the records on your case.

You'll be at the top of his list but there are a lot of other people who will be drawn into this debacle before he's done."

"That was never my intention," Ganson said recalling when the baby girl's tiny fingers had first brushed across his own. He hadn't realized it at the time but it was as if he'd entered into a handshake agreement to do all he could to save her.

"You should have thought about that when you were cooking up that insane scheme of yours."

"Sir, I've already told you that none of my actions were premeditated."

"You told me but I don't believe you," Nix said. "Let me tell you where we are with this. We've sent all the records to BOMEX. I also plan to send them a full report. I advised them you are under indefinite suspension. If the district attorney doesn't bring charges against you and the rest of these things work out in your favor I'd be open to recommending Dr. Murphy consider accepting you back into the program."

"Is that all?" Ganson asked, knowing he had about as much of a chance of Murphy inviting him back into the residency as he did of Nix inviting him over for dinner.

"You'll need to surrender your ID to my receptionist," Nix said as he notated something in Ganson's folder. "I can't believe you show so little remorse over what you've done. If I were in your position I'd be feeling pretty broken up by all this."

"How about shattered?" Ganson asked.

"That's a good way to describe it," Nix said looking up.

"You don't remember me, do you?"

"I seem to recall you once had a medical school admissions interview with me."

"Do you remember what you asked me at the end of that interview?"

"No, I don't."

"You asked me if I felt shattered."

Nix cracked a smile. "I'd have to say nothing's changed since then."

Ganson dropped his ID onto the receptionist's desk. As he was walking across the lobby the cork inside his head holding in a decade of bottled emotions blew. He turned around and stormed back into Nix's office.

"Sir," he said in as calm a voice as he could muster, "something has changed."

"What might that be?" Nix asked, not bothering to look up from his desk.

"There's something I'd like to say to you."

Nix dropped his pen on the desk in disgust. "I've heard more than enough from you already."

Ganson leaned over and placed his hands on Nix's desk. "I'm going to tell you anyway, you Freudian fuck."

Nix knocked over his coffee cup as he came out of his chair. "What gives you the idea you—"

"You might have once gotten away intimidating and humiliating me with all your psycho bullshit," Ganson interrupted, "but I now know you're just a pernicious prick."

Three

Ganson stood watching the weary mothers crowded outside the windows of the Medical Center's Neonatal ICU. The blinds had been drawn and the mothers had been asked to leave after one of their newborn children had crashed. None of them would be allowed back in until the crisis had been dealt with. The women's faces were filled with anguish; anguish for the newborn whose heart monitor was screaming in distress and anguish for the newborn's mother whose heart was racing in terror.

There was a sense of community amongst these women. Many of them had been together for weeks, holding vigil over their critically ill babies. A few traded watch with their husbands but most stayed day and night, leaving only to run to the bathroom or grab something to eat from the cafeteria. They understood their children were at the mercy of pathological processes they couldn't fully comprehend; yet they carried on as if their presence ensured a more favorable outcome. The mothers were bonded by the uncertain fate of their children. This bond bridged barriers that would have otherwise kept them at a distance. In the weeks they'd been together they'd shared more of themselves than at any other time in their lives. They rejoiced with those whose babies were getting better and wept with those whose babies weren't.

One mother not there was Angela Miller. Technically she had died during childbirth. The medical examiner had concluded her death was due to cardiac arrest. The autopsy report stated her toxicology screen was positive for both cocaine and heroin. What it couldn't say was to what degree either of those drugs contributed to her death.

Ganson spent his late nights lying awake in bed trying to convince himself the drugs would have killed Angela whether he'd operated on her or not. He'd never know for sure. When he returned to the County Hospital to dictate her death summary he saw on her record that she was a full-blooded Apache, born in Whiteriver, Arizona. Her home address, however, was in a neighborhood of gated golf course communities north of Tucson at the foot of the Santa Catalina Mountains. The next of kin were William and Lucille Miller. They lived at the same address.

Ganson suspected William Miller was the white man who had picked up Angela the first time she'd come to the County Hospital ER. Since her death Ganson had seen him on several occasions hanging around outside the Neonatal ICU. One time there was a sickly looking woman with him who Ganson assumed was Miller's wife, Lucille. Ganson wasn't sure Miller knew who he was but whenever he noticed him at the window Ganson got up and left the unit. He rarely saw Miller in the hospital after eight in the evening, so that's when he had started showing up to hold his own watch over Angela's baby.

After the staff opened the blinds and gave the all clear Ganson followed the women filing back inside. Before he got to the door he stopped at the sink to wash his hands and slip into one of the yellow gowns hanging from the wall. He smiled at the woman sitting at the desk as he walked by. She neither asked him to show her the ID he no longer had nor asked him to scribble his name in the logbook.

The inside of the ICU reminded Ganson of a scaled-down version of the Ford garage where he took his truck to be serviced. The unit was separated into bays, each of which was filled with one or more high-tech machines run by a personal attendant. Only instead of Mustangs, Broncos and F-250s, the bays were full of miniature babies, most of whom were fighting to survive the multitude of misfortunes that came with being born too early.

The miracle of creating and carrying life into the world had taken an unfathomable amount of time to evolve. Whereas the design was perfect, the process was not. The majority of babies born sailed through gestation, labor and delivery without incident. After being warmed and weighed they got to room in with their mothers. The less blessed babies ended up stuck full of tubes in the ICU. Suffering from a variety of congenital and gestational insults they lingered between life and death while the newborn specialists worked night and day to revitalize their twisted hearts and expand their stiffened lungs.

Every baby in the nursery was at risk but not all of them were in need of individual care. Positioned near the front of the unit were the jaundiced ones, there primarily to get a tan. They wore makeshift sunglasses to protect their eyes from the ultraviolet lights hanging above them. All they had to do was lie around waiting for the lights to bake the bilirubin out of their skin before it had a chance to precipitate in their brains. These babies weren't that sick and acted as if they knew they'd be going home shortly.

Grouped at the center of the unit were the critical newborns. The baby who had crashed earlier was alive but Ganson could tell by the looks on the faces of the staff that things weren't going well. He slipped by that bay and made his way to the isolette with the Indian blanket folded over the top. Inside the clear enclosure lay Cassie, the newborn daughter Angela Miller hadn't lived long enough to know she'd delivered. She weighed not much more than a pound and was hooked up to a ventilator cycling air in and out of her premature lungs. Her eyes were taped shut and a pink bow encircled the few strands of black hair sticking out the back of her otherwise shaved head. There was an ET tube running down her throat and a feeding tube running up her nose. Her wrist was wrapped in a splint that looked like a Popsicle stick. The needle connected to the IV tubing was taped to the back of her hand. An infusion pump was pushing a premixed solution of glucose and electrolytes into the network of delicate veins lying just beneath her transparent skin.

Ganson pulled a rocking chair up to the front of the isolette and sat down to look in on the life he'd given his best to save. He opened the port and slipped his hand inside. He touched the tips of her matchstick sized fingers, fingers that had once reached out to him from the depths of her uterine tomb. One of Angela's silver rings encircled Cassie's tiny wrist. Ganson had found the ring on the floor of the ER when he was cleaning up after Angela's death. He'd stuck it in his pocket and taken it home, only to forget about it until it fell out in the wash the following week. He'd intended to turn it in when he returned to County to clean out his locker but ended up bringing it to the unit and slipping it over Cassie's miniature hand.

He'd never been a parent and could only imagine how he'd feel if Cassie were his daughter. He came every night to sit next to her and carry on one-sided conversations in a voice soft enough for only her to hear. The conversations sometimes lasted for hours. He'd talk about whatever happened to be on his mind. Whenever his rambling came out in the form of a question he wouldn't hesitate to answer it himself. He was there as much out of fear as out of compassion. He was afraid that she could only hold on for so long and that if she gave up, so would he.

Ganson rocked back and forth to the rhythm of the ventilator. After an hour he fell asleep. He awoke when one of the nurses covered him with the woven blanket that had appeared the night before. Black and gray with an interconnecting pattern of hexagons surrounded by a zigzag border, the blanket had the scent of juniper.

He didn't know how it got there until he returned to the unit the following evening and came upon the Indians at the window. On them he could smell the juniper he'd smelled on the blanket. There were three, a short elderly couple and a taller young woman. The couple's faces were the texture of leather. The man was wearing jeans and a beaten up cowboy hat. His wife had on a lavender camp dress and a tattered green scarf. The two were holding hands and conversing in their native language with the young woman, who had her back to Ganson. She had on a blue blouse and khaki pants. He couldn't see her face until he passed by and looked at her reflection in the window. She looked so intriguing he tripped over his feet as he stumbled to a stop and turned back toward her.

"I don't mean to seem rude," he said in a voice loud enough to gain her attention, "but do you speak English?"

"Yes," she answered.

"Are you by any chance related to Cassie?"

The young woman said something to the old man, who nodded back at her. "If you're talking about the Apache baby in there, she's my niece."

"Are they related to her also?"

"They're her great grandparents."

"Have you been inside to see her?"

"She won't let us."

"Who won't let you?"

"The woman guarding the door."

"Did you tell her who you were?"

"We told her when we brought the blanket yesterday. She took the blanket but wouldn't let us in."

"Why not?"

"She said we weren't on the list."

"These are your grandparents?" Ganson asked.

"Yes," the woman answered.

"Ask them if they'd like to go in."

The young woman spoke to her grandparents in Apache. They said something back to her as they nodded their heads. "They'd like to as long as it doesn't get them in trouble."

"The hospital has some kind of rule about how many family members can be in the nursery at one time," Ganson explained, "but I'll see if I can't get all of you in together."

"Just take my grandparents."

"Are you sure?"

"If there's no problem I'll go in later."

Ganson motioned the elderly couple to follow him down the hall to the sink. After he got them to wash their hands and put on yellow gowns he led them to the door of the unit. A woman he had never seen before was at the desk.

"Where do you all think you're going?" she demanded.

"These people would like to go inside for a few minutes and see Cassie Miller. They're her great grandparents."

"Are they on the list?" she inquired.

"What list?" Ganson asked.

"Who are you?" she asked

"My name is Michael Ganson. I'm one of the residents here."

"Can I see your hospital ID?"

"I left it at home."

"I'm sorry but rules are rules. You can't come inside either unless—"

"Look lady. I've been inside the unit every night for the past month and nobody has ever asked me for my ID."

"Don't 'look lady' me," she snapped. "I've been out on medical leave for the past six weeks but I've worked this desk for the last seven years. I don't know if you are who you say you are or not but

I'm not going to let you in without proper ID. If those Indians aren't on the list they can't come in either."

"Have a heart, Jewel," Ganson said as he read the woman's name off her badge.

"What did you say your name was?" she asked as she started thumbing through the notebook lying in front of her on the desk.

"My name is Ganson, Dr. Michael Ganson."

"Well, Dr. Ganson, if you really want to go inside I suggest you go home and get your ID. As for these two," she said as she pointed an arthritic finger at the elderly couple, "they will not be allowed through these doors until someone adds their names to the patient visitor list."

"Who makes out that list?"

"That would be the parents."

"What if there are no parents?"

"Then it would be the legal guardians."

"Would that be the Millers?" Ganson asked.

"I'm not at liberty to give you that information," Jewel snorted.

"These people came all the way from Whiteriver. Why don't you just look the other way for a minute and let them slip inside so they can see their great granddaughter? You don't even have to let me in."

"Neither you, nor them," she said. "If you don't stop harassing me I'm going to have to call security."

"Harassing you," Ganson yelled. "What the hell are you talking about?"

"That does it," Jewel said as she reached over to pick up the phone.

Ganson was getting ready to rip the receiver out of her hand when the neonatologist taking care of Cassie came through the door. "What's going on here?" he asked.

"Thank God," Jewel said. "This fellow claims he's a doctor but he has no ID."

"Dr. Ganson, right?" the newborn specialist asked.

The neonatologist's name was Khan. Ganson had seen him attending to the newborns in the nursery, but the two had never spoken. Ganson didn't know if all the doctors at the Medical Center held him in the same disregard as Dr. Nix and Dr. Murphy did but whenever he came to the unit he did his best to be as inconspicuous as someone could be who carried on lengthy unilateral conversations with a four-week-old baby. Since he suspected the neonatologists and nurses knew who he was and what he'd done he went out of his way to stay out of theirs.

Ganson reached out and took hold of the Apache couple before they could back away from the doorway. "Sir, these are Cassie Miller's great grandparents. They came all the way down from the reservation to be with her but Jewel refuses to let them inside."

"Is that so, Jewel?" Khan asked.

"They're not on the list," she answered, "and rules are rules."

"I think we can bend those rules a little," Khan said.

"Well I never," Jewel said throwing up her hands. "Do you know I could lose my job over this?"

"I'll take full responsibility for Dr. Ganson and his guests," Khan said as he hit the button that unlocked the door to the unit.

When Ganson got to Cassie's isolette the first thing he noticed was that the blanket was gone. He pulled up a pair of rocking chairs and motioned for the elderly couple to each take a seat. He opened the port to the isolette and encouraged them to reach inside and touch their great grandchild. Their faces lit up as they took turns running their gnarled fingers up and down her bony little arms and across her sunken cheeks. The fact that she looked to be in such poor shape did nothing to dilute the joy they showed while they were with her.

Not wanting to risk another confrontation with Jewel Ganson remained with them and left the young Apache woman standing at the window. The elderly couple sat with Cassie until Dr. Khan came over and suggested Ganson get them out of there before Jewel changed her mind and called security on all of them. Khan was carrying the Indian blanket, which he handed to Ganson. He said he'd had to store it in his locker after Mr. Miller had gone to the hospital administrator to get it removed from Cassie's isolette.

Ganson led the Apaches past Jewel without incident. She glared at them but didn't say a word. He offered the young woman the blanket and explained why it was being returned. She accepted it but after a lengthy discussion in Apache with her grandparents she handed it back to Ganson.

"My grandparents thank you for what you did for them and they insist I tell you about Patrice."

"Who's Patrice?" Ganson asked.

"The baby's mother," she answered.

"I don't understand," he said.

The woman and her grandparents had another exchange in Apache before she resumed her conversation with Ganson. "Patrice is, excuse me, Patrice was my younger sister. Our mother was from Cibecue, on the Fort Apache Indian Reservation. She had us when she was very young and ended up giving both of us to the pastor at the Lutheran Mission in East Fork. He in turn adopted us off reservation to two different Anglo families."

"So the two of you didn't grow up together?"

"Patrice grew up here in Tucson. I grew up in Flagstaff. Our real mother died in a car accident in 1966. Shortly after that I moved back to the reservation to live with my grandparents. None of us heard a thing from Patrice until she showed up last fall at the Lutheran Mission. Her behavior was as foreign to us as the new name her adoptive parents had given her."

Ganson's attention shifted to the man coming down the hall. It was William Miller. He was dressed in his signature western suit and string tie. Ganson was tempted to say something to him about the blanket but didn't. After apologizing to the Apache woman he asked her to continue her story.

She smiled and started in again. "My grandparents opened up our home to her and even paid to have a medicine man from Cibecue named Bronco Dazen conduct a healing ceremony. She did okay until she started drinking, doing drugs and staying out all night. Right after New Year's she disappeared. We didn't hear another thing about her until the woman from the Mission called me at work last week to tell me Patrice had died giving birth. When Bronco Dazen found out about it he gave us this blanket to give to Patrice's baby for protection."

Ganson looked down at the blanket's complex patterns and thought about all the effort that had gone into weaving it. "I'd like to tell you I could take it back in there and place it next to Cassie," he explained. "If I did, it would be gone again by morning."

"I understand," she said, "but my grandparents believe she'd have a better chance if you held onto it. That way it can give its power to her through you."

Ganson shared none of the grandparents' beliefs of the power of the blanket but he took hold of it anyway. He watched as they and their granddaughter walked down the hallway and disappeared into the elevator. He wondered how receptive they'd have been to his keeping the blanket if they'd known the role he played in the death of Angela. He folded the blanket under his arm and headed toward the stairwell that would take him to the parking garage.

As he turned the corner he was drawn to the muffled sounds of a woman's sobs. They were coming from the room off the ICU that everyone referred to as the "Pod." None of the mothers still standing watch over their newborn babies had ever gone in there. They prayed to God they never would. The Pod was where the doomed babies went to die. They were taken there after their parents and doctors yielded to the reality that it was pointless to try to keep them alive any longer. Disconnected from all the machines and removed from all the onlookers, they were cradled in the arms of their brokenhearted parents and held long past the last gasp of their collapsed little lungs, long past the final beat of their failed little hearts and long past their despondent souls having left their little bodies and floated away from all the unanswered prayers.

Four

"Excuse me, I'm trying to find out how to get to this address," Ganson said as he stood in front of the secretary to the Psychiatry Department. "I've never heard of this place and have no idea how to get there."

"Let me see," the woman said in a surprised voice as she plucked the appointment slip out of his hand. "That's Suite Three at the South Campus."

"Where is the South Campus?"

"I believe it's somewhere south of here."

"I'm afraid that doesn't help me much."

"I apologize but I've never been there either."

"How do this doctor's patients know where to go?" Ganson asked.

"I guess he tells them," she said as she rummaged through a pile of folders in her desk drawer. "He rarely comes to this office."

"Isn't he affiliated with the department?" he asked.

"Yes, he is," she answered, "but I bet I haven't seen him five times in the past two years."

"Out of curiosity could you tell me approximately how many patients the department has sent to him in the past year?"

"You're only the second one I can remember," she answered.

"How did the other know how to get to his office?" Ganson asked.

The woman continued to sift through the folders and didn't answer until she pulled one of them out from the bottom of the drawer. "Ah-ha," she said as she opened it up and pulled out the map lying inside. "He dropped this off last winter, right after we'd sent him that other doc—" she stopped and cleared her throat. "I mean patient. Right after we'd sent him that other patient. Let me make you a copy," she said taking it to the Xerox machine. "It shouldn't be all that hard to find. It looks like it's just a little way down I-19."

On his way through town Ganson passed by two David Dunbar billboards. They both said the same thing as the newspaper ad. One of them had the picture of the malpractice lawyer on his horse, wearing his cowboy hat and slicker. The other had him sitting astride an Indian motorcycle, wearing shades and dressed in a suit. His phone number for a free consultation was 1-800-DOC-BSTR.

A little way down I-19 turned out to be almost half way to the Mexican border. In route Ganson started thinking about his friend Aaron Silver, the first year resident whose slot in the residency Ganson had filled after Silver dropped out of the program. Silver was blessed with a brilliant mind but suffered from manic-depressive disorder. He did a credible job until he unraveled one night in the OR. He'd been working all weekend holding retractors and cutting suture for Dr. Cassidy. He'd gotten little sleep and forgotten to take his prescribed medications. Cassidy had been all over him for months, never missing an opportunity to tell him how ill prepared and incompetent he was. On that particular night Silver took exception.

He asked her to give it a rest. When she didn't he came across the operating table and buried her face in what was oozing out of the surgical patient's ruptured colon. The anesthesiologist told Silver to let Cassidy up before she smothered to death. When Aaron didn't the anesthesiologist floored him with a karate chop to the neck.

The police came and carted Silver off to the county jail. After they released him on his own recognizance, Murphy sent him to Nix, who suspended him and reported him to BOMEX. When Silver's urine came back positive for amphetamines and pot the board gave him the choice of surrendering his license or shipping out for six months of finger painting and basket weaving at the physician rehab center in Atlanta. He agreed to go into treatment but walked out of the center a week later. Facing assault charges brought against him by Cassidy he moved out into the desert south of Tucson and went to work as a yardman at a retirement village in Green Valley. It was Silver who had suggested Ganson go see Luther Shock.

Ganson exited the freeway at Green Valley and turned southeast toward the Santa Rita Mountains. The pavement turned to gravel, then to dirt. He wound through miles of cactus-studded desert before entering a vast mesquite bosque. He was beginning to wonder how many prospective patients had given up and turned back when he braked down a steep wash, slid through a sharp left turn and came upon the gate to the South Campus. He slowed the truck and rattled over a worn-out cattle guard missing half its pipes. On each side of the gate lay the rusted remnants of a barbwire fence. Watching over the entrance were two aging saguaros. The giant cacti each had strands of Christmas ornaments dangling from their bird pecked arms.

The South Campus consisted of three Quonset huts. The half cylindrical steel structures paralleled each other in the middle of a crumbling asphalt lot. Driving through pothole after pothole Ganson bounced his truck past the first two buildings, each of which appeared deserted. He pulled up in front of the third building and parked next to a wooden sign that read "Department of Psychiatry." The only vehicles in the lot were a white Mercedes convertible and an orange Volkswagen van with a camper top. He walked up a shaded flagstone path that was lined with potted flowers. He pulled open the metal door that had "Suite Three" engraved on it.

Once inside he had to hesitate to allow his eyes to adjust to the diminished light. There was only one window in the waiting room and it was half blocked by an air conditioning unit laboring to keep the temperature in the low 80s. The walls were full of photographs of the West. A coffee table in the middle of the wooden floor was covered with hardbound picture books of Arizona and stacks of *Arizona Highways* magazines. There was an oak desk, a cloth covered couch and several well-worn chairs. Nobody was there. No receptionist. No patients. No doctor.

There was, however, a parrot guarding the closed door to the psychiatrist's inner office. The parrot, an African gray, was strutting back and forth on top of a wicker cage. The door to the cage was wired open and above it was a silver plaque with the name "Wallace" inscribed on it. When the bird saw Ganson it let out a squawk and flapped its wings.

Ganson ignored the bird and poured himself a cup of water from the bottled dispenser. Even though he hadn't counted on the South Campus being half way out in the middle of the Sonoran Desert he'd arrived with time to spare. He sat down on the couch and picked up a book entitled *Ghost Dancers: A Century of Apache Medicine Men*. On the jacket was a painting of a white wooden cross. It was decorated with a recurrent pattern of black zigzags and gray hexagons like the ones Ganson had seen on Cassie's blanket. He flipped to the back flap to read about the author, an anthropologist from the University of Arizona. The first section of the book was devoted to Geronimo, by far the most famous Apache medicine man. The chapter that caught Ganson's eye was about Noch-ay-del-klinne, a contemporary of Geronimo who had practiced in the village of Cibecue on the Fort Apache Indian Reservation.

Ganson began to read about how the Cibecue medicine man created his own Ghost Dance long before the Paiute version had spread across the northern plains and taken hold of the Sioux. Promoted as the way to return their fallen leaders from the dead and rid the white soldiers from their land, the dance was the desperate act of a spiritual leader trying to reverse the fortunes of his fallen race.

Ganson found Noch-ay-del-klinne's story fascinating but before he could get all the way through it he started to nod off. As he was falling asleep a voice spoke out to him. It said "God grant me the serenity to accept the things I cannot change, the courage to change the things I can and the wisdom to know the difference." It wasn't the voice inside Ganson but the voice of the African gray. From its new perch atop the water cooler the bird was parroting the "Serenity Prayer."

Ganson was about to engage it in conversation when the door to the inner office swung open and a smiling woman with a platinum hair-do appeared. Accompanying her was Dr. Shock, who was also smiling until he saw Ganson. After walking the woman out to her

Mercedes the psychiatrist returned and reentered his office without looking at or saying a word to either Ganson or the bird.

When he didn't reappear, Ganson got up and knocked on the door. There was no answer. He gave it a harder knock, causing the door to drift ajar. He called out to the psychiatrist and waited for a response. The only sound coming from inside the office was the shuddering of the ceiling fan. He pushed the door open and peered inside. Stuffed full of Indian décor, the room looked more like a cultural center than a psychiatrist's office. Blankets, baskets, pottery and crafts were everywhere. The walls were filled with photos and paintings of American Indians. Hanging above an oversized couch was a mobile with half a dozen dream catchers. Shock was sitting at his desk.

"I apologize for interrupting you," Ganson said.

"This is the second time you've barged in on me," Shock said, obviously still put off over what had happened between the two of them the night their patient had died in the ER.

"I thought you might have forgotten about me."

"I was hoping you'd go away."

"Didn't you know I had an appointment?"

"I knew someone was coming at eleven. I just didn't know it was you."

"Do you mind if I come in?"

"Why are you here?"

"For another opinion."

"On what?"

"Dr. Nix doesn't believe I'm fit for the medical profession."

Shock motioned for Ganson to take a seat on the couch. "I've known Frederick Nix for years. He's written several books on human sexuality. Most of the therapists in this part of the country hold him in the highest regard."

"He's an asshole," Ganson said.

Shock let out a laugh.

"How familiar are you with what happened that night in the ER after you left?" Ganson asked.

"I read about it in the paper."

"I have a date with BOMEX next week. With all the publicity I'm pretty sure they're going to crucify me."

"What is it you want from me?"

"I want you to treat me as well as you did Aaron Silver."

"I have no idea what you're talking about," Shock said through tightened lips.

"Yes, you do," Ganson said. "I've spoken with Aaron since he returned from Atlanta. He told me you'd helped him emotionally get through his ordeal with BOMEX."

Shock relaxed his face. "Even if that were the case it doesn't seem to have done a whole lot of good for his medical career. Someone said they'd seen him on a riding lawnmower in Green Valley."

"I spoke with Aaron last week," Ganson said. "He told me how much better he felt working out of doors. He recommended you to me. That was after I informed him of our little disagreement in the ER. He said you'd be open and honest."

Shock lit up a button of juniper incense. He leaned back and watched the ribbon of smoke rise and scatter in the draft of the overhead fan. "What is it you think I can do for you?"

"Officially, the Surgery Department and Dr. Nix have proclaimed their support of me. All they're really trying to do is feed me to BOMEX."

"Even if what you say is true, what do you expect me to do about it?"

"You can't do anything about it but I'd feel better having the opinion of another psychiatrist before going up against the board."

"What if I test you and come up with the same conclusions you expect to get from Dr. Nix?" Shock asked.

"If that's the case I'll go quietly," Ganson replied.

The psychiatrist took a moment to stare at the smoke filtering through the mobile of dream catchers. "I'd like to know something."

"What's that?"

"What was going on inside your head at that moment?"

"The moment I did the operation?"

"The moment you decided to do it."

"I can't tell you."

"You can't or you won't?" Shock asked.

"I can't tell you what was going on inside my head because I felt like I was somewhere outside my body at the time," Ganson answered honestly.

"I don't think that's going to wash well with BOMEX," Shock said with a reflective look on his face. "Did you tell Dr. Nix how you felt?"

"Are you kidding? If I would have told him he would have tried to commit me right then and there."

"Dr. Nix is a brilliant man. I can't believe he'd say such things about you if he didn't believe them to be true."

"Why don't you test me and find out for yourself?" Ganson suggested.

Shock tapped his pen on the pad of paper on his desk and scribbled some notes. "Tell me a little about your parents."

"I was pretty much raised by my father, who was a physician."

"What kind?"

"General practitioner."

"Were you close to him?"

"Extremely."

"How about your mother?"

"I felt close to her too, until she left."

"What happened to her?"

"When I was ten years old she and her friend Mimi packed up the station wagon and moved to San Francisco. I haven't seen her since."

Shock scribbled another note. "Have you ever used illicit drugs?"

"I smoked pot a few times when I was in college."

"How about since then?"

"No."

"Other drugs?"

"Like?"

"Like cocaine, heroin, amphetamines or psychedelics."

"No."

"Have you ever abused alcohol?"

"I don't believe so."

"But you do drink?"

"I used to drink about a six-pack a week. When I started working in the ER the six-pack in my refrigerator lasted four months. Right now I'm drinking three to four beers a night."

"Do you think that might be too many?" the psychiatrist asked.

"How many are too many?" Ganson asked.

"What do they do for you?" the psychiatrist asked.

"Not much," Ganson answered. "I get a little buzz that gives me a few minutes of freedom from the fear I might not be able to live the life I'd envisioned."

"Do you think you might be depressed?"

"Wouldn't you be?"

"Maybe you need to be on some medication?" Shock suggested.

"I'll get through this," Ganson responded.

Shock reached into his file cabinet and pulled out a folder. "There's a lengthy questionnaire inside here. It's a personality inventory developed for health care professionals. Take it to the waiting room and answer every question the best you can."

When Ganson walked out of Shock's inner office the African gray was back on top of its cage. Ganson sat down at the desk and was about to start in on the questionnaire when the parrot started in on him.

"My name is Wallace and I'm an alcoholic."

"Thanks for sharing," Ganson said.

"Did you know that if you don't drink you won't get drunk?" the bird continued.

When Ganson didn't answer, the bird started spitting out bits and pieces of Twelve Step jargon. Its favorite phrase was "trust God, clean house and help others." Ganson finally became so aggravated he told the bird to shut up. The African Gray retreated into its cage but continued to chatter.

Ganson did his best to ignore it while concentrating on getting through the lengthy questionnaire. It started with simple questions about family and childhood before progressing to more complex ones concerning attitudes and emotions. One page was devoted entirely to dreams. A great number of the questions dealt with the issues of addiction and low self-esteem, conditions prevalent in health care providers.

The phone never rang and no one entered the office while he was working on the questionnaire. Other than the Alcoholics Anonymous catch phrases from the parrot the only sound in the room was the air conditioner straining against the stifling heat. By the time he answered the last question the scent of juniper incense filtering out of Shock's office had given way to the smell of the smoldering asphalt radiating through the walls from the outside. The afternoon sun had baked the west side of the steel building to the point Ganson felt he was in a sweat lodge.

He reentered the inner office to find Shock asleep with his corduroy jacket folded across his chest. The psychiatrist's head was hanging over the back of his chair and his feet were propped up on the desktop. When Ganson called out his name Shock's head snapped forward and his feet slid off the desk. The psychiatrist stretched and yawned before asking for the folder, which he opened and perused while Ganson walked around the room taking in the Indian artwork. Shock spent half an hour slashing through Ganson's answers with a red Marks-a-Lot. When he finished he placed the questionnaire back in the folder and looked over at Ganson, who had taken a seat on the couch.

"As soon as I have time to review your answers in more depth I'll draft you a letter detailing my findings," he said.

"Is that it?" Ganson asked.

"That's it," Shock replied.

"Don't you have any other questions for me?"

"Don't you think you've answered enough questions for one day?"

"I thought there might be some others you'd like to ask."

"Just one. What happened to the little baby?"

"She's still in the Neonatal ICU."

"Most of those real early births end up with a lot of neurological problems, don't they?"

"Yes they do," Ganson replied.

"How does it look for her?" Shock asked.

"She has a good chance of going home."

"Home to where?"

"Her adoptive grandparents live here in Tucson."

"Let me guess," Shock said. "Her mother was adopted into an Anglo family convinced they could provide her with a better life than the one she was facing on the reservation."

"Something like that," Ganson answered.

"The mother never told me but I'm pretty sure she was full blooded Apache."

"She was. I met her sister and natural grandparents at the Neonatal ICU. They said she was originally from Cibecue, a little place on the Fort Apache Reservation."

"I know the place well," Shock said.

"You do?" Ganson asked.

"Before I went into psychiatry I spent five years as a General Medical Officer on that reservation. I was stationed in Whiteriver but made many trips to Cibecue to attend ceremonies put on by Bronco Dazen, a well-known medicine man."

"Angela's sister mentioned him to me."

"Earlier this summer he and his home town were all over the news."

"For what?"

"For the disappearance of a child."

"Is such an occurrence that unusual?"

"This one was a thirteen year old white boy. He and his mother were living on the reservation but they were originally from the

Mormon polygamist colony in Colorado City. The rumor was that the boy somehow got involved with Bronco Dazen and that the boy's disappearance was the result of an Apache ritual that got out of hand."

"I take it the boy hasn't been found."

"Not yet."

"Is Cibecue that dangerous a place?" Ganson asked.

"Cibecue is an isolated community on the west end of the reservation. It has a reputation for not taking to outsiders."

"I know very little about the Apaches," Ganson said, "but I found Angela Miller's sister and grandparents to be genuine and warm."

"That was pretty much my experience with those people," Shock said.

After thanking Shock for his time Ganson told the psychiatrist he needed the evaluation in his hand by the middle of the following week. He gave Shock his phone number and address and told him he'd be happy to drive back down and pick it up. When he passed through the waiting room the African gray was waiting for him. It let out another squawk and advised him to "go with God and take life one day at a time."

Five

By Thursday evening of the following week Ganson was convinced Luther Shock had either forgotten about him or blown off his request to get him a copy of his evaluation. After calling several times and getting no answer he'd driven back down to the South Campus only to find the parking lot empty and the metal door to Suite Three bolted shut. His meeting with BOMEX was scheduled for ten thirty the next morning and he was facing the prospect of confronting the board with little to offer in the way of a defense. He'd left Shock's office without bothering to leave a note.

The registered letter he received from the board had advised him of his right to bring a lawyer. Early on he'd decided he was going to go it on his own. He'd told himself for weeks that the best thing he could do was give his side of the story and hope for the best. As the date drew closer he'd become more anxious about what was going to happen to him. Not only could BOMEX jerk his license, it could forward its findings to the district attorney's office for the filing of criminal charges against him. He didn't see Shock's evaluation being much of a defense but he wanted to have something to put up against the no doubt devastating opinions of Frederick Nix.

By nine o'clock Ganson had given up. He was stretched out on the couch of his apartment sipping on a Tecate when he heard a knock at the door. With beer in hand he walked to the window and split the blinds. Shock was standing on his porch. The psychiatrist was carrying a leather briefcase and had a corduroy jacket slung over his shoulder.

"You make house calls?" Ganson asked as he opened the door.

"I'm afraid this evaluation won't be of much help to you," Shock said offering Ganson the folder he pulled from his briefcase.

"That bad, is it," Ganson uttered as he took the folder and gestured for Shock to come in.

"Not at all," Shock responded. "Other than you being depressed I found you quite functional."

"Would you like a beer?"

"No thanks."

"Why do you say your findings won't be of any help to me?"

"What kind of contact have you had with BOMEX?" Shock asked.

"Not much," Ganson answered. "They sent me a registered letter informing me I was under investigation. The investigator assigned to the case was this guy named Jumbo Grimes. He requested a narrative summary detailing my version of what happened and followed that up with an interview. I haven't seen or heard from him since."

"If you had, he would have told you that you'd be wasting your time trying to introduce an evaluation from a physician who is not pre-approved by the board."

"How do you know that?"

"I asked the board."

"They spoke to you about my case?"

"Of course not. All I did was to pose a hypothetical question to one of the administrative assistants and that's what she told me."

Ganson drained the Tecate and dropped the can in the trash.

"Are you going to have a lawyer with you tomorrow?" Shock asked.

"No," Ganson answered.

"Why not?"

"I can't stand lawyers."

"You can bet BOMEX will have at least one of their own there."

"I'm sure they will."

"Have you ever been in front of the board before?"

"No, I haven't."

"Let me tell you what you're in for. The meetings are open to the general public. There's enough seating available to accommodate members of the press, the public and any other interested parties, like the district attorney's office. The medical school even sends its students there to witness what could happen to them if their professional or personal lives should stray off course."

"Sounds like I've got a lot to look forward to," Ganson said.

"I had to go in front of the board last year," Shock continued. "I was there because your cohort Helen Cassidy accused me of contributing to the death of one of her patients. The patient was a sixty-year old woman dying from colon cancer. There was no hope for her but Dr. Cassidy kept offering her more surgeries anyway. The woman's family doctor got me in on the case to see if I could do anything for her depression. I conducted a healing ceremony for her right there in her hospital room. The next day she got herself dressed and had her next-door neighbor take her home where she died a few weeks later."

"What in the world was the board's beef with you?"

"Dr. Cassidy claimed I'd offered the patient false hope through the use of unproven practices. I told the board I'd informed the patient I was there not to cure her cancer but to heal her spirit so she could get ready for the final leg of her life journey. Even though the board acted as if they understood what I was trying to tell them they still issued me a letter of concern criticizing my lack of documentation in the patient's chart."

"Did you take a lawyer with you?" Ganson asked.

"A friend of mine got me in touch with this attorney from Phoenix named Duane Jamison. He didn't have much to say about my methods but he provided me with emotional as well as professional support. I was confident the board wasn't going to do much to me but having Duane there made the experience much less intimidating."

Ganson grabbed another beer from the refrigerator. "Are you sure you don't want one of these?" he asked.

"I'd love one," Shock answered, "but I swore them off years ago."

"Maybe if I drink enough of these tonight I'll be able to convince myself BOMEX will show me leniency tomorrow."

"I wouldn't count on it. You're big news and I can't imagine the board not wanting to show everyone how tough they've gotten when it comes to protecting the public interest. I know it might be too late but why don't you see if you can get them to delay the hearing until you can get yourself hooked up with someone like Duane?"

"Fuck it," Ganson said. "I think I'll go in there and try a novel approach."

"What's that?"

"I'll tell the truth."

Shock almost choked. "You're in deep denial if you think the board cares more about your view of the truth than it does about the public's view of the board."

"To tell you the truth," Ganson said, "I'm at the point where I just want to get it over and done. At least then I'll know my fate."

"Is anyone going to be at the meeting for you?" Shock asked.

"The Surgery Department told me they'd be there in support of me, but I haven't heard from them in weeks," Ganson said.

Shock's attention turned to the Indian blanket draped across the back of Ganson's rocking chair. "Where did you get this?" the psychiatrist asked.

"Bronco Dazen gave it to Angela Miller's grandparents to give to their great granddaughter. When Angela's adoptive father complained about it to the hospital administrator the grandparents gave it to me."

Shock spread the blanket out on the coffee table and rubbed his fingertips across its borders. He placed his nose to the fabric and inhaled the juniper scent. "Did they say anything about the patterns on this blanket?"

"No, they didn't."

"I'm not sure whether the zigzags represent lightning power or snake power but the hexagons are definitely snake," Shock said.

"I have no idea what you're talking about," Ganson said.

"The Apache religion embraces the belief that the natural world is full of powers capable of commingling in the affairs of the people," Shock explained.

"What kind of powers?"

"There are many. Some come from natural phenomena like

lightning, thunder, wind and rain. Others come from animals like eagles, snakes, coyotes and mountain lions. The Apaches look upon the few who have acquired these powers as being blessed."

"Is it the medicine men who possess these powers?" Ganson asked.

"A medicine man might possess one or two of them," Shock answered, "but every power out there is potentially available to anyone."

"How do you get them?"

"The power can find you or you can find the power. It might seek you out in the form of a vivid dream, a close encounter or even a haunting voice. The other way is for you to make a conscious effort to seek it out. It can only be acquired by mastering the dozens and dozens of different chants and prayers that define it. The learning process takes place under the supervision of a medicine man and can take months to years to complete."

"What do you do with the power once you have it?"

"The way it was described to me was that it's as if the power is a living being, there to offer comfort and support."

"Does it stay with you all your life?" Ganson asked.

"Usually," Shock answered, "but it will leave if it's not treated with respect."

"How does that happen?"

"It happens if the one who has acquired it chooses to live a life lacking in kindness and consideration for the nonliving as well as living things on earth."

Ganson could see where the message wasn't unlike the one he'd been taught growing up Catholic. The imagery was different but the intent seemed the same. "Are these medicine men like high priests?"

"For centuries they were the most influential members of the tribe. Part priest, part prophet, part psychiatrist and part soothsayer; they were the ones in charge of the tribal psyche. A lot has changed in the last hundred years. Not long after the Apaches were conquered and confined to the reservation the Anglo missionaries started showing up. By the mid-twentieth century there were half a dozen different denominations spreading their gospel."

"And the Apaches accepted it?"

"Many of them did. The people were so emotionally impoverished from all that had happened to their once mighty race that they were more than willing to listen to any dogma promising a more bountiful life."

"Where does that leave the medicine men?" Ganson inquired.

"At the brink of extinction," Shock answered. "What followers they haven't lost to the influx of Christianity they've lost to the influx of drugs, promiscuity and rock music.

"How many of these medicine men are left?"

"Just a few. The most well known is Bronco Dazen. He used to be pretty active but I doubt he's done a thing since the federal agents tried to link him to the disappearance of that white boy."

"How come?"

"Bronco Dazen used to perform a lot of ceremonies with rattlesnakes until the Tribal Council ordered him to stop."

"Why did they do that?"

"Their reasoning was that snake rituals were not only dangerous but also primitive. He ignored their decree and continued with the ceremonies until the Council had the police pick him up and throw him in jail. They kept him there until the snakes went back into hibernation for the winter. When he started using them again the following spring the police put him back in jail and kept him there until he finally agreed to quit the snakes. Over the years he continued to throw a snake or two into some of his ceremonies but I can't imagine him even doing that with all the attention he's attracted lately."

"Why do the Feds think he had something to do with the missing boy?" Ganson asked.

"I have an Apache friend who's a tribal police officer. He told me Dazen and the boy knew each other. After the boy disappeared Dazen was nowhere to be found. The last place the boy was supposedly seen alive was in a clearing across the creek and not that far upstream from the medicine man's camp. The boy was in the company of this crazy old Apache woman who later claimed she witnessed God coming down from the sky and taking the boy away."

"I don't suppose there was anyone else who could verify that."

"When the authorities searched the clearing they found hoof prints. The shod prints led them to believe that if the boy indeed died there he left the scene not in the arms of God but on the back of a horse. When they questioned Dazen about his whereabouts the medicine man told them he'd been out in the hills meditating."

"That doesn't sound like much of a case to me," Ganson said.

"There was something else the Feds found in the clearing that led them to believe the medicine man was in some way involved."

"What was that?"

"An enormous rattlesnake."

"Dead or alive?"

"Fried to a crisp."

"Over a fire?"

"No, it was just lying there on the ground."

"That's all they have on Mr. Dazen?"

"Pretty much."

"What about the old woman?"

"There are these four brothers who have a drinking camp close to the clearing. They claimed they found the old woman all busted up in the weeds. At the hospital she was diagnosed with a concussion, a fractured cheek and a broken collarbone. The authorities came and questioned her on several different occasions. The only consistent response they got was her insisting the power of God was responsible for what happened to the boy."

"What do you think happened to him?" Ganson asked.

"I have no idea," Shock answered while glancing at his watch. "I'm sorry to cut this short but there is somewhere else I have to be. My conclusions are on the back page of the evaluation. For what good it will do you I don't believe you are any more maladjusted than the rest of us in this profession."

"Thank you for your time and effort."

"I still know some people in the Indian Health Service. Depending on what happens between you and the board I'd be happy to do what I could to help you get a job with them some day."

Working on the reservation was the farthest thing from Ganson's mind. He accompanied Shock to the door and was about to tell him how much he appreciated him dropping by when he realized the psychiatrist had left his corduroy jacket on the back of the chair. "I think you're forgetting something, Dr. Shock."

"What's that?"

"Your jacket."

"That one's for you. I have another at home."

"Are we expecting some sort of cold wave tonight?" Ganson asked as he opened the door to the blast furnace heat outside.

"Not that I know of," Shock answered, missing Ganson's humor. "I thought you might need it for protection."

"Protection from what?"

"From whatever might be threatening you."

Ganson thought about asking the psychiatrist if that's why he wore his all the time. Instead, he thanked him and watched as he drove away in his orange Volkswagen camper. Ganson wasn't looking forward to attending his hearing the next morning with a hangover but he still stopped at the refrigerator and reached in for what he'd decided would be his last Tecate of the night. He walked over to his stereo and pulled out Pink Floyd's *Dark Side of the Moon.* He was loading it onto the turntable when he heard another knock at the door. Suspecting it was Shock having second thoughts about giving up his sacred corduroy jacket Ganson hollered for the psychiatrist to let himself in.

When he looked up he was startled to see it wasn't Shock but Helen Cassidy standing in his kitchen. Her perfectly formed store-bought breasts were pushing their way out of her low cut shirt. She'd had so much to drink she had to balance herself against the counter to keep from keeling over on the floor. It had been nine years since she'd last set foot inside his apartment and Ganson felt a flood of conflicting emotions as he took her by the arm and helped her to a chair.

"What brings you this way, Helen?" he asked.

"Yellow Cab," she answered.

"Would you like a glass of water?"

"You wouldn't happen to have a cigarette, would you?" she asked.

"Sorry," he said as he leaned over the counter and turned on the coffee maker.

"What are you doing with this?" Cassidy asked when she noticed the corduroy jacket lying across the back of her chair.

"It's a gift from Luther Shock."

Cassidy pulled herself up and stumbled away from the table. "If I were you I'd get rid of that thing."

"Why?"

"It's probably full of some kind of infestation."

"What is it you have against Shock?" Ganson asked.

"The man's a menace to the medical profession," she answered. "I've written him up on several different occasions. Once I even had to report him to BOMEX."

"Your visit wouldn't have anything to do with the fact that BOMEX is where I'm headed in the morning, would it?" he asked.

"What are you doing hanging around such a freak?"

"He dropped by to wish me well tomorrow."

"I suppose he also offered to cast some sort of bullshit Indian spell over the board members?"

"How did you know that?" Ganson asked.

"You're going to go out of your way tomorrow to try to implicate me, aren't you," she said.

"You know I'd never do anything to hurt you, Helen."

"You have no idea what all you've done to me."

"What are you talking about?" Ganson asked.

"I'm talking about the death of a baby," she replied.

"What baby are you talking about?" Ganson asked, knowing Cassie was doing so well she was about to be discharged from the Neonatal ICU.

Helen didn't answer.

When Ganson returned from pouring her a cup of coffee he found her passed out on the couch. Asleep and off guard she had a look of innocence to her. He went to cover her with the Indian blanket. When he tucked it over her shoulders his face came close enough to hers to smell the scent of her most recent menthol cigarette. The aroma brought back memories of the months they'd spent together.

They'd met in college and become lovers. Two to three nights a week he'd wake up to the sound of her unlocking the door to his apartment. She'd undress and place her neatly folded clothes on the chair before slipping between the sheets to give him a trembling kiss. She was the only girl he'd ever been with who smoked, yet the taste of tobacco on her lips did nothing to diminish his anticipation over the places on his body those lips would soon be seeking.

Their intimacy never made it beyond the bedroom. Helen had already interviewed and been accepted into medical school. When Frederick Nix rejected Ganson, she seemed to lose interest in him. Her late night visits spaced out to the point they eventually ended altogether. Ganson was never in love with her but he missed her more than he thought he would.

Their paths next crossed in the fall of his first year of medical school. When he ran into her one morning on the way to class he hardly recognized her. Her face was gaunt and her skin was pale. The defining curves in her body that had so appealed to him were no longer there. At the time he knew nothing about anorexia or bulimia. It was later he came to suspect her relentless drive to excel had been fueled by secrets dredged up from her childhood, secrets she'd tried to starve back into the depths of her subconscious mind.

By the time Ganson started his internship the metamorphosis of Dr. Helen Cassidy had reached another stage. She'd regained her weight and color, her hair had gone from straight brunette to curly blond and she was sporting a new set of full C's. She'd also adopted a different demeanor. She complained about everything and made sure whatever went wrong in the operating room was someone else's fault. Much of her wrath was directed toward the hospital personnel who worked with her. It was they who struck back at her by giving her the nickname she would never shake. She insisted she be addressed as Dr. Helen but behind her back everyone called her Bitch Cassidy.

Although Ganson and most of his classmates had started medical school determined to make a difference in other people's lives they'd ended up desperate to salvage whatever they could of their own. He and Helen had both experienced the degradation and dehumanization of the training years but had dealt with it in different ways. They were at odds with the human race, but whereas he'd chosen to retreat, she'd chosen to attack.

After turning off the coffee maker Ganson slipped a pillow under Helen's head. He turned down the AC and was about to go to bed when a smile crossed his face. He removed the blanket that was covering her body and replaced it with Shock's corduroy jacket.

Six

Sitting at a picnic table in the park across the street from the BOMEX parking lot Ganson felt ill. Neither the caffeine he'd guzzled nor the aspirin he'd popped had done much for his splitting headache. The bottle of Tums he'd gone through that morning had done nothing to neutralize the effects of the Mexican beers he'd downed the night before.

He'd fallen asleep on his bed with his clothes on and hadn't moved until the sunlight shining through his bedroom window woke him. He'd arisen to find Helen long gone and the corduroy jacket in a wad underneath the coffee table. After straightening up the jacket he'd taken a few minutes to read through Shock's evaluation. He'd showered, shaved, put on a shirt and tie and jumped in his truck for the hour and a half drive up I-10 to Phoenix.

As he sipped on another cup of coffee and thumbed through the Valley and State section of the *Arizona Republic* he came upon yet another article about him being called up in front of the board. Accompanying the story was a related one detailing a potential custody battle for Cassie. Angela Miller's death had become a rallying point for Apache self-determination. One of the lawyers for the Tribe was preparing to file a lawsuit in federal court claiming Angela's daughter should be returned to her blood relatives on the reservation. Ganson knew little about the law but didn't see the tribe having a ghost of a chance getting a judge to remove Cassie from the custody of her adoptive grandparents.

When he was finished reading the paper he walked across the street to the conference room. He had his evaluation in one hand and the corduroy jacket in the other. He'd brought along the jacket even though he knew it would be of no more use to him than the bulletproof Ghost Shirts the Sioux were wearing when they were massacred at Wounded Knee Creek.

The BOMEX conference room was on the second floor. The gallery was packed and Ganson had to find a place to stand in the corner. The board was way behind schedule. As its member physicians were busy meting out justice to the ophthalmologist who had accumulated over a hundred patient complaints and the family doctor accused of sexual impropriety Ganson was thinking about Helen.

Seeing her at his apartment had stirred up memories of their college days together. There was a vulnerability about her that he had never been able to let go of. He'd suspected she'd in part drifted away from him due to his initial failure to get into medical school but he'd never held that against her.

Ganson looked at his watch. The board had two more cases to hear before his. The first involved an anesthesiologist with a drug problem. In medical school the Chief of Psychiatry had told Ganson's class that one out of every eight physicians in Arizona was suffering from some kind of addiction. Luther Shock had told him he thought the number was much higher than that.

BOMEX spent a great deal of time and money in pursuit of these wayward physicians, most of whom proved difficult to apprehend. They lived in the shadows of their addictions and revealed themselves willingly to no one, not even their significant others. From a menu that included drugs, alcohol, sex and gambling they had each selected their own mind-numbing method of escape. When apprehended they blamed their behavior on the pressures and demands of their profession. The truth was their souls had been suffering since childhood. They had grown up acquiring the knowledge and skills necessary to give comfort to others but had no idea how to care for themselves.

With only one case left before his Ganson began to get nervous. He tried to blank everything out of his mind but couldn't keep his eyes off the physician sitting in front of the board.

He was a Chinese obstetrician accused of the wrongful death of a woman who was also a Chinese physician. He'd performed a mid-trimester abortion on the woman, who was carrying a fetus with Trisomy 13, a condition incompatible with life. The woman subsequently went into shock and bled to death from a perforated uterus. Accompanied by his lawyer the obstetrician stared straight ahead into the emptiness that had taken hold of his life. He had comforted thousands of patients throughout his career but at this moment the only patient that meant anything to him was the one who had died under his care. By the time the board finished with him his shoulders were stooped so far forward that his forehead was almost flush against the top of the table.

The Chinese obstetrician and his lawyer had barely vacated their metal folding chairs when the board chairman called for Ganson's case. As Ganson passed by the gallery he recognized David Dunbar. In person the malpractice lawyer didn't look nearly as impressive as his billboard pictures. His face had little color to it and his hairline had started to recede.

There were fifteen board members present that day. Most of them were physicians. They were positioned around the outer side of a massive horseshoe shaped table. The physician under investigation was forced to sit at a flimsy table at the open end of the horseshoe. The table had two chairs. One was for the physician. The other was for his lawyer, who was there primarily to create enough legal resistance to curb the board's punitive appetite.

When Ganson got to the table he hung Shock's jacket over the back of the one chair and took a seat in the other. The chair was still warm from the ass frying the obstetrician had received. The board chairman remained silent as if he were expecting someone to appear and sit down in the other chair. When nobody did he spoke out.

"Doctor Ganson, my name is Willard Russell. I'm a board certified general surgeon and I've practiced here in the Valley for the past twenty-five years. On behalf of this board I'd like to thank you for coming today. Am I correct in assuming you will not be represented by legal counsel this morning?"

"Yes sir, you are."

"Then without further delay I'm going to ask our investigator Mr. Grimes to give us the particulars of your case."

Jumbo Grimes took up a position next to Ganson at the open end of the horseshoe and spent the next fifteen minutes going over what had happened that night in the ER at County. He also discussed the interviews he'd conducted with Drs. Helen Cassidy, Alexander Murphy and Frederick Nix. When prodded by Russell, Grimes confirmed that all three had characterized Ganson as being unpredictable in his response to crisis and disrespectful in his response to authority. The statements came as no surprise to Ganson, nor did the fact that Grimes had made no attempt to interview the intern, the pediatrician or any of the nurses who'd been there the night Angela Miller died.

After Russell thanked Grimes for the work he'd put in on the case he paused to remove his glasses and rub his eyes. "Doctor Ganson," he said with a sigh, "I've studied this case from every conceivable angle. For the life of me I can't come up with much to hold onto in your favor. Not only does the record suggest your actions contributed to the loss of a woman's life but your statements suggest you have little regret for having done what you did. Is that true?"

"Sir, if you're asking me if I feel remorse over the death of Angela Miller, my answer is obviously yes. If you're asking me if I regret what I did that night, my answer is no. I know if I had made a different decision I wouldn't be here in front of you today but I did what I thought was the right thing."

"That's an awfully bold statement coming from someone who has had so little training in either obstetrics or surgery," Russell observed.

"I was the only one in the room that night with any training in either of those fields."

Russell shook his head. "I'm going to leave the obstetrical aspects of this discussion to our OB-GYN expert, Dr. Strickland. From my point of view as a general surgeon your knowing more than a nurse or an intern hardly qualifies you to take on a potentially life threatening procedure. According to both Dr. Cassidy and Dr. Murphy your duties at the time were limited to triaging and stabilizing the patients who came to the ER. You had yet to be trained, much less cleared, to perform any kind of surgery. Is that correct?"

"Yes."

"Yet you chose to ignore the specific instructions of your chief resident and took on the case all by yourself, didn't you."

"Yes, I did."

"That doesn't sound like a good precedent for a respected residency program, now does it."

"What doesn't sound like a good precedent for a respected residency program is to leave its residents hung out to dry."

"Is that the way you see this?"

"Yes, it is."

"You were the one in charge in the ER that night, weren't you?"

"Yes, I was."

"Could you please tell the board members what it is that makes you think you made the right decision?"

"I was convinced the baby was going to die if I didn't get her delivered."

"What about the mother?"

"What about her?"

"Did you think she was going to die too?"

"To tell you the truth I wasn't thinking about her at the time."

"Why not?" Russell asked.

Ganson thought for a moment before answering. "I felt I had a far less chance of changing her fate than I did that of her baby."

"So you decided to risk the fate of both of them."

"That's not the way I looked at it."

Russell shook his head again and turned the floor over to the OB-GYN on the board. "Doctor, my name is Harold Strickland. I'm board certified in obstetrics and gynecology and have served this board for the past two decades. I received my obstetrical training at Mayo. Could you please tell us where you received yours?"

"I spent a month as a student delivering babies at County in Tucson and two months doing obstetrics as an intern, also at County."

"That's it?" Strickland asked.

"I also spent a year and a half delivering babies in my father's practice."

"And your father is?"

"My father is deceased. He was a general practitioner."

"That's the extent of your obstetrical experience?"

"Yes sir."

"How many babies would you say you've delivered in your career?"

"Maybe two hundred."

"That's all?" Strickland asked.

"That's all," Ganson answered.

"Before the night you operated on Angela Miller had you ever done a Cesarean section on your own?"

"No, only assisted."

"Can you tell me at what point of the pregnancy a baby has a realistic chance of surviving an early delivery?"

"Somewhere around twenty-four weeks."

"Did you have any idea how far along Angela Miller's baby was?"

"Angela wasn't in any kind of condition to give out that information."

"So there was a possibility she could have been way earlier, say eighteen or twenty weeks?"

"I thought she was farther along than that."

"Why did you think that?"

"When I did a vaginal exam I felt the baby's fingers sweeping across mine."

Strickland let out a laugh. "If you're telling me that you can tell the gestational age of a baby by feeling its fingertips you're a far better clinician than I."

"I had the feeling the baby had a legitimate chance of surviving if it were delivered right away."

"Did you have the feeling that you had enough training and experience to make the critical decisions required of a complicated patient like Angela Miller?"

"I didn't look at it that way."

"When you first discovered Angela was pregnant why did you call Dr. Cassidy and not an obstetrician?"

"I called Dr. Cassidy because she was in house and the closest obstetrician was across town."

"According to her interview with Mr. Grimes, Dr. Cassidy told you there was no way that patient should be operated on at County and you should seek to transfer her immediately. Is that true?"

"Yes."

"But you didn't do that, did you."

"I pleaded with Dr. Cassidy to come down to the ER."

"When she didn't you disobeyed her directive and operated on a pregnant patient you essentially knew nothing about. Is that right?"

"Yes."

"Son," Strickland said, "I've been in this business for thirty years and I must admit I've never come across a case quite like this one. You claim you did what you did to save the baby's life but there is nothing to indicate the baby was in any kind of distress until you took it upon yourself to deliver her. In addition to that we have a psychiatric report suggesting you suffer from a variety of disorders that could well impair your decision-making ability. What do you have to say to that, Doctor?"

"I say you're full of shit," Ganson said, stunned by his own self-destructive response.

The response also stunned Strickland, whose jaw dropped open like a trap door. The room became quiet and remained that way until Russell pounded his fist on the table. "This board will not tolerate being spoken to with such disrespect. If you can't conduct yourself in a more civilized manner I will have you removed from this room and we will take care of this matter without you."

"Sorry, sir," Ganson answered apologetically, "it won't happen again."

"Is there anything you'd like to say on your behalf before this board rules on your case?" Russell asked.

"If you don't mind, I'd like to ask you a question or two," Ganson said.

"Go ahead," Russell said.

"Did you get a chance to read Angela Miller's autopsy report?"

"No, I didn't, but I have a copy of her death certificate sitting here in front of me."

"If you would have read the report you would have seen that Angela had enough drugs in her to put down a horse."

"Is it your contention that she was going to die anyway?" Russell asked. "Is that your defense?"

"No, it's not," Ganson answered. "My defense is that I did the best I could under the circumstances."

"I'm afraid you're going to have to come up with something

a little more compelling than that to influence the opinion of this board."

"I brought with me a copy of an evaluation from another psychiatrist."

"And who might that psychiatrist be?"

"Dr. Shock."

Russell paused for a moment before breaking into a frown. "That wouldn't be Dr. Luther Shock would it?"

"Yes sir. I met with him last week."

"I'm sorry, Dr. Ganson, but Dr. Shock is not on our consultant list."

"I'm aware of that. It seems to me if you were really interested in getting to the truth of my alleged psychiatric disorders you'd be willing to consider another physician's opinion."

"Thank you for yours, doctor, but this board doesn't need you to tell us how to conduct our business. Now if there are no further questions I'm open to accepting recommendations from anyone on the board. Dr. Strickland?"

"I first have a question or two," one of the women on the board spoke out.

Russell raised his eyes. "Go ahead, Dr. Newell."

"Dr. Ganson, my name is Delinda Newell. I'm a pediatrician here in Phoenix. Could you tell me what's become of Angela Miller's baby?"

"She's off the ventilator and it looks like she'll be able to go home in another month or so," Ganson answered.

"I know this is in your report but could you tell me again exactly what it was that led you to do the Cesarean section on Angela?"

"Yes ma'am. Her baby's heart rate had dropped into the fifties and there was no one else available to operate on her."

"So is it your position that the baby would have died or suffered irreversible brain damage if you hadn't done something right away?" she asked.

"That's correct," Ganson answered.

"Willard," Newell asked, "doesn't the Good Samaritan principle somehow apply to this case?"

"You've got to be kidding, Delinda." the board chairman answered. "The only principle that applies to this case is 'Primum non nocere.' You've heard of that one, haven't you, Dr. Ganson?"

Of course Ganson had. It was Latin for "First, do no harm." Every student heard it from the first day of medical school. It meant that the welfare of the patient came first and that the physician should avoid doing anything that might make the patient worse.

"I thank you for your insight, Willard, but don't you think this board has dished out enough vindictiveness for one morning?" Newell asked.

"What are you talking about?" Russell responded.

"What I want to talk about needs to be done in private. Before we vote on what we're going to do with Dr. Ganson there are a few things I'd like to get cleared up in executive session."

"You can't be serious, Delinda."

"But I am, Willard."

Russell looked around the table seeking support from the other board members. Most of them seemed as surprised as Strickland, whose mouth was still hanging half open. When none of them spoke out Russell threw up his hands and asked for all non-board members to leave the room. Ganson didn't know what he was supposed to do. He remained where he was until one of the secretaries walked over and told him he had to leave too. As he was standing up, Dr. Newell motioned for him to hand her Shock's report. He knew there was no way she was going to be able to do that much to protect him and he would have just as soon stayed in his chair and had his punishment dished out to him right then and there.

As Ganson made his way through the crowd in the hallway he came face to face with David Dunbar. The king of the state's personal injury lawyers had a look of elation on his face.

Seven

On an August monsoon morning a year after his meeting at BOMEX Ganson loaded his truck with what belongings he hadn't given away, gave his cat to the next-door neighbor and left Tucson for the unknown. The board had suspended his license and presented him with a series of demands he'd had to meet before petitioning to get it reinstated. He'd survived a three-day psychiatric evaluation, passed a five-day medical competency exam, completed a hundred and fifty hours of continuing education, taken two medical ethics courses, attended an anger management workshop and performed three hundred hours of community service. He was grateful for the opportunity he'd been given to salvage his license, yet there were times when he thought about how much simpler his life would be if he pulled an Aaron Silver and got out of the medical profession altogether.

Every three months he had to return to Phoenix to give a progress report to his case physician Dr. Delinda Newell, the pediatrician who had somehow saved him from the unbridled wrath of the board. He never knew why she'd stood up for him but at every one of their quarterly meetings she had encouraged him to hang in and handle whatever tasks were assigned him. A year after suspending his license the board granted him a provisional one allowing him to either enter another residency program or do general practice in an underserved area of the state. The board also put him on probation for five years, requiring him to return to Phoenix for yearly reviews and prohibiting him from treating any patient who was pregnant. Ganson had wanted to get into another residency but couldn't find a program interested in taking on his baggage. One of the directors told him they'd be willing to have another look at him if he kept a clean record for the next two years.

Heading east on I-10 Ganson feared he'd made a wrong turn. The highway was familiar to him but the direction his life had taken was not. He'd never felt more alone. He had no family. No brothers. No sisters. No children. His mother had been gone for over twenty years. His father was gone forever.

At Benson Ganson left the freeway and drove out to the farm where he'd grown up. He wanted to see where he'd come from one last time. His father had planned to hold onto it but when his health had taken a downward turn he'd sold it to pay his escalating medical bills. A developer had purchased the farm at a bargain basement price and was in the process of dividing it into lots. Ganson's childhood home looked pitiful, all boarded up and waiting to be bulldozed. He spent a few minutes sitting on the old swing in the front yard before walking across the weed-filled field and down the embankment to the San Pedro River.

From its origins in the mountains of Mexico to its confluence with the Gila River in central Arizona the San Pedro was the only river in the Southwest that ran in a south to north direction. It was the route Coronado had followed on his way to laying claim to the region. In the spring of 1540 the Spanish conquistador and his Catholic crusaders entered present-day Arizona with an expeditionary force of 1,500 men and several hundred head of livestock. Coronado rode through hundreds of miles of Apache Land on his way to the Great Plains in search of the legendary Seven Cities of Gold. When he found only the rock and mud mortared huts of the Pueblos he took out his frustrations by slaughtering a good number of the Indians who lived there. He would have no doubt done the same to the Apaches if he had ever found them.

Once a powerful and proud river, the siphoned off San Pedro had reached the point it was little more than a ribbon of water winding through a riverbed of tamarisk and sand. There were lengthy stretches where the river had disappeared underground, much like Ganson had done for the past year. Looking down into one of the few riparian areas still full of water and life he feared he'd never again feel so connected and content.

He'd spent his childhood years turning rocks and parting

watercress in an endless search for the creatures living there. He was a catch and release kid and could never uncover enough of the frogs, salamanders and crawdads to satisfy his curiosity. When he'd tire of crisscrossing the riverbed and dumping the sand out of his tennis shoes he'd lie down and listen to the leaves of the cottonwoods fluttering in the breeze.

His favorite spot was a patch of grass next to a cliff that contained a well-preserved petroglyph of a line of men on horseback. Each of the men in the rock etching was outfitted in the cape and wide brimmed hat of a Spanish soldier. Resting with his back against the trunk of a fallen tree Ganson would stare at them for hours, trying to comprehend the fear and wonder running through the mind of the Apache artist who centuries before had witnessed the Spanish intrusion of Coronado and his Catholic army.

Other than the day his mother had left, the most vivid memory of his youth was of an event that had taken place in the river bottom. He was eleven years old at the time and on horseback searching for stray calves. He was riding along a game trail when his horse suddenly spun around and threw him into a thicket of tamarisk. By the time he scrambled to his feet the horse had taken off for home and he was staring across the river at a hundred pound cat. The cat was feasting on the leg of one of the calves Ganson had been looking for. With little more than a trickle of water separating them Ganson figured it would take only three or four bounds for the cat to cover the ground between them and pounce on him. He stood waiting for that to happen. It didn't. Instead, the two of them stared at each other at a distance of less than twenty yards.

He would later be terrified by nightmares and flashbacks of the encounter but at the time he was in awe. The cat was crouched sideways, giving him a full-length view. It had a huge head and its orange colored pelt was covered with dark rosettes. Looped above its back, its tail was almost as long as its body. The back half of the tail was black, as if it had been dipped in a giant inkwell.

His father had once told he him that big cats went out of their way to stay away from humans. If one happened to come his way the worst thing he could do was to try to run away. Instead he should get tall. Stand on a rock. Raise his hands above his head. Make noise. Do anything to appear different from the four-footed animals the feline predator was genetically programmed to attack.

Ganson kept his eyes on the cat and started backing up the embankment. When he got to the top he turned and sprinted for home. He didn't dare look back for fear he was about to get run down. It was dusk by the time he yanked open the screen door to the house and breathlessly told his father about the cat he'd seen.

Heavily armed they returned to the site at dawn. The cat was long gone, having left the remains of the calf in a brushy ravine on the other side of the river. After inspecting its prints and asking Ganson again to describe the animal his father said he must have seen a jaguar. He went on to tell him the jaguar was no longer native to the state and hadn't been for over a century. The rare sightings came when one wandered up from the mountains of Sonora, Mexico, hundreds of miles to the south.

As Ganson stood there reliving what had happened some twenty years before, he could still taste the terror he'd felt as an eleven year old confronting the giant cat. He thought about the white boy who'd disappeared off the reservation. If the boy were indeed dead, Ganson hoped he hadn't had to face that fate. Although he'd never heard of anyone being eaten by a jaguar the mountains of Arizona were full of mountain lions. The lions tended to leave humans alone but every now and then there was a report of an attack by one.

Maybe the boy died from the bite of a rattlesnake. More likely he fell off a cliff, drowned in a river or met his death in some other encounter with nature. The bothersome part was that the authorities had been unable to find even a remnant of the body. And there was the medicine man. Ganson wondered what role he might have played in the boy's disappearance.

After saying his final goodbye to the life he was leaving, Ganson returned to his truck and headed north along the river. At Winkelman, where what was left of the San Pedro emptied into the

Gila, he stopped for a cup of coffee. He continued on into Globe where he came upon the photographically enhanced face of David Dunbar staring at him from yet another billboard. This one had the lawyer dressed in jeans with a pair of six guns hanging from his belt. The billboard assured everyone driving by that Dunbar "wasn't going to rest until he cleaned up the West."

Staying on 77 Ganson followed the general course Coronado had taken into the heart of Apache Country. The highway cut across the southeast corner of the Tonto National Forest before dropping into the Salt River Canyon. The canyon was so deep that from the top the river looked like a twisted thread. Ganson wound his way down the south side and crossed a narrow two-lane bridge. On the other side of the river a sign informed him he was entering the Fort Apache Indian Reservation. He drove past a small store sporting two palm trees and one gas pump before starting his ascent into the homeland of the White Mountain Apaches.

Out of the canyon and back into the ponderosa pine he came upon the turnoff to Cibecue, the place he'd signed up to be his homeland for the next two years. He stayed on the main road and continued on to Carrizo Junction where he turned to the southeast on 73. It had rained all summer and the reservation was overgrown with vegetation. The rolling hills were covered in carpets of green. Rows of sunflowers crowded the shoulders of the highway like they were lined up to watch a parade.

The scenery was spectacular but did little to soothe Ganson's disconnected soul. The vastness of the land emphasized his isolation. The life he'd left no longer existed. He yearned to feel he belonged somewhere but couldn't imagine that happening in a place that felt so foreign to him.

Just south of Whiteriver he came upon the sign for the Apache Culture Center. Hoping to get a better feel for the people amongst whom he'd be seeking redemption he turned off the highway and crossed the bridge taking him to the legendary Fort Apache. The restored remains of the fort sat on a bluff overlooking the confluence of the East and North Forks of the White River. For half a century it had served as a Bureau of Indian Affairs boarding school. Multi-storied wood and brick buildings bordered a grassy parade ground overgrown with goat dandelion and bull thistle. Half a dozen Indian boys were playing basketball in front of one of the barracks.

Ganson stopped next to a small building with a hand painted sign identifying it as the Apache Culture Center. A handful of white haired Apaches were sitting on the porch. They looked to be as ancient as the original fort. Standing at the door was a middle-aged man with long black hair and soft brown eyes. He welcomed Ganson with a smile and invited him to come in and have a look around.

The walls were covered with photographs and paintings. The front room was full of modern day crafts. There were baskets, beadwork, blankets, dream catchers, leather goods and an assortment of turquoise and silver jewelry.

The back room was bursting with Indian artifacts. Inside one of the locked display cases was a collection of Apache playing cards, something that caught Ganson completely by surprise. Made of leather, they were suited in the colors of mustard yellow, royal blue, rust red and black. Ganson could identify two of the suits as coins and clubs but wasn't so sure about the other two. One was a cup or a chalice and the other a spear or an arrowhead. Three of the suits appeared to be of Old World origin but the spear or arrowhead looked Indian. Ganson knew gambling and games of chance were integral parts of the Indian way of life but he had a hard time envisioning Apache warriors sitting around a campfire playing rummy.

He was on his way out the door when his eyes were drawn to the photograph of a spectacular looking Apache woman. She was holding a pistol in each hand and her right foot was resting on the head of a gigantic bear. The caption read "Fannie Hoffman with Silvertip west of Cibecue, 1928." Ganson didn't know when the last grizzly bear was killed in Arizona but he doubted it was more than a few years after the one Fannie stood over in her photo.

He drove back past the boys playing basketball and out to the road that led to Whiteriver. Entering the town from the south the first thing he came upon was a shopping center. It had a motel, a restaurant, a grocery store, a movie theater and several small businesses. Just past it on the same side of the highway was the new Alchesay High School. The school was named for the early twentieth century chief who had taken on the overwhelming task of leading the White Mountain Apaches out of the spiritual decimation they'd suffered following their confinement on the reservation.

Across the street from the school was a drive-through liquor store. A hundred yards beyond the store was a bar. The sign for the liquor store had fallen down or been blown away but the one atop the bar read "Apache Flame." Between the liquor store and the bar was an open field that was littered with busted bottles and broken Indians.

It was raining by the time Ganson turned left at the BIA Office and followed the signs directing him to the Indian Health Service hospital. He drove along a tree-lined street bordered by immaculate yards and took a left at the far end of the government compound. Situated next to a grassy field was a two-story brick hospital that looked like it had been built around the same time Fannie shot her grizzly bear. Adjoining the hospital was a newer wooden one-story structure that housed the outpatient clinic and the administration offices. Ganson parked his truck in the gravel lot and sprinted through the downpour to the front entrance of the clinic. At the other side of a waiting room full of fussy Apache babies and pregnant

Apache mothers he found a round-faced woman who showed him to the Clinical Director's office.

The office was filled with unpacked boxes. Behind the desk sat a strait-laced looking physician. "Can I help you?" the doctor asked with an annoyed look on his face.

"I have a one thirty appointment," Ganson replied.

"With whom?"

"With Dr. Richard Stevens."

"I'm afraid you're a bit late."

Ganson checked his watch. It read 1:25, which was also what the clock on the wall read. "Are you sure?" he asked.

"Quite sure," the physician answered. "Dr. Stevens no longer works here."

Ganson couldn't conceal the disappointment on his face. Richard Stevens and Luther Shock had worked together in Whiteriver. It was Shock who had called his old friend and talked him into giving Ganson a chance to go there and work off the first two years of his probation. Ganson had never been to Whiteriver but had met Stevens on three different occasions at the Indian Health Service Area Office in Phoenix. Without Stevens' cooperation and support Ganson would have never been able to get BOMEX to sign off on letting him use his license to work on the reservation.

At issue was the fact that Indian Land fell under federal

jurisdiction. The Fort Apache Indian Reservation was located inside the state of Arizona but about the only thing the state had a say in was the patrolling of the highways. BOMEX had no jurisdiction whatsoever. The only reason the board agreed to let Ganson use his license to work there were the reassurances Stevens had given them on how closely Ganson would be monitored.

"What happened to him?" Ganson asked.

"Who are you?" the sandy haired doctor countered.

"I'm sorry," Ganson said as he strode forward and offered his hand. "My name is Dr. Michael Ganson. I'm here for orientation."

"Oh yes," the doctor said as he stood up. He was a good half-foot taller than Ganson and looked down on him with disinterest as he shook his hand with a halfhearted grip. "I'm Dr. Bryce Peterson. I guess you might call me the clinical director pro tem."

"Did you know I was supposed to report today?" Ganson asked.

"Now that you mention it I remember Stevens having said something about you coming."

"If you don't mind me asking, what happened to Dr. Stevens?"

Before Peterson had a chance to respond the phone rang. He picked up the receiver and started arguing with someone on the other end of the line about how the hospital wasn't equipped to handle such a critically ill patient. Ganson took a chair and surveyed the diplomas propped against the wall, waiting to be hung. There was a

BA from Brigham Young University, an MD from the University of Utah, a certificate of Board Certification in Internal Medicine and a framed document identifying him as a commissioned officer in the Public Health Service.

Next to the diplomas were half a dozen photos of a leaner Bryce Peterson in a BYU basketball uniform. In one of them he was dunking the ball behind his head. In another he was releasing a fall away jumper from the corner of a jam-packed arena. Ganson had no reason to dislike the handsome doctor but found himself feeling a bit intimidated in his presence. Not only did Peterson have the will and intellect to get through medical school, he also possessed the drive and physical talent to play major college basketball.

When Peterson finished his phone call he slammed the receiver down. "You'd think someone in this organization would have the fortitude to stand up to this nonsense," he bemoaned as he took the chart on his desk and tossed it onto the floor next to a pile of others. "Our forefathers conquered these people, only to turn around and give them sovereignty, along with over one and a half million acres of the most abundant land in Arizona. Now does that seem right to you?"

"To tell you the truth, Dr. Peterson, I've never given it much of a thought."

"We give them government subsidies and free health services. They act as if they're doing us a favor to let us come and take care of them on their reservation. They even charge us to camp and fish on their land."

Peterson paused as if he were awaiting a response from Ganson. When none came he continued. "This spring the Indian Health Service started construction on the new hospital north of town. When the groundbreaking ceremony was held the only thing the Tribal Chairman could talk about was how he couldn't wait until the day the new facility was totally staffed with Apache doctors."

"Are there any Apache doctors on staff here?" Ganson asked.

"If there were I'd be delighted for them to take care of the Tribal Chairman."

"Is there something wrong with him?

"A couple of months ago the old goat got so sick he checked himself into a private hospital in Phoenix. Now he's telling everybody he wants to come back to the reservation. The Indian Health Service is under pressure from the Tribe to transfer him back up here but I keep telling the Area Office we are in no way equipped to care for such a sick patient."

"Has there ever been an Apache physician stationed here?" Ganson asked.

"We used to have one but he left. That's how it is with these people."

"How's that?"

"It's part of the Apache paradox. The government provides assistance for them to go get continuing education and job training but few of them take advantage of the opportunity. Those who do often don't return to the reservation. Those who do return often turn right back around and leave."

"Why is that?"

"The Apaches who go off reservation to better themselves face great resentment from those they've left behind. I have this theory that within the Tribe there exists this massive inferiority complex that leads them to look with suspicion and distrust upon any of their members who have left their world to better themselves in ours."

"Are they all that way?"

"The majority of the adults living on the reservation are unemployed. A great number of them are alcoholic. The way I see it they've made a conscious decision to escape their miserable existence by drinking themselves into oblivion. They are quite successful at it. If not killing themselves from cirrhosis of the liver or some other medical complication of alcohol abuse, they're dying from gunshots, stabbings, beatings and car wrecks."

The phone rang and Peterson got into another heated discussion. This one was with someone over the lack of funds available for the rest of the fiscal year. When he finished he stood up from his desk. "I've got some things I need to tend to. If you don't mind showing yourself around I'll meet you back here at four o'clock."

Ganson was on his way to a self-guided tour when a female voice called out to him through a half open door.

"Dr. Ganson?" The voice belonged to a middle-aged Indian woman with a perfectly round face and beautiful brown eyes. "You are Dr. Ganson, aren't you?" she asked.

"Yes ma'am, I am," he answered as he stepped into the woman's office.

"My name is Nella Sydney," she said as she reached up to shake his hand. "I'm the drug and alcohol counselor for the reservation."

Ganson had a puzzled look on his face.

"I recognize you from your picture," she said with a grin. "I worked with Dr. Stevens on the committee that reviewed your Indian Health Service application."

"I was sorry to hear Dr. Stevens had left," he said.

"So was I," she said.

"What happened to him, if you don't mind me asking?"

"He came to work one morning and told us he would be transferring to Tucson. Two weeks later he was gone."

"Did he say why?" he asked.

"Family problems," she answered as she stood up. "Let me show you our little hospital."

She led him down the hallway past the delivery room and through the nursery where two babies were sleeping strapped in their cradleboards. After introducing him to the director of the lab she took him to the inpatient ward. The rooms were small and sparse. The tile flooring reminded Ganson of the County Hospital. There were two nurses at the nursing station, one Apache and one Anglo. They both looked up and smiled at Ganson when he walked by the desk. Nella finished up the tour on the back porch over a cup of coffee.

"If you hadn't already noticed," Nella said, "we have a bit of an alcohol problem."

"Did you grow up around here?" Ganson asked.

"I'm from Second Mesa."

"Second Mesa?"

"On the Hopi reservation."

"So you're Hopi?"

Nella laughed. "I'm a Hopi hybrid, half Hopi and half Navajo.

"Do the Hopis sell alcohol on their reservation?"

"Not legally."

"Why do the Apache's do it?"

"The liquor store is owned and operated by the Tribe. The official spin is that the Tribal Council made alcohol available so there wouldn't be as many deaths from tribal members wrecking their cars when driving back drunk from the off-reservation bars and liquor stores. I think a more compelling reason is that the Tribe got tired of losing all that revenue."

"Since we gave the Apaches alcohol I guess it only seems fair we should give them the free enterprise tools necessary to maximize their profits," Ganson offered.

"The Apaches may have picked up their business sense from you," Nella replied, "but they were using alcohol long before any of your European ancestors showed up on the continent. They got their first taste of it when they raided the native Indians of northern Mexico and discovered the intoxicating effects of fermented corn. They call it tulapai and they drink it even though it's only about two per cent alcohol."

"I think they'd have to drink an awful lot of that to get buzzed."

"The Apache brew masters discovered how to ferment malt syrup with sugar and yeast. They call it home brew. It's what those who don't have the money for beer or wine get drunk on and get their guts eaten up by."

"I can understand the economics of it," Ganson said. "I just can't see tribal leaders sponsoring the sale of something so destructive to their people."

"It's not that simple," Nella said. "Alcohol is a form of currency on the reservation and drinking is an integral part of the Apache culture. It's illegal to drink in a public place but it goes on all the time."

"Why doesn't the tribe do something about it?"

"There are many social settings where drinking is considered perfectly acceptable. Whether it's a wedding or a wake, there will always be a bunch of people standing around getting drunk. Some experts say we Indians are genetically inclined to abuse alcohol. The way I see it, the devastatingly high rates of alcoholism are the result of many different factors including complex cultural beliefs, loss of self-determination, cripplingly high rates of unemployment and sub-zero levels of self-esteem."

The rain had stopped and streaks of sunlight illuminated the vast stand of pine on the ridge to the west. It was a setting as beautiful as any Ganson had seen. It disturbed him that the people living there seemed to be in so much pain. "I'd guess there would also be a few street drugs around."

"That there would," Nella confirmed.

"The people sound a lot like the inner city ones I treated in Tucson," he said.

"It looks like you're about to get the chance to find out," she answered as she glanced at her watch. "I'm sorry to leave you but I have a meeting to attend. There is, however, someone else I think you should meet."

She left him at the entrance to the ER where he found a bearded doctor with a ponytail giving wound care instructions to an older Apache man.

"Now try to keep it clean," the doctor said, "and don't wait so long to get the stitches out this time." He walked the man to the exit before turning to speak to Ganson. "Can I help you?" he asked.

"I didn't mean to interrupt," Ganson said.

"You didn't," the doctor responded. "Carlyle and I were just finishing up. The last time he had his head sewn he didn't show back up to get his stitches out for over a year. Is there something I can do for you?"

"My name is Michael Ganson. I'm the new recruit for Cibecue."

"Oh, yes," the young doctor said extending his hand. "I'm Jim Mackenzie. Dr. Stevens told us you'd be coming sooner or later. I wish he was still here to greet you."

"Ms. Sydney said he'd had some family problems," Ganson said.

"You could say that," Mackenzie responded. "He left to try to get more help for his wife. For years she's been in and out of treatment centers for drug and alcohol addiction."

"There's not a place on this planet immune to that problem, is there," Ganson observed.

Mackenzie nodded. "Not even in Cibecue."

"What are the people like out there?"

"They're a little different, more distant and detached. The ones here in Whiteriver at least make an effort to appear as if they tolerate the presence of the white man."

"They don't in Cibecue?"

"Cibecue is at the western end of the reservation. The residents out there have lived a far more isolated life than the ones here. Most of them didn't have electricity until the fifties. It wasn't that long ago that the road in from the highway wasn't much more than a track of mud bogs and washouts."

"What is the housing like out there?"

"The town has its share of HUD homes with telephones, televisions and washing machines, but there are still a number of wickiups, squaw coolers and one-room huts with dirt floors. Many of the older people live as they have for most of their lives. In contrast there's the younger group who drive around in their pickups, smoking dope and listening to Led Zeppelin. The general impression is that no one out there cares much for outsiders, white or any other color."

"Do you believe that?" Ganson asked.

"I didn't give it much thought until that white boy disappeared last summer. Have you heard anything about him?" Mackenzie asked.

"A few things," Ganson answered.

"It made national news. One of the networks published a story speculating the boy's death was the result of some kind of snake ritual."

"Do you think that's true?"

"The BIA has an ongoing investigation but has had little to say about it. The reservation's rumor list of suspects includes the Cibecue medicine man, Mother Nature, numerous unidentified witches and Major Mendoza."

"Who's Major Mendoza?" Ganson asked.

"He was this Apache renegade," Mackenzie answered. "He disappeared a couple of years ago after trying to single handedly rid the community of Cibecue of all organized religion."

"How did he do that?"

"At the time he was studying as an apprentice under the medicine man Bronco Dazen. One day he crashed his truck through the front door of the Mormon Church, started a fire on the front porch of the Lutheran Church and busted all the windows out of the Native American Church. He then held up the trading post and stole one of the owner's horses. On his way out of town he shot the tires out of every vehicle parked at the police station. The Feds went searching for him with helicopters and dogs but never found him or the horse."

"He hasn't been seen or heard from in two years and he's still a suspect?" Ganson asked.

"I'm afraid so," Mackenzie answered. "Whenever there's an unexplained event on the west end of the reservation his name comes up as the possible perpetrator."

"What kind of event are you talking about?"

"Someone's horse runs off. Someone's cow drops dead. Someone's house burns down."

"Was he really a major?"

"He was in the service for a brief period of time but got discharged. I never saw him as a patient but he apparently suffered from mental illness. When he came back to the reservation somebody nicknamed him the 'Major,' and it stuck."

"Do you believe he had anything to do with the disappearance of the boy?" Ganson asked.

"A lot of the people around here do," Mackenzie answered, "but I'm not one of them."

"What do you think happened?"

"To the boy or to the Major?"

"Both."

"I have no idea what happened to the boy but I've got to believe something or somebody got to the Major. The boy didn't turn up missing until months after the Major had run off. By that time the Major had probably rotted away in some crevice or cave."

"I've heard Bronco Dazen might be connected to the disappearance of the boy."

"The boy and the medicine man disappeared the same day. When Dazen showed up a couple of weeks later the BIA brought him in for questioning. Somebody told me they wanted to give him a polygraph test but he refused because he said he was afraid to get hooked up to all the wires. To this day nobody has been charged with anything."

"Have you been out to Cibecue since the boy disappeared?" Ganson asked.

"Many times," Mackenzie answered. "There was this Apache doctor living and working out there. Shortly after the boy disappeared he loaded up his family and left. Stevens and I tried to keep the clinic open. For a while we alternated going out there but we ended up having to close down all physician services."

"Were you at all apprehensive about being there?"

"I have never felt unsafe on the reservation. Part of that is because I was born and raised here. My parents moved from Minnesota in the early forties to help run the Lutheran Mission at East Fork. Except for the years I left to go to school I've lived here all my life."

"You've never felt threatened or at risk?"

"I've always been of the opinion that being an Apache on this reservation is a far greater danger than being a white man. The Apaches feel great frustration over having lost most everything. When they get drunk they direct their anger toward their fellow tribal members. It's as if the different clans have held onto century-old animosities that are rekindled with the consumption of alcohol. Didn't Stevens tell you anything about what you would be getting into?"

"He did."

"And you still decided to come."

"I don't know how much you know about my situation. I didn't have a whole lot of choices."

"I don't know about your other choices," Mackenzie said, "but everyone here knows about your situation."

"They do?" Ganson asked somewhat surprised.

"When the Tribal Council got wind of the fact there was a doctor with a provisional license coming here to practice they had a fit. They were threatening to file a formal complaint with the Area Office until Stevens and some Tucson psychiatrist friend of his who used to work here met with them and talked them into giving you a chance."

Ganson was grateful to learn of the support Luther Shock had given him but at that moment he felt like someone had taken a bone saw to his sternum. He'd wanted to go some place he could get a fresh start and serve his sentence in anonymity. If there was any place like that, he'd thought it would have been in an isolated community at the west end of an Apache Indian reservation. "I know we can never escape ourselves," he said, "but I came here hoping to escape a few other things."

Mackenzie gave Ganson a reassuring look. "I have no idea what went on between you and BOMEX but if it's of any consolation to you Cibecue is in desperate need of a doctor."

Eight

Ganson's quarters were at the south end of the hospital grounds where four one-room apartments were nestled amongst a grove of Arizona sycamore. He had a kitchenette, a fold out bed, a table with two chairs and a TV that didn't work. The only luxury item in the entire complex was the hammock hanging from the limbs of two of the sturdier trees out back. Scheduled to be there a month before moving on to Cibecue, he filled his days seeing clinic patients and learning the Indian Health Service system. He spent his free time reading medical journals while listening to either his stereo or the AM radio station that blasted rock music all across the Southwest from somewhere south of the border.

Late one afternoon he dropped by the Apache Pizza Parlor. The only person in the place was the proprietor, a middle-aged white man with a shaved head. The man was standing behind the counter reading the local newspaper, the Apache Scout.

"Can I help you?" he asked looking up from his paper.

"It looks to be a bit slow tonight," Ganson remarked.

"Payday's not until tomorrow. What would you like?"

"Something to go."

"How about some fresh pepperoni slices?"

"I'll take three."

"I don't believe I've seen you before."

"I live down by the hospital."

"I wouldn't live here if they paid me," the man said as he removed the pizza slices from under the warmer and placed them in a Styrofoam box.

"Why not?" Ganson asked reaching for his wallet.

"These people are pretty crazy."

"How's that?"

"You can never tell what they're thinking."

"Maybe they think the same about us."

"Most of them don't seem to care for us white folks."

"The one's I've met seem quite pleasant."

"How long have you been here?"

"A couple of weeks."

"I'd like to hear how you feel in a couple of months."

Ganson paid for the pizza and drove his truck north past the site of the new hospital under construction. He turned east on a road descending into the canyon carved out by the North Fork of the White River. At the bottom of the canyon next to a one-lane bridge he parked and got out of the truck. He left the pizza in the box on the front seat.

The rocks below him were littered with shards of glass and he had to make his way through a graveyard of busted beer bottles to get to the water's edge. He found a narrow game trail and followed it upstream. Half an hour later he came upon an eight-foot wall of granite jutting out into the river. He couldn't get around it without wading through the waist high water so he tried climbing over it. Growing out of a crack was a pine sapling he was able to use to pull up onto the massive rock. When he discovered the other side was too steep to descend he found a spot where he could stretch out and watch the water tumble down the boulder-strewn canyon as it had for eons.

Listening to the rush of the river Ganson felt as if he were alone in the middle of what Coronado had once referred to as "The Wilderness." Four and a half centuries earlier the Spaniard had passed through in search of fame he'd never realize and fortune he'd never find. He rode right through the heart of the Apache domain yet never knew they were there. The task of finding and subduing them would fall upon his Spanish descendents, who spent the next three hundred years trying but failing.

Ganson was starving by the time he made it back to the truck. He took a minute to pick the cockleburs out of his shoestrings and sweep the pine needles out of his hair before reaching through the open window for his pizza. The box was open and the only thing left of the three slices was one piece of crust. He whirled around and looked up and down the road but didn't see a living thing.

Driving back to Whiteriver he came around a corner and upon an Apache man in the middle of the road. Ganson slammed on his brakes to avoid hitting him. Unfazed, the man opened the passenger door and let himself into the truck.

"Thanks for stopping," he said after taking a swig from the bottle of Colt 45 he was carrying. "Would you like a drink?"

"No, thanks," Ganson answered.

"You can drop me off at Memorial Hall. My cousin's playing ball tonight."

"What's your name?" Ganson asked as he restarted the truck.

"Lester," the man answered.

Ganson shifted into gear and started back up the road. "Where do you live, Lester?"

"On the other side of river."

"You didn't happen to see anyone on your way, did you?"

"Nope."

"The strangest thing just happened to me," Ganson said as he reached down and opened up the empty Styrofoam box. "Something or somebody got into my truck and ate all my pizza."

The Apache scratched his chin. "There've been a lot of bears around here this summer."

"You don't say," Ganson said. "I feel bad I don't have any left to offer you."

"Thanks but I just finished eating," the man said breaking into a wide smile. Stuck between his teeth was a sliver of pepperoni.

Across the street from the BIA Offices and next door to the Tribal Offices stood Memorial Hall, an elongated building with a basketball gymnasium and seating for several hundred fans. It was where the Apaches held their city league games and hosted their weekend invitational tournaments. Basketball was king on the reservation and the Apaches played it all year long.

Ganson dropped Lester off at the front door. As he was driving past the packed parking lot he decided to ignore his hunger and go in and catch what was left of the game. Above the front door hung a butcher paper banner that read "Welcome to the Apache Tribal Fair Shootout." Two large women were selling tickets at the door. Lester was standing there arguing with them.

"I had the money but somebody stole it."

The women ignored him.

"I'll get it to you tomorrow night. I promise."

One of the women looked up. "How many times have you told us that, Lester?"

"Please, Josie. My cousin's playing."

"How much does it cost to get in?" Ganson asked as he walked up beside Lester.

"Two dollars," the woman answered.

"Ganson pulled out a five dollar bill and handed it to her. "This is for both of us."

"Hey, thanks," Lester said with another big smile on his face.

Ganson wove his way through the crowd of youngsters playing in front of the concession area. The stands were half full. Except for the white players on the one team Ganson was the only non-Indian in the building. He sat down next to Lester, who was already yelling at the referees.

Both teams were running up and down the court at a frenzied pace. Ex-collegian Bryce Peterson was leading his team's attack. It was early in the second half and they were up by three points. Looking at the players on the floor Ganson thought they would have been up by thirty. Peterson stood at least six and a half feet tall. He had with him two other hulks towering over everyone on the opposing team.

The Apache frontcourt players were about as wide as they were tall. Even after watching how they used their bulk to block out and get rebounds Ganson couldn't see how they'd be able to keep their team in the game. That was until he saw the Apache guards in action. They were lightning quick as they raced up and down the court stealing passes and drilling jumpers. In a two-minute stretch one of them pulled up and drained four shots in a row from about twenty-five feet out.

Ganson figured the fans would be overwhelming in their support for the Apache team but that wasn't the case. Even when the one Apache guard buried a leaner from the corner that gave his team the lead the crowd didn't get that excited. The most emotion they showed was when they all broke out laughing after one of the heavyweight Apache forwards tripped and went sliding out of bounds on his belly.

With less than six minutes left and his team behind by a bucket Peterson called time out and started screaming at his teammates. When they got back on the court he took over the game. The Apaches double and triple teamed him the rest of the way and he still scored at will. Pull up jumpers, running one-handers, reverse dunks and a tip-in off a missed shot. He handled every possession down the stretch and won the game doing things Ganson would never have dreamed of doing himself.

Just before the final buzzer Ganson said goodbye to Lester and left. He returned to the hospital to catch up on his charting. Entering through the ER he said hello to the night nurse and walked down the hallway to the small office he was using. In addition to Peterson and Mackenzie there were four other doctors stationed at the hospital, all committed to seeing their share of both the clinic and the hospitalized patients. They went out of their way to befriend Ganson and make him feel welcome. They answered his questions, assisted him with his patients and helped him wade through the reams of government paperwork.

Ganson repaid them by doing as much as he could to help out. He came in early, worked through lunch and was always willing to stay and see the walk-ins who straggled in later in the day. He'd gone almost fifteen months without treating a patient but it had only taken him a few days to get comfortable with the ones in the clinic. He'd offered to help take care of the in-patients but for some reason Peterson had seemed reluctant to let him do anything on the hospital side.

After Ganson finished charting he left and followed the brick walkway that led to his apartment. He was so worn out he went straight to bed. That night he dreamt he was playing on a basketball team coached by Dr. Frederick Nix. Ganson was one of the scrubs and rarely got into the game. He spent most of his time at the far end of the bench where he wouldn't have to listen to his own coach criticize and make fun of his teammates on the court. With less than two minutes left Nix sent him into the game. Their team was behind by twenty-five points but Ganson still wanted to give his best and make a positive impression on the coach. Unfortunately, every time he touched the ball he either turned it over or fired up a shot that missed everything. What was worse was that he suddenly realized he was half naked. He had on his tennis shoes and shirt but no shorts or jock strap. As Nix howled at him from the bench and the crowd roared at him from the stands he continued to run up and down the court with his dick jiggling beneath his jersey.

When he walked to work the following morning he noticed the parking lot was full of pickup trucks. Peterson had lost his battle with the Area Office to keep the Tribal Chairman in Phoenix and an airplane had been dispatched to fly the ailing leader home. Ganson made his way through the crowd that was waiting in anticipation of the Chairman's return. He spent the morning in the clinic seeing walk-ins. Just before noon he heard stomping and whooping coming from the inpatient side of the hospital signaling the arrival of the Chairman. He finished his last patient and walked over to the nursing station where he found Peterson thumbing through a four-inch thick chart.

"The Chairman's records?" Ganson asked.

"He's tucked away in Room 201," Peterson responded.

"What's wrong with him?"

"What isn't? He has diabetes, hypertension, congestive heart failure, atrial fibrillation and renal failure. He's on insulin, oxygen, warfarin, digoxin, furosemide and three different blood pressure medications. He was scheduled to have a vascular shunt placed in his forearm so he could go on dialysis but he refused."

"Maybe he just wants to come home to die," Ganson suggested.

"Not according to him," Peterson said. "He rolled in here this morning predicting he will be resuming all his duties once he gets well."

"What does he think is going to make him well?" Ganson asked.

"A medicine man," Peterson said with laugh of disbelief.

The picture running through Ganson's head was that of an Apache dressed in full regalia, dancing around a hospital bed occupied by a man who looked like Howard Hughes in his final days. "It sounds like a huge challenge," he said.

"It's a huge waste of money," Peterson said. "The U.S. Government is footing the bill to fly him here just so he can have some native soothsayer slinking around spouting a bunch of gibberish."

"I guess I don't see the big deal," Ganson said.

"There is one," Peterson said. "For openers the cost of the flight will be deducted from our Service Unit's capital budget. Of more concern to me is the possibility that the Chairman will croak before the medicine man gets the chance to treat him. If that happens we're going to have another public relations disaster on our hands."

"How's that?"

"The Tribe will say it's our fault for not getting the Chairman back sooner. I know that might sound a bit paranoid to you but I've been around here long enough to know how these people think."

"Is the medicine man on his way?" Ganson asked.

"He is," Peterson answered, "but he probably won't get here until late tomorrow."

"Where is he coming from," Ganson asked, "Alaska?"

"No," Peterson answered. "He lives in Cibecue."

"Is it Bronco Dazen?"

Peterson nodded. "The last of the snake charmers."

"Why can't someone drive out there and pick him up?" Ganson asked.

"It's not that simple," Peterson answered. "When the Tribal Councilwoman from Cibecue tried to get him to come in earlier this week Dazen informed her he wasn't going to leave his camp until the Chairman made it back to the reservation. The Tribal Police went out to notify him as soon as the Chairman's plane landed but they haven't been able to get him to come in either."

"Why not?"

"Dazen has had several run-ins with the police over the past few years. He's gotten to the point where he's afraid to get in any of their vehicles, or anyone else's for that matter."

"So what's he doing," Ganson asked, "walking to Whiteriver?"

"He's coming by horseback," Peterson answered.

"Does he have some kind of special relationship with the Tribal Chairman?"

"The two of them are from the same clan."

"What does that mean?"

"It means we have to do everything we can to keep the old man alive until Dazen gets here."

"Is the Chairman that close to dying?" Ganson asked.

"You can go see for yourself," Peterson answered, "but first I have a favor to ask of you. This weekend is the Tribal Fair and there's a huge basketball tournament going on at Memorial Hall. There are teams here from all over the Southwest and ours has a great shot at winning the whole thing. My problem is that I'm scheduled to be on call."

"You want me to take yours?"

"Mackenzie usually covers for me but his wife is about to have a baby and I can't count on him to be around the whole time. I've asked the other docs if any of them would be willing to trade call but they all have other plans."

"You know I've yet to treat a single in-patient here."

"I'd like you to watch over the Chairman and the rest of the hospital for the weekend. If you can hold down the fort I'll be back and forth and help you out between games. I can cut you loose from here by the middle of next week so you can go ahead and get started in Cibecue."

If Ganson hadn't gone through what he had with BOMEX he'd have accepted Peterson's offer without a second thought. He hadn't taken care of a critically ill patient in over a year. The confidence he'd once had in his ability to handle a crisis had died with Angela Miller. As often as he tried to remind himself that he'd done the best he could for her, he couldn't move beyond his feelings of doubt. They had encrypted his thoughts and invaded his dreams. He'd tried reading self-help books, exercising to exhaustion and attending counseling. He'd even spent a weekend with Luther Shock at a sweat lodge ceremony in New Mexico. Nothing had helped.

His father had once told him that service was the most worthy form of human endeavor and Ganson had often seen the feeling of worthiness on his father's face after he'd come home from taking care of someone late at night. Ganson hoped he'd someday get to the point in his professional life where he could experience that same feeling of worthiness. He'd adjusted to living with the stigma that came with working under a restricted license but was fearful of making a mistake.

"When's your next game?" he asked.

"Tonight at eight," Peterson answered, looking relieved. "It's a double elimination tournament. Win or lose, we play again tomorrow afternoon. I'll come by in the morning to free you up so you can at least watch the parade."

Later, after Ganson finished his afternoon clinic, he spent an hour going through the Chairman's voluminous chart. The

Chairman's name was Amos Cromwell and Ganson marveled at how he'd managed to hang on as long as he had. In Phoenix he had coded three different times and been on and off the ventilator but he refused to die. His chart was full of detailed documentation from multiple specialists. The entry Ganson found the most intriguing was the one made the previous night by an intern. The intern noted how the Chairman perked up and all his vital signs improved after he found out he was going back to the reservation.

It wasn't until well after visiting hours had ended and the hospital hallways had cleared out that Ganson opened the door to room 201. The first thing he noticed was the attractive young Apache woman curled up in a chair in the corner. She was wearing a nurse's aide uniform and had an *Advanced Principles of Nursing* textbook open on her lap. Inside the textbook was a copy of *The National Enquirer*. When she saw Ganson she closed the textbook over the tabloid and placed both of them on the windowsill. It had been over a year since she'd handed him the blanket outside the Neonatal ICU in Tucson. If she knew who he was she didn't show it.

"Hello," he said with a smile as he recognized her immediately. "I'm Dr. Michael Ganson."

"I'm Olivia," she said with an expression that still didn't reveal whether or not she remembered him.

Ganson turned his attention to the Chairman, who had a cannula blowing oxygen up his nose and an IV infusing fluids and electrolytes through a vein in his neck. His sunken face was the color of paste and his hair the texture of cotton candy. A salty residue caked the corners of his mouth and he gurgled with every breath. When Ganson approached his bed the old man tried to say something but couldn't clear his throat. Olivia gave the Chairman a sip of water and wiped the crust off the corners of his mouth. He said something to her in Apache before speaking to Ganson in a hoarse whisper.

"Who are you?" he asked in English.

"My name is Michael Ganson. I'm going to be your doctor for the next couple of days."

The Chairman motioned for him to draw closer. "Are you going to take care of me until my doctor gets here?"

"Are you talking about Dr. Peterson?" Ganson asked.

The Chairman took another sip from Olivia before answering. "I'm talking about Bronco Dazen." He started coughing and didn't stop until a dark gob of phlegm flew out his throat and stuck to the railing of the bed. "Are you new here?" he asked Ganson as Olivia wiped away the phlegm with a tissue.

"Yes, I am," Ganson answered.

"Why did you come?"

"I came to be the doctor in Cibecue."

"My home," the Chairman said after catching his breath. "That's what Cibecue means in Apache, my home."

Ganson stood at the railing until the Chairman dozed off. "Thank you for the help," he said to Olivia.

"Do you think he's going to make it through the weekend?" she asked following him out the door.

"Not without divine intervention," Ganson answered.

He ordered morning labs for the Chairman before returning to his apartment. After heating up a bowl of Top Ramon he walked out on the porch to watch as one lightning strike after another lit up the sky to the west. He imagined that somewhere out there Bronco Dazen was holed up in the rocks, waiting for the weather to break so he could climb back on his horse and continue his journey to Whiteriver. It was after midnight before Ganson climbed into bed and fell asleep to the sound of the raindrops peppering the tin roof of his apartment.

Two hours later he was summoned to the ER to treat a man who'd ended up on the losing end of a disagreement outside the bar the local Apaches referred to as the "Flame." A knife was stuck in his sternum and he was bleeding from multiple cuts across his right forearm. Ganson recognized him immediately.

"Can you hear me, Lester?"

"Loud and clear," Lester answered, too drunk to open his eyes.

The nurse in the ER was much calmer than Ganson, who hadn't handled a trauma case since his suspension. The nearest trauma center was two hundred miles away and Whiteriver Hospital had neither a surgeon nor an anesthesiologist, much less an operating room.

"Would you like me to call in one of the other doctors?" the nurse asked as she was wrapping the cuts with gauze.

"Are any of them around?" Ganson asked as he watched the knife handle rise and fall with Lester's respirations.

"I'm pretty sure Dr. Mackenzie is home."

"Isn't his wife about to have a baby?"

"She is, but she hasn't yet. Dr. Mackenzie is a great guy and he's always willing to come in and help us out."

Mackenzie lived in the government compound and made it to the hospital in less than five minutes. "Nice first night of call," he commented to Ganson as he came through the ER door grinning. He walked over to Lester. "Hey, fellow. How are you doing tonight?"

"Not so good," Lester answered, his eyes still closed.

"Do you know where you are?"

"Yes, I do."

"Where?"

"Somewhere on this earth."

Mackenzie broke out laughing. "You're right about that, brother." The ponytailed doctor put on a pair of gloves and motioned for Ganson to do the same. "Let's get this gentleman over to x-ray and see where the tip of that knife is."

The x-rays revealed the knife hadn't penetrated through to the heart or the lungs. Mackenzie waited until they got back to the ER before grabbing hold of the handle with both hands and yanking it free. After dressing the chest wound he placed two different blood pressure cuffs around Lester's upper right arm and pumped each one of them up to two hundred and fifty millimeters of mercury. He cross-clamped the tubing so neither one could deflate and injected a syringe full of local anesthetic into a vein in the back of Lester's right hand.

"Do you know what this is?" Mackenzie asked Ganson.

"I believe it's a Bier block," Ganson answered.

"That it is. It's good to know how to do things like this when you're practicing medicine out here at the edge of the frontier. With the blood flow cut off to that arm it will take a few minutes for the anesthetic to seep in and deaden everything. After that you can sew all this up without him feeling a thing. Just make sure when you've finished you only let down one cuff at a time. There's enough anesthetic in his forearm to kill him if it were to all go to his heart at once."

Mackenzie left to go back to bed and Ganson set about sewing up Lester, who had passed out and was snoring. Ganson used a Betadine solution to scrub up the wounds and spent an hour approximating the shredded muscles and closing the skin. Lester had gotten lucky in that he'd suffered no major nerve or tendon injuries. Ganson knew the anesthetic would be fixed to the tissue with little risk of it getting to the heart but he still deflated each of the cuffs separately and slowly. After instructing the nurse to give a tetanus shot and start IV antibiotics he wrote orders to admit Lester for overnight observation.

He left the ER and returned to the ward to check on the Chairman. When he opened the door he found Olivia half asleep in her chair and the Chairman motionless in his bed. Fearing the old man was dead Ganson rushed to the bedside. By the time he got there the Chairman had begun breathing again. His respirations started as shallow gasps, advanced to deep breaths, retreated to shallow gasps and then stopped. After a few seconds of silence the cycle started in again. The pattern of waxing and waning respirations like those of the Chairman was known as Cheyne-Stokes breathing. It was never a good sign.

"How long has he been doing this?" Ganson asked Olivia, who had woken up and was standing next to him.

"Ever since I got here," Olivia answered.

"He wasn't that way when I saw him earlier," he said.

"He only does it when he drops into a deep sleep," she explained. "The nurses have been in and out of here all night listening to him and haven't said a thing."

Ganson picked up the copy of *The National Enquirer* that had dropped onto the floor and placed it back inside Olivia's textbook. "Why don't you take a break," he said. "When you come back you can bring us both a cup of coffee."

As he sat at the side of the bed listening to the Chairman's irregular respirations he wondered what had become of Olivia's niece Cassie. He'd lost track of her after she'd been discharged from the Neonatal ICU in Tucson. He thought about asking Olivia but decided against it. He had no idea what she knew about him, but with the news of his restricted license having spread across the reservation, he could imagine her thinking he'd come there to practice because no other place would have him.

Olivia returned with two steaming cups of coffee and revealed no emotion when he told her he was going to help her keep watch over the Chairman for the rest of the night. He dragged in a chair from the room across the hall and curled up in it much like she had done in hers. There was a mesmerizing effect to the Chairman's stuttering breathing pattern and before long it was Ganson who couldn't keep his eyes open. He fell asleep with a half empty cup of coffee clamped between his knees. When he awoke, the coffee cup was on the windowsill and there was a hospital blanket draped over him. The daytime RN was in the room tending to the Chairman, whose condition hadn't changed.

"Thanks for the blanket," he said, "I guess I must have drifted off for a while.

"For a couple of hours," she said, "but don't thank me. It was Olivia who tucked you in."

Ganson got up and went to the lounge to wash up. When he returned to the nursing station Bryce Peterson was leaning over the desk. The Clinical Director looked rested and in good spirits.

"How did it go?" he asked Ganson.

"Other than the Chairman Cheyne-Stoking all night, I guess it went all right."

"I heard you had it pretty easy in the ER."

"Not bad."

"There are Indians here from all over the Southwest attending the rodeo and fair. This is usually the busiest weekend of the year for the ER."

"I saw one patient that got cut up pretty bad. I was just getting ready to go down to his room and see how he's doing."

"No need to bother," Peterson said.

"What happened to him?" Ganson asked with a sickening feeling in his gut.

"The fool got up this morning and ran out the door dragging his IV pole behind him."

"I was afraid you were going to tell me he died."

"The police found the pole in the middle of the road. The patient's whereabouts are unknown."

"Have you heard anything about Bronco Dazen?" Ganson asked.

"One of the tribal cops saw him crossing Carrizo Creek last night at dusk. I suspect he'll be here by late afternoon or early evening."

Neither time seemed early enough for Ganson, who was convinced the Chairman was destined to die on his watch.

Nine

Bronco Dazen was in no hurry to break camp. The monsoon storm had caught up with him and he'd spent the night huddled under an overhang at the bottom of Carrizo Canyon. He'd started an early morning fire to take the chill out of his bones but didn't feel up to riding on to Whiteriver.

The medicine man stirred the ashes to generate enough heat for another cup of instant coffee. He knew Chairman Amos Cromwell was dying and doubted there was anything he could do about it. Dazen no longer had confidence in his ability to heal because he'd lost his two major sources of power, lightning and snake. The lightning had turned against him. The tribe had taken the snakes away from him. He had agreed to ride to the government hospital out of respect for the Chairman, even though it was the Chairman's Tribal Council that had forced him to abandon his most reliable source of power.

It was another hour before he doused the coals and collected his gear. The mare was grazing under a tree and acted as disinterested as he was in going anywhere. For years the two of them had traveled as one. They anticipated each other's moves, felt each other's fatigue and sensed each other's uncertainty. That had all changed when he'd forced her to carry the dead boy on the back of the saddle. Now they were like a pair of dance partners who could never agree on who should take the lead.

As soon as she saw him coming toward her she started pawing at the ground and pulling at the rope. He followed her around to the other side of the tree and threw the blanket and saddle over her back. Before she could throw them off he tightened the cinch and fastened the breast collar. He eased the bit into her mouth and slipped the bridle over her head.

When Dazen stepped up into the stirrup and swung his leg over the saddle the coyote came running out of the bushes. The medicine man pulled a piece of beef jerky out of his saddlebag and tossed it into the air. The coyote caught it before it hit the ground. Dazen kicked the mare into a lope. He didn't have to look around to know the coyote would be right behind because the coyote had been following him ever since he'd carried the boy off and buried him in the canyon of the Ancient Ones.

Ten

Ganson stayed in the shower until the hot water ran cold. After putting on a clean cotton shirt and pair of jeans he walked the four blocks to State Route 73, the two-lane highway that ran through the middle of Whiteriver. Both sides of the road were filled with arts and crafts booths. Hundreds of onlookers had arrived early to watch the Labor Day weekend parade celebrating the annual Tribal Fair. Ganson found an unobstructed view of the highway on the skeletonized porch of what used to be one of the town's two trading posts. The remains of the other trading post stood right across the street. The two had long served as the center of commerce for the reservation. Both were now out of business, victims of the government subsidized shopping center at the south end of town. The two relics were wasting away, their fate paralleling that of the Apache way of life they'd serviced for the greater part of the century.

The parade was scheduled to start at nine but the reservation ran on Indian Time, not Greenwich Mean. It was almost ten o'clock before the master of ceremonies standing in front of the temporary grandstands turned on his microphone and tested it with three ear-splitting thumps. After turning the volume down he identified himself as Ronald Massey, the director of tribal public relations. Speaking in both English and Apache he thanked everyone for coming and reminded them of the afternoon events at the rodeo grounds. He then asked the crowd to join in a moment of silent prayer for the Tribal Chairman.

The first entry in the parade was the Alchesay High School Marching Band. Led by half a dozen banner-carrying cheerleaders, the blue and yellow uniformed musicians were high stepping it to the rhythm of the Apache percussionists, who, with their hair flying in the breeze, were beating away on their drums. When they reached the grandstands, the rest of the band took up their instruments and erupted into a tuba-dominated version of "Another One Bites the Dust."

With each additional stanza of the hit song by Queen, the horse positioned behind the band became more agitated. It tossed its head, pawed at the asphalt and started crow hopping sideways across the highway. The rider was an Apache girl who couldn't have been more than ten or eleven years of age. The ends of her flowing black hair brushed back and forth across the cantle of her saddle as she struggled to keep her seat. She was wearing a miniature camp dress with a sash across the front that read "Apache Princess." The sash had worked its way up in front of her eyes. When she tried to readjust it, the sash slipped over her head and fluttered to the pavement. To make things worse, a bunch of Apache boys who appeared to have been drinking were laughing at her and telling her she needed to take control of her mount. She ignored them and relaxed her legs, steadied her hands and coaxed her horse back into line. After one of the Apache women in the crowd retrieved her sash and handed it to her the little girl looked back at the rowdy boys and waved.

The parade went on for over an hour. Innumerable horse and riders were interspersed between the makeshift floats, antique cars and fat motorcycle-riding white men with burgundy fezzes stuck atop their heads. There were also several groups of dancers representing the different Southwestern tribes. The Tribal Council members, minus the Chairman, cruised by in a pair of Cadillac convertibles. Right behind them was a carload of county and state officials.

The crowd didn't seem all that interested in the dignitaries but broke out in applause when the Apache Hot Shots passed by in the back of what looked like an old paddy wagon. The vehicle was designed to transport firefighting crews. The Hot Shots were one of the nation's elite. They'd spent an exhausting summer battling blazes all across the western United States and it was all they could do to muster a smile as they rolled by.

Following the Hot Shots was a group of young riders who called themselves the Tucson Troopers. They were fully uniformed and rode in tight formation. They stared straight ahead as they paraded their chestnut colored mounts down the middle of the highway. It had only been a hundred years since the army had sent its horse soldiers into Apache Land to subdue the natives and Ganson found it puzzling that the tribe would allow themselves to be reminded of such things by a bunch of cavalry clad cadets from white suburbia.

As the teenaged troopers were riding by, an Apache man wearing a black Stetson took up a position next to Ganson on the porch. Ganson recognized him from the Apache Culture Center.

"Michael Ganson," he said offering his hand.

"Tiswin Richards," the Apache replied returning Ganson's firm handshake.

"I saw you over at Fort Apache," Ganson said.

"I remember," Richards replied.

"I enjoyed looking at all the historical displays."

"I wish more of our own people would drop by."

"I guess things have changed a bit in the last hundred years."

"Are you here for long?" Richards asked.

"I'm a doctor at the hospital," Ganson answered. "Next week I'll be moving to Cibecue."

"Why would you want to do that?"

Ganson chuckled. "I can't say I had much of a choice."

"I used to live in Cibecue but don't think I'd ever move back."

"Why's that?"

Richards wiped his brow and readjusted his Stetson. "Something out there is not right."

Before Ganson could ask him what he meant, Richards stepped off the porch and disappeared into the crowd.

The master of ceremonies announced the arrival of the band, Apache Dreams. Armed with a drummer, a keyboard player, three guitarists and a female lead, the band rolled up on a trailer. They were all Apache and the woman looked like a dream. She was dressed in tight jeans and a Jefferson Starship t-shirt that clung to her willowy body. Drifting back and forth across the flatbed stage, she flailed her limber arms and pounded her bare feet to the band's rendition of Fleetwood Mac's "Rhiannon." Ganson kept his eyes on her until she and her band rolled out of sight.

The parade's final entry was the Apache Crown Dancers. There were five of them, four Mountain Spirits and the Clown. The Mountain Spirits were masked and decked out in wooden headdresses. They were clad in buckskin and their bodies were painted reddish-brown with white markings. In a semi-crouch they rocked and swayed as they shook the wooden crosses and daggers they held in their hands. The Clown was also masked but he had no headdress and his body was painted white with black spots. In contrast to the discipline displayed by the Mountain Spirits the Clown was all over the place.

When he wasn't mocking the other dancers he was darting in and out of the crowd terrifying the little children.

When the parade ended Ganson found a booth selling Navajo fry bread and cream sodas. He sat down at a picnic table and watched the Apache people stroll in and out. Laughing and carrying on, they seemed unaware of the paradox of celebrating a parade on Labor Day weekend when over two thirds of their own people were unemployed.

The Apache warriors of centuries past had devoted their lives to fighting an inevitable fate that had come stalking them from the other side of the world. From the time Coronado put them on notice in 1540 until the Cibecue Massacre of 1881, these "Merchants of Death" had fought to maintain their way of life. Experts in guerilla warfare, they'd held their own for hundreds of years before falling to the U.S. Government's thirty-year campaign to destroy them.

Most of the parade watchers were just three generations removed from the end of the Apache wars. They carried within them their ancestors' undiluted DNA. The double helical combinations of nucleic acids that determined who they were ran through their hearts and whispered to their souls as they had for centuries. Before the reservation years, star status within the tribe came from the ability to raid, hunt and fight. The concept of work was as confusing to them as the flood of Christian doctrine that would later adulterate their aboriginal beliefs. Those Apaches fortunate enough to have adjusted to the new way of life woke up every morning to a job that would pay them so they could provide for their families and to a religion that would comfort them in that endeavor. The rest woke up to a hangover that had hung over them ever since their ancestors had fallen victim to America's Manifest Destiny.

Ganson made it back to the hospital by twelve thirty. Entering the ER he asked the nurse if she'd heard anything about the status of the Chairman. She said as far as she knew nothing had changed. When he walked over to the ward to see for himself he encountered a hallway full of Apaches. They were lined up outside the Chairman's room, waiting their chance to pay their respects. Ganson was thinking about wading through them when he saw Jim Mackenzie sitting at the nursing station.

"What are you doing here?" he asked.

"Peterson called me," Mackenzie replied.

"He told me his game didn't start until one."

"He gets pretty anal about his basketball. He asked me if I'd cover until you got here."

"What did he say about the Chairman?"

"Not much. He gave the poor man a couple of extra doses of lasix to see if he could get him to pee a little more."

Ganson sat down at the desk next to Mackenzie. "I apologize for you having to come over here. I told Peterson when I'd be back."

"He wasn't mad or anything," Mackenzie said. "He said he just didn't want to be late for school."

"What's he talking about?" Ganson asked.

"When he's getting ready for a ballgame he claims he's getting ready to 'school' the Lamanites."

"Who are the Lamanites?"

"What do you know about the Mormon religion?"

"Not much. I know they believe Christ came over here after he finished his business in the Middle East."

"They also believe the American Indians are direct descendants of the Lost Tribes of Israel."

"Really."

"According to the Book of Mormon the displaced Israelites came to America long before the birth of Christ. They later splintered into two groups, the god fearing group led by a guy named Nephi and the not so god fearing group led by his brother Laman. The descendants of the two remained at war until the dark skinned Lamanites prevailed and wiped out the light skinned Nephites. The Mormons claim the American Indians are the direct descendants of the Lamanites."

"Are any of these claims certified by the Smithsonian Institute?" Ganson asked.

"Do you know any religion that's scientifically certified?" Mackenzie answered with a chuckle.

Ganson had to think about it for a minute. He'd grown up with a set of Christian beliefs ancient enough to survive historical and scientific scrutiny. The Mormon religion was but one hundred and fifty years old, which made it far more vulnerable to modern day research. "Are the Mormons on a mission to save the Indians?" he asked.

"My guess would be they're on a mission to enlighten them."

"Is that what Peterson believes he's doing every time he drops in another jumper over the Apache's drawn-in defense?" Ganson asked.

"I've never asked," Mackenzie answered.

"Before he left did he tell you if he'd heard anything about the ETA of Bronco Dazen?"

"No, he didn't."

"Assuming the medicine man makes it in time, do you have any idea how long a ceremony he'll do?"

"When I was growing up on the reservation there was this Apache man working at the Mission who was dying from tuberculosis. My parents kept trying to get him to go see the doctor. He finally sought the services of a medicine man, who conducted a five night curing ceremony."

"Five nights?"

"The first night was to diagnose the disease. The next four nights were to cure it."

"What happened to the patient?"

"He made it through the ceremony but died shortly thereafter."

Ganson told Mackenzie to go home and headed toward the Chairman's room. The hall was full of women in their multicolored camp dresses and men in their denim shirts and jeans. They reluctantly stepped aside for Ganson. The only people inside the room were the patient, the daytime aide and an elderly woman in a yellow camp dress. They were busy bathing the Chairman and didn't pay much attention to Ganson when he entered. After they finished washing the Chairman's wispy white hair they dressed him in a pair of jeans and a black and red western shirt with pearl colored snaps. The elderly woman was the Chairman's wife. After she finished straightening up her dying husband she went back out into the hall to mingle with the crowd.

Ganson told the aide to take a break. The room had a stale smell to it. When he went to crack the window he noticed the copy of the *Enquirer* Olivia had been reading the night before. The front-page story was about a Phoenix neurologist who'd ordered a hit on another neurologist who was scheduled to testify against him in a malpractice case. The hit man was actually an undercover cop and both physicians turned out to be cocaine addicts.

More business for BOMEX Ganson said out loud as he laid the tabloid newspaper down and turned his attention back to the

Chairman. He lifted the vital signs clipboard from the rack at the foot of the bed and looked at the recorded blood pressure, pulse rate and respiratory rate. They were all moving in the wrong direction. When the aide returned, Ganson left to get some fresh air before devoting the remainder of the afternoon to treating the steady stream of patients seeking care through the ER. There were the usual sick kids as well as a number of rodeo casualties. By the time he got caught up the sun was deep in the afternoon sky. On his way back to the Chairman's room he came upon a crowd gathered on the porch. They were all watching the approach of a horse and rider.

The pair had descended the ridge to the west and were making their way across the grassy field in front of the hospital. Sagging under the swelter of the heat and humidity, the horse was laboring to throw one foot out in front of the other. At the edge of the parking lot the rider dismounted next to a metal hitching rail that was half hidden behind a clump of blue spruce trees.

As he was unsaddling his horse a coyote appeared. It came halfway across the field before pulling up. The crowd of people on the porch seemed to disturb it. After pacing back and forth for several seconds the coyote turned and took off. It ran with a hitch in its left back leg and Ganson kept his eyes on it until it disappeared into a patch of foxtails.

Bronco Dazen toweled off his worn out mare while one of

the janitors brought out a bucket of water for her. The medicine man waited for her to finish drinking before walking over and climbing up the back steps to the hospital. When he reached the porch the Apaches stepped back in a show of reverence and allowed him to pass. He had the hardened body of a tested warrior but the beleaguered face of a man full of doubt.

Ganson waited for the medicine man to disappear into the Chairman's room before returning to the ER. It was change of shift before he got back to the nursing station and saw Olivia at the other end of the hall. The crowd had parted for her and she was pushing the portable defibrillator Peterson had ordered kept at the Chairman's bedside. After rolling it into the adjacent room she walked down to where Ganson was standing.

"What's going on, Olivia?" he asked.

"I hope you're not mad at me," she answered. "I know Dr. Peterson told us to have the defibrillator in there at all times but the medicine man asked me to remove it."

"Did he say why?"

"He claimed the machine interfered with his power."

"Is he getting ready to perform some kind of ceremony?"

"He didn't say."

Ganson listened for chanting coming from the room. There was none. All he could hear were the animated voices of the Apaches in the hall. They'd been there all day and were still in a heightened state over the arrival of Bronco Dazen.

"How's the Chairman doing?" he asked.

"The same," she answered.

Ganson was about to go see for himself when a stat page summoned him back to the ER. Lying on the ambulance gurney was a woman who'd been scalped. She'd gotten drunk, fallen out the back of a pickup truck and skated down the middle of the highway on the crown of her head. The road had peeled back the top of her scalp and ground a strip of asphalt into her skull. The paramedics had placed her neck in a soft collar, taped her to a backboard and brought her to the hospital.

"What's your name?" Ganson asked the woman, who appeared to be remarkably alert.

"Roberta Ivy. What's yours?"

"My name's Dr. Ganson. Can you tell me where you hurt?"

"Yes, I can."

"Where?"

"My head."

"What about your neck?"

"What about it?"

"Does it hurt?"

"No, it doesn't," she answered.

"Are you sure about that?" Ganson asked.

"Are you sure you're a doctor?" Roberta replied.

Ganson laughed and looked over at Evelyn Shaw, the nurse he'd worked with the night before. "I don't guess we have any neurosurgeons or plastic surgeons in the facility tonight, do we."

"Would you like me to call Dr. Mackenzie?" Nurse Shaw asked, looking no more confident in Ganson's abilities than she had the night before.

"I don't think so," Ganson answered.

He instructed her instead to call in the radiology tech, who took Roberta for x-rays of her skull and cervical spine. When they showed no fractures or dislocations Ganson rolled the woman back to the ER. She had fallen asleep but immediately awoke when he lifted up the top of her scalp and started picking at the asphalt and grit lodged underneath.

"What are you trying to do to me?" she yelled as she attempted to wiggle her head free of the tape that was holding her to the wooden backboard.

"Where do you hurt now?" Ganson asked as he released the flap of scalp and let it fall back over her skull.

"The same place I hurt before."

"Your head?"

"That's right."

"How about your neck?"

"I already told you it doesn't hurt."

"How about your back?"

"It doesn't hurt there either."

At County, Ganson had seen drunken patients survive serious car crashes with minimal trauma. The standard ER explanation for their good fortune was that the excessive amount of alcohol they'd consumed had relaxed their bodies to the point that they'd rolled with the impact. Ganson had never been totally convinced of the truth of that explanation but he had to admit that something had saved Roberta from a far worse outcome than having the top of her scalp separated from her skull.

"Do we have anything around here we can clean this up with?" he asked Nurse Shaw.

"How about a Waterpik?" she suggested.

He'd never used one for anything other than cleaning his teeth but he could see how it could be used to irrigate a dirty wound. "Let's try it out," he said.

While Shaw got the Waterpik out from under the sink and filled the reservoir with a mixture of Betadine and water, Ganson explained to Roberta how important it was to get her head cleaned. She seemed quite agreeable until she saw him coming at her with the nozzle of the Waterpik.

"You're not going to shoot that shit in my mouth," she yelled.

"Don't worry," Ganson laughed. "I'm just going to use it to clean out the top of your head."

He waited for her to calm down before turning on the pump and directing the pulsating spray into the space between her skull and her scalp. The golden brown stream bounced off the bone and flooded into the recesses of the wound, flushing out the debris the road had deposited there. After taking a brush to the asphalt that was tattooed into her skull he used a pair of tissue forceps to pick out what was left. He then re-irrigated the wound with the Waterpik.

Roberta's scalp had been sheared off from the peak of her forehead. After anesthetizing the tissue he closed it in a way that hid the scar in her hairline. It was the first procedure of any kind he'd attempted since operating on Angela in the County ER. Although Nurse Shaw made no mention of the cosmetic result Ganson could tell she was surprised at what he'd been able to do. He admitted Roberta to the hospital for overnight observation.

He returned to the floor to find the hallway deserted. Olivia was the only other person in the Chairman's room.

"What happened to everybody?" Ganson asked.

"They all went home for the night," Olivia answered.

"What about the medicine man?"

"He left too."

"When's he coming back?"

"He didn't say."

"What about the ceremony?"

"He sprinkled some sacred pollen around the room," Olivia explained.

"That doesn't sound like much of an effort to me," Ganson observed.

All the time Ganson was putting Roberta back together he'd been thinking about Bronco Dazen. He had this vision of the medicine man dancing through an abandoned field, throwing handful after handful of cattail pollen amongst the rotting cornhusks. He knew Dazen didn't have a ghost of a chance of warding off the diseases besieging the Chairman but he still felt drawn to him. It was as if their fates were intertwined.

Bronco Dazen was a mere mortal devoted to doing what he could to protect the Apache tradition. The medicine man's calling was to preserve their beliefs while providing emotional support for those who still believed in them. His power came from his ability to offer comfort through ritual and prayer. Even though his face reflected the doubt and suffering of his people, there was something about him that held the promise for spiritual realization and inner peace. To those who believed in him, he was the last of the spiritual leaders of the tribe and the keeper of the faith. To the hard rocking Apache pill poppers he was nothing more than a vestige of a vacated past.

Eleven

Bronco Dazen returned at dawn but that was too late to help Amos Cromwell. The Chairman had been pronounced dead an hour earlier and his body was already starting to stiffen. With the help of the two RNs and Olivia, Ganson had worked on him for an hour. He'd intubated him, shocked him nine times and given him every drug in the crash cart, all to no avail. One of the nurses had called Peterson when the Chairman crashed but by the time the Clinical Director got there from his home in Pinetop Ganson had already called the code.

Peterson had lost a late night game to a team of scrappy Navajos from Window Rock and seemed in none too pleasant a mood as he went over the details of the Chairman's death at the nursing station. "Can anybody tell me why the flipping defibrillator wasn't in the room when the Chairman went down?"

Ganson answered before Olivia could. "Bronco Dazen requested it be removed."

"That defibrillator should have never left the Chairman's bedside."

"It couldn't have taken fifteen seconds to get it in there. Surely you're not suggesting the outcome of the code would have been any different."

Peterson slammed the Chairman's chart down on the desktop. "That's not the point."

"What is the point?" Ganson asked.

"I don't know how it was where you came from, but around here we don't allow a medicine man to override a physician's order."

"He didn't change the order, Bryce. I did."

"I can see how you got into trouble with the Arizona Board."

Peterson walked away shaking his head. Even though he returned a few minutes later and apologized, Ganson suspected the Clinical Director would screw him the first chance he got.

The nursing supervisor had dispatched the police to notify the wife but Ganson was the only one in the Chairman's room when Bronco Dazen arrived at daybreak. The medicine man picked up the Chairman's ice-cold right hand and held it between his. After laying the arm over the Chairman's chest and folding the other one across it he reached into his pouch and offered a pinch of sacred pollen to his dead friend.

"We did everything we could to save him," Ganson offered.

"You waited too long to call me in on the case," Dazen replied.

The funeral took place the following Friday and was attended by many of the same dignitaries who had participated in the parade the previous weekend. The Tribal Council designated it a day of mourning. Most of the businesses in town, including the liquor store, were closed. Peterson and Mackenzie went as representatives of the medical staff.

As the services were going on Ganson was preparing for his move to Cibecue. He packed up his clothes, boxed his books and albums and wrapped his stereo in the Indian blanket. Not knowing whether or not the Tribe would hold him accountable for the death of the Chairman, he felt apprehensive about venturing deeper into the territory of a people he knew so little about.

The Apaches were late arrivers to the Southwest. Of Asian descent they were members of the Athapaskan speaking family of American Indians that also included the Navajo. Before the end of the last Ice Age they crossed the Bering Land Bridge and entered North America. It took another eight thousand years for them to migrate from the far western tip of Alaska to the southwestern portion of the present day United States. The White Mountain Apaches settled into their homeland in eastern Arizona sometime between the disappearance of the ancient Mogollon culture and the arrival of Coronado. The Spaniards called them Coyoteros, which meant wolf men, but the name Apache came from the Zuni word for enemy.

Before being confined to the reservation the Apaches were

nomads, living in small groups of extended families. They spent their summers in the cooler mountain country farming and gathering before retreating to the relative warmth of the lower river canyons. They hunted game all year long, but mostly in the fall when they could top up their supply before returning to their winter camps. Their lives cycled the same way year after year, decade after decade, century after century.

The first hint of change came when Coronado passed through and proclaimed Spanish ownership of everything he saw. It was a claim his mother country was never able to back up. Waging an ongoing war of terror against settlers and Indians alike, the Apaches ruled the region for the next 350 years.

Armed with the knowledge of the terrain they used their guerilla hit and run tactics to resist every military campaign directed against them. The land they'd never relinquished to Spain was later claimed by Mexico, who eventually sold it to the United States. Under the terms of the Gadsden Purchase thirty million acres of Apache Territory were acquired for ten million dollars. The signing of the treaty marked the culmination of Manifest Destiny, which was the United States' self proclaimed mission to expand all the way from the Atlantic to the Pacific Ocean and annex every acre of land in between.

The U.S. purchased the land in 1853 but it took another thirty years to wrest it away from the Apaches. During the 1860s the government made the mistake of breaking too many promises and pissing off too many war chiefs. The result was another fifteen years of warfare costing the U.S. thousands of additional lives and millions of additional dollars.

In spite of their superior numbers and weaponry the Army wasn't able to take control of the region until General George Crook came up with the idea of employing Apaches as scouts. Age-old tribal hostilities provided a constant source of recruits willing to go to war against their hated kindred. There was no way the Army could have brought in the renegade Apaches without them. The scouts knew every foot of the terrain and could track a coyote across it. When engaged in battle against their hostile brethren they fought right along side the government troops.

The Fort Apache Indian Reservation was established by executive order on November 9, 1871. Things were relatively quiet until the spring of 1881 when a Cibecue medicine man named Noch-ay-del-klinne started to stir up the natives. The Apache medicine man, who was also known as the "Prophet," claimed he could resurrect the dead. He traveled the reservation, holding dances designed to drive his audience into a state of hallucinogenic exhaustion. He'd position himself in the middle of a small circle with his followers arranged in lines running out from the center like the spokes of a wheel. Swaying back and forth they'd dance until dawn.

The dances continued into the summer. When they failed to bring a single soul back from the grave, Noch-ay-del-klinne announced he'd been in communication with two dead chiefs. He claimed they'd both told him they couldn't make the journey back to earth until the white man had been driven from their land. The medicine man also told his followers that one of the chiefs had provided him with a shirt that would protect him from the bullets of the soldiers.

Living in Whiteriver at the time was a levelheaded Apache named Alchesay. He was one of the most respected tribal leaders and often served as a mediator between his people and the Army. When Noch-ay-del-klinne started getting the warriors on the west end of the reservation worked up, Alchesay went to Fort Apache to speak to the commander about what was going on in Cibecue. Alchesay referred to Noch-ay-del-klinne as a harmless witch doctor and advised the commander to leave the medicine man alone so his prophecies could die an unfulfilled death. The commander chose to ignore Alchesay's advice and led a force of seventy-five soldiers and twenty-three Apache scouts to Cibecue to bring the medicine man in for questioning.

They took him into custody without incident but a battle later broke out between his followers and the troops. Eight soldiers and dozens of Apaches were killed. Among the dead was Noch-ay-del-klinne, whose ghost shirt offered no protection from the hatchet one of the soldiers buried in his skull.

The Army's Apache scouts scattered with the first foray of gunshots. Their role in what would come to be called the Cibecue Massacre was never fully established. Most of them were captured and imprisoned. Three were later hanged. None of them ever admitted to any wrongdoing and it was the only incident in the history of the Apache Wars where an Apache scout was accused of treason against the United States.

Also killed during the massacre were Noch-ay-del-klinne's wife and son. The medicine man had a second wife who survived. She was pregnant at the time and gave birth to a baby boy in the spring of 1882. The boy grew up an outdoorsman, tracking and hunting game all across the west end of the reservation. He didn't take a wife until after his mother died in the influenza epidemic of 1918. Six years later his one and only son was born. This boy, the grandson of Noch-ay-del-klinne, spent his youth hunting with his father but later became interested in following in the footsteps of his grandfather.

The grandson spent years learning from one of the older Cibecue medicine men before moving to Whiteriver to study under the most influential Apache medicine man of the twentieth century, Silas John Edwards. In 1961 the thirty-seven year old grandson of Noch-ay-del-klinne moved back to Cibecue to devote his life to practicing his religion and perfecting his religious ceremonies. Like his mentor Silas John, the grandson claimed to have acquired both lightning and snake power. He'd mastered a litany of songs and chants for both. He never married and spent much of his time alone in the hills in spiritual retreat. The older tribal members looked upon him as a man worthy of great respect. The younger ones looked upon him as irrelevant. His God-given name was Bronco Dazen but a Led Zeppelin loving Apache pothead had later re-christened him Dazen Confused.

Twelve

The road Ganson took from Whiteriver to Cibecue approximated the route the soldiers from Fort Apache had taken a century before to arrest Noch-ay-del-klinne. The farther west he went, the farther back in time he felt he was going. About an hour out from Whiteriver he crested a small pass and started a gradual descent that led him into a green valley surrounded by red hills. A shallow creek bisected the valley and an assortment of structures dotted the fields sloping down toward the creek from the east. The Cibecue Apaches lived in everything from brick houses to wooden shacks. Many of them still had brush-covered wickiups and squaw-coolers on their adjoining land. There were only three paved roads in the entire town. Other than a day school and a police station, the business establishments consisted of a few churches, a sawmill, a Laundromat, a hamburger joint called the West End Café and the Cibecue Trading Post.

Ganson skirted the trading post parking lot before crossing the creek on the town's only bridge. He turned south and drove past a cluster of houses with TV antennas on the roofs and pickup trucks in the carports. When he reached the sawmill he turned right into a tract of trailers. The first trailer had a hand painted sign that read "Cibecue Clinic." The gravel parking lot was empty and the clinic appeared to be closed for the weekend.

The adjacent trailer was Ganson's new home. It was so run down that even in Cibecue it looked out of place. When Peterson handed him the keys he'd told him it was a dump. He'd also told him the Service Unit wouldn't have the funds to fix it up until sometime after October first, which was when the new fiscal year began.

Ganson parked his truck in the crumbling cement carport that was missing its roof. He entered the front yard through a gateless opening in a broken down fence. Exfoliated strips of paint crunched under his shoes as he walked across the wooden porch. Things inside weren't as bad. The electricity and water were on and someone had made a modest attempt to make the place livable. The two-bedroom trailer had a stove, a refrigerator, a table and chairs, a couch, a bed, a chest of drawers and a TV that looked like it might work. The kitchen cabinet held a few plastic dishes and some silverware. The bathroom had half a roll of toilet paper.

A black rotary phone sat on the counter on top of a Navajo County phonebook. The receiver was off the hook. When Ganson went to replace it, an electricity-like surge rushed through him. The surge came not from the phone, which was disconnected, but from the phone book, which had a full-page ad for David Dunbar on the cover. It was as if the malpractice attorney were stalking him.

What most appealed to Ganson about Cibecue was its remoteness. It was an opportunity to get as far away as he could from the memories of the past fifteen months. Having the state's most notorious personal injury lawyer lying in wait for him in his own trailer was a shocking reminder of his vulnerability. He tore off the cover of the phonebook and threw it in the trashcan.

After unpacking his belongings and draping the Indian blanket over the back of his couch he drove back across the creek and visited the trading post. The building had a wooden floor with high-beamed ceilings. The walls were crowded with the mounted heads of animals native to the region. There was a black bear, a bobcat, a coyote, an antelope, a javelina and two mountain lions. The store carried a variety of perishable and nonperishable goods. It also had clothing, jewelry, tennis shoes, guns and ammunition. Working behind the counter were two women conversing in Apache. Neither paid him much mind when he walked in and they stopped talking just long enough to take his money. The price of everything was marked up to reflect the reality that the closest place to shop was the off-reservation town of Show Low, which was over fifty miles away. Ganson bought only enough goods to last him until he had the opportunity to make the one-hour drive north.

On the way to his truck a commotion broke out at the side of the trading post. He dropped his purchases in the front seat and walked over to see what was going on. Next to the building was a kennel full of hounds and hunting dogs. They were all at the fence, howling at a stray dog that had somehow gotten its head stuck inside a restaurant sized plastic Mayonnaise jar. The dog was staggering around the parking lot like it had gotten into somebody's home brew. It couldn't see where it was going and kept running into the side of the dumpster. One of the caged dogs, a massive caramel colored male with a ridge running down its back, was trying to climb over the fence.

As Ganson approached the stray an Indian carrying a hunting rifle stepped out of the back door of the trading post. The man was wearing a cowboy hat with the head of a rattlesnake mounted on the brim. He motioned for Ganson to get out of the way. After rapping the butt of his rifle against the section of fence the ridge-backed dog was attempting to scale, the man pumped a shell into the breech and drew a bead on the stray. The blast blew a hole in the plastic jar and penetrated the dog's skull, killing it instantly. The moment the dog dropped dead the hounds stopped howling. The man walked over to the dead dog, picked it up by the hind leg and threw it into the dumpster. He passed by Ganson and was halfway through the back door when he stopped and turned around.

"You never know about that kind of an animal," he said with a smirk. "It was acting like it might have rabies or something."

Ganson was tempted to say it might have just been acting like a stray dog that had a Mayonnaise jar stuck over its head but he wasn't all that sure the Indian wouldn't shoot him too. He drove back to his trailer and walked over to the clinic. The facility had remained open for triage and the dispensing of chronic medications. Staffing it were two Apache women, one an RN who had previously worked at the hospital in Whiteriver. Inside the double-wide trailer was a waiting room with seven chairs, a reception area with a bookcase full of charts, a doctor's office, another smaller office, three exam rooms, a closet full of drugs, an area for drawing blood and a room with an x-ray machine. The waiting room could use a carpet upgrade but for the most part the clinic appeared clean and well cared for.

He went in and out of every room before sitting down at the desk in the office. The chair was a little low but he figured he could adjust it later. The only thing on the desktop was a phone and a laminated listing of several reservation and government phone numbers. He opened the drawers looking to see if there was a phone book with David Dunbar's picture on it. All he found was an empty stapler and a box full of paper clips.

The sun had dropped below the hills and the air felt calm as he walked the short distance from the clinic back to his trailer. The sawmill had shut down for the weekend and the only living thing in sight was a horse running up the road. As the horse got closer

Ganson could see there were two Apache boys riding bareback. The boy in front was holding onto a rope halter, the boy in back was holding onto the boy in front. Both of them were bouncing up and down to the jackhammer gait of the horse. The boys appeared to be no more than nine or ten years old and he marveled at how they were able to keep from being thrown.

Back in his trailer Ganson fixed himself a bowl of trading post priced Top Ramon and a tuna fish sandwich. He had his dinner on the porch steps where he remained until the stars came out for the night. Gazing up into the heavens he felt isolated and alone. When he was a little boy his mother and he would often sit on the swing and study the nighttime sky. She knew all the constellations and the brightest stars in each. She was always naming off the ones she claimed were at work that night, sending him encoded messages. He'd tell her he had no idea what the stars were trying to tell him. She'd promise some day he would.

Ganson spent that first weekend working on his trailer. He found the TV antenna lying out back in a pile of weeds. It took him half a day to secure it to the roof and hook it up to the television. He could only pick up two channels, neither one clearly. Both stations were boosted in from Tucson. It felt strange for him to be in such a far-off place watching the same local NBC station that had once reported on him and his disastrous night at the County ER.

He found the front gate behind the carport and hinged it back into place. The fence was missing several sections but he felt he'd upgraded his quarters by getting the gate back on. Growing up on the farm, one of his duties had been taking care of the yard. The near compulsive drive he developed for doing this chore had followed him into his adult life. He made a mental note to pick up a shovel, a rake and something to beat back the weeds when he took his first shopping trip to Show Low.

Sitting on his porch on Sunday afternoon he was aware of a feeling he hadn't experienced since childhood. He knew his rundown trailer wasn't much but it felt like home to him.

Early that evening he ventured into the Laundromat. The place had eight washers and four dryers. The only person using them was a young mother who had three little boys with her. The boys had buzz haircuts and each was carrying a can of Coke and bag of potato chips. The floor of the Laundromat looked like it hadn't been mopped in a month and the machines were coated with detergent and grime. Ganson stayed and washed two loads of clothes anyway. He'd depleted all his savings serving the mandates of BOMEX but promised himself he'd take his next paycheck and apply it toward a washer and dryer.

Before he went to bed that night he carried a box full of books over to the clinic. There wasn't a bookcase for them in his office so he arranged the books side-by-side on the floor next to his desk. They were the text and reference books he'd carried around with him since medical school and he couldn't get along without them. His year of internship, eighteen months working in his father's practice and four months of residency had given him a good learning foundation, but he knew he was years away from acquiring the experience and knowledge necessary to be a skilled practitioner.

He awoke the next morning to his alarm clock, which he'd set to a talk radio station out of Phoenix. After showering and shaving he put on a clean shirt and jeans and headed to work with a cup of coffee in hand. There was an old Chevy pickup in the clinic parking lot but no patients in the waiting room. An angular faced woman with glasses and graying hair was sitting at the reception desk talking on the phone in Apache. Ganson waited for her to finish her conversation.

"I'm Michael Ganson, the new doctor," he said as he extended a hand she seemed reluctant to accept.

"I'm Daisy," she said with a shy glance.

"Are you the only one here?" he asked.

"The nurse will be back soon," she answered.

"Where are all the patients?"

"We have none scheduled today."

Ganson told her it was nice to meet her and walked down the

narrow hallway to his office. He picked up his pediatric textbook and was reading about childhood communicable diseases when he heard a tap at the door. Looking up he saw a middle-aged Apache woman with sparkling eyes and an engaging smile.

"Welcome to Cibecue," she said offering her hand. "My name is Gwendolyn Price. I'm the clinic nurse."

"I'm Michael Ganson," he said as he stood up from his chair.

"Sorry I wasn't here to greet you," she apologized. "Twice a week I have to go out in the field and dispense medication to some of our tuberculosis patients."

"So, you're the public health nurse as well as the clinic nurse."

"I guess you could say that. There hasn't been much to this clinic since Dr. Roper left. Two of the doctors from Whiteriver used to come out here but we haven't seen either of them in almost a year."

"What about the emergencies?"

"There was an EMS provider out here but he got tired of getting called out for every little thing and moved back to Whiteriver, which is where the closest ambulance is now stationed. Most of the people don't have a phone. If they need anything they come to the clinic."

"What about after hours?"

"If they can't find anyone at the police station, which is often the case, they'll come to my house or Daisy's."

"And now probably to mine," he said.

"Probably so," she agreed.

"Daisy told me we didn't have any appointments today."

"These people aren't too keen on appointments. Most of them live on Indian Time, if you know what I mean. Sooner or later they'll come in."

Not a single patient came in that morning but a few mothers brought their sick children in that afternoon. Since there wasn't anyone waiting to be seen Ganson was able to devote a great deal of time going over each of the children's health histories and shot records. The mothers were somewhat aloof but they spoke good English and seemed attentive to the needs of their children. Pediatrics had never been one of Ganson's strong subjects. Luckily there was an immunization schedule tacked on the wall in the medication room, and Gwendolyn, or Gwen as she preferred to be called, was familiar with the current Center for Disease Control recommendations.

Ganson stayed at the clinic well past five and again took dinner on the steps of his porch. He had a Vienna sausage sandwich and a can of Spaghetti O's as he reflected on his day. Seeing well children in a walk-in clinic was a far cry from the adrenaline rush he was used to experiencing while dealing with the disasters at the County ER but he was happy to be getting into an established routine. He remained on the porch until dark. As he watched the stars come out again he wondered if he would ever understand the secret messages his mother had assured him they were sending.

Waiting for him at the clinic the next morning was Gwen's mother, a white haired woman who smelled like smoke from a campfire. Her face was the texture of a dried hide but her eyes had the same sparkle as those of her daughter. Gwen took her into the first exam room and worked her up for an office visit. As soon as Ganson picked up her chart and read the name Fanny Hoffman he realized she was the woman he'd seen standing over the grizzly bear in the photograph at the Apache Culture Center.

When Ganson asked her why she was there she responded by lifting up the top half of her blue two-piece camp dress. Underneath were crossing cartridge belts that holstered a pair of pistols appearing old enough to be the ones she'd used to drop the grizzly. She pushed the gun belts out of the way and showed Ganson a large abscess on her left breast. He tried to explain to her what it was but she didn't seem to understand.

"How good is Fannie's English?" Ganson asked.

"It's not," Gwen answered.

"Is she diabetic?"

"For the last twenty years."

"This looks like an infection from where those gun belts rubbed back and forth on her breast. How long has she been suffering with this?"

"She just told me about it last night."

"How long has she been packing those pistols?"

"She didn't wear them for the longest time but put them back on a little over a year ago."

"Does she shoot them?"

"She'd like to but she's not allowed to have any bullets."

Fannie didn't flinch as Ganson took a scalpel to her left breast and drained almost half a cup of pus out of the abscess. He packed the open wound with gauze so it could continue to drain. He told Gwen she'd need to bring Fannie in every day that week to have the wound repacked. He gave them two weeks worth of antibiotics to take home and recommended Fannie stop wearing her guns, at least for the time being.

"I keep telling her she doesn't need to be carrying them around but she insists they are protecting her," Gwen said.

"Protecting her from what?" Ganson asked.

"Fannie thinks someone tried to sic a witch on her."

"Does she know who?"

"She won't say."

"Has anyone around here ever seen a witch?" Ganson asked.

"Not and lived to tell about it," Gwen answered with a hint of a smile. "However, my mom did once tell a federal agent she'd seen God."

Ganson immediately thought of what Shock had told him about the crazy woman who claimed to have witnessed God's abduction of the missing boy. "Was it your mother who was with that white boy the day he disappeared?"

"That white boy's name was Harley. He and my mother were together almost every day. It was shortly after he disappeared that she put on her pistols again."

"Do you have any idea what happened to the boy?" Ganson asked.

"I don't," Gwen answered, "but there are a lot of rumors running around out there."

"The one I heard involved the medicine man."

"That would be Dazen Confused."

"I thought his name was Bronco Dazen?"

"Everyone out here calls him Dazen Confused."

Dazen Confused's name wasn't mentioned for the rest of the week, a week in which Ganson saw an increasing number of patients each day. Most of them were sick kids suffering from ear infections and asthma. There were a few older Apaches who came in for their uncontrolled diabetes and hypertension. Fannie appeared every morning to get her abscess repacked. She refused to stop carrying her guns but agreed to wear the belts over her dress so they wouldn't rub as much against her breast.

When Ganson wasn't seeing patients he was working with Gwen and Daisy to reorganize the way things were done at the clinic. There hadn't been a physician there for a year and the supplies needed to operate the facility were lacking. The pharmacy was also in a state of neglect. Most of the medications were either backordered or outdated. Many of the ones that were available for dispensing hadn't been properly logged in. On Tuesday he sent two pages full of requisitions for updated drugs and additional supplies to Whiteriver. As of the end of the week no one had responded to his requests.

Friday afternoon Gwen walked into his office with a plastic bag full of pills. "If you don't mind," she said, "I'm going to leave early to see if I can catch up with the Buffalo brothers before they check out for the weekend."

"Who are the Buffalo brothers?" Ganson asked.

"They're four of our TB patients. They're supposed to come in twice a week to take their medication. More often than not they don't show up and I have to hunt them down."

"Are they that hard to find?"

"Not really. They have a drinking camp across the creek. It's the first place I look. If they're not there, they're most likely in jail."

"Do you mind if I go with you?" Ganson asked.

"You really want to?" Gwen responded with a look of surprise.

"If you give me a few minutes to finish up with these charts I'll even drive."

Ganson was done in ten minutes and the two of them climbed

into his truck and drove off in search of the brothers. It had recently rained and the scent of dampened pinon hung over the valley. Following Gwen's directions he drove back across the bridge and turned south. She pointed out the Buffalo brothers' house, a two-room shack located off the paved road in the middle of a field full of Russian thistle. Gwen said there was no use walking through the mud and weeds to see if the brothers were home because the only time they were there was when it was too cold to be outside.

They turned onto a muddy two-wheel track that took them closer to the creek. They parked on a rise and followed a path toward a ribbon of smoke curling up from the middle of a grove of cottonwood trees. In a grassy area next to the creek they found all four Buffalo brothers stretched out around a smoldering campfire. Two of the men were shirtless and they were all wearing red headbands. Their shoulder length hair was littered with pine needles.

Ganson couldn't believe how native they looked. Take away the beer bottles they'd bartered from the bootlegger and the scene could have come straight out of the 1880s. The brothers were the direct descendants of a line of warriors who had fought the Spaniards for centuries before finally falling to an army of United States soldiers guided by Apache scouts. Although they didn't appear anywhere near as lethal as their ancestors they still had an air about them that would scare the life out of most any white man having the misfortune of stumbling upon their camp.

Ganson accompanied Gwen over to the campfire where she began conversing in Apache. She had a put off tone to her voice but her words didn't seem to impress the brothers. When she held up the bag of medication she'd brought with her they all got a serious look on their faces and nodded their heads. Then they looked at each other and broke out laughing. Gwen pointed to the pills and grabbed hold of her chest as she faked a wheezy cough and made out like she was having trouble breathing. One of the brothers said something to her and all four of them started laughing again.

Undeterred she walked around the camp picking up empty beer bottles until she found one that was half full. She handed it, along with a handful of pills, to the brother closest to her and stood over him until he swallowed the pills and chased them down with a swig of the stale beer. After doing the same for the other three brothers she dropped the beer bottle in the grass and went over to the creek to rinse her hands.

As she was walking back through the camp one of the brothers waved his arms at her. "Who's the white man?" he asked in English.

"His name is Dr. Ganson," she answered in English. "He's the new doctor at the clinic."

The brother gave Ganson a long look. "Is he going to last longer than the last one?" he asked.

Ganson smiled at the brother. "I expect to see you all at the clinic Monday morning to get your medicine."

Gwen led Ganson on a more direct route back to the truck. They were halfway up the hill when he tripped over a metal stake and fell into a clearing. The open area was about a quarter of an acre in size and roughly the shape of a square. In the middle of it was a white wooden cross. The cross was missing half its arm. Each corner of the clearing was marked with a post anchored in a pile of rocks. The posts were painted different colors. Black, white, yellow and blue. They were all leaning at an angle toward the ground.

"What is this?" he asked.

"It's a shrine," she answered. "About a hundred years ago there was this battle out here between the soldiers and the Indians. A lot of people on both sides got killed. The papers called it the 'Cibecue Massacre.' The New York Times called it another 'Little Big Horn.'"

"This seems like a pretty out of the way place to put a shrine."

"A couple of years ago some people from the University of Arizona came up here wanting to establish exactly where the battle had taken place. They spent a week scanning both sides of the creek with metal detectors. It was right around here they unearthed an army cartridge box, several cartridge casings and some other metal artifacts. Convinced this was the site, they marked it with that stake you tripped over."

"Does anyone ever come here?"

"Have you met Bomar Shanks yet?" Gwen asked.

"I can't say I have," Ganson answered.

"He run's the trading post."

"Is that the guy with the rattlesnake head on the brim of his hat?"

Gwen nodded yes. "Bomar had this idea he was going to turn this site into a memorial that would draw tourists who would drop by his trading post and spend a bunch of money on his overpriced goods. The problem was there were a lot of people out here that were against the idea."

"Is the site sacred to them?" Ganson asked.

Gwen laughed. "You see that big rock out there," she said pointing down to where a huge boulder was sitting out in the middle of the creek. The boulder was about the size of the Buffalo brothers' two-room shack and had a pine tree growing out of the top of it. "They call it Fantasy Island. The only thing sacred about this place is that it's where they come to drink."

Ganson thought back to the incident at the trading post when Bomar shot the stray dog. "Doesn't Bomar do whatever he wants around here?"

"He knew no one would want to visit a memorial if he couldn't get rid of the resident drunks so he decided to stink them out. For two weeks he showed up every night and chucked another dead skunk into the underbrush. The scent got so thick we could smell it all the way over at the clinic. When the drinkers still refused to leave, Bomar killed a great horned owl and strung it up by its talons from one of the limbs of that pine tree growing out of the top of Fantasy Island. As soon as they saw the dead owl they exited en masse."

"Is there something about a great horned owl?" Ganson asked

"Any owl," Gwen answered. "Most Apaches believe the owl embodies the spirit of their dead relatives and that it's not a good thing to hang out in the presence of one, whether it's alive or dead."

"The Buffalo brothers are still here," he noted.

"They left but came back a few days later. The dead owl was still there but the brothers kept their distance and the owl eventually rotted away."

Ganson circled the shrine, stopping to stand up each post as best he could. "What is the significance of the different colors?" he asked.

"Each one stands for a different direction in the Apache world," Gwen answered.

He walked into the middle of the clearing and picked up the busted-off arm of the cross. It had a blue snake painted on it. "Is this the place your mother says she saw God come down and get Harley?"

"If what she says is true, this is also the place God came down and tried to get Fannie. My mother claims she has little memory of what went on that morning. What I remember is that she left the house with Harley and ended up in the hospital with a concussion, a fractured face, a broken collarbone, a shredded camp dress and no shoes. Right after that she started wearing her guns again."

Thirteen

Ganson came to Cibecue intending to serve out the first two years of his five-year probation. His plan was then to petition the board to get the restrictions lifted from his license so he could reenter a residency and get on with his life. He never considered staying any longer than two years but the longer he was there, the better he felt about himself. Every morning he woke up ready to go to work.

He updated the drugs in the clinic and started a campaign to get the children in for their immunizations and the elderly in for their checkups. Those who came in for appointments were almost never on time but he made it a policy to treat whomever, whenever they showed up. He opened the clinic every morning at eight and stayed until the last patient was seen, which was often long after five. He kept additional drugs and supplies at his trailer to treat the after-hours traffic.

It took almost two months for Fannie's abscess to heal. During that period Ganson came in contact with patients suffering from diseases he'd learned about in medical school but never dreamed he'd see in practice. One was a fifteen-month old girl whose mother brought her in because the bottom of her foot was red and swollen. Right after the little girl got there she seized. Ganson stopped the seizure with a small dose of IV Valium but was clueless as to what was going on until the grandmother showed up with what was left of the scorpion the little girl had stepped on and been stung by. He shipped her to Whiteriver where she remained in the hospital overnight before being sent back home the next day.

Another case involved a twenty-one year old sawmill worker who came to the clinic agitated and complaining of severe abdominal pain. Ganson thought the man might need an operation for appendicitis so he sent him by ambulance to Whiteriver. The accepting physician was Jim Mackenzie. Mackenzie was in the process of authorizing an emergency flight to Phoenix when the man happened to tell him the pain had started shortly after he'd felt a small pinprick on his scrotum while taking a crap in his neighbor's privy. After canceling the plane and admitting the man to the hospital for IV therapy Mackenzie called Ganson to give him some good-natured grief over missing his first chance to diagnose a patient suffering from the neurotoxic effects of a black widow spider bite.

By far the most memorable patient was a teenage boy who staggered through the front door of the clinic reeking of gasoline. It was the day before Halloween and the boy's head was blown up to about the size of the premium pumpkin Daisy had carved and stuck in the window. The boy's eyes were swollen into slits and his nose looked like a pomegranate. He could only breathe through his mouth, which was wide open and had a continuous drool dribbling from it. The boy collapsed onto the floor of the waiting room and would have died if Ganson hadn't been there to resuscitate him. Having no idea what had happened, Ganson accompanied him on the ambulance ride to Whiteriver where Bryce Peterson took over and flew with the boy to Phoenix.

Ganson caught a ride back to Cibecue in the van. When he got to the clinic Gwen told him there was more to the story. A Cibecue cop had gone to the boy's home where he found another teenage boy. The second boy was lying dead on the dirt floor of the shed out back of the house. The shed was full of open gasoline containers. The cop first assumed the boys had both fallen victim to the gas they'd been sniffing. When he was looking around he noticed the swirls the rattlesnake had left when it had slithered out of the hole at the back of the shed. At that time of year the snake should have already gone into hibernation but the Indian summer must have kept it above ground longer than usual.

The dead boy showed no evidence of having been bitten and the autopsy would confirm he died of gasoline asphyxiation. The boy who made it out of the shed had been bitten between the eyes by the snake. The strike had apparently shocked him far enough out of his gassed-out stupor to get him out of his vapor deathtrap. The cop speculated the gas fumes stirred up the snake and forced it out of its hole. The Cibecue senior citizens suspected Major Mendoza was in some way involved. When Fannie heard about it she told Gwen that God had saved the one boy's life by drawing the rattlesnake out of the ground so it could strike him and drive him out of the shed.

When not working, Ganson spent much of his free time exploring the western end of the reservation. He hiked the hills, fished the creeks and drove his truck down to the Salt River Canyon to search out Indian ruins. He filled his evenings rereading the books he'd carried around with him in a cardboard box since college. Among his favorite authors were Dostoyevsky and Tolstoy, William Faulkner and Hermann Hesse.

He made monthly trips to Show Low to stock up on groceries and supplies. Once he stayed long enough to knock down a couple of Coronas at a concrete floored bar called Gerald's Club. The bar had a local band playing to a mostly redneck crowd but there was one table full of flashy looking Apache girls. One of them was Olivia, who Ganson hadn't seen since the morning the Chairman died. He thought about walking over to her table but instead finished the beer in front of him and left. Driving back to Cibecue he wished he had at least gone over and said hello.

Two to three times a week he'd buy lunch for the office. He'd leave after seeing the last patient of the morning and drive over to the West End Café where he'd pick up three orders of cheeseburgers with fries from the white woman working behind the counter. Daisy always sat and ate hers at the front desk while Ganson and Gwen took theirs into his office. Even though Gwen had a great sense of humor and was easy to talk to, it took Ganson weeks to feel comfortable enough to ask her about her personal life.

"Are you from Cibecue?" he finally asked her at lunch one day before shoving a handful of fries into his mouth.

"Born and raised," she answered.

"Where did you get your schooling?"

"I started at the Lutheran Mission in East Fork. When I turned thirteen, I moved to Oklahoma to go to boarding school. I finished high school there before coming back to ASU, where I got my degree in nursing."

"How long have you worked out here at the clinic?"

"After graduating college I returned to the reservation and went to work at the hospital. I didn't move back to Cibecue until two years ago."

"How many children do you have?" Ganson asked.

"Nine," Gwen answered proudly.

"Nine!"

"Five boys and four girls."

"Do they all live on the reservation?"

"All but one. My youngest daughter is at the University of Arizona."

"How many of your children went to college?"

"My two oldest boys were all-state basketball players in high school. They both had scholarships to Eastern Arizona JC but neither one of them lasted past their first year. The only one who has ever showed any interest in school is my youngest. She has her undergraduate degree and is working on her masters in fine art."

"If I'm asking too many questions or getting too personal just tell me and I'll shut up," Ganson said as he brushed the salt from the fries off his lips.

"Ask me anything you like," Gwen said.

"What prompted you to move back to Cibecue after all these years?"

"My mother," she answered. "She got to the point her memory was beginning to fail her. She could recall events from fifty years ago but was starting to have problems remembering what she'd done the day before. I tried to get her to come live with me in Whiteriver but she was set on living out her life here in Cibecue."

"How hard was it to get your family to leave Whiteriver?"

"None of them came with me. My husband died five years ago and most of my children are married and have children of their own."

"Was moving out here what you expected it would be?"

"My only regret is that I wish I'd had the opportunity to work with Dr. Roper a little longer."

"Doctor Roper?" Ganson asked.

"He's the Apache doctor who was out here for about a year," Gwen answered.

"What was it like to work with an Apache doctor after being around Anglo doctors all those years?" he asked.

Gwen hesitated before answering. When she spoke her voice had a measured tone to it. "Most of the doctors on the reservation either come to get their medical school loans paid off or to fulfill a service obligation. They're here for two to three years and leave. I'm not saying they don't do a good job but most of them don't seem to have their heart in it."

Ganson wondered if that was how Gwen felt about him. "Why did Dr. Roper leave so soon?" he asked.

"I'm not sure," she answered. "He came from the San Carlos Reservation, supposedly to be groomed for the Clinical Director position in Whiteriver. He worked awfully hard while he was here and I think he might have gotten a little burnt out. I also think he got tired of battling the belief system of the traditional Apaches."

"How's that?" Ganson asked.

"The older Apaches like my mother believe most of their

suffering is the result of witchcraft. They think the witches make people sick by casting spells on them or shooting invisible objects into their bodies. They put far more faith in the mystical powers of the local medicine man than in any clinic doctor, whether that doctor is Anglo or Apache."

"How many medicine men are there on the reservation?"

"When I first moved back to Whiteriver, there were a number of active ones. Most of those have either died or gotten too old to practice. Of the ones left, Dazen Confused is by far the most respected."

Ganson didn't see how anyone with a name like that could command much measure of respect. "How did he get that name?"

"Years ago there was this teenage boy living out here who smoked marijuana all the time. When his mother finally realized he had a problem she hired the medicine man to rid her son of the evil spirits that had taken over his mind. Arrangements were made for a weekend ceremony. Things went okay Friday night but by Saturday afternoon the boy had become quite agitated. He grabbed one of the medicine man's sacred sticks, stuck the end of it in the campfire and used it to light a joint he'd been carrying around in his underwear. The ceremony ended shortly thereafter. When the boy later told his pothead buddies about the look of disbelief on Bronco Dazen's face he referred to him as Dazen Confused. The name has been with him ever since."

"When I was at the hospital in Whiteriver he rode in to do a ceremony for the Chairman. Did you hear about that?"

"Everybody on the reservation heard about that."

"He didn't stay very long and when he left he accused me of mishandling the Chairman's case."

"So I heard."

"Was he critical of Dr. Roper's work?"

"Even though they were both Apache practitioners neither one had much use for the other."

"Did they ever have a direct confrontation?" Ganson asked as he wadded up the cheeseburger wrapper and tossed it in the trashcan.

"Once," Gwen answered. "It was right after Dazen Confused's apprentice went crazy."

"Are you talking about Major Mendoza?" Ganson asked.

"The Major was mentally ill. Someone in the army had diagnosed him with schizophrenia. He refused all treatment until Dr. Roper arrived and talked him into trying anti-psychotic medications. The next time the Major came into the clinic he told us the voices he'd been hearing for years were beginning to go away. Soon after that he began studying under Dazen Confused."

"Do you think the medicine man had something to do with the Major going off?"

"About a week after the Major disappeared Dazen Confused

walked into the clinic and accused Dr. Roper of using white man's medicine to make the Major crazier than he already was. After setting the Major's pill bottles on the front desk he started sprinkling his sacred pollen all around the waiting room full of patients."

"What did Dr. Roper do?"

"In English he told Dazen Confused to get out of the clinic and take his magic powder with him. He pulled the broom out of the utility closet and started sweeping up the pollen from the floor. It was the maddest I ever saw him."

Ganson understood Dr. Roper's frustration over dealing with the mindset of Dazen Confused, yet he identified with and felt great empathy for the medicine man, a man struggling to hold onto his own beliefs. "What I heard about Dr. Roper was that he left because he was concerned for the safety of his family. Did he think the medicine man had something to do with what happened to Harley?" Ganson asked.

"If he did, he didn't say anything to me about it," Gwen answered.

"Other than you, I've never heard a soul around here say a word about Harley. I don't even know his last name."

"His last name was Johnson. Around here people don't like to talk about the dead."

"Then why do they talk about Major Mendoza?" Ganson asked as he stood up and refilled his and Gwen's water glasses at the sink.

"They don't believe he's dead," Gwen answered

"Do you?"

"I believe the Major has long since met his maker."

"And Harley?"

"If you believe my mother, Harley died that day at the shrine."

"Is that what you believe?"

"I have no idea who or what killed Harley but I believe someone carried him off after he died."

"Why would anyone want to do a thing like that?"

"I don't know. There was something very different about that boy. A lot of the people around here were afraid of him."

"Why's that?"

"His eyes were blue."

"Gwen," Ganson said with a smile, "lots of white peoples' eyes are blue."

"I know that," she said. "What do you call the white part of your eye?"

"Are you talking about the sclera?" he asked.

"That's it," she said. "Harley had blue sclera."

"Solid blue?"

"Light blue."

Ganson thought back to medical school but couldn't remember what it meant to have blue sclera. "Was there anything else about him that made him different?"

"He had some kind of a limp and he was in here all the time. He wasn't eligible for Indian Health Service benefits but Dr. Roper treated him anyway."

"For what?"

"His mother kept bringing him in for broken bones. If it wasn't a finger or a forearm it was a toe or a foot. Daisy and I both thought his mother was beating him until Dr. Roper showed us the films of all the metal Harley had in his body."

"You mean like plates and screws and things?" Ganson asked.

"Gwen nodded. "He told us the boy had some kind of disease."

"What kind of disease?"

"I can't remember. It was a couple of foreign words with a bunch of syllables in each one."

"Did Roper keep a chart on Harley?"

"He didn't want the Service Unit to get hold of anything they could bill Harley's mom for so he kept an unofficial chart hidden away in medical records."

"Let's have a look at it."

"We can't."

"Why not?"

"The Feds took it."

"What about the films?" Ganson asked.

"I don't think they even looked for them," Gwen beamed.

The two of them walked back to the room where the films were stored. The unit used to shoot them was a dinosaur of a machine made by Xerox. The technology wasn't suitable for shooting much of anything other than an extremity. The images came out in a hazy green color that made them appear to have been shot underwater. It was difficult to discern the soft tissue from the calcified bones but Harley's films were easy to read. His right femur had a steel rod in it from end to end. His right ankle was held together with five screws. He also had a plate with several screws in his left wrist and more screws in his left elbow.

"It looks like he had osteogenesis imperfecta," Ganson said as he belatedly linked the blue sclera with the broken bones. "The patients with this disease have a defect in their bones that leaves them brittle and apt to break with the most trivial of injuries."

"That sounds like Harley."

"With all that metal in him he had an awful lot of orthopedic surgery done somewhere."

"That had to have all taken place before he moved here."

"How long had Harley been living here in Cibecue before he disappeared?"

"Maybe two years."

"Isn't his mother the woman with the long black hair and no makeup who cooks our cheeseburgers at the West End Café?"

"That's her."

"What's her name?"

"Amanda Johnson."

"I always say hello to her but I bet she hasn't said a hundred words to me total."

"She pretty much keeps to herself."

"I would have thought she would have moved on by now."

"I don't think she has anywhere to go."

"I've often seen her riding a horse around town," Ganson said as he placed Harley's films back inside the x-ray folder.

"I believe she rides out into the hills almost every weekend," Gwen commented as she took the folder from Ganson and refiled it in the cabinet.

"I take it she's not afraid of Major Mendoza."

"The rumor is she's still searching for her son."

"After all this time?" Ganson asked.

"So it seems," Gwen answered.

"Where does she live?"

"In a trailer on the other side of the creek."

"Do you know how she and her son ended up in Cibecue?"

"An Apache named Tiswin Richards brought them here."

"The curator at the Culture Center?"

"You know him?" Gwen asked.

"We've spoken once," Ganson answered as he recalled the conversation the two of them had at the Labor Day parade. He wondered how Richards and Amanda were connected but didn't ask. He stepped back in to his office and finished off the rest of his fries before going back to work.

By the time he'd seen the last of his patients and sent Gwen and Daisy home for the Thanksgiving weekend the sun had dropped beneath the red rock cliffs to the west, leaving the valley in a sluggish chill. He locked the front door and was walking to his trailer when Gwen came driving back into the parking lot.

"Dr. Ganson," she called out after rolling down the window to her truck, "what are you doing this weekend?"

"Having a quiet time at home," he answered.

"Why don't you come over to the house tomorrow? Fannie turns eighty on Saturday and we're going to celebrate it over Thanksgiving dinner."

"I wouldn't want to be an intruder," Ganson said.

"About the only thing you'll be is outnumbered," Gwen responded with a laugh. "There will be at least fifty people there. If my youngest makes it up from Tucson you'll be able to meet every one of my children."

Ganson thought about the turkey potpie he'd been saving in the freezer for his Thanksgiving meal. "Tell me when and I'll be there."

"You can come anytime. We'll probably eat around three."

"What can I bring?"

"Nothing. There will be plenty there to eat."

"What about a gift for Fannie?" he asked.

"My mom doesn't need a thing," she answered.

"How about a few bullets?" he asked.

"That's very funny." Gwen said as she threw the floor shift into reverse and started backing out of the driveway.

The first thing Ganson did when he entered his trailer was turn on the heat. After taking a Tecate out of the refrigerator he pulled the pen out of his shirt pocket and drew a line through another week on the calendar. Each week marked was one less week of the exile he'd signed up to serve. He fell asleep on the couch but awoke in the middle of the night in a drenching sweat. He'd had a dream that he'd unknowingly gotten Helen pregnant and that she'd had an abortion without telling him.

Wide-awake he lay there with his heart throbbing. He thought back to the night before his meeting with BOMEX. Helen had shown up at his apartment drunk and later said something about the death of a child. A chill passed over him as he recalled how their final weeks together in college had been such a strain. In a moment of perfect clarity he realized what he'd dreamt about that night had really happened a decade earlier.

Fourteen

By the time Ganson woke up Thanksgiving Day the sun had already burned the frost off the ground. The day was crystal clear and he spent most of the morning sitting on his porch thinking about the revelation from his dream. He was remorseful about not being included in her decision but sympathetic over what she'd gone through to make that decision. He couldn't imagine her choice being as simple as having a child versus pursuing a career. He knew that the lifelong defenses she'd built around her had to have cracked when she was trying to decide whether or not to abort her baby. He also understood how her ambivalence toward him all these years was fueled by the blame she must have put on him for getting her pregnant.

It was early afternoon when he put on his corduroy jacket and set out on foot for Gwen's house, which was right across the street from the trading post. The traffic was brisk and many of the Apache women and children huddling together in the beds of their pickup trucks waved at him as they drove by. Three different families stopped to offer him a ride. Even though Ganson was a white man living in Cibecue for fewer than three months he felt the community had in some ways accepted him.

On the bridge he met the two young boys riding bareback on their rough gaited horse. Both of them grinned at him as they bounced by. When he got to the trading post there was a black jeep with Texas plates parked in front of the gas pump. Stretched across the hood of the jeep was the skinned pelt of a mountain lion. Its head was positioned atop the grill like a hood ornament. Ganson walked over to what was left of the animal and gazed into its empty eyes as he stroked its broad head and ran his fingers along its killer canines.

"I'd appreciate it if you'd get away from there," a gruff voice growled out.

Ganson pulled his hand back and looked over to the porch of the trading post where a tanned white man dressed in combat fatigues and wearing a Texas Rangers baseball cap was glaring at him. The man had a holstered 9MM pistol hanging from one hip and a hunting knife hanging from the other. He reminded Ganson of a survivalist he'd treated at the County ER for an unfortunate grenade accident that had blown off the tip of the man's penis.

"Did you shoot this magnificent animal?" Ganson asked.

"No, I ran it down and slit its throat with my Bowie knife," the man said with a disgusted look on his face. "Of course I shot it. I'd just as soon you kept your hands off it."

Ganson walked past the man without saying another word and entered the store. He collected up an armful of chips and dip. After paying what seemed like an arm and a leg for them he wished the woman behind the counter a happy holiday and left. Joining the white man on the porch was Bomar Shanks, who was again wearing his cowboy hat with the rattlesnake head. Bomar and his buddy were in the midst of discussing the thrill of shooting coyotes from helicopters. Ganson hadn't seen Bomar since the stray dog incident and as he brushed by him he noticed something he couldn't believe he'd missed the first time. Bomar's skin was devoid of hair follicles. He had no hair, no beard, no eyebrows, no eyelashes.

Ganson left without speaking to either man and crossed the street to Gwen and Fannie's. The dirt road running next to the house was full of parked pickup trucks. There were twenty or so little kids running around in the front yard. At the edge of the driveway a half dozen teenage boys were shooting baskets. With them were two men Ganson recognized as two of the ballplayers he'd watched lose to Peterson's team at Memorial Hall. The two were taking on the teenagers in a game of horse, destroying them with long distant bombs launched from the edge of the front porch and the other side of the hedge. On one of their rare misses the ball ricocheted off the rim and bounced over to Ganson, who rolled it back toward the basket. One of the men asked if he'd like to play but Ganson declined. He loved the game but hadn't picked up a ball since med school.

Inside the house the smell of roast turkey and dressing reminded him of being at home with his parents for the holidays. A handful of men were crowded around the TV watching the Thanksgiving Day football game. They all looked up to say hello before going back to rooting for the Dallas Cowboys, who were receiving an ass kicking from the Washington Redskins. The women were out in the kitchen. They were busy preparing the food and moving it to the back porch where it was to be served buffet style. After Ganson placed his chips and dip on the counter and gave Fannie a birthday kiss he found Gwen at the serving table. She told him she was happy he'd come and took him around and introduced him to everyone. He offered to help with the dinner but she sent him back into the living room to watch the football game.

Toward the end of the first half he got up and gave himself a tour of the house. It was a wooden structure that had been added onto in stages. On the walls were a variety of paintings of southwest scenes inhabited by bear, coyote, bobcat and mountain lion. At the far end of the house was a room full of twined baskets and water jars, beaded goods, leatherwear and an entire bookcase of figurines carved from wood. The room also had a small fireplace. Above the mantle was a portrait of a stunning Apache woman in her early twenties. He was still staring at her when one of Gwen's daughters came up behind him.

"Dinner's ready," she said.

"Who's that in the picture?" he asked.

"My mother," she answered as she walked back out of the room.

With everyone gathered around the back porch one of Gwen's brothers speaking in English offered a prayer of thanks for having the family safely together. Afterwards he blessed the food. There was a lot of food to bless. Three turkeys, two hams, dressing with gravy, corn casserole, pinon stew, fry bread, fruit salad, sweet potatoes, mashed potatoes, baked beans, cranberry sauce, whole wheat rolls, homemade pies and a two tiered vanilla birthday cake for Fannie. One thing noticeably absent was alcohol.

The group filed through and filled their plates before scattering throughout the house to eat. Ganson found a place to sit at the end of a picnic table occupied by a bunch of Gwen's grandchildren. The kids were dividing their time between cramming their mouths full of turkey and jabbering away with each other. They were all speaking in English laced with an occasional Apache word or phrase. Gwen was sitting at another table with Fannie, who was wearing a smoke free green camp dress. Both of them were laughing and carrying on in Apache with some of Gwen's brothers and sisters.

Sitting in the midst of four generations of full-blooded Apaches

Ganson found it hard to believe they would be so enthusiastically celebrating the holiday that symbolized the beginning of the European thrust into the New World, a venture that was destined to strip the autonomy away from every American Indian. He figured whether they thought of themselves first as Indians or as Americans, they had every reason to be more than a little distraught over what had gone on with them and their brethren since that first little New World picnic.

However that wasn't the case. His Apache hosts embraced Thanksgiving with as much enthusiasm as any Anglo family Ganson had spent the holiday with. If they had any issues with its historical significance they seemed to have gotten over them long ago.

Whereas the kids at his table ate in a hurry and were back running around the yard within twenty minutes, Ganson took his time. He couldn't recall the last time he'd eaten a homemade meal and he was determined to get a second helping of everything, including the pie. By the time he was finished he was stuffed. He felt so content he knew he was going to fall asleep if he didn't get up and move around.

"Let me do the dishes," he offered to Gwen, who he found in the kitchen with two of her daughters.

"Leave this to us," she said. "After we get things cleaned up we're going to give Fannie her birthday cake."

Ganson settled into a cushioned chair in the living room and quickly dozed off into a deep sleep. It was dark when he awoke. For a moment he didn't know where he was. As a medical student working twenty-four hour shifts in the hospital he'd often woken up in the middle of the night disoriented and apprehensive. There was something so disconcerting about it that he'd never forgotten the feeling. He didn't like sleeping anywhere other than at his own place but for some reason he felt quite safe waking up that evening at Gwen's.

He pushed himself out of the chair and returned to the kitchen where Gwen and two of her daughters were finishing off Fannie's birthday cake. The daughters were talking about Dazen Confused and Bomar Shanks and all the other "crazy Indians" who lived in Cibecue and how they couldn't believe Gwen had chosen to return and live amongst them.

"Where is everybody?" Ganson asked with a yawn.

"Gone back to Whiteriver," Gwen answered.

"I guess I should be going home too."

"We saved you a piece of cake," Gwen said as she motioned for him to take a seat at the table.

Ganson had consumed enough sugar that day to last him the rest of the holidays but the nap had given him enough time to crave a little more. "Where's the birthday girl?" he asked as he looked around the room for Fannie.

"She's down for the night," Gwen answered.

"Is she okay?" he asked.

"Oh, yeah," Gwen answered. "I think today's excitement was a little too much for her. After she had a piece of cake she put herself to bed."

"I wish someone would have woken me," he said.

"I thought about it," Gwen said, "but you looked so comfortable."

Ganson was about to say something when the sound of three rifle shots cracked through the evening calm. "What's going on out there?" he asked.

"It's Bomar," Gwen answered.

"What's he going to kill at this time of night?" Ganson asked.

"Most anything that moves," she answered.

"Isn't it illegal to discharge a firearm within the village limits?"

"He does it all the time."

"Why doesn't someone report him?"

"It wouldn't do any good."

"Why not?"

"He's buddies with the cops. He used to be one."

"Here in Cibecue?"

"Bomar worked in Whiteriver but quit and moved out here to take over the trading post. The previous owner was this old German. One day the guy was bootlegging booze out of the back of the store and the next day he was gone."

"Do you know what happened to him?" Ganson asked.

"I believe Bomar and his dogs scared him off," Gwen answered.

"What's Bomar do with all those dogs?"

"Hunters from all across the country pay big bucks to come here and have Bomar take them out with his dogs."

"What do they hunt?

"Everything that's out there. Bomar leaves the dogs at home when he's after deer or elk but he couldn't track down a bear or a lion without them. There was this story about how he and his dogs chased a jaguar around the reservation for three days. Some rich client from back east paid him tens of thousands of dollars to shoot it out of the tree."

Ganson thought back to the jaguar he'd seen on the bank of the San Pedro River. He was amazed that one of them could have made its way as far as the reservation, which was a good four hundred miles north of its Mexican birthplace. "The jaguar has got to be on some kind of protected list," he said.

"I don't know about that," Gwen said, "but I doubt Bomar pays much attention to lists. He and his clients kill whatever they come across."

"That must have been one of his clients I saw standing with him in front of the trading post today."

"Almost every other weekend there's another fancy truck with out of state plates parked over there in his lot."

"What happened to Bomar's hair?" Ganson asked.

"He lost all of it," Gwen answered.

"So I noticed."

"I think it had something to do with what happened to Butch."

"Who's Butch?"

"Butch is that devil dog in the kennel, the dog with the stripe running down its back. Bomar bred one of his hounds to some African hunting dog and ended up with that ferocious animal. The dog's as apt to tear into one of the other hunting dogs as he is to tear into a lion. Once he even tore into Bomar."

"From what I've seen of Bomar it surprises me that he didn't shoot the dog right then and there."

Gwen chuckled. "The day it happened Bomar came into the clinic with the backs of both his hands shredded and the top of his scalp ripped open. That was when he still had his hair. All of us at the clinic thought that would be the end of Butch but when I got home from work that evening Bomar and Butch were sitting together on the porch of the trading post acting as if nothing had happened. The next day I saw them driving down the road together in the front seat of his truck."

"That sounds to me like a very unhealthy relationship," Ganson said.

"Bomar went out and bought Butch a gold collar after that."

"Butch must be quite the dog."

"Everyone in Cibecue is terrified of that beast. He runs around killing everyone's chickens, calves and goats. He's also hell on stray pets."

"Why doesn't someone just shoot him?"

"A lot of people would like to but they're afraid of what Bomar would do to them if he found out who did it."

"He wouldn't kill them, would he?" Ganson asked.

"I don't know about that," Gwen answered. "Bomar is unpredictable, just like Butch."

"What did Butch have to do with Bomar's hair falling out?"

"Butch ran off the day Major Mendoza went berserk. After shooting up the trading post the Major let every one of Bomar's dogs out of the kennel. They took off running up and down the valley. All of them returned by nightfall, all except Butch. When Butch didn't come home the following morning Bomar fell apart. For days he rode up and down the creek bottom and out into the hills in search of his beloved dog. He spent his nights drinking on the front porch of his trading post. When Butch finally showed up three weeks later Bomar's hair had already started to fall out."

Ganson recalled how such a thing could happen when the body's immune system went on tilt and started attacking its own hair follicles. No one in the medical field knew exactly why, but one of the primary triggers seemed to be stress. The medical term for the condition was alopecia totalis. Not counting Bomar, Ganson had seen two cases. One was a woman who had seen her fourteen-year old daughter decapitated by a drunk driver. The other was a man whose wife of twenty-five years had left him to move in with a methadone addict.

"Dinner was great," Ganson said as he gave Gwen a hug. "Thank you for having me over to celebrate the holiday with your family."

"Thank you for coming," Gwen replied as she handed him a plate full of food wrapped in cellophane.

"Do you think you could save this for me?" he asked as he gave the plate back to her.

"You don't want to take it with you?"

"I'm on foot."

"Where's your truck?" she asked.

"In my carport."

"Let me drive you home."

"Thanks, but the walk will do me good."

"Wait here," she said. She returned a minute later with a flashlight that she gave to him. "I wish you'd had the chance to meet my youngest daughter."

"Maybe next time," Ganson said as he stepped out the door.

A cold front sweeping down from the northwest had pushed

aside the warm air that had bathed the valley for most of the day. Ganson buttoned up his jacket before setting off down the street. Since midday the temperature had dropped forty or fifty degrees with the wind chill. He could feel the lobes of his ears burning and the hairs in his nose freezing as he marched down the deserted road. There were no streetlights and he had to swing the flashlight back and forth to avoid stepping into the countless potholes. He hadn't gone a block before he had to get off to the side of the road to avoid the Toyota pickup that rattled by.

When he got going back down the road he heard a rustling in the woods off to his right. He shined his flashlight but couldn't make out anything through the thick underbrush. The rustling had stopped, but when he started back up, so did it. He called out and asked if anyone were there but there was no answer. He picked up his pace but so did whatever it was that seemed to be following him. He broke into a jog. By the time he got to the bridge he was sidestepping potholes at a full sprint. He was halfway across when the Toyota pulled up beside him.

"Hop in and I'll take you home," the female voice said through the half open window.

Ganson had no idea who the woman was until he opened the passenger door and the interior light went on. She looked a lot like the young Gwen he'd seen that afternoon in the portrait and he instantly recognized her as the alluring lead singer of the Apache band he'd watched perform in the parade at Whiteriver.

"Dr. Ganson, I presume," she said. "I'm Nikki, Gwen's daughter. My mom sent me out to rescue you."

"I'm Michael," he said. His lungs were burning so badly he could barely speak.

"You look like you've just seen a ghost," she said.

"More like heard one," he said.

"What do you mean?"

"I thought something or somebody was shadowing me from the bushes off the side of the road."

"Did you see anything?" she asked.

"No," he answered. "It was probably nothing more than my overactive imagination."

"I never lived out here but my mother has told me how jumpy the people are since that white boy turned up missing. What was his name?"

"Harley."

"That's right, Harley. What do you think happened to him?"

"There are a lot of crazy stories involving shamans and ghosts swirling around out here."

"That's the reservation for you," Nikki said as she shifted her pickup back into gear. "Where am I taking you?"

"I live in the trailer next to the clinic."

Ganson wished he had more time to talk to her but by the time he caught his breath the Toyota was already at his driveway. "Sorry you had to come back out for me. How long are you going to be at your mother's?"

"I'm leaving in the morning," she said as she reached out and shook his hand again.

Ganson got out of the truck and stood in the driveway watching the taillights of the Toyota disappear in the distance. Meeting one of the reservation's most exotic looking women had boosted his spirits but the feeling rapidly gave way to his concern that someone might be stalking him.

Fifteen

That night Ganson had another dream. This one was about Cassie. He'd smuggled her out of the ICU inside the blanket her great grandparents had brought her and taken her with him to a swap meet where they came upon a golden colored booth. Inside the booth was a baldheaded fat man with a gray beard who was selling herbal supplements. Dressed in a black robe the fat man claimed the supplements would ensure an everlasting life. He offered a money back guarantee if Ganson would give him all his money. Ganson was taken by the idea and was getting ready to write him a check when it suddenly dawned upon him that if the supplements didn't live up to the herbalist's claim Ganson wouldn't be able to collect on the guarantee because he'd be dead. When Ganson pointed this out the man became angry and called him a nonbeliever. The man pulled a snake from beneath his robe and began twirling it above his head. Ganson grabbed Cassie and tried to run away but the man lassoed them with the snake and dragged them back into his booth.

He made it through the rest of the night dream free. When he woke the next morning everything outside was covered with a thick blanket of snow lying in perfect undulation with the terrain. The valley had an eerie silence to it and the only signs of life were the wisps of smoke rising from the chimneys of the houses to the west. Growing up in the high desert of southeast Arizona he had never cared for the cold, but as he stood at the kitchen window sipping a cup of coffee, he felt blessed to be witness to such beauty.

He dragged the tote bag from the back of his closet and pulled out a pair of insulated rubber boots. They were at least twenty years old. He had worn them when he'd mucked stalls at the farm and had brought them with him as an afterthought. Toward the bottom of the bag he found a pair of fur-lined gloves and a woolen headband. The only thing he had for shoveling snow was a short handled garden shovel. He pushed the snow off his porch. Although he had no intention of going anywhere that day he also cleared a path to his truck.

Nothing made it down the road until Gwen pulled up in his driveway at noon. "I would have brought your plate of food with me but I thought you might want to get out for a while."

"In this weather?" he asked.

"I promised Fannie I'd bundle her up and build her a snowman."

"It's freezing."

"We'll give you hot chocolate and feed you lunch."

"I think I'll pass."

"Are you sure?"

"Cold weather and I don't get along."

"We've got a great fire going."

"You didn't have to make a special trip over here."

"I would have called but the phone lines are down."

"How often does that happen?"

"This is the first time I can remember."

"Thanks for the invite. I really appreciate you thinking about me but I think I'll stay inside and stay warm."

"Are you sure you won't change your mind?" Gwen asked.

"I'm sure," Ganson answered. "If you don't mind, the next time you get a chance to speak with your daughter would you thank her for giving me a ride?"

"I'll do it as soon as I get home."

"I thought you said the phones were out?"

"They're not working but neither are the snowplows," Gwen explained. "Nikki is stuck out here for the time being."

Ganson saw no graceful way to save face for reneging on his stated desire to stay home so he didn't try. "I'll be over within the hour."

He used the broom to sweep the snow off the windows and side mirrors of his truck. After locking the hubs into four-wheel drive he climbed into the cab and keyed the ignition. The diesel engine started rattling like a bunch of marbles bouncing around inside a wooden box. He let it warm up for a minute before shifting into reverse and backing out of the driveway.

He followed Gwen's tire tracks up the road and across the bridge. Before he reached the trading post he pulled off to the side. The woods didn't look dangerous in the daytime. He had all but talked himself out of the notion he'd been followed the night before but he wanted to get a closer view. Even though he knew the snow had covered up any chance of finding a footprint or a track he waded out into it anyway. He soon found a break in the brush that led to a game trail winding through the woods.

Confident his supposed stalker was nothing more than one of the innumerable animals making their way across the valley he turned to go back to the truck. That's when he noticed the tattered strip of blue fabric stuck in the tree limb. It appeared like the limb had ripped it from someone's denim shirt. The piece of fabric was a good seven feet off the ground, leading Ganson to believe that whoever was wearing the shirt had to have been weaving their way through the woods on horseback. He had no idea why anyone would be after him but as he trudged back to his truck he vowed to be more vigilant when wandering out at night.

He pulled into Gwen's driveway behind Nikki's Toyota, which was half buried in the snow. Gwen met him at the front porch. After he dusted off his boots and jeans he followed her inside. The living room was comfortably warm from a fireplace loaded with splintered oak and juniper. The wood snapped and hissed with delight as it spit its burning embers against the screen. Fannie sat on the couch, all bundled up and ready to go. Nikki was nowhere to be seen.

After accepting a cup of hot chocolate topped with whipped cream Ganson moved closer to the fireplace so he could absorb as much heat as possible. Gwen left for the kitchen and returned with two yardsticks and a bag full of fixings for the snowman. The three of them walked out onto the front porch where Fannie remained while Ganson and Gwen waded out into the snow.

"Nikki told me you thought somebody was following you home last night," Gwen said as she rolled up a snowball and hit Ganson in the back of the leg with it.

"It was probably nothing," Ganson said as he turned around with a snowball of his own and sent it sailing over the top of Gwen's head.

They squared off and threw a few more at each other before getting down to the business of building Fannie's snowman. The wet snow rolled up heavy. Half way across the front yard Ganson could feel his breath funneling out his pursed lips. It formed a white mist in the air. By the time he got the bottom of the snowman to the edge of the porch his inner shirt was soaked with sweat and his legs were shaking. He paused to catch his breath and throw a couple more snowballs at Gwen. The two of them rolled up the torso and the head, stacking one on top of the other.

After Ganson finished molding the three balls together he grabbed hold of Fannie's arm and escorted her off the porch. He held onto her coat and led her to the snowman along the path he kicked in front of them. Fannie pulled the avocado pit eyes out of the bag and stuffed them into the empty face. She stuck the carrot nose right between the eyes and seemed satisfied with the placement even though it was far from anatomically correct.

While Gwen pulled the mittens over the ends of the yardsticks to make the hands and arms Ganson folded the potpie tin in half to make the mouth. The tin was so cold it split down the middle. Fannie broke out in a grin when Ganson pushed the tin into the bottom of snowman's face because it looked more like a duckbill than a mouth. They all laughed when Gwen tried to shove the pipe through it.

Fannie took exception to Frosty wearing a knit cap and went back inside to get a cowboy hat. When she returned with the hat she also had her guns. She hung a cartridge belt over each of the snowman's yardstick arms and flashed a toothless smile when Gwen snapped a picture. They were all smiling as they trudged up the stairs of the porch and into the warmth of the living room.

Wearing a pair of sweats and an Eagles t-shirt, Nikki was sitting in a chair she had pulled up next to the fireplace. She had a cup of coffee in one hand and a cigarette in the other. The glow on her face was every bit as radiant as the one emanating from the fire. There was also a glow radiating from the diamond she wore on her left hand.

"You told me you were going to quit those cigarettes," Gwen said.

"I know," Nikki replied. "I came across this one little orphan in the bottom of my purse and couldn't resist." She got up from her chair and gave both her mother and Fannie a hug. "Well hello Michael, how are you today?"

"A bit chilled," Ganson said, describing not so much the weather as the disappointment of seeing the ring he hadn't noticed the night before.

"Pardon my appearance," she said," but I can't seem to get it going today. I think all those late nights have finally caught up with me."

"Studying too hard?" Ganson asked as he tried to appear concerned about something other than her unavailability.

"I wish," she answered.

"Performing too much?"

"Did my mom say something to you?"

"Not a word. I saw you at the Tribal Fair."

"At the parade or the concert?" Nikki asked.

"The parade," Ganson answered. "I would have liked to have gone to the concert, but had to go back to the hospital."

"I'm sorry you missed it. The Tribal Fair is always a great time."

"How often do you play?"

"Apache Dreams doesn't do that many dates but I'm in a Tucson band that's booked three nights a week."

"How long have you been singing?"

"Since I was six."

"Where do you perform in Tucson?"

"All over town. You name the club and we've more than likely closed it down for the night."

During his college days Ganson had closed them all down at some time or other. He went out not so much to drink as to dream of linking up with the women he hoped he'd find there. He'd sometimes get wasted but most of the nights ended in a sober trip to Taco Johns for a late night serving of chips, dip and cheese enchiladas. He used to look back and beat himself up over having wasted all that time sipping on whiskey sours and lusting over coy coeds but he'd come to accept the fact that life was as much about yearning as it was about learning.

While Fannie, Gwen and Nikki relocated to the kitchen, Ganson thawed out in the living room. He could hear the three of them chattering away. He had no idea what they were saying because the only words they were speaking in English were ones the Apaches had no translation for, like "Long Distance Phone Calls" and "TV Miniseries." Their mysterious sentences flowed from their lips in rhythms broken by words that seemed to bubble out of the back of their throats. Ganson knew nothing of the field of linguistics but he could feel the passion in their speech.

Gwen had taught him a few Apache words. As he listened to her and Nikki converse he was quite proud of himself for being able to pick out two of them, "doctor" and "bullshit." However, he began to fret when he thought they might have been using the two words in combination to describe him. When he finally got up the nerve to walk into the kitchen the women's smiling faces melted away his unfounded fears.

The table was set for a second feast. Everything he'd had the previous day was there to tempt him again. He settled for a small plate and sat across from Nikki, who was cutting up tiny pieces of turkey for Fannie. The women were back to speaking English. After they finished eating, Nikki started asking about everyone who'd been there the day before. When she got around to her four-year old nephew Benjamin, Gwen broke out in laughter.

"What's so funny?" Nikki asked.

"I just remembered something Benjamin told me last summer," Gwen said after she caught her breath. She took a sip of water and looked over at Ganson. "All my children are fluent in Apache but I can't say that about a single one of my grandchildren."

"Come on Mom," Nikki interrupted, "They can speak some Apache."

"They recognize a lot of the words but have trouble carrying on a conversation," she explained to Ganson. "Last August I was sitting on the porch one morning drinking my coffee when little Benjamin came screaming around the corner. The words for snake and vagina sound almost the same. When I asked him to explain to me in Apache what was wrong he told me he'd seen a giant black and white vagina in the backyard.

When they all stopped laughing Gwen continued. "There was this king snake living under the house last summer and I suspected that was what Benjamin had seen. We walked into the backyard together and there it was, a beautiful black and white king snake. Benjamin asked me if I was going to cut off its head and butcher it. I told him that it was a good snake and that his butchering of the Apache language was enough butchering for one day."

After Nikki stopped laughing she got serious. "Don't you find it depressing that our own language is no longer the primary one spoken in any of your grandchildren's households?" she asked.

"When you have children it won't be the one spoken in yours either," Gwen answered.

"I can at least make my children more aware of their heritage," Nikki said.

"That's a noble thought, Nikki, but if you haven't noticed, English is the only language taught in the schools. It's spoken more and more at the Council Meetings. There will come a day when the majority of the representatives on the Council won't even be able to speak Apache. When that happens, the tribe will have lost not only its past but also its identity."

"Why can't somebody reintroduce the Apache language into the schools?" Nikki asked.

"I think today's kids would look upon that the way I looked upon the BIA school in Oklahoma trying to make me learn Latin. You know how difficult our language is to master. For centuries it was unwritten. There wasn't even an English-to-Apache dictionary until the Culture Center published the first one about ten years ago. If you don't grow up speaking Apache you're never going to get it."

"That seems like such a tragedy to me," Nikki said. "I don't understand how you can sit there and sound so matter of fact about it."

"It is a tragedy," Gwen agreed, "but nothing is going to change the way things are. I've learned to accept that."

"I'm not ready to give up on the Apache race just yet."

"I never said anything about giving up. I didn't move out here just to watch over your grandmother," Gwen said glancing over at

Fannie, who was beginning to nod off at the table. "I also came back to do what I could for these people."

While Fannie shuffled off to her room for a nap Nikki and Gwen went on about how their culture was disappearing. Ganson listened as they talked about everything from the lack of respect for tradition to the influx of street drugs. When they finished cleaning the kitchen the three of them moved to the living room. The fire had died down but the room was warm. Even though Nikki was seemingly off limits Ganson stretched out his stay as long as he could. About four o'clock the phone rang and Nikki took it in the bedroom. She returned minutes later to tell them the roads had been plowed and she needed to be on her way. Ganson figured the phone call must have been from her fiancé. He stood up immediately and explained he also needed to get going. He told Gwen he'd see her Monday and wished Nikki a safe trip. On the way to his truck he stopped and cleared the snow off her Toyota.

When he got home he put on Led Zeppelin's first album and huddled over the heating vent in the floor of his living room. The setback he'd suffered over the revelation of Nikki being engaged had triggered the greater realization that he had no idea where he belonged.

Sixteen

Ganson had for years felt little joy for the holidays. As far as he was concerned everything after Thanksgiving could be cancelled. He only looked forward to New Year's Day because it marked the end of another seasonal surge of holiday suicides and other depression related illnesses. To make things worse Bryce Peterson showed up unannounced at the clinic two weeks before Christmas. Ganson hadn't spoken with the Clinical Director since their disagreement at the hospital and he doubted his boss had driven all the way out to Cibecue for a social visit.

After going through all the cabinets and drawers, Peterson had Gwen pull several charts, including the one of the boy who'd been bit in the face by the rattlesnake. Peterson and Gwen seemed to know each other and they had an easy rapport. Ganson had just finished up with his last patient of the day when Peterson walked into his office.

"I need a few minutes of your time," Peterson said.

"Sure thing," Ganson answered.

"I have some concerns about this office that need to be addressed," the Clinical Director stated.

"What kind of concerns?" Ganson asked.

"You are now in your fourth month out here and you have yet to update the Policies and Procedures Manual for the clinic."

"I have to admit that hasn't been one of my higher priorities."

"Not only have I found government forms improperly filled out, I've also found errors in the logging in and out of medications."

"How many errors?"

"Two."

"That many," Ganson commented.

"There's more," Peterson continued. "We've received some patient complaints about you."

"How many of those?"

"Two."

"Who were they from?"

"One was from Sharon Nevermissashot. I don't know if you know this, but Sharon is on the Tribal Council. She came into my office last week to tell me of her concerns over the way you'd treated her daughter."

"Are you talking about Zenith?" Ganson asked.

"That's right," Peterson replied. "Sharon claimed you saw Zenith twice for a bad sore throat but never gave her any antibiotics. Sharon ended up having to drive her all the way to Show Low where they did some blood work and put her on ampicillin."

"Did you look at her whole chart, Bryce?"

"I have it right here, although I can't read some of your writing."

"Did you read where I thought she had a viral illness?"

"I did."

"Did you read my next note when she came back in with a total body rash?"

"What's your point?"

"She developed a rash after she started taking the antibiotics they prescribed for her presumed bacterial infection. It wasn't the kind of rash you get with a drug allergy but the kind you get when you give ampicillin to someone who has mononucleosis. That rash is as reliable an indicator of mono as any blood test. The only good the antibiotics did her was to help me confirm her diagnosis."

"You could be right about that, but judging from your track record and reputation I'd think you'd want to do everything you could to win over the confidence of these people."

"You're not telling me you think I should be treating viral illnesses with antibiotics, are you?" Ganson asked.

"Of course not," Peterson answered. "What I'm telling you is that the practice of medicine is an art that often requires the use of nonscientific principles."

It was all Ganson could do to not react. "You said there was a second complaint about me?"

"It came from the family of the Palmer boy."

"The boy who got bit between the eyes by the rattlesnake?"

"That's the one."

"What was that one about?"

"The family claims, and I happen to agree with them, that you should have diagnosed the snake bite earlier so he could have gotten the antivenom sooner."

"We didn't even have any antivenom in Cibecue at the time."

"If you would have diagnosed the boy correctly we could have had it waiting for him in Whiteriver."

"Would it really have made that big a difference?"

"It might have saved him from all the plastic surgery he's looking at."

Ganson again had to calm himself down. "If it were that critical a call why didn't you pick up on it before you flew him to Phoenix?"

"You were the one here when the boy came in. When I took over his care I had to depend on what you told me about him."

"Let me ask you something, Bryce. Do you ever receive a complaint on any of the other doctors in Whiteriver?"

"Every now and then."

"What do you do with it?"

"I go over it with them."

"Do you attack that doctor in the same spirit you do me?" Ganson asked.

"I have no idea what you mean by that," Peterson said.

"What I mean is that I think you drove all the way out here to mess with me."

"You're wrong about that but you have become a burden to me."

"How's that?"

"The Area Office has told me I need to keep a closer eye on you."

"Is that why you're here?"

"I've got better things to do with my time than to be your babysitter."

"Fuck you, Bryce."

"Would you please refrain from using that kind of language around me?"

"Would you please get out of my clinic," Ganson responded as he tried to push Peterson toward the door.

They squared off against each other with clenched fists but no punches were thrown. Peterson left without saying another word.

"I should have handled things better," Ganson told Gwen as the two of them watched Peterson peel out of the gravel driveway. "He's the one person I needed on my side."

"He can be difficult," Gwen said.

"How well do you know him?" Ganson asked.

"I was his nurse for a year."

"That must have been an adventure."

"He's extremely bright but most of his patients don't care that much for him."

"I can see why."

"When I was working in Whiteriver he was always asking me to help him get a date with Nikki. She wasn't interested."

"Do you mind if I ask you something?" Ganson asked.

"What's that?" Gwen responded.

"I might be way off on this but over Thanksgiving I got the impression you really wanted Nikki to meet me."

"Nikki had been asking me questions about you before you even came to Cibecue."

"Isn't she engaged?"

"On and off."

"How did she know about me?"

"Olivia Parker told her."

"Olivia, the nurse's aide at the hospital?"

"They've been friends since Olivia moved back to the reservation. I don't know what Olivia told her but Nikki got to where she was asking me about you every time she called. I finally suggested she come out here and meet you the next time she made it back to the reservation."

"Who is Nikki's fiancé?"

"His name is Teddy Yazzie. He's a Navajo from Tuba City and a second year law student at the U of A."

Ganson had several unanswered questions about Nikki but

decided he'd already asked Gwen more than enough about her daughter. "Did our Clinical Director lead you to believe the clinic was in as poor a shape as he stated it was to me?"

"He didn't say much about the clinic. However, he did say something about you."

"What was that?"

"He told me the reason you came to Cibecue was because you didn't have anywhere else you could go to practice medicine."

Ganson felt his face go flush. He wanted to tell Gwen the whole story but feared all that would do would make him appear as if he were going out of his way to try to defend himself. He silently swore to himself not to ask her another thing about either Nikki or Peterson. "Please tell Nikki I wish her and her fiancé well."

He spent the remainder of the month in a major funk. He was afraid Peterson had undermined whatever trust and respect he'd been able to establish in the office. He was pleasant with both Gwen and Daisy but was hesitant to engage either one of them in lengthy conversation. He continued to see as many patients as he could and stayed late to work on the things in the clinic Peterson had criticized. On the day before Christmas he was at his desk writing a letter for one of his patients to the Social Security Administration when Daisy came back and told him there was a white man at the front desk looking for him.

"Who is he? " Ganson asked.

"I don't know," she said. "I've never seen him before."

"He isn't a government agent, is he?" he asked half joking.

"He doesn't look like one," she answered.

Ganson wasn't sure what she meant by that until he walked out into the waiting room. A man about Ganson's age was standing at the reception window. The man was wearing a rumpled black suit but that's where his resemblance to a federal agent ended. His hair had something in it that made it stand straight up in the air and his face sported a two-day stubble. He also had only one eyebrow. He actually had two eyebrows but they'd grown together across the gap between his eyes.

"Can I help you?" Ganson asked.

"Are you Dr. Michael Ganson?"

"I am," Ganson replied. "Who are you?"

"Sir, my name is Felix Lash. I have some papers for you."

"Are you serving me?" Ganson asked, already knowing the answer.

"Yes, I am," Lash said as he reached into the briefcase he was carrying and pulled out an all too familiar file of legal looking documents.

In medical school Ganson had listened to a lecture given by a lawyer on how to survive a lawsuit. The attorney suggested medical malpractice should be looked upon as nothing more than a cost of doing business. The insurance was there for the doctor's protection and the plaintiff's allegations shouldn't be taken personally. The advice sounded reassuring. The problem was that for most doctors the emotional cost of being sued far outweighed the financial cost of carrying malpractice insurance. It was absurd to suggest a malpractice lawsuit not be taken personally.

"Who is this from?" Ganson asked.

"Sir, it's all in the document."

Ganson looked down and saw David Dunbar's name on the letterhead at the top of the first page. The man who had been stalking him from the front of billboards and the back of phonebooks had finally attacked. "Am I supposed to sign something?" he asked.

"Yes, sir, just sign right here. Then I need a few things from you."

"What kind of things?" Ganson asked as he scribbled his name on the line marked with an "X."

"This will only take a minute," Lash said as he pulled a notepad out of his briefcase. "I need to know your hair color, height, weight and the color of your eyes."

"What does my physical appearance have to do with any of this?"

"Sir, I've been instructed by the court to secure a physical description of every person to whom I serve papers."

"Which court is that?"

"Pima County."

"Do you think I might be someone else?" Ganson asked.

"No sir," Lash answered. "I'm confident you are who you say you are. I still have to ask these questions. Can you tell me the color of your hair?"

"See for yourself."

"Brown," Lash said as he wrote it down in his notebook. "You look like you're maybe five foot, ten inches tall."

"Try six foot," Ganson said.

Lash gave Ganson a second look and wrote down five eleven. "I'd have to say you weigh around a hundred and eighty pounds."

"That would be one seventy."

A smile formed at the corners of the process server's mouth as he wrote down one seventy-five. "I'm afraid I won't be able to tell the color of your eyes unless you step a little closer to me."

"They're green," Ganson said, "green with envy over the great job you have."

"Sir, there's no need to shoot the messenger."

Ganson knew the process server was nothing more than an arm of the court. He was doing what he'd been commissioned to do and probably wasn't happy about having to drive all the way to Cibecue to do it. None of that mattered. "Why don't you get an honest job?"

"Have a good day," Lash said as he drew a line through the space for eye color and placed his notepad back inside his briefcase.

Ganson retreated to his office and closed the door. He threw the papers on his desk and tried to settle down. When Frederick Nix had shown him the newspaper ad of David Dunbar, Ganson had made out like he had no idea who the malpractice lawyer was. The truth was he knew him all too well. David Dunbar had once sued his father. Like Ganson's, the case against his father was an obstetrical one. His father was one of several defendants in the case. Although he'd eventually gotten out of the case his father's love for medicine had never seemed the same after that.

Fearing he too would soon be losing a sizeable slice of his soul to the legal system Ganson picked up the document and began reading through the allegations against him. The wrongful death lawsuit had been brought on behalf of William and Lucille Miller and their granddaughter Cassie. Ganson stopped reading the document halfway through the second page and threw it inside the bottom drawer of his desk.

Since it was Christmas Eve and looking like it was getting ready to snow, Ganson sent Gwen and Daisy home early. Gwen had invited him to drop by for dinner the next day but he had already committed to work at the hospital in Whiteriver. There had been a death in Jim Mackenzie's family and he had called Ganson the night before and asked him if he'd be willing to cover from Christmas Eve to Christmas evening. After receiving Mackenzie's reassurance that Peterson had signed off on it Ganson had agreed to work the twenty-four hour shift.

When he got on the road that evening the snow was coming down in sheets. Driving down the highway he found himself spellbound by the stroboscopic effect of the wipers whipping back and forth across the windshield. He stopped for a cup of coffee at the gas station at Carrizo Junction before continuing on. He arrived at the hospital a little after seven and checked in with Mackenzie. The Apaches had been celebrating the holiday in full force and there were already half a dozen injured ones lined up in the hallway outside the ER.

"I feel bad about leaving you with all this," Mackenzie said apologetically, "but I have a 1 AM flight out of Phoenix I'm trying to catch."

"Don't worry about it," Ganson said as he motioned for Mackenzie to be on his way.

The scene reminded him of a typical night at County. He quickly took inventory of the patients and prioritized them as to the severity of their needs. No one was critical but several needed to be x-rayed and sewn up. One was a boy with an obvious wrist fracture. Another was a man with a hip injury. While Ganson was waiting for the films to come back he sewed up a drunk with a facial laceration and admitted a diabetic with a gangrenous toe.

He was able to reduce and cast the boy's fractured wrist. The man, however, had a dislocated hip and had to be sent by ambulance to Phoenix. Around three in the morning a teenage girl came in complaining of cramping and passing blood clots. Ganson was getting ready to examine her when she bowed her back and let out a scream. Riding a wave of blood rushing out her vagina was an intact sac and placenta. Inside the sac was a fetus. It looked to be about twelve weeks along, which left it another twelve weeks short of the earliest gestational age it could survive. Separated from its mother's lifeline the fetus lay floating face down in its amniotic pod, a celestial traveler jettisoned much too soon from its earthbound uterine craft.

When he went to remove the dying fetus from between the mother's legs the lemon-sized sac ruptured. Ganson cut the threadlike umbilical cord and placed the male fetus on a towel next to the sink. After watching its last aborted gasp Ganson covered it with the towel. He asked the mother if she wanted to see her baby but she didn't answer.

As he was preparing to get her cleaned up Olivia arrived. She'd been sent over from the floor by the nursing supervisor to help out in the ER. She gave Ganson a sweet look before helping him finish up with the girl and get her on a gurney.

"What happened to her baby?" Olivia asked after she returned from wheeling the girl to the floor.

"I don't know," he answered. "For some reason he came out way too early."

"I feel bad for her," Olivia said. "It's the second time this has happened."

"Does she have a history of doing drugs?"

"Not that I know of."

"Most of the time we have no idea why miscarriages happen," Ganson explained.

"I'll tell her that," Olivia said.

"Do you think she'll want to see her baby later?" he asked.

Olivia nodded yes. "She wants to wait until her mother comes. They'll take the baby home and have a service for it."

After the ER had emptied out and Olivia had left to go back to work on the floor Ganson lay down on the couch in the doctor's lounge. He awoke at daybreak to see a baby with a croupy cough and spent the rest of the day tending to a steady trickle of patients. One of the night nurses came in at four in the afternoon with a tray full of food and for the next hour the staff sat around the nursing station eating turkey, dressing, green beans and sweet potatoes.

At change of shift Bryce Peterson arrived to take over call. Neither Ganson nor he said a word about their encounter in Cibecue earlier that month. Ganson checked out to him before looking in on the girl who had miscarried. It wasn't until he was walking into her room that it occurred to him that he'd violated the terms of his agreement with BOMEX by caring for a woman who was pregnant.

The room was full of female family members. On the table next to the girl's bed were a bouquet of flowers and a hand carved miniature casket. Everyone stared at Ganson when he walked in, everyone except the girl, who seemed hesitant to make eye contact.

"How are you feeling?" he asked.

"I want to go home," she said.

"Dr. Peterson will release you in the morning," he said as he gently placed his hand on her shoulder.

As he was leaving the room he ran into Olivia. She'd been off all day but was back for the nightshift.

"Still here I see," she said.

"I wonder if she's upset with me." Ganson said.

"Why would you think that?" Olivia asked.

"She refuses to look at me."

"I doubt she's the first person around here that's done that to you."

"No, but I sense in her some kind of anger or hostility toward me."

"You're wrong about that," she said.

"How do you know?" he asked.

"I talked to her before I left this morning. She told me she was afraid you thought she did something that caused her to lose her baby."

"That couldn't be farther from the truth."

"A great number of these people don't think too well of themselves."

"Do you think I should go back and say something to her?"

"I already did."

"You did?"

"I assured her you'd never think such a thing."

"Maybe she didn't believe you," he persisted.

"I'll tell her again before she leaves," she responded.

"I'd appreciate that," Ganson said.

"You're not staying for another night, are you?" Olivia asked.

"No," Ganson answered, "I'm done working here at the hospital for the holidays."

"If you're not doing anything special on New Year's Eve a group of us are going to be celebrating at Gerald's Club," she said.

"I'll see if I can make it," he said as he walked away still not knowing whether or not she was aware of the role he'd played in the death of her sister.

Seventeen

Ganson's current malpractice policy was under the umbrella of the Indian Health Service. His previous coverage had been with the Medical Center. The day after Christmas he notified them of the lawsuit David Dunbar had filed against him. Due to all the publicity on the case the insurance company had long since opened a file on him. The representative seemed less than surprised when Ganson informed him of his being served. Ganson could only imagine how the company's risk manager looked upon him.

There was nothing he could do about it except keep working. The week after Christmas was a busy one with several patients coming to his trailer after hours. By the time New Year's Eve came around he was exhausted. He closed the clinic early and took a three-hour nap. He woke up in the dark and spent another two hours trying to decide whether or not he was going to get out of bed. He ended up yielding to the anticipation of spending an evening with Olivia and her friends.

The roads were clear and he made it to Show Low in time to fill the dual diesel tanks in his truck before heading on to Gerald's Club.

It was almost eleven by the time he got there. The parking lot was packed but he found a spot out back between two pine trees. After paying the five-dollar cover he squeezed between the two bouncers at the front door. The smoke-filled bar reminded him of an old roller skating rink. There was an oval dance floor in the middle with a wood railing of finished 2x4s around it. Against the far wall was the stage. The band was on break and the sound system was blasting out "Don't Look Back" by Boston.

Most of the patrons were Anglo and he had no trouble finding the Apache girls. They were crowded around two tables pushed together at the far edge of the dance floor. When he got over to them Olivia stood up to greet him. Over the blare of Boston's distorted guitar riffs she introduced him to everyone. It wasn't until he went looking for a chair that he noticed Nikki sitting at the other end of the table, looking as irresistible as ever. She was smoking a long thin cigarette and drinking shots of Tequila with a couple of Anglo guys who had pulled their chairs up next to hers.

Ganson took a seat at the table between two girls Olivia had introduced him to but whose names he'd already forgotten. He spoke briefly with each of them as he sipped on a Tecate. It was a long way home and with no designated driver in sight he didn't want to be driving impaired on the most dangerous night of the year. Besides the chance of getting run off the road by a drunk there was the risk of crashing into a horse or a cow or even an elk.

The band was a collection of burnt out rockers who called themselves "Of Questionable Origin." All five of the members looked super stoned and every song they sang was from the acid sixties. As they closed in on midnight they took off on a twenty-minute rendition of "Light My Fire." Several of the girls' boyfriends had drifted into the bar and Ganson was thinking about heading for home when Nikki came over and pulled up a chair next to him. She was wearing jeans and an aqua blue halter-top. As she leaned over to speak to him her leg pressed against his, causing his dick to do a double clutch. "Happy almost New Year," she said as she toasted his Mexican beer with a shooter of Tequila.

"Same to you," he said, raising his voice above the noise of the band.

"How's my mom?" she asked, placing her face close to his so he could hear her.

When he smelled the sweet scent of perfume on her cheek the rest of his body went into sensual overload. "She seemed fine this afternoon," he said as he stole a glance at her left hand.

Undaunted by the fact Nikki was still wearing a ring he downed what was left of the beer he'd been swigging and ordered a fresh one for each of them. He drained his as he entertained fantasies of Nikki's naked body gliding back and forth over his on a frictionless layer of sweat. The voice inside him told him he was headed for deep trouble. He didn't want to hear it.

He excused himself to go to the bathroom and picked up two Tequila shooters on his way back. When he got to the table he found his chair occupied by one of the Anglo guys who'd been drinking with Nikki earlier. Nikki's chair was empty and she was out on the dance floor with the other guy. Ganson could have sat down and waited for her to return but for some reason he didn't. Instead he took his two shooters and wandered down to the other end of the table where Olivia was sitting.

She was facing the other direction, nursing a blended Margarita while carrying on with one of her female friends. When she turned to see who had sat down beside her, Ganson was unprepared for what he saw. He was used to her in a nursing uniform with her straight black hair streaming down her cheeks. Since she'd introduced him earlier she'd taken off her jacket and pulled her hair above her head with a tortoise shell clip. She was wearing a black spaghetti strap blouse that revealed most every ripple in her toned upper body. Ganson couldn't stop staring at her.

"Do you remember speaking with me at the hospital in Tucson?" he asked after he'd inhaled one of the shooters and offered the other to her.

"Of course," she answered as she took the shooter and poured it into her half empty Margarita.

"How are your grandparents?"

"Not well. After Patrice died they went downhill fast. They're now both in a nursing home in Phoenix."

It took a second for Ganson to recall that Patrice was the name of Olivia's sister before the Millers adopted her and changed it to Angela. "What happened to Cassie?"

"One of the tribal lawyers is trying to get us visitation rights but I haven't seen or heard of Cassie since she left the hospital."

With Olivia having gone out of her way to invite him to the bar Ganson had come to the conclusion she either had no idea of his role in the death of her sister or didn't hold him responsible for it. He hoped it was the latter but feared it was the former. Either way he wanted to tell her. He was thinking about how best to bring it up when the lights went on and the burnouts in the band started slinging confetti. The other couples at the table were all over each other as the lights flashed on and off and the confetti continued to fly.

The next day when Ganson tried to recollect the night's events there was a gap or two in his mind. One minute he'd been sitting next to Nikki, lusting over what he wanted to do to her. The next, Olivia was sitting on his lap with her tongue half way down his throat. He couldn't remember making a play to take her home but after last call the two of them ended up together in his truck. He hadn't made it out of the parking lot before he had both his hands up her spaghetti strap blouse and she had both her hands down his Levi jeans. With his pants pulled below his knees he made it all the way down the hill to Whiteriver steering his truck with one thigh. Near the north end of town she had him take the turn-off to North Fork. She showed him a place to park next to the river where they spent the rest of the night doing things he'd all but forgotten. When he drove her home at dawn all he could think about was how wonderful it had felt to hold a woman again.

Olivia lived in One Step Beyond, a housing development on the other side of the cemetery. After Ganson walked her to the door and kissed her good morning he got into his truck and drove back through town. A tribal police car pulled him over before he cleared the cemetery. A young Apache officer walked up to the door, rapped on the window and instructed him to get out. Ganson showed him his driver's license and told him he was one of the physicians working on the reservation. The officer responded by telling Ganson he'd be in need of the services of one of his doctor colleagues if he didn't leave Olivia alone. Ganson was about to tell him to mind his own business but thought better of it. He couldn't be sure the officer wouldn't shoot him right there and bury him in the cemetery.

As Ganson drove west toward Cibecue he wondered whether the Apache policeman was Olivia's current lover, ex-lover, overly protective relative or some other lunatic. He concluded it didn't matter because he was going to avoid whichever one it was. In spite of his night with Olivia all he could think of at the moment was how his life had taken such a twisted path. His mother used to tell him he was on a miraculous intergalactic journey. She said it was a trip that could carry him all the way to the stars but that out in the nebulae another fate would always be lying in wait for him. Ganson didn't know whether or not it was fate that had led him to Olivia but he did know he needed to leave her alone.

The rest of the winter turned out to be a quiet one in Cibecue. There were no new Major Mendoza sightings, no new Harley disappearance theories and no new evidence of hair growth on Bomar. Harley's mother Amanda continued to sling burgers at the café and ride her horse out into the hills of the reservation. Bomar's dog Butch was still slaughtering domestic animals and the medicine man Bronco Dazen was still being followed by the coyote.

Ganson's trips to Show Low were restricted to the purchasing of groceries and other supplies. He stayed away from Gerald's Club and all the other bars in the off-reservation town. He drove into Whiteriver once a month to attend meetings at the hospital. On one of these occasions he ran into Olivia in the hall. The sight of her set into replay the thoughts of the night they'd spent together. She, however, appeared to be as standoffish toward him as he had vowed to be toward her.

Stories traveled across the reservation at a faster and more predictable rate than the mail. If Gwen had heard anything about Ganson's New Year's encounter with Olivia she hadn't let on. She stayed busy with her clinic work as well as her public health duties, which still included hunting down the Buffalo brothers twice a week to give them their TB medications. She had Ganson over for dinner a couple of times a month but never revealed any new information about Nikki, and he never asked.

Ganson's malpractice case was in the early stages of a process that would take one to two years to complete. He'd requested legal representation from Luther Shock's attorney, Duane Jamison. They met once in Globe. Duane was constantly sending Ganson copies of all kinds of things being filed with the court on his behalf. The documents came to him in official-looking envelopes mailed from Duane's office. Whenever Ganson got one he chucked it on top of the others accumulating in the bottom drawer of his desk. He'd stopped opening them because all they did was make him feel more anxious about what lay ahead. It was like waiting for a beating.

The clinic days were full and Ganson found himself spending a great deal of time trying to get to know his older patients. Most of them suffered from multiple medical problems including hypertension and diabetes but he didn't have a single patient with heart disease. He suspected that was because the Apaches had not yet had enough years of devouring fast food to clog up their arteries.

The winter brought with it innumerable upper respiratory infections. He had to send several patients, adults as well as children, to Whiteriver to be admitted for the treatment of their pneumonias. He couldn't see any pregnant patients so all the Cibecue women who were pregnant had to go to Whiteriver for their prenatal care. He was permitted to see them postpartum and take care of their newborns when they came home from the hospital.

When he wasn't treating patients he was getting into better shape. He stopped drinking altogether and went for a walk whenever he had the chance. He had a three-mile course in and out of the creek bottom he'd do after work. On the weekends he'd hike out for a day in the hills if the weather were decent.

He was returning home from one of these when one of the Apache boys he'd seen riding bareback came running up his driveway. In a panic the boy told him Chico had been bit by a snake and couldn't breathe. When Ganson asked him where Chico was, he pointed toward the creek. Ganson told the boy to wait on the porch. He raced over to the clinic and pulled the first aid box off the shelf. He also grabbed the ten vials of antivenom he'd talked Whiteriver into sending him after the previous incident with the snake.

Ganson and the boy hurried down to the creek. Standing at the bank were the Buffalo brothers. The other boy was nowhere to be seen. The brothers were watching the boys' horse, which was standing out in the middle of the creek. They paid Ganson little mind until he asked them if they'd seen Chico. When they looked up and stared at him in disbelief Ganson suddenly realized that Chico, the victim of the snakebite, was a horse.

When he looked closer he saw that Chico's nose was swollen up bigger than a basketball. The horse's chest was heaving and his ribs were retracting as his lungs made noises that sounded like someone trying to pull their boots out of a mud bog. Chico was bobbing his head in and out of the creek as if he were hoping the cold water would reduce the swelling enough to allow him to draw a deeper breath.

At that moment the second boy came running up the creek bottom. In his right hand he was carrying a piece of green garden hose that reminded Ganson of a relay race baton. The boy ran up to the Buffalo brothers and began pleading with them in Apache as he pointed the hose toward the horse. The oldest of the brothers made a gesture with his hand and looked over at Ganson.

"The boy wants you to save his horse," the brother said.

"I have no idea how to do that," Ganson replied.

"You're a doctor, aren't you?"

"I doctor people, not animals."

After speaking with the boy the brother again spoke to Ganson.

"Dazen Confused told the boy to take the hose and shove it in there so the horse can get more air. The boy says he'd do it but he's too scared."

Ganson could have suggested one of the Buffalo brothers take on the task but they were all quite drunk and he could see Chico's legs beginning to buckle. He took the foot-long piece of hose from the boy and entered the creek. The boys followed him. He had them push Chico's nose up out of the water. His plan was to intubate the horse as he would a human but when he tried to thread the hose through Chico's mouth the Buffalo brothers started laughing at him.

"What are you trying to do there, Doc?" the oldest one called out.

"Didn't you ask me to try to save this horse?" Ganson replied as he continued to try to get the hose around Chico's clinched teeth.

"Yes, I did. There's one little thing you should know."

"What's that?"

"A horse can't breathe through its mouth."

Ganson dislodged the tube from Chico's teeth and shoved it up his swollen right nostril. Chico jerked his head sideways and blew a stream of blood out the end of the tube. The horse started shaking his head in an attempt to dislodge the tube but settled down when he discovered he could breathe through it. He stood his ground in the middle of the creek, struggling to get enough air into his lungs to satisfy the massive oxygen debt his body had built up.

Ganson returned to the bank and dumped the vials of antivenom out of the first aid box. Snake antivenom was designed for use in humans but was harvested from horses. It was produced by injecting a horse with sub-lethal doses of snake venom. The horse then developed antibodies to counteract the effects of the venom. The antibodies were collected from the serum of the horse and concentrated for commercial use. Depending upon the amount of venom released by the snake, the victim could require as many as thirty to forty vials of antivenom to survive with all his body parts intact.

Ganson only had the ten vials. He was reluctant to use them because he had no idea how effective they'd be on an animal the size of Chico. The vials were also outrageously expensive. He had lobbied long to get Whiteriver to release the ten he had. He could only imagine Bryce Peterson's response when the clinical director discovered Ganson had used all ten of them on a horse. He was about to place the antivenom back in the first aid kit when he took another look at Chico. The horse was listing to the left. The boys were standing beside him in the creek, stroking his neck and begging for him to get better.

The voice inside Ganson said "fuck it." He mixed and drew up all the antivenom in a giant syringe and waded back into the creek. Chico's veins were bulging with every attempt he made to breathe and Ganson had no problem finding a suitable site to inject the antivenom. He rested the needle against Chico's neck. With the horse's next breath he thrust it into the vein. He aspirated a stream of blue colored blood before pushing the antivenom directly into the horse's circulatory system.

As Ganson was pulling the needle back out, Bronco Dazen came riding up. The medicine man was carrying a piece of garden hose similar to the other one. He leapt off his horse and into the water. When Dazen reached Chico he put the palm of his hand in front of the piece of hose Ganson had stuffed up Chico's nose. He held it there to feel how much air was moving in and out. He put the second piece of hose up to his mouth, spit on the end of it and slipped it into Chico's other nostril.

The hoses hung from the horse's nose like a pair of javelina tusks, giving Chico the look of a prehistoric animal. The additional flow of air was of immediate benefit and Chico's appearance began to improve within a matter of minutes. After he regained some of his strength the boys were able to lead him out of the creek.

Bronco Dazen followed Chico to the bank and sprinkled the horse's face with some of his sacred pollen. Following a lengthy discussion in Apache that included several uses of the Apache word for doctor the medicine man climbed aboard his own horse. He gave Ganson a half salute and took off downstream. As he passed by Fantasy Island the coyote scurried out of the brush and followed him.

While the boys and the Buffalo brothers gathered around Chico, Ganson capped the needle to the syringe, collected all the empty vials and closed the first aid box. He snapped the box shut and was getting ready to go when the one of the Buffalo brothers spoke up.

"Aren't you going to do some kind of checkup on the horse?" the brother asked.

"I hadn't planned on it," Ganson answered.

"Dazen Confused told the boys they could lead the horse down to his place after you gave the okay."

"He did, did he?"

"He said you'd know when the horse was ready to go."

Having already been laughed at for not knowing a thing about equine airways, Ganson couldn't believe any of them would have confidence in his ability to evaluate a horse's health status. Ganson figured if the hoses stayed up Chico's nose long enough to give the antivenom time to work, the horse had a reasonable chance of surviving. To give the boys a little reassurance he pulled the stethoscope out of the first aid box and listened to the horse's chest. He could hear coarse wheezing but the air seemed to be moving fairly well through the horse's lungs.

Ganson was about to proclaim Chico well enough to be walked

to Bronco Dazen's when he noticed the left forearm of the second boy. It was bent at a thirty-degree angle. "'What's your name?" he asked.

"Reggie," the boy answered.

"What happened there?" he asked pointing to the boy's wrist.

"I hurt it when Chico bucked me off."

"You were on him when the snake bit him?"

"We both were," the boy answered.

"What's your name?" Ganson asked the other boy, the one who had come to get him at his trailer.

"Rickie."

"Are the two of you brothers?"

Rickie nodded. "I'm a year older."

Ganson looked back at Reggie. "What do you say we go find your mother so we can get this arm of yours fixed up?"

"I want to stay with Chico," Reggie said.

"Why don't we let Rickie take care of Chico," Ganson suggested.

Reggie didn't answer as he walked around to the other side of the horse.

"Why don't you let the doctor take care of you?" one of the Buffalo brothers spoke out.

Reggie shook his head and looked like he was getting ready to run off into the trees.

Manifest West

"Let him fix your arm, boy," one of the other Buffalo brothers said in a harsher tone.

Reggie would have taken off if Rickie hadn't grabbed hold of him. After a few words between the two of them in Apache it was Rickie who spoke. "We'll come see you after we get Chico down to Mr. Confused's."

"Don't forget to bring your mother," Ganson advised the boys as they led their horse downstream in the direction of the medicine man's camp.

"I don't think she'll be able to make it today," the one Buffalo brother said as all four of them started upstream toward their drinking camp.

"Why's that?" Ganson asked.

"She's been dead for a while," the brother answered over his shoulder.

"What about the father?"

"He's in jail."

By the time Ganson reached his trailer it was dark. He spent the next two hours waiting for the boys. He was about to give up on them when he saw their flashlight bobbing up the driveway. They came with no legal guardian but Ganson took them to the clinic anyway. The films he shot of Reggie's forearm revealed greenstick fractures of the radius and the ulna, with significant angulations of both bones.

The name greenstick came from the fact that younger bones were more inclined to bend and split open than to snap in half. They were much easier to realign than complete breaks. After Ganson explained what he was going to do he positioned his thumbs over the site of the fracture and pressed down while pressing up from the bottom with his fingers. He bent the arm back straight and splinted it without a word from Reggie. He didn't cast it because he didn't want to risk it swelling up and cutting off the circulation. He told Reggie to come back in two days for a full cast.

When Ganson arrived at the clinic the next morning Gwen was busy cleaning up the treatment room. "I heard you had a little excitement," she said.

"Where did you hear that," he asked.

"The Buffalo brothers told me when I gave them their medicine this morning."

"What did they have to say?"

"They said they hoped you know more about doctoring humans than you do about doctoring horses."

Ganson laughed. "I thought I did rather well under the circumstances."

"I see you used up all the antivenom," Gwen said as she dropped the last of the empty vials into the waste container.

"The situation called for it," Ganson said as he cleaned up the unused casting material from the previous night.

"The Buffalo brothers said the rattlesnake was a giant. Maybe six feet long."

"I didn't know they even saw it."

"They were right there when it happened."

"They were?"

"They told me they were on their way to their camp when the boys rode up to the creek to let their horse get a drink. There were a bunch of cattails there by the bank. When the horse pushed its nose through them to get to the water, the snake bit it. The snake's fangs must have gotten stuck in the horse's nose because when the horse pulled back its head and reared up, the snake as well as the boys went flying."

"Didn't anyone hear the snake rattling beforehand?"

"I asked the brothers the same question and they said no."

"I thought those snakes were supposed to sound a warning before striking some unsuspecting soul."

"They generally won't rattle unless they feel threatened."

"Are you sure about that?" Ganson asked

"When I was in college I took a course in herpetology," Gwen remarked.

"Really."

"Since I was a little girl I've always been interested in reptiles."

"You're kidding me."

"I love Gila monsters and horned toads," Gwen said picking up a wet towel to scrub the dried plaster off the floor.

"How about rattlesnakes?" Ganson asked as he took the towel away from her and got down on his knees to do the job himself.

"I find them unfairly maligned and grossly misunderstood."

"Don't try telling that to Chico."

"Who's Chico?"

"The boys' horse that damn near died."

"A rattlesnake can't see that well but is well aware of its environment. It can smell things through the tip of its tongue and feel vibrations through the sensors in its body. It's called a pit viper because of the pits on each side of its head. The pits can detect minute changes in temperature. The rattlesnake's response to other animals is based on how its brain processes all this."

"Doesn't it strike out at anything crossing its path?" Ganson asked.

"Not necessarily. It determines whether whatever is coming is a potential meal or a potential threat. If the intruder is small enough to be killed and eaten, the snake isn't going to scare it off by rattling at it. If the beast approaching is too big, the snake is going to rattle to warn it away. That way it can avoid the risk of being injured while not wasting its precious venom trying to defend itself."

"So why didn't it give a warning to Chico before it struck him?"

"Maybe it tried."

"How's that?"

"What could have happened was that the snake tried to tell the horse to stay away but couldn't. A rattlesnake will do whatever it can to keep its tail dry. If it does get wet its rattles get all watered down and don't work. One time I took the hose to this rattlesnake sunning itself on my front porch. I could see its tail vibrating but there wasn't a sound coming from its rattles."

Ganson spent the next several days watching for snakes everywhere he went. One afternoon he'd just finished making sure there wasn't one underneath the picnic table out front of the West End Café when he saw Chico and the boys bouncing down the road. Chico's nose was scabbed over and still swollen but he was without tusks and seemed as spunky as ever. Reggie hadn't returned to the clinic to have his arm casted and the splint had all but fallen off. The top half was completely missing. The bottom had pieces of gauze dangling from it like strips of unrolled toilet paper.

The boys were laughing and paying no attention to the logging truck bearing down on them from the west. About the time the truck got even with them the driver hit his airbrakes. Chico spooked and spun around. Rickie was able to hold onto the rope reins but Reggie was unable to hold onto Rickie. He went sailing out into the road and just missed getting run over by the truck. By the time Ganson got to him the boy was already on his feet. He was rubbing his broken arm but not shedding a tear. Ganson took him to the clinic where he removed the remnants of the splint and replaced it with a long arm cast. He was just finishing up when a fully uniformed Bryce Peterson walked in the front door.

The Clinical Director gave Reggie a long look before confronting Ganson in front of everyone in the office. "Where are this boy's parents?" he demanded.

"One of them is in the cemetery and the other is in jail," Ganson answered.

"You know it's illegal to treat a minor without the consent of a legal guardian," Peterson said.

"Is that what you came all the way out here to tell me?"

"What I came all the way out here to tell you is that I am formally placing you under notice."

"Notice of what?"

"Notice of—" Peterson hesitated as he looked over at Gwen and Daisy. "I suggest we discuss this in private."

"Sure thing, Bryce," Ganson said as he led the Clinical Director back to his office and closed the door behind them.

Peterson was carrying a manila folder with him that he laid on the desk. "Do you recognize this?" he asked as he pulled out a sheath of papers with the BOMEX official letterhead at the top.

"All too well," Ganson answered as he stared down at the copy of the stipulations the board had placed on his restricted license.

"On page four it specifically states you are not to render any kind of treatment to any woman who might possibly be pregnant. Last week I contacted this office and had Daisy send me a copy of the charts of all the pregnant patients. When I reviewed them I was shocked to see how many of them had been seen and treated out here by you."

"Good God, Bryce. What I treated those girls for had nothing to do with their pregnancies."

"That might be so but the board was very specific on this point."

"So you think I should be sending those patients all the way to Whiteriver to spend the day waiting in your walk-in clinic to be treated for their colds and rashes and ingrown toenails?"

"If I were in your position I wouldn't be letting a pregnant woman get any closer to me than the sign-in sheet at the front desk."

"If that's the case how did it happen that you left me to treat the pregnant patients I saw in the ER while I was taking call at the hospital?"

"That was an oversight on my part and I can assure you it won't happen again. I've notified everyone in Whiteriver that you will no longer be taking call at the hospital. After I get finished with you, you won't be working out here either."

"So this is your formal notice of how you're planning to get me off the reservation?"

"My recommendation to the Area Director will be that if he thinks you deserve another chance he should send you to the Dakotas for a stint at Pine Ridge or Wounded Knee. You and the Sioux would be a good match for each other."

"You don't much care for Indian people, do you Bryce," Ganson said.

"They don't much care for themselves," Peterson responded.

"Have you always had such a humanitarian nature?" Ganson asked.

"You hardly have the right to ask me that," Peterson answered. "I've read the reports of how you killed that Apache woman in Tucson."

Ganson started in Peterson's direction. "I suggest you get out of here before I kill you too, you arrogant cocksucker."

Acting as if he believed him Peterson backed out of the clinic and leapt off the porch on his way to his car. Ganson closed early and walked his three-mile trail through the river bottom three times. It was dark by the time he got back to his trailer. He opened a can of sardines and a box of Wheat Thins and took his dinner on the steps of the porch. There was no moon and the galaxies were ablaze. Ganson's mother had once taught him the constellations and the major stars in each. Other than Ursa Major, the Great Bear, the only one he could still identify was Orion. He recognized Orion by the three stars lined up in a row forming the astrological hunter's imaginary belt. As he gazed into the heavens he thought again about how his mother claimed she could pick out the stars flickering their cryptic communications back and forth across the horizons.

Before his mother had left, Ganson had been a child in awe of the universe. He'd longed to experience all the magical things in life beckoning to be explored. Now thirty-four years of age, he wondered what was out there to look forward to.

Eighteen

Ever since he'd seen the pelt of the mountain lion tied to the hood of the Jeep at Bomar's store he'd dreamt of coming across one in the wild. He was certain he'd never be fortunate enough to see another jaguar but a mountain lion was a possibility because its natural habitat covered the entire West. To Ganson the lion was the West. It was powerful, mysterious and enduring. There was something unpredictable about its predatory nature but Ganson knew his chance of being attacked by one were far less than his chance of being attacked by Butch, or Bomar for that matter.

On a Saturday in early May he got the chance to find out. He had hiked several miles south of Cibecue to explore a series of ruins encircling a rock amphitheater when something told him to turn around. Hurdling in his direction was a large mountain lion approaching in twenty-foot leaps. Ganson recalled his father's advice about getting tall and standing up to the lion but this one looked far too focused to be deterred by such a tactic. Fortunately for Ganson the lion bounded by without giving him as much as a look and raced up the lone pine tree at the far end of the amphitheater.

Ganson had no idea what the lion was up to until he heard the baying of the dogs. Led by Butch the five of them crested the entryway to the amphitheater and yelped in unison as they flew across the rocks. They gave Ganson no more attention than the lion had. When they closed in on the lion's position they broke into a barking frenzy. The dogs took turns taking runs at the tree and doing back flips off the base of the trunk. Not content to keep the lion treed, Butch tried to climb up after it. He made it to the third limb before falling and landing on two of the other dogs.

The tree was dying. A lightning strike had stripped the limbs on one side. Crouched on one of the living limbs fifteen feet above the ground was the yellow-eyed lion. Its body was designed for brief attacking sprints, not long distance runs, and it was exhausted. While its heart pounded and its lungs heaved to clear the excess lactic acid from its fatigued muscles, the lion was content to remain in the tree. It could have made a run for it but millions of years of instincts were telling it that it was safe to stay where it was.

Ganson knew Bomar and his bloodhound tracker would be hot on the trail. He climbed up a set of ancient Mogollon steps and handholds to get a better vantage point. He was close enough to hear the lion hissing and spitting at the dogs. He wasn't sure his survival instincts were any better than those of the lion but he figured that if he could get it to jump out of the tree it wouldn't bother to attack him when it took off.

He hollered and swore but the lion's attention stayed focused on the dogs. Standing at the edge of a ruin he resorted to chucking pieces of the wall at the tree. He kept missing the lion but on several occasions hit the dogs. He had just thrown a rock that bounced off the lion's tree limb and onto Butch's head when Bomar came into view, clattering across the rocks on his sweat-soaked horse. He had his rifle drawn and pointed in the direction of the lion.

Ganson reached down and found a baseball sized rock half buried in the rubble. He rose up and fired a strike. The rock hit the lion square in the back of the head and sent it clawing toward the end of the limb. It leapt out of the tree and scrambled up a cliff too steep for the dogs to follow. Bomar got off several shots before the lion disappeared over the ridge but none of them slowed it down.

Ganson's joy over the escape of the lion rapidly gave way to the realization of the danger of his own position. Bomar galloped up to the base of the ruins. He stared up at Ganson with his rifle still drawn.

When Butch gave up trying to scale the cliff he joined them. The ridge running down the middle of the big dog's back was sticking straight up in the air and the hair around his neck was fluffed up to the point it obscured his gold plated collar. He rose up on his back legs and started scratching at the handholds in the rocks. It appeared to Ganson that Bomar was going to keep him at bay long enough to give Butch the opportunity to tear him apart.

"What's on your mind, Bomar?"

"Do you have any idea how long I've been trying to shoot that one lion?"

"For a moment I thought you were thinking about shooting me," Ganson said with a feigned smile of relief.

"I still am," Bomar responded flatly.

"Why would you do a thing like that?" Ganson asked as he looked around for another rock to throw.

"Why did you do what you did?" Bomar asked as he raised his rifle in Ganson's direction.

"I thought the lion needed someone on its side."

"So do you."

The crack of the rifle came simultaneously with the bullet sailing over Bomar's head and splintering a crease of rock off the canyon wall. The shot came from the far ridge where a rider and his horse were silhouetted against the sun. Before Bomar could draw a bead on the rider a second shot exploded at the foot of Bomar's horse. Bomar dropped his rifle into its sheath and backed his horse away from Ganson. He turned his horse around and took off across the amphitheater with Butch and the rest of the pack close behind.

Ganson stayed where he was until Bomar was no longer in view. He climbed down from the ruin and looked back up at the horse and rider, who were working their way across the horizon. Trotting along behind them was a coyote.

Ganson had no way of knowing whether Bomar intended to shoot him or just scare him. He suspected Bomar hadn't known either. As soon as he got home he dug into the bottom of his tote bag and pulled out the handgun his father had given him. He hadn't fired it in years. He'd never shot a living thing with it. He spent the rest of the night worrying over whether he should carry it with him when he ventured out. By the next morning he'd decided to leave it at the bottom of his tote bag underneath his wool headband and fur lined gloves.

Nineteen

A tropical storm had spun its way up from the Gulf of California, bringing with it days of rain. When Ganson stepped out onto his porch to greet the first cloudless morning Cibecue had seen in a week he saw the bones. There were four of them lined up on the railing of his porch. The first two were roughly the size and shape of the sugar cubes he dropped into his coffee cup every morning. The third one was also cuboidal but larger. The last one looked like the handle to a mallet and was almost a foot in length.

Ganson left the bones where they were and walked out into his yard, which was full of fresh horse tracks. The tracks came up his driveway, through his busted gate and over to his porch, where it appeared someone had dropped off the bones without ever getting off their horse. The tracks looped around the carport and left the same way they'd come.

He looked up and down the street. The only sign of life was Daisy unlocking the front door to the clinic. After calling her and telling her to reschedule whoever was coming in that morning, he pulled out the phonebook that no longer had a picture of David

Dunbar on the back cover and found the number for the Bureau of Indian Affairs.

Two hours later Agent Gus Martin rolled into town. He parked his black Lincoln out by the street and was careful to avoid stepping in the horse tracks as he made his way up the muddy driveway. Dressed in a dark suit that couldn't conceal the bulge of his middle-aged belly he was a pleasant man with salt and pepper hair and a small scar in the middle of his forehead. He introduced himself and gave Ganson a tired handshake that mirrored the look in his eyes. He pulled a camera out of his pocket and snapped several pictures of the bones before sitting down on the steps and pulling a small notebook out of his suit pocket. If he were in any way excited over the appearance of the bones he didn't show it.

"You haven't been here that long, have you?" the agent asked as he started scribbling in his notebook.

"September will be a year," Ganson answered.

"I heard they had lots of problems getting somebody to come out and work since that Apache fellow left. I can't remember his name right this minute."

"Dr. Roper."

"That's right. Dr. Steven Roper. I'm sorry it didn't work out for him. He seemed like a decent man to me."

"How well did you know him?"

"How familiar are you with Major Mendoza?" Martin asked.

"I've heard stories about him," Ganson replied.

"After the Major tore up the town and disappeared into the hills I interviewed Dr. Roper. The doctor was treating the Major for some kind of mental illness. He seemed concerned over what had happened but didn't act as if he were worried about the Major making any trouble for him. Unfortunately, there were some other events that later drove the doctor and his family out of town."

"Did one of those have to do with Harley?"

"Harley Joseph Johnson. If I don't some day find his grave, I'm afraid I'll be carrying his name to mine. It wasn't two weeks after he disappeared that Dr. Roper and his family up and moved to Phoenix."

"How long had Major Mendoza been missing when Harley disappeared?"

"Almost a year."

"Do you have any idea why Dr. Roper got in such a hurry to leave?"

"There was something else that happened after Harley disappeared that I'm not at liberty to divulge."

"What do you think happened to Harley?" Ganson asked.

"I wish I knew," Martin answered.

"You don't give any credence to Fannie Hoffman's claim that she saw God come down and get him?" Ganson asked with a smile.

"Not really."

"Why not?"

"Everyone knows Fannie is mental. She has been for some time. I know she says she was with Harley when he disappeared but that's not the first time she's suggested it was a divine act that created a missing persons case. On more than one occasion she's informed me that God also had a hand in the disappearance of the Major."

"What do you think happened to the Major?" Ganson asked.

"I think he's taken up residence out there with all the other ghosts," Martin answered.

The BIA agent dropped the notebook in his pocket and walked back to his car. He returned carrying a suitcase, which he opened up on the porch. After putting on sterile gloves he used a pair of tongs to pick up the three smaller bones and drop them into a small evidence bag. He placed the long bone in a second bag.

"How many of these do you think are human?" Martin asked.

"The two smallest ones look like carpal bones to me," Ganson answered.

"Carpal bones?"

"Bones from a wrist."

"A child's or an adult's?"

"I can't tell for sure."

"What about the other two bones?"

"They look like they came from the leg of some animal."

"Like a cow or a horse?" Martin asked.

"I have no idea," Ganson answered. "I suppose they could be from a bear, an elk, a lion or whatever else lives out there."

Martin dusted the porch railing and the broken gate for prints. He made plaster casts of the hoof prints in the front yard much the same way one would for tire tread marks at a crime scene.

"And you have no ideas about who would want to bring you these bones?" he asked Ganson.

"None whatsoever."

"Has anyone given you anything since you came out here to work?"

"Like what."

"Like a gift."

"I've received lots of those. These people are so appreciative of having someone willing to take care of them that they bring me things all the time. Cookies, bread, tamales, acorn stew, beadwork, even jewelry."

"Do you think you could make me a list?"

"Do you think these bones are a gift or a threat?" Ganson asked.

"They could be either," Martin answered.

After asking Ganson if he'd mind waiting while the casts hardened, Martin took off on foot, following the horse tracks across the road. He returned thirty minutes later half covered in mud.

"Did you find anything out there?" Ganson asked, trying not to laugh.

"Only what ended up on my suit," the agent said with no emotion on his face.

"Where did the tracks lead?"

"Down into the creek. I couldn't get across because the water's too high. I'm going to have to drive across the bridge and get one of the Cibecue policemen to help me."

"That bottomland can be pretty rough," Ganson observed.

"Believe me, I know," Martin agreed. "I've gone back and forth over every square foot of it."

"Looking for Harley?"

"And for the Major before that."

"Could the bones be the Major's?" Ganson asked.

"They could be anybody's," Martin responded. "I've been working on this reservation since 1972 and there have been a handful of unsolved disappearances since then. Add to that the centuries of people dying and not being disposed of well enough to keep them away from the critters and you have the potential for a great number of unaccounted for corpses." Martin washed off as much mud as he could at the outside faucet before handing Ganson one of his cards. "The agency will be doing all it can to find the distributor as well as the owner of these bones. If anyone drops any more of them off you can call me at my office in Whiteriver. My home phone number is on the back. In the meantime I'd advise you to keep this to yourself."

"What do you suggest I tell them?" Ganson asked as he pointed across the parking lot at Gwen and Daisy, who'd been watching all morning from the waiting room window of the clinic.

"I wouldn't tell them a thing. Who's to say they're not in some way involved?"

"You're kidding, right?"

"I've seen stranger things."

"I'm sure you have but there is no way either of those women had anything to do with this."

"Even if you are absolutely certain about that I'd still recommend you tell them nothing. Make up some other story about my visit. Later on I'd like you to ask them to help put together a list of everyone who has given you anything."

Ganson watched Martin drive away before walking over to the clinic. The two women were waiting for him at the front desk. He said nothing to them and went directly to the x-ray room. After pulling Harley's films he spread them out on the table and held each one up to the light. He was looking for the pictures of Harley's hands. When he found them he placed them on the view box. There were multiple views of both wrists. As he studied the cube shaped carpal opacities he wondered if he wasn't looking at a picture of the two wrist bones that had found their way to the railing of his porch.

Neither Gwen nor Daisy asked him about his morning and the three of them worked late into the evening taking care of the patients they'd rescheduled. The morale at the clinic hadn't been that good since Peterson had paid his most recent visit but Ganson hadn't yet heard any word from the Area Office. He had continued to work as if he was going to be there for the full two years of his contract and he had continued to cross another week off his calendar every Friday.

"How large of a man was the Major?" he asked Gwen as they were getting ready to close up for the weekend.

"Which part of him are you interested in?" she responded.

Ganson couldn't help but laugh at Gwen's Apache humor. "How tall was he?"

"Not very. Before he joined the service and became the Major his nickname was Stump. Why do you ask?"

"Just curious."

"Does your curiosity have anything to do with what Agent Martin was doing over at your trailer this morning?"

"He told me I should keep that to myself."

"Keep what to yourself?"

"The nature of his visit."

Gwen laughed.

"What's so funny?" Ganson asked.

"You can keep the nature of his visit to yourself if you want but most everyone else in town already knows about it."

"How's that?"

"The Cibecue policeman who went hunting hoof prints through the creek bottom with Agent Martin is Daisy's cousin. Daisy was one of the first people he called after Martin left to go back to Whiteriver."

"Did he find out where the tracks led?" Ganson asked.

"If he did, he didn't tell Daisy," Gwen answered. "What he did say was that Agent Martin showed him the bones from your porch and told him there's a chance they could be Harley's."

"That's strange, "Ganson said. "This morning he didn't seem that confident about finding out who those bones belonged to."

"He doesn't give out a whole lot of information. He also has some strange ideas about this case."

"Like what?"

"According to Daisy's cousin, Martin thinks Harley's mother and Dazen Confused were both involved in the disappearance of Harley."

"Why would he think that about Harley's mother?" Ganson asked.

"I have no idea," Gwen answered. "Maybe you can ask him sometime."

By the time Ganson got home he was too tired to fix dinner. He stretched out on the couch but his mind wouldn't shut down. Prior to Peterson's most recent visit his sleeping patterns had improved. Now they were back to the way they'd been before. It often took

Kenneth D. Jackson

him two hours to fall asleep and he'd awaken in the middle of the night and take another two hours to doze off again. If he wasn't thinking about his court case with David Dunbar he was thinking about the case Bryce Peterson was building to use against him at the Area Office. If he wasn't thinking about either one of those he was thinking about what a basket case he'd become.

He closed his eyes but could still see the bones lined up on the railing. The ones from the unidentified animal were of no matter to him but he couldn't get away from the human ones. He lay there exhausted yet wide-awake, his mind obsessing over what had happened to the skeletal remains from which those bones had come. Were they tucked safely away in some subterranean sepulcher, where the skull, ribs and the spine all lay close enough to comfort one another into eternity? Or had they ended up above ground, a pile of disarticulated bones baked by the sun and scattered across the water-eroded slopes of the reservation.

Around ten o'clock there was a knock at the front door. Ordinarily Ganson would have assumed it was a mother making an after-hours visit with her sick baby. After what had showed up on his porch that morning he wasn't so sure. He peered out the window and saw a woman who had no baby in her arms. She was pacing back and forth and looked like she was getting ready to leave when Ganson opened the door.

"Mrs. Johnson?" he asked.

"I'm sorry to bother you," she apologized.

He believed it was the first time he'd heard a complete sentence come out of her mouth and he couldn't hide the surprise on his face. "Come on in."

"Thank you," she said with a look of relief on her face.

"Would you like something to drink?" he asked.

"I'll take a glass of water," she answered.

"Please sit down," he said as pulled up a chair for her at the kitchen table.

She fidgeted with the string that ran along the border of the sweatshirt she was wearing. She was tall and thin with an anxious face. She wore no makeup and her hair was pulled back and tied on the nape of her neck. Her nervousness gave her the look of a woman in her early forties, yet there was something about her eyes suggesting she was much younger. "I'm sorry," she said again. "It's not like me to come over to someone's house in the middle of the night."

"What can I do for you Mrs. Johnson?" Ganson asked as he poured them each a glass of water.

"You can call me Amanda." She tried to force a smile but the anguish on her face wouldn't permit it. "I heard about the bones you found this morning. I came here hoping you could tell me whether or not you think they belong to my son Harley."

As soon as she said his name she burst into tears. Ganson scooted his chair next to hers and put his arm around her. She stopped crying long enough to apologize to him a third time before burying her head in his shirt and starting in again. He held her until she'd sobbed herself so limp it felt like she was going to slide out of the chair. He pulled her up and led her over to the couch where he sat her down and unfolded the Indian blanket over her shoulders. She closed her eyes and looked like she might drift off to sleep. A few seconds later she sat straight up and asked if he had any Kleenex. He apologized and said he didn't, then walked into the bathroom and brought her a wad of toilet paper.

"I know you have no idea whose bones those are," she said after wiping her face and blowing her nose, "but I have to talk to somebody. If this is going to be too much of a burden you can tell me now and save us both the embarrassment."

"You're welcome to stay here and talk to me as long as you wish," Ganson offered.

"What do you know about Colorado City?" she asked after blowing her nose again.

"Isn't that where all the polygamists live?"

"Polygamists live all across the West. Most of the ones in Arizona live in Colorado City, which is on the border between Arizona and Utah. That's where I was born and raised. The house I grew up in had thirty people living in it. Twenty-five of them were children.

In addition to my mother there were—" She stopped and gave Ganson a questioning look. "Are you sure you want to hear this?"

"Absolutely," he said as he brought the glasses of water over from the kitchen table.

"I grew up with four mothers, my own and my father's other three wives. My mother was fourteen when she married my father. He was seventy-three. He lived to be eighty-nine years old. Less than three months after he died the three older wives gave me to Warren Johnson, who already had two wives and eighteen children of his own."

Amanda took a drink of water. "Warren got me pregnant right away. There weren't any doctors in town and this old midwife who'd lived in Colorado City all her life delivered me. She had to be at least eighty-years old. She was so frail that if I'd have cut a huge fart in labor it would have probably blown her out the delivery room and across the border into Utah."

Ganson spewed the swig of water he was drinking onto the coffee table. He followed that with a burst of laughter and a prolonged coughing spell. "Sorry about that," he said after he caught his breath.

"My delivery was a disaster," she continued. "Harley came out breech and his head got stuck. By the time the old woman pulled him out of me he was so limp and blue I thought he was dead. He must have suffered some kind of brain damage because he always had this weakness on the right side of his body. To make things worse I caught some kind of infection. I got so sick the midwife had to send me to an obstetrician in St. George. I stayed in the hospital on antibiotics for two weeks. When I was released the doctor told me I'd never be able to have another child. I didn't believe him, but that was fifteen years ago, so I guess he was right. Do you have any children?" she asked.

"I don't."

"I wished I'd had more," she said with a sad look on her face. "After I came home from the hospital I lost interest in everything. I spent most of the time holed up in my room and never left the house. It was a struggle to do even the simplest things for Harley. The wives went out of their way to shame me because I couldn't have any more children. Have you heard enough of this yet?" she asked.

"What was it like growing up there?" he asked.

"We didn't have a TV or a radio. There were no newspapers in the house. The only magazines were the ones my husband kept locked up in the basement. I knew nothing of the world outside Colorado City."

"What about your schooling?"

"Done at home. Mostly religious teaching."

"What was your social life like?"

"It wasn't. The elders ran all the boys out of town before they reached the age of twenty. That was so they could have all the young girls to themselves. By the time I entered puberty I knew I was destined to become the teenage wife of some old man who had a scrotum full of white hair."

"Why didn't you leave?"

"All I knew to do was live my religion."

"What changed your mind?"

"I can still remember the first time I ever thought about another life. Harley and I were lying on a blanket in the backyard. Harley had fallen asleep. I was stretched out on my back, staring up at the stars. I picked out one that was traveling across the sky and watched it until it disappeared beyond the horizon. I didn't know much back then but I did know that it wasn't a star but an airplane. Lying there I felt in some strange way connected to the passengers. As I watched them being transported across the heavens I wondered what it would feel like for Harley and me to be flying away with them."

"What finally got you out of there?"

"My son had an accident when he was ten years old. He was riding his bicycle on one of the few sidewalks in town when a boy in a pickup truck peeled out of the alley and knocked Harley all the way across the road. By the time I got to him the paramedics were already there. Blood was oozing out his nose and his body was all broken up. He looked so small and helpless."

Before Amanda could go on there was another knock at the front door. This time it was a mother holding a sick baby. Amanda stood up and offered to leave but Ganson assured her it would only take a few minutes. The mother was apologetic for coming so late but her two-year old son was having problems breathing. After looking in his ears and throat and listening to his heart and lungs Ganson gave the boy two different shots and two different medications to start taking. He told the mother to bring him back that night if he got worse and to bring him to the clinic in the morning for follow-up.

After he carried the boy out to the mother's truck he returned to the living room. Amanda once again asked him if he really wanted her to go on with her story and he again assured her he did.

"I thought my son was going to die that day," Amanda continued. "Until the day I die I'll remember crying over how the two of us were never going to be able to take that airplane flight together. The doctors in St. George were in surgery with Harley all night. When they came out of the operating room the next morning they told me they expected him to recover. They also told me he had brittle bone disease. Do you know what that is?" she asked.

Ganson nodded yes.

"I'd always suspected there was something not right about the white part of his eyes being blue but I had no idea there was something wrong with his bones. Have you seen his x-rays?"

"Yes, I have."

"They're all full of metal, aren't they?"

"Yes, they are."

"Harley spent three months mending in the hospital in St. George. I stayed there the whole time. The hospital let me eat in the cafeteria and they put me up in a tiny apartment adjacent to the grounds. When I started going stir crazy the pink lady hospital volunteers became my saviors. They took me out to eat and drove me all over town. They were also instrumental in my getting out of Colorado City."

"The pink ladies?" Ganson asked.

"They helped me get a library card."

"A library card got you out of Colorado City?"

"With the help of the librarian I took an eight-week crash course introduction to life. When I wasn't hanging out with Harley or riding around with the pink ladies, I was reading about white whales, scarlet letters and purple sage. I read books by Mark Twain, Ernest Hemingway and John Steinbeck. I even made it through one of William Faulkner's. I read almost a book a day and started keeping a journal in this three-ring notebook that had a raised metal emblem of a cross on its front cover. When it came time for Harley and me to go back to Colorado City I took the journal with me."

Amanda rose up from the couch. With the blanket still draped across her shoulders she walked over to the sink to refill her water glass. She offered to do the same for Ganson but he motioned he was okay.

"I got a job at the convenience store and talked this eighteen year-old boy who was working there into teaching me how to drive. At the age of twenty-seven I got my first driver's license. When Warren found out about it he tore up the license and got the boy fired. He also stepped up his visits to my bedroom."

"If you don't mind me asking, how did it work with all those wives in the house?"

"We lived in a three-story house and all three of us had our own bedrooms. Mine was on the top floor. Each one of us had our own designated night of the week. On that night Warren would appear wearing his sacred undergarments. From the beginning of our marriage I had never liked having sex with him. After Harley was born I hated it."

"Was he ever physically abusive to you?"

"He never beat me but it felt like he was trying to hurt me every time he crawled on top of me. He didn't have sex with me every time he came to my room but I always knew what was in store for me before he made it up the stairs. If the stairs were groaning it was because he was climbing them at a weary pace and wasn't up to doing anything to me that night. If the stairs had a bouncy squeak to them I'd get a sick taste in my mouth and want to throw up." Amanda took a deep breath. "Are you sure you haven't heard enough?" she asked.

"Not unless you want to stop," he answered.

"My bedroom door had a brass doorknob on it. From the way the door was open I could see my husband's reflection as he came down the hallway. The closer he got to my bedroom the more distorted and grotesque his image appeared in the doorknob. I'd make out like I was asleep but it wouldn't matter. He'd pull up my gown, pull down my panties and climb on top of me anyway. I always kept my journal hidden under my side of the mattress. I think it was the pain of the notebook's metal cross digging into my spine that allowed me to focus on something other than how much longer he was going to be grinding away."

"Your husband sounds like quite the guy."

"Warren's room was in the basement and he always kept it locked. One morning I noticed the door had swung open. He must have accidentally left it unlocked because he'd just left the house with his other two wives to go to the post office to pick up his social security check and all the welfare checks for the kids. I tiptoed down the steps and into his room. The air was so heavy I felt like I was in a crypt. There weren't any dead bodies there but there were stacks of magazines full of pictures of naked women. On top of one of the stacks was a package of photographs. I sat down on the bed to look through them. They were all of naked children. When I saw my son in one of them I threw up all over Warren's comforter."

Amanda choked back the tears and continued. "Harley and I ran away that day with the clothes we were wearing and the twenty dollar bill I had in my pocket. I got the boy who had taught me how to drive to take us as far as Fredonia. He dropped us off at the south end of town with a package of cheese crackers and two bottles of water. As we were walking down the road we came upon a coyote puppy whining in the drainage ditch. I told Harley to leave it alone because it might have some kind of disease but he picked it up anyway. When he climbed back up to the road with it in his arms he told me he was going to name it Garfield," Amanda said breaking into a smile.

"After the cat?" Ganson asked.

"No," she said, "after a basketball player. The coyote had a circular marking on its forehead that looked just like a basketball. While watching TV in the hospital in St. George Harley had become a Phoenix Suns fan. The name Garfield came from the name of a player on the Suns who had made some miraculous shot in a playoff game."

"That shot," Ganson said, "was in the fifth game of the championship finals against the Boston Celtics. Even though the Suns lost the game and the series the shot is considered one of the greatest in the history of the NBA playoffs. It was a turnaround jumper from above the key. The guy who buried the shot was Garfield Heard." Ganson immediately regretted his choice of the word "buried" but he couldn't take it back and Amanda didn't seem to take offense.

"Less than five minutes after Harley had given his coyote a name," Amanda went on, "an angel entered our lives. He was an Apache gentleman on his way back home from an Indian Powwow in Montana. I told Harley he would have to leave the coyote but the man told him he could bring it along. He introduced himself as Tiswin Richards, the curator for the Culture Center at Fort Apache."

Ganson didn't mention the conversation he'd had with Richards. "Tiswin is a pretty strange name for a man, isn't it?"

"His name is really Owen. In his younger years his buddies called him Tiswin because of all the alcohol he drank. After he gave it up he continued to hold onto the name. He said it reminded him of where he'd once been and never wanted to be again. He brought us all the way to Cibecue and put us up in the trailer he used to live in. He also helped me get a job at the café and gave me enough money to get started. He used to spend a lot of time telling Harley about the history and traditions of the Apache people."

Amanda looked at her watch. "Good God," she said as she stood up and returned the blanket to the back of the couch. "I had no idea of the time. I'm so sorry I've kept you up so late." She gave

Ganson a hug. "I can't tell you how much it's meant to me to have you listen to my story."

Ganson knew her story didn't end there but he also knew it wasn't the right time to be asking about the disappearance of her son. "Can I drive you home?" he asked.

"Thank you for the offer," she answered, "but Caesar's waiting outside for me."

"Caesar?"

"My horse."

"I didn't see him," Ganson said.

"He's tied up down at the other end of your driveway."

With flashlight in hand Ganson directed Amanda through the gate and down the driveway. Amanda's horse was one of the ugliest Ganson had ever seen. Not only did it have a massive overbite, it also had a Roman nose, a nose that must have prompted its original owner to give the horse its Roman name. Ganson gave Caesar a pat on the nose while Amanda stepped up into the saddle. It wasn't completely dark but the quarter moon did little to illuminate the landscape.

"Are you sure you don't want to leave your horse here for the night and let me give you a ride home?" he asked.

"It's a quick trip," she answered, "and Caesar and I both have to be up at first light."

"Why don't you take the flashlight," he suggested.

"Thanks but I won't need it. Caesar is sure-footed and can see things in the dark better than most people can in the daylight."

Ganson wished Amanda and her horse a safe trip home. As he watched their shadowy forms fade into the darkness he wondered about the nature of the business beckoning her to ride out again at dawn.

Twenty

Although the appearance of the bones on Ganson's porch caused quite a stir, two days later the community was rocked by an event of even greater impact, the second disappearance of Bomar's dog Butch. According to Fannie, who was across the street in her garden at the time, Bomar had entered Butch's pen with a fresh bucket of water when a pack of coyotes came yapping down the road. Butch went crazy and ran over Bomar as he rushed out the open gate in pursuit of the coyotes.

That happened on a Thursday. When Butch hadn't returned by the following Monday Bomar flooded the valley with reward posters. The posters had a picture of the two of them sitting on the front porch of the trading post. Both were posing proudly and Butch was wearing his gold engraved collar. Underneath the picture was a pledge to give one hundred dollars of shopping credit to anyone providing information leading to the recovery of Butch. The reward was destined to go uncollected, not only because no one cared if the dog were ever seen again, but also because everyone knew the gold in the dog's collar was worth far more than one hundred dollars worth of overpriced goods at Bomar's trading post.

Everyone in the village wondered how Bomar was going to react to this disappearance of Butch. The joke around town was that since it had been his hair that had fallen off the first time, maybe it would be his penis this time.

Their answer came within a few days. While still searching for his missing dog, Bomar started a campaign to kill every coyote he came across. Once he killed them he hung their carcasses out by his kennel. The sight and smell of the dead animals didn't do a thing for the business but that didn't deter Bomar. By the end of the week there were twelve coyote corpses dangling from the fence. Coyotes were classified as varmints and Bomar could legally kill them until there were no more left to kill.

Gwen filled Ganson in on what was happening. "Every time Bomar strings up another coyote Fannie crosses the street and lifts up its forehead to see if it's the one that used to hang out with Harley and her."

"Are you talking about Garfield?" Ganson asked.

"You know about him?" Gwen asked.

"Harley's mother paid me a visit the night the bones showed up on my porch," Ganson explained.

"Really?" Gwen asked with a look of surprise. "What did she have to say?"

"She told me a little about her and Harley's life and how they ended up here in Cibecue. She also told me how they found Garfield."

"Harley and Garfield used to come over to the house all the time to get Fannie. Harley would walk up to the porch and knock on the door while Garfield stayed out at the far edge of the yard, pacing back and forth. The three of them would take off together."

"Where would they go?"

"According to Fannie they always went to the shrine."

Ganson recalled the time he and Gwen had visited the Buffalo brothers there. "Why that place?"

"That was their place."

"What do you mean?"

"After those people from the University of Arizona determined that was the site of the Cibecue Massacre, Fannie and Harley decided to mark it with something more than a metal stake. With the help of Tiswin Richards they painted and set the corner posts and the cross."

"What did they do there after they finished setting it up?"

Gwen shook her head. "Fannie never said."

"What happened to Garfield after Harley disappeared?" Ganson asked.

"He disappeared for a while too," Gwen answered.

"Almost every time I've seen Bronco Dazen he's had a coyote tailing him."

"That would be Garfield."

"Are you sure?"

"Garfield has a very distinctive circular marking on his forehead. He also walks with a hitch in his back leg from when Butch once got hold of him and tore off two of his toes."

"Was Garfield in with the pack of coyotes Butch took off after?"

"Fannie says he wasn't."

"And Garfield is not one of the dead coyotes hanging from Bomar's fence?"

"Bomar cut all those coyotes down last night. Fannie and I watched him drag them into a pile, drench them in five gallons of gasoline and ignite them with a firecracker."

"I take it Bomar believes it was coyotes that did Butch in."

"I suppose. Fannie told me she thought Bomar was killing all of them so he could cut them open and see if any of them had chunks of Butch inside them."

Bomar was unsuccessful in his search for Butch's remains and the dog's whereabouts were still unknown when Ganson was paid a second visit by Gus Martin. The BIA agent had telephoned in advance, advising Ganson he was going to be in the area and had a few more questions he wanted to ask him.

"What do you think happened to Butch?" Martin asked after he drove into Ganson's driveway and got out of his Lincoln.

"I hope you didn't drive all the way out here just to ask me that," replied Ganson, who was sitting on his porch sipping on a

Mountain Dew. "Was Butch ever a suspect in the disappearance of Harley?"

Martin nodded. "Everybody was a suspect in the disappearance of Harley. Butch would have been a legitimate one if he hadn't had a rock solid alibi. He and his kennel mates were with Bomar west of Canyon Creek on a guided hunt with some bigwig banker from Oklahoma City." Martin accepted a soda from Ganson and sat down next to him on the porch. "My reason for coming here today was to ask you about Amanda Johnson. I heard she paid you a visit."

"How did you know that? Ganson asked.

"She told me," Martin answered.

"When?"

"She called me the following evening to inform me there was no way the bones belonged to her son."

"I hope you didn't think she got that idea from me," Ganson said.

"I've spoken with Mrs. Johnson on several occasions and I can say she is a woman of both unique and original thought."

"Somebody told me you thought she might in some way be involved in Harley's disappearance."

"That's not exactly true. What I thought and still think is that she knows far more about what happened to her son than she lets on."

"Why do you think that?" Ganson asked

"I have my reasons," Martin answered. "What did she tell you when she came over to see you?"

"Not a lot," Ganson answered. "She talked some about her life with Harley before they found their way to Cibecue."

"Did she say anything about her husband Warren?" Martin inquired.

"A little."

"About a month after Harley disappeared I took a trip up to Colorado City to interview Mr. Johnson."

"That must have been quite a treat."

"When I drove into town I thought I'd entered a time warp. The houses and vehicles didn't look all that different than those in other parts of rural Arizona but the people sure did. There were all these teenage girls dressed up in their prairie dresses, shepherding bunches of little children up and down the side of the road. I found Mr. Johnson sitting in his front yard. It was his opinion that Amanda had come under the influence of the devil."

"Did you happen to ask Mr. Johnson for an alibi?" Ganson asked.

"I ask everyone for an alibi," Martin answered. "He told me the only time he'd gone out of town in the past two months was to buy groceries in Fredonia. He said he went shopping about once a week and was never gone more than a few hours."

"Did you believe him?"

Martin shrugged his shoulders. "For what it's worth he claimed he had a house full of witnesses who could back him up."

"I know you've told me you have no idea what happened to Harley but I can't imagine you don't have a working theory or two."

"To try to solve this case I've used helicopters, bloodhounds, other agents, tribal cops, countless volunteers and two psychics from Sedona. I have all kinds of theories about what took place. Without a body that's what they'll remain, just theories."

"What about the bones?" Ganson asked. "Have you got an ID on them yet?"

Martin didn't answer right away, as if he were contemplating just how much he was willing to reveal. "Before I left the office today I received a call from one of the FBI's forensic pathologists. She hadn't yet determined the sex or the age group of the two human bones but she said you were correct in identifying them as from the wrist. She called one of them the lunate and the other the trapezium."

"What about the other bones?" Ganson asked.

"A cannon and a carpus," Martin answered. "Both from the leg of a horse."

"That's interesting," Ganson reflected out loud. "If you don't mind coming inside for a minute there's something I'd like to show you that could be of some help." Out of the corner of Ganson's eye he could see the "yeah right" look on Martin's face as the agent followed him into his trailer. Ganson picked up the folder of x-rays he'd brought over from the clinic and pulled several of the films. "Tell me what you see," he said as he held them up to the sunlight.

Martin took hold of the films and studied them as if he knew what he was looking at. "I see a lot of different bones."

"What else do you see?"

"A lot of things that look like they came from the Ace Hardware Store in Show Low."

"They did come from a hardware store, an orthopedic hardware store."

"That's nice to know but what does that have to do with helping solve this case?"

"These are Harley's x-rays. All those things you see in there are made out of metal."

"So?"

"When I first moved here my nurse told me of the group who had gotten together to locate the site of the Cibecue Massacre. She said they came out here and spent days scouring the creek bottom with—"

"Metal detectors," Martin interrupted. "They used metal detectors."

"I take it you didn't use anything like that when you were searching for Harley."

Martin didn't answer as he replaced the films in the folder. After asking Ganson's permission to take them with him he left saying he had to make another stop before going back to Whiteriver.

When Ganson got to the clinic the next morning Gwen was waiting for him. "What's up with the BIA man?" she asked.

"How should I know?"

"Didn't he come see you yesterday?"

"Are there no secrets in this community?" Ganson asked.

"A few," Gwen answered. "When I went over to give the Buffalo brothers their medication this morning I saw Agent Martin at the shrine. He had a metal detector with him."

"That was quick," Ganson commented.

"Did you have something to do with that?"

Ganson nodded. "I showed Martin the x-rays of all the metal Harley had inside him. Would you like another cup of coffee?" he asked as he walked over to pour himself one.

"Why would you do a thing like that?" Gwen asked.

Ganson stopped in midstride and turned back toward Gwen. "Ask you if you wanted another cup of coffee?"

"No. Why would you show Harley's x-rays to Martin?"

"I thought it might help him find the boy's body and solve the case."

"There are a lot of people out here who would just as soon not see the case solved."

"Why's that?"

"They're afraid Dazen Confused could end up getting arrested and thrown into prison."

"Do they think he had something to do with Harley's disappearance?"

"They think he'll be blamed for it whether he had anything to do with it or not."

"If he did have something to do with it don't you think he should be prosecuted?" Ganson asked.

"I guess that depends on how much he had to do with it," Gwen answered. "He claims he's lost his power and he's all but stopped performing ceremonies. To the older people living here he represents the last hope they have of holding onto the life they've been used to living. They're likely to give up if the last medicine man of any influence is removed from the reservation."

Ganson thought back to when he'd first seen Bronco Dazen at the hospital. The medicine man seemed to command a reverence amongst his people but it appeared to Ganson he'd moved well beyond his once powerful prime. "When was the last time Bronco Dazen held a major ceremony?" he asked.

"About two years ago he conducted a curing ceremony on a girl from Carrizo," Gwen answered.

"What was wrong with her?"

"She was paralyzed. It started in her feet and was working its way up. It got to where she lost the complete use of her legs and could barely breathe."

"Why wasn't she in the hospital?"

"She was at one time. Dr. Peterson thought she had polio. He wanted to ship her to Phoenix but the family pulled her out of the hospital and took her home to be treated by Dazen Confused. I didn't agree with what they did but I couldn't convince them to take her back."

"What happened to her?"

"Dazen Confused tried to get her to lie down on a blanket but she got so short of breath he had to prop her up against a log. When he realized how sick she was he cautioned the parents that if he wasn't successful they should consider taking her back to the hospital. He dumped a rattlesnake out of a gunnysack. He grabbed the snake behind its head so it couldn't open its mouth to strike. To this day I can hear the snake's tail buzzing and see it wrapping its body around Dazen Confused's arm."

"What did he do with the snake?"

"He rubbed its head back and forth across the girl's chest. It was as if he were trying to create a boundary that would prevent the paralysis from rising any higher in the girl's body. When he finished with the snake he kissed it on the top of its head and released it into a nearby gully. After singing for the next four nights he told the parents their daughter would be better by the next full moon. He promised to refund his fee if she wasn't. The girl survived but it was way more than one full moon before she was able even to get out of bed. I think it was a full year before she could stand and walk."

Ganson wondered how much credit Gwen gave the medicine man for curing the girl. Her description of the illness was a textbook case of Guillain-Barre syndrome, an ascending muscular paralysis triggered by a viral infection. Most of the patients got back to normal with nothing more than supportive care. It was Ganson's opinion that if Bronco Dazen's snake power contributed to the girl's recovery, it was simply by instilling in her mind the belief she was going to get better.

That belief however could only take her so far. If the disease had moved up her spinal cord to the level of cervical nerves number five, four, and three, the girl's diaphragm would have become paralyzed and she would have needed to be intubated and placed on a ventilator to survive. No amount of songs, chants, prayers, positive thoughts or snake power would have saved her from an agonizing death by asphyxiation.

"How much was it?" Ganson asked.

"How much was what?"

"Bronco Dazen's fee."

"Since she didn't get better in a month did he give the family a refund?"

"I don't know but I can't imagine he didn't."

"Why not?"

"Because Dazen Confused has always been a man of his word."

Also a man of his word, Agent Martin was determined to find Harley's body or finish out his career trying. For three days he swung his metal detector back and forth as he worked his way up and down the bottomland bordering Cibecue Creek. He unearthed shell casings, a pickax head and several other rusted artifacts seeming to confirm the officially selected site of the Cibecue Massacre, but he found none of the hardware that had once held Harley together.

Convinced he'd reached another dead end, he was crossing the creek a quarter of a mile south of Bronco Dazen's camp when his metal detector went off over a pile of driftwood. The signal was so strong his heart began to flutter. He dropped the detector and began pulling the tree limbs out of the pile. There was so much tangled debris he had to stop several times to catch his breath and wipe the sweat off his forehead. Lifting off the last of the driftwood he came face to face with Butch. The dog's partially submerged body was half rotted away but he was still wearing his gold collar.

After telling Bomar where he could find his dog, Martin dropped by the clinic to return Harley's x-rays. Ganson was in the middle of removing a sebaceous cyst from the back of one of Daisy's brothers-in-law and Martin waited for him to finish.

"Why don't you hold onto these," the BIA agent said as he handed Ganson the films. "They are less likely to get lost here than in my possession."

"I don't guess you found anything out there, did you?" Ganson asked.

"As a matter of fact I did."

"What?"

"Butch's collar."

"What about Butch?"

"Parts of him were there too."

"Was it the coyotes that got him?" Ganson asked.

"I doubt it," Martin said. "Not unless they've taken up the bearing of arms."

"What are you talking about?" Ganson asked.

"It could have been Butch's gold collar that set off my metal detector but I'm more inclined to think it was the three lead bullets I dug out of his skull."

Twenty-One

The Apache version of the Ghost Dance sprung from the tortured mind of Noch-ay-del-klinne, who in the spring of 1881 sought the supernatural to soothe the psyche of his followers. He made his final stand on the east bank of Cibecue Creek on August 30, 1881. One hundred years later his grandson Bronco Dazen seemed destined for the same fate.

Through the few followers he had left the medicine man let everyone know he was planning to lead a ride along the route his grandfather had taken from the original Noch-ay-del-klinne camp north of town to the shrine marking the site of the Cibecue Massacre. Bronco Dazen hadn't been the same since the Tribal Council had taken away the snakes and the lightning had turned against him. The rumor around town was that he was doing the ride as a last-ditch effort to reclaim his lost power. Fannie and her friends were excited but the Cibecue citizens as a whole showed little interest in the event.

On the morning of the day the community would come to call the "Second Cibecue Massacre," Ganson was sitting on his porch sipping a cup of coffee when Gus Martin came driving up.

"What happened to the Lincoln?" he asked pointing to the dent in the hood of Martin's car.

"Some idiot threw a rock at it."

"In Cibecue?"

"At the rodeo last night in Whiteriver."

"That's right," Ganson remarked, "this is the weekend of the Tribal Fair, isn't it."

"The place is crazy," Martin replied. "People everywhere stumbling over each other. The Chief of Police has called in every cop on the reservation to cover the parade."

"So what are you doing in Cibecue?" Ganson asked.

"I heard Dazen Confused plans to have a little parade of his own today."

"If you drove all the way out for that, you're showing far more interest than the majority of the people who live here."

"I came because I have a bad feeling about this."

"Are you thinking Major Mendoza might do something to disrupt Dazen's ride?" Ganson asked with a boyish grin on his face.

"No, but I'm thinking this guy might," Martin answered as he pulled a folded flyer from his pocket. "I suppose you've seen a few of these around," he said showed it to Ganson.

"They're all over the valley," Ganson replied.

The tan colored flyer had a picture of Bomar and Butch on it with the offer of a one hundred dollar reward for information about the dog's death.

"Bomar has been calling me ever since I dug that dog of his out of the creek. He's usually drunk and carrying on about Dazen Confused. One time he asked me to confiscate the medicine man's rifle and run a ballistic test comparing a slug fired from it with one I dug out of Butch's skull."

"Did you?"

"I informed him that Butch's death was not a capital crime. Since it had nothing to do with any other ongoing investigation there would be no ballistic testing."

"You think he's crazy enough to want to harm Bronco Dazen?" Ganson asked.

"If he gets drunk enough he just might be crazy enough to want to try to harm you too."

Ganson thought back to incident with the treed mountain lion. "If you really believe that why don't you take him in?"

"He hasn't done anything, yet."

"What about Dazen? Have you told him of your concerns?"

"Earlier this morning."

"What did he say?" Ganson asked.

"Not a thing. It didn't seem to bother him," Martin answered.

Ganson tried to make out like it didn't bother him either. "I think Bomar's basically harmless."

"I hope you're right."

"Are you planning on hanging around for Dazen's little procession?"

"I'd like to but I have to get back to Whiteriver for the parade." Martin reached out and shook Ganson's hand. "Be careful today, Doc."

As Martin was backing out of the driveway Ganson witnessed something he never thought he'd see, all four Buffalo brothers up and on the move before noon. They were across the street, walking stiffly in the direction of the bridge. Reggie and Rickie were riding right behind them on Chico, whose coat had been painted white with blue dots.

Gwen had left for Tucson the night before to visit Nikki and Ganson had promised to keep an eye on Fannie. The plan was for the two of them to watch Bronco Dazen's ride through town from Fannie's backyard. Driving over to her house he saw very few people along the route. He assumed the majority of the holiday enthusiasts had gone to Whiteriver to catch the Labor Day parade. When Ganson got to Fannie's she was sitting in a lawn chair wearing her lavender camp dress. She'd tied a red bandanna over her head and strapped her pistols across her chest.

"Are you planning on using those today?" Ganson asked.

A smile flickered across Fannie's face as she raised a bony

finger and aimed it across the street. With his rattlesnake hat atop his head Bomar was seated on the top step of the trading post porch eating sunflower seeds and guzzling cans of beer. He didn't appear to be armed.

Ganson pulled up another chair and sat down next to Fannie in the shade to wait the arrival of the medicine man. Although Bronco Dazen had announced he'd be coming through town at midday, Indian Time was in full effect and he still hadn't made it by mid-afternoon. The few who had turned out to watch the event had gone back inside their homes to get out of the heat and humidity.

Around three o'clock the dogs in Bomar's kennel started barking. Ganson pulled at the sleeve of Fannie's dress and pointed to where Dazen and his entourage had arrived at the north end of town. The medicine man was wearing a blue shirt that was color coordinated with the blue snakes painted across the neck and along the withers of his horse. Strung out on foot behind him were the Buffalo brothers. Bringing up the rear were Reggie and Rickie on Chico.

Oblivious to the reservation's public ban on open containers the brothers were drinking beer from the cans they'd kept chilled in the ice-filled saddlebags draped across Chico's neck. They were dressed in their usual denim with red headbands wrapped around their foreheads. The headbands were the same as those worn by the

Apache scouts a hundred years before. Employed by the government to track down the hostiles, the scouts had worn the headbands so the army wouldn't fire on them by mistake.

Ganson took Fannie by the hand. As they were walking toward the street to get a closer look, Bomar stumbled off the porch and over to the freezer where he stored the meat from the wild game he shot. He hoisted a 50-gallon black trash bag out of the freezer and dragged it across the parking lot.

"Hey witch doctor. I got something in this bag you and that old woman over there might be interested in."

The medicine man checked his horse to a stop. He raised his hand, signaling for those behind him to stop also. The brothers were paying little attention and the one of them walked right up the rear end of Dazen's mare. Already nervous over what was in the trash bag, the mare kicked out at the brother, who seemed more concerned over the loss of the beer he'd accidentally poured up the mare's ass than over the possibility of having one of her horseshoes planted up his.

When Ganson saw Bomar pull the hunting knife from the back of his belt he let go of Fannie's hand and broke into a run. "Look out, Bronco," he yelled.

Before Dazen had the chance to respond Bomar took the knife and sliced open the side of the trash bag. He picked up the bag by the bottom and dumped out its contents, a frozen coyote. "This is partial payment for Butch," he said as he placed his boot on the body of the coyote and sent it sliding across the pavement.

The mare bolted sideways. As Dazen struggled to rein her in Bomar raised the knife and cocked it behind his head. Before he could release it a half empty can of Miller High Life whizzed past his nose. He spun around to see where it came from, catching the second can flush in the face. The knife flew out of his hand and skated across the parking lot. He went to retrieve it but was beaten there by one of the beer-flinging Buffalo brothers. The brother picked up the knife and sent it zinging in the direction of the trading post. The knife stuck fast in the wood siding. After breaking into a fist pumping celebration the brothers started laughing at Bomar, who retreated through the side door of the trading post.

Not knowing what kind of a weapon Bomar would have in his hand when he reappeared, the Buffalo brothers, Reggie, Rickie and Chico scattered for the creek bottom. Bronco Dazen seemed more concerned about the coyote and dismounted to get a closer look. He gathered up the frozen animal and carried it over to Fannie, who had joined Ganson at the side of the road. She wrapped her arms around the coyote and fell to her knees. Dazen said something to her in Apache before getting back on his horse and continuing alone on his ride toward the site of the massacre.

By the time Ganson was able to separate Fannie from the coyote her chin and her forearms were ice cold. He led her back into the yard and returned for the animal. Its frozen face appeared to be looking up at him through a third eye, confirming what he already knew to be true. It wasn't an eye at all, but a spherical marking in the fur of its forehead that had prompted a young white boy to name the creature after a black basketball star. Ganson was afraid Fannie might pull out her pistols and make a run at the trading post but all she did was insist he bury Garfield at the back end of her garden. He promised he'd do it later and told her to go inside and lock her doors until he returned.

Hoping he could find someone who could do something about Bomar, Ganson climbed in his truck and headed for the police station. When he arrived he found only a note tacked to the front door. The note said that due to the Tribal Fair the police officer on duty would be in Whiteriver for the day. He drove home and got his gun. He popped in a loaded clip and dropped it into the right hand pocket of his corduroy jacket.

Knowing Bomar was nowhere near done with Bronco Dazen, Ganson hoped the medicine man had enough sense to cut short his ceremonial ride and cut out for a safe place. He returned to Fannie's to find the front door open and nobody inside. When he couldn't find her out back or down the street he panicked.

He was about to jump in his truck and go driving around looking for her when he noticed that the front door of the trading post was also wide open. There was no way he wanted to go over there but the more he thought about it the more convinced he was that's where Fannie had gone. The fact he was carrying a gun was of no comfort to him and he left the gun inside his jacket pocket as he approached the trading post. When he got to the top step of the porch he called out through the open door. "Hello, is anybody there?" When there was no answer he called out again. "Hello. This is Dr. Ganson. Is it okay for me to come in?"

"You're not going to rob me, are you?" a woman's voice called out to him.

"Of course I'm not going to rob you," Ganson said as he stepped inside with his hands partially raised so as to pose no threat. "I'm looking for Fannie."

"You're sure you're not going to rob me?" asked the Apache woman hunkered down behind the cash register.

"Why do you keep asking me that?"

"Because that's what Fannie just did."

"She robbed you?"

"At gunpoint."

Ganson gave the woman a look of disbelief. "Everybody knows those pistols of hers are worthless."

"Those pistols of hers were both pointed at my chest and I wasn't about to ask her whether or not they worked."

"They're never loaded."

"They are now."

"You know that for sure?"

"The only thing she took was a box of .44 caliber bullets."

"Oh, shit," Ganson said. "Where's Bomar?"

"He took off right after he had the run-in out by the road," the woman answered.

"No doubt carrying a few weapons."

"One rifle. Lots of ammunition."

"He didn't happen to say where he was headed, did he?"

"No, but he did something strange before he left."

"What's that?"

"He painted up his eyebrows."

"I didn't think he had any eyebrows."

"He painted where they used to be."

"Why do you think he did that?" Ganson asked.

"I don't know," the woman shrugged. "Maybe he's going on the warpath."

"Maybe so," Ganson said. "I need you to call the police in Whiteriver."

"I already have."

"Call them again and say there's an emergency at the Cibecue Massacre shrine."

Ganson ran back over to Fannie's, jumped in his truck and sped toward the turnoff to the shrine. When he left the pavement and turned onto the muddy road he gunned the engine. The weeds growing up between the two tracks grabbed at the underbelly of the truck, causing it to skid sideways. He got out and locked in the hubs. As he continued on in four- wheel drive he could feel the mud sticking to the tires and hear the power steering groaning with every turn of the wheel.

At the end of the road he slid to a stop underneath the limbs of a massive alligator juniper. The Buffalo brothers' camp was deserted. The shrine was hidden behind a cluster of scrub oak but he could see Bronco Dazen's mare tied to one of the posts. He found the medicine man in the middle of the clearing. Fannie was hunched over on the ground. The right side of her face had a hematoma the size of a tomato and her right eye was swollen completely shut. Ganson rushed toward her. Before he could get there Bomar and his purple painted eyebrows stepped out of the bushes with his rifle pointed at Ganson's head.

"You didn't have to shoot her," Ganson yelled.

"I didn't shoot her," Bomar said in a voice that sounded as if he'd sobered up some since having had one of the Buffalo brothers bounce a beer can off his skull, "but I did have to use the butt of my rifle to gain her attention."

"Why would you do a thing like that, Bomar?" Ganson asked as he dropped down to tend to Fannie.

"She told me she was going to kill me," Bomar said.

"And you believed her?" Ganson asked as he took off his jacket and draped it over Fannie.

"She pulled her pistols on me."

When Ganson saw her pistols lying on the ground, it dawned on him that he'd become separated from his own gun. "You know those pistols aren't any good," he said as he tried to get closer to the right pocket of his corduroy jacket.

"I don't know shit about those pistols and I wasn't about to wait until she shot me with one of them."

"Bomar, she's hasn't got the strength to—"

"Shut up and go stand next to the witch doctor," Bomar said as he reached out and pressed the barrel of his rifle against Ganson's cheek.

Ganson reluctantly left Fannie to join Dazen. The medicine man was standing by the cross. There was a gunnysack hanging from the part of the arm that hadn't fallen off. In Apache Bomar said something that prompted the medicine man to slip the sack off the arm. He untied the top of it and shook it upside down until a thick gray snake with a triangular head wiggled out the opening and fell to the ground. The rattlesnake landed on top of Fannie's pistols and immediately wound itself into a spiral with its head in the center and its tail at the outer edge. The tail was buzzing.

The snake wasn't three feet away from Dazen's feet. Bomar acted as if he was waiting to see if it would strike the medicine man. When it didn't he stuck his rifle in the snake's face. The snake rose up to defend itself and Bomar pulled the trigger. The blast blew the snake's head into a thousand fragments of protoplasm. The snake's body began to quiver and its tail continued to buzz until Bomar walked over and ground off its rattles with the heel of his boot.

Even though it was missing both of its ends, the snake wasn't ready to give up. Driven by the primitive reflexes housed deep within its serpentine spinal cord, it recoiled, uncoiled and recoiled again before thrusting its headless neck into the air. Bomar slapped at it with his rifle. The snake responded by coiling around the barrel. With a look of disgust Bomar swung his rifle, slinging the snake out behind him into a thicket of scrub oak.

"I'm here to make a citizen's arrest," he announced as he levered another round into the chamber. "It seems our local voodoo doctor has gone against the wishes of our trusted tribal leaders and gone back to his old ways. He's threatened to use his powers against me. Fortunately for me I've yet to see a thunderbolt come out of the sky and I believe he's fresh out of snakes." Bomar raised his rifle. "Do you have anything you need to tell me about the death of my dog?"

When Dazen didn't answer, Bomar swung around and shot the medicine man's horse. The bullet entered the mare's skull right below her left ear. She dropped to the ground, pulling the post she was tied to with her. She groaned and struggled to get to her feet but collapsed a second time.

"You're next," Bomar said as he ejected the empty shell casing. "This is your last chance to confess to the murder of Butch."

"Bomar, you don't really want to do this," Ganson said in as level of voice he could manage.

"I told you to shut up," Bomar barked as he pointed his rifle it at Dazen's head.

All of a sudden there was a rustling in the underbrush. When Bomar whirled around to see what it was Ganson broke for Fannie. He grabbed his jacket but before he could get his gun out of the pocket Bomar turned with his rifle raised. Ganson threw the jacket at him as he rushed forward.

Bomar fired off a shot that ripped through the shoulder of the jacket but missed Ganson. He sidestepped Ganson and hit him with the barrel of his rifle, knocking him to the ground. He snapped another round into the breech. Before he could put a bullet into Ganson, Dazen put two into him, one from each of Fannie's pistols.

Bomar stumbled forward and died under the shadow of the shrine's one armed cross.

Ganson scrambled to his feet and picked up his jacket as he ran over to Fannie. He covered her back up before washing her wounds with the water from Dazen's canteen. He was about to leave and go for help when he noticed Dazen off to the side of the shrine where the rustling noise had come from. The medicine man was standing over the headless snake, which was still twisting around in the bushes.

"Thank you," Ganson said putting his hand on Dazen's shoulder.

The medicine man nodded but didn't speak as he continued to stare at the snake with an inspired look on his face.

Calling what took place that day the "Second Cibecue Massacre" was pure Apache. The naming of the event referred not so much to the death of Bomar as to the massacre of all the animals leading up to his death. No one on the west end of the reservation missed Bomar or his vicious dog Butch, but many came to the shrine to pay their respects to Bronco Dazen's mare, Harley's coyote Garfield and all the other animals Bomar and Butch had slaughtered over the years.

The Cibecue Apaches also gained a renewed respect for Bronco Dazen. It arose from their belief in the power he'd summoned to get a headless snake to thrash around in the underbrush loud enough to divert the murderous intentions of a hairless madman.

Twenty-Two

Ganson's pretrial deposition in front of David Dunbar had taken place in the conference room of the Paint Pony Restaurant in Show Low. Following the advice of his lawyer Duane Jamison, Ganson had done his best to remain focused and keep his answers direct and concise. Duane had advised him that not a single case was ever won at a pretrial deposition but that a great number were lost. That was because the plaintiff's lawyer was going to do everything he could to attack the defendant's credibility. Every loose answer given during deposition provided the plaintiff's lawyer with another opportunity to take the most trivial inconsistency and present it to the jury as if it were a key indicator of the witness's lack of credibility. In a court of law perception always trumped fact. In a malpractice trial the facts of the case were often left scattered about the courtroom floor, scientific debris discarded by a jury ruled more by emotion than rational thought.

All the depositions had gone well but Duane had warned Ganson that they were well behind in the case. At the pretrial settlement hearing David Dunbar had offered to accept the policy limit of $1,000,000 in exchange for not going after Ganson's assets and future earnings. The strategy was obvious. By striking that deal Dunbar could collect $1,000,000 of the insurance company's money and keep forty percent for himself without having to go to trial and face the risk of not winning a cent.

The incentive for Ganson to take the deal was that the settlement money wouldn't come out of his pocket. He also wouldn't risk paying out hundreds of thousands of dollars in future earnings, assuming he were to have any future earnings. One of the problems he had with that decision was that his malpractice company had stood by him throughout the case. He felt he'd be betraying whatever faith they had in him if he caved in and settled for the maximum amount for which they were at risk. He knew that wasn't the most self-protective stance for him, but not unlike the jury he'd soon be facing, his decision was governed more by emotion than rationality. His inner voice kept reminding him how much more was at stake but he couldn't get away from the memory of the elated look on David Dunbar's face when they'd passed by each other at BOMEX.

In making his decision there was one other thing he'd chosen to discount, the increased publicity the trial had generated. The Attorney General had shown some interest in the case when it had first hit the papers but apparently no one in that office had felt compelled to pursue it. No criminal charges had ever been filed against Ganson but there was always the possibility the trial could stir up something that would rekindle the prosecutor's interest.

"You can do this," Ganson told himself as he sat in his car in the parking lot of the Pima County Superior Court. He had on dark slacks and a white shirt he'd ironed the night before. Folder across his arm was his corduroy jacket. Before driving down to Tucson for the trial he'd gotten Gwen to mend the bullet hole in the shoulder.

As soon as he opened the door a handful of reporters encircled him. Most of them were the same ones who had feasted on him three summers before.

"Do you still have no regrets over what you did?" a chunky brunette asked as she shoved a microphone in his face.

"What's the current status of your medical license?" a man in an orange polo shirt asked.

Ganson broke through the circle and jogged up the marble steps to the courthouse. Duane was waiting for him in the lobby.

"Show time," Duane said as he reached over and adjusted Ganson's tie.

They walked down the center aisle together and took their seats at the table on the defendant's side of the room. David Dunbar sat across the aisle. He had another lawyer with him. Also at their table were Angela's adoptive parents, William and Lucille Miller. Cassie was sitting right behind them along with a young woman who looked to be the child's nanny. Cassie was fidgeting with the bow on her pink dress when Ganson walked by. Although Duane had advised him it was best to ignore the whole group Ganson couldn't help but smile at Cassie. Duane didn't see him do it but David Dunbar did. Dunbar immediately instructed the nanny to move away from the aisle and sit on the other side of Cassie so she could block the little girl's view of both Ganson and Duane.

Ganson took a seat while Duane emptied out the satchel full of records and reports he'd brought with him. One of the many things Ganson liked about his lawyer was his laid back manner. On this particular morning Duane didn't look so easygoing.

"Are you okay?" Ganson asked.

"I will be as soon as we get into this," Duane assured him.

"You look like you want to throw up," Ganson observed.

"I already have. Three times. Once at the hotel and twice on the way here."

"Are you sick?"

"No, just nervous."

"Is our case that weak?"

"I always throw up at the beginning of a trial."

"But not at the end?"

"The beginning is the most perilous part."

"More perilous than the closing argument?" asked Ganson thinking it would be the other way around.

"The closing argument is worthless if we don't have a favorable jury. The judge can dismiss potential jurors for obvious biases or conflicts of interest and we can strike others who we think might hurt us. We're still going to be in trouble if the jury we end up with isn't open to what we're trying to prove to them."

That morning Cassie remained only long enough to be viewed by the prospective jurors. Shortly after they arrived the nanny took Cassie by the hand and led her out of the courtroom. The judge trying the case was a Hispanic woman named Joanne Martinez. She had a fastidious look to her that spilled over to the selection of the jury, a process that dragged out all day.

Some of those in the jury pool had already heard about the case. When interviewed they jumped at the opportunity to express their distrust of the medical profession in front of all the other prospective jurors. There were other candidates who knew nothing about the case but still joined in to complain about everything from medical misdiagnoses to botched surgical procedures to excessive billing. By the end of the day it was hard to believe there was a one of them who hadn't in some way been negatively influenced by what they'd heard.

"What a fucking feeding frenzy," Duane lamented as he and Ganson left the courthouse. Duane looked like he might be spending much of the night on his hands and knees with his face centered over the toilet bowl. "I can't believe the judge didn't dismiss the whole lot of them."

"How often does that happen?" Ganson asked.

"Never," Duane answered. "That's why a jury trial is such a crapshoot. I could have used twice the number of strikes allotted us for this bunch and I still wouldn't have ended up getting a jury I felt comfortable with."

"What can we do?" Ganson asked.

"I could file for a mistrial but the judge would just deny it."

"That's it?"

Duane hesitated before answering. "We could surrender and take what Dunbar offered us."

"You don't really want to settle this out of court, do you?" Ganson asked with an anguished look.

"Michael, this is not about doing what I want, it's about doing what's best for you and your future."

"What do think our chances are of winning this case?"

"Not nearly as good as they were yesterday."

"All because of that jury?"

"The jury is everything."

"That sucks."

"I could cut a deal with Dunbar in the judge's chambers and you wouldn't even have to go back into the courtroom."

Ganson shook his head. "I can't believe you'd even consider giving in to that dickhead."

"Sleep on it," Duane said patting him on the shoulder. "You can let me know in the morning."

Ganson skipped dinner and turned in early. He couldn't stop thinking about how sickening it would feel to give up. When he awoke he was more tired than when he'd gone to bed.

"What do you think?" Duane asked him when the two met at Denny's for breakfast the next morning.

"I think you might want to go a little light on the French toast. I don't want to have to watch you puking all over your satchel when you're defending me in court today."

Duane smiled. "I was hoping you'd want to continue."

"You could have fooled me."

"I needed to know your resolve."

"That's one thing I thought you would have known."

"This is going to be a very difficult experience for you to process."

"I've had worse," Ganson said recalling the night Cassie's mother died under his care in the ER.

The second day of the trial started out like the first with Ganson running through a gauntlet of reporters to get into the courtroom. There were more spectators in the gallery than the day before. The

Millers had an entourage of family and friends filling several of the rows on the plaintiff side of the courtroom. Cassie was also there with a teddy bear cradled in her arms.

Sitting three rows deep on the defendant side was Dr. Luther Shock. He'd called before the trial and suggested Ganson bring the Indian blanket with him. Ganson had told him he was okay with the corduroy jacket but felt carrying the blanket into the courtroom was a bit over the top.

"Thanks for coming," Ganson said giving Shock a big hug.

"Good to see you wearing the jacket," Shock said.

Ganson smiled. "I'm counting on it to help get me through this."

After everyone had risen for the arrival of the judge Duane and Dunbar approached the bench and entered into a brief conversation with her. Before Dunbar addressed the jury with his opening remarks he returned to his table to confer with the other lawyer. Duane had told Ganson that Dunbar had attended medical school at the U of A for three years before dropping out to enter law school. His medical school experience had undoubtedly given him great insight into the workings of the profession he'd chosen to devote his life attacking. As soon as he passed the bar he began building a statewide network to draw medical malpractice cases into his practice. He'd gotten rich pursuing premium cases that were usually settled out of court. His reputation as a trial lawyer wasn't that great and that's why he'd brought the other lawyer into the courtroom to help out. Duane wasn't sure which one of them was going to put on the plaintiff's case until Dunbar picked up a folder full of notes and strode to the podium to address the jury with his opening remarks. There were nine jurors; five women and four men, eight voting members and one alternate. Dunbar made eye contact with each and every one of them as he spoke out.

"Ladies and gentleman of the jury, the great American lawyer Clarence Darrow once said 'chase after the truth like all hell and you'll free yourself.' That's all I'm asking you to do. Chase after the truth. We are all here today to right a wrong, actually a series of wrongs, perpetrated against my client and her family. This beautiful little girl," he said as he turned and pointed to Cassie, "may look like the picture of perfect health, but in her short life she has suffered immensely. Because of the ill-advised acts of the defendant Mike Ganson, Cassie was forced to enter this world almost four months earlier than she should have. This caused her to have to spend a horrific eight weeks hooked up to a ventilator in the ICU. Eight weeks," Dunbar reemphasized. "During that time and for the next two and a half years her adoring grandparents William and Lucille Miller have been at her side trying to help fill the void created by the untimely and inexcusable death of her mother Angela, a death that was the direct result of the defendant Mike Ganson's actions.

"Every death has a tragic nature to it," Dunbar continued. "Angela's was even more so because it didn't have to happen and wouldn't have happened if Mike Ganson had heeded the advice of his supervising physician, Dr. Helen Cassidy. Angela would be alive and well today if he had only done what he had repeatedly been told to do and transferred her from the County Hospital to the Medical Center. Instead, he tried to be a hero, performing a surgical procedure he had never been trained to do. If that wasn't enough, he did this procedure in a non-sterile environment without even the use of anesthesia. As the result of his actions, Cassie was delivered perilously premature and Angela died right there in the emergency room."

After spending another half an hour touching on what he identified as the critical aspects of the case Dunbar paused for a minute to look down at his notes before looking back up at the jurors. "Over the next two weeks you will be hearing from several different witnesses, some of them ours and some of them theirs. What you will need to do is to establish the truthfulness and relevance of each and every one of their testimonies. When they have all finished there is no doubt in my mind that you will feel both comforted and compelled to right this despicable wrong and find in favor of Cassie and her grieving grandparents, William and Lucille."

Duane, looking a bit better than he had the previous day, waited a full sixty seconds before standing up to address the jury. It might have appeared to them as if he were writing down a few last minute thoughts but Ganson could see that all he was doing was doodling on his notepad. Duane's suit and tie weren't nearly as dapper as Dunbar's and his shoulders sagged ever so slightly as he stood up and walked slowly across the hardwood floor that would serve as his and his opponent's stage for the next two weeks. His close-cropped hair and wire-rimmed glasses gave him the look of an accountant or administrative assistant preparing to give a presentation to his governing board. When he spoke it was in a conversational tone that seemed to put everyone in the courtroom at ease.

"Ladies and gentlemen," he said, "I will be brief with my opening statement. For the rest of this week Mr. Dunbar will parade a collection of witnesses through this courtroom. They will all attempt to portray my client as a loose cannon that went off, causing the death of a mother while delivering her premature infant daughter. These so-called experts will paint you the picture of a resident physician doing the unthinkable, performing an unnecessary operation, an operation for which he'd received no training. They will tell you that the actions were irresponsible and the outcomes avoidable. As I cross examine these witnesses this week and bring in our own witnesses next week I will show you what my client did was a courageous act to save the life of a baby whose mother's poor choices had put both her and her baby at great risk."

Duane didn't spend nearly as much time as Dunbar had previewing his presentation of the case. Before finishing he paused to allow time for what he had said to sink in. He took a sip of water and cleared his throat. "For someone to suffer an untimely death is indeed a tragedy. For someone else to suffer from being wrongly accused of causing that death is also a tragedy, a tragedy you as a jury can prevent from going any farther than this courtroom."

Dunbar's first witness was William Miller, who spent the rest of the morning on the stand in tears. Miller told the jury how Angela had been the love of his life and how he still had a difficult time accepting the fact she was gone. He said that he and his wife Lucille had been unable to have children of their own and that Angela's coming to live with them was a gift from God. Every few minutes he'd break down while recounting memories of his "little Angel's" childhood. He spoke of how she grew up to be a junior high school honor student, a member of the student council and a high school homecoming attendant. He told of how she planned to pursue a career as a mental health worker. He related anecdote after anecdote of their family life. By the time he was finished there wasn't a dry set of eyes in the jury box.

What Miller didn't tell them about were the DUIs, the drug possession charges and the shoplifting convictions, all of which happened while Angela was still in high school. He also failed to bring up the fact that his adopted daughter had been thrown in jail in Whiteriver one New Year's Eve for assaulting a police officer outside the local bar.

Duane knew of all these offenses. He'd told Ganson about them long before the trial had begun. He'd explained how focusing on Angela's longstanding history of legal problems relating to her alcohol and drug abuse could be of benefit to their case but he was afraid the jury might interpret it as a shameless attack on the character of a dead woman. He limited his cross-examination of William Miller to a few questions about Angela's adoption and was finished with him by noon.

In what would be a recurring pattern throughout much of the trial Cassie and the nanny left before the lunch break and didn't return for the afternoon session. According to Duane, David Dunbar's strategy was to keep Cassie in view of the jury for as long as he could. No one would expect a two and a half year old to be able to sit and behave herself in court all day, but the longer the jurors looked at her, the more likely they were to empathize with her motherless plight and rule in favor of the plaintiffs.

Lucille Miller's testimony that afternoon was much the same as her husband's, only with less emotion. There was emptiness in her look and her words evoked little empathy from those in the courtroom. When it was Duane's turn to cross-examine her he didn't ask a single question.

Dunbar's first witness on Wednesday was Joshua Smith, senior VP at the Medical Center. "Mr. Smith, can you please tell the jury why the Medical Center decided to end its affiliation with the County Hospital."

"Certainly," Smith answered. "We had ongoing concerns over our ability to provide coverage to County."

"What kind of concerns?"

"At the time we had contracts with several different hospitals and felt our residents were being spread too thin to give quality care to all of them."

"So you pulled your residents out of County?"

"It was a very difficult decision but we had no other choice."

"Did you just have all the residents up and leave one day?" Dunbar asked.

Smith chuckled. "Oh no. We had a detailed step-by-step plan signed off by me and Roberto Cabrera, who was the CEO at County at the time. We removed the OB residents first because we felt that was the service whose care had been the most compromised. We instructed the emergency room physicians to divert all pregnancy related problems to the other obstetrical hospitals in town."

"After the OB residents left, how many more babies were delivered at County?"

"I am only aware of one."

"And that would be the one performed in the ER by Mike Ganson?" Dunbar asked.

"That's correct," Smith answered.

"Your witness," Dunbar said returning to his chair.

"I just have a few questions," Duane said. "Mr. Smith, could you tell me if the Medical Center's decision to pull out of County System was driven by financial as well as safety concerns."

"Unfortunately, all health care decisions have a financial aspect to them."

"Do you think your decision to remove your residents from County Hospital contributed to its closing?"

"I suppose it might have played a role. The viability of that hospital was not our business."

"But it was your business to make sure the health care was provided in a proper manner while you still had a presence there. Is that a correct statement, Mr. Smith?"

"Yes it is?"

"And those details were under your responsibility?"

"Yes."

"How familiar are you with what went on the night Dr. Ganson performed the emergency Cesarean section on Angela Miller?"

"Very."

"At that time didn't County Hospital have both an anesthesiologist and a general surgeon in house twenty-four-seven?"

"I believe so."

"With that in mind, wouldn't it be your opinion that County could take on most of the life threatening emergencies in need of immediate surgery?"

"Objection," Dunbar said coming out of his chair. "Mr. Smith is a hospital administrator, not a physician. You can't expect him to render an opinion on what County Hospital was or was not capable of handling, or 'taking on,' as Mr. Jamison put it."

The judge called both lawyers to the bench. After a lengthy discussion she allowed Duane's question to stand.

"Would you like me to repeat the question? Duane asked.

"That won't be necessary," Smith answered. "At that time County was theoretically capable of handling a variety of surgical emergencies."

"Would you include an emergency Cesarean section in your theoretical list, Mr. Smith?" Duane asked.

"I suppose so," Smith answered.

The next witness was Dr. Alexander Murphy, head of the Surgery Residency Program. Murphy had late in life developed a tremor that had forced him to retire from the operating room. The more upset he became, the more pronounced his tremor became. By the time Dunbar got around to asking him about Ganson's performance Murphy's head was shaking so hard his jowls were flapping.

"Mike Ganson tried to single handedly destroy the reputation of our residency program," he stated.

After an objection from Duane, which was sustained by Judge Martinez, Dunbar rephrased his question. "How would you characterize Mike Ganson's emotional demeanor as a resident?"

Duane again objected but the judge overruled him and advised Murphy he could answer the question.

"He was a rebellious young man whose work in the ER was mediocre at best. He clashed with the attending staff and continually got into it with the chief resident. He'd only been in the program a few months, yet we were already considering taking disciplinary action against him for his nonconforming behavior and lack of professionalism."

"Doctor," Duane asked as he approached Murphy after Dunbar had finished with him, "what kind of turnover rate do you have in your residency program?"

"We have six new residents entering each year to replace the ones graduating."

"I'm sorry, sir. Let me ask this in another way. What I want to know is how often do you have a resident drop out before he's completed the program?"

"I object Your Honor," Dunbar yelled jumping up from his seat. "What is the relevance of that question?"

"Your Honor," Duane responded," if you'll just bear with me one minute I'll show you the relevance."

"That's about what you have, Mr. Jamison," the judge said looking at her watch, "one minute."

"Thank you, Your Honor," Duane said turning his attention back to Murphy. "What I'm asking, sir, is how often do you have a resident up and leave the program?"

"That certainly happens," Murphy answered, "but not that often."

"Does 'not that often' mean once every few years or so?" Duane asked.

"That sounds about right."

"Does the name Aaron Silver mean anything to you, Dr. Murphy?"

"Yes. He was one of our residents."

"Could you tell us what happened to him?"

"All I can say about Aaron Silver is that he had some personal issues and was asked to leave."

"Did these personal issues you're speaking of come to light following a confrontation he had with the chief resident at the time, Dr. Helen Cassidy?"

"I suppose you could say that."

"Would it surprise you if I told you that in the last five years, seven of your surgery residents have left your program early?"

"Is that the number?" Murphy asked.

"Yes it is," Duane answered.

"Your Honor," Dunbar interrupted," I fail to see where this is going."

"Where is this going, Mr. Jamison?" the judge asked.

"My point, Your Honor, is that over the past five years seven residents have left this program early. Several of those seemed to have had issues with Dr. Cassidy, who happens to be one of the plaintiffs' star witnesses. I just wanted to have this in the record so I can refer to it when I cross examine her."

"Very well, Mr. Jamison," the judge said. "Now can we move on?"

Duane finished up with some questions pertaining to the overall responsibilities of the residents. When he was done court was adjourned for the day. That evening Ganson and Duane met over dinner. Neither of them made it past the soup and salad.

"Try to get a good night's sleep," Duane suggested as they left the restaurant. "Dunbar's bringing in his big hitter tomorrow morning."

Ganson didn't answer. He knew Duane was referring to Dunbar's expert witness, Dr. Hudson Barnes.

Barnes was an OB-GYN from Tucson who retired from medicine at the age of 46 and moved to Aspen to perfect his skiing technique. He supported his new lifestyle by offering his services to any personal injury lawyer willing to pay his extravagant fees. Non-practicing physicians who made a business out of testifying against other doctors were referred to as hired guns. Duane called them whores.

Barnes's Curriculum Vitae was impressive. He'd received innumerable academic and performance awards and participated in a variety of research projects. He'd also spent months as a resident moonlighting in emergency rooms.

The more Ganson thought about the man who was going to try to destroy him the more convinced he became that he was screwed.

Twenty-Three

Sitting upright in the witness chair Dr. Hudson Barnes looked like he'd been lifted right off a magazine cover. He was tall, thin, tan and more nattily dressed than David Dunbar, who was standing in front of him asking him the questions that would solidify his credibility as an expert witness with the jury. After spending much of the morning leading Barnes through the events leading up to Angela's death Dunbar asked his expert witness some specific questions about Ganson.

"Dr. Barnes, do you have a problem with Mike Ganson's medical care that night in the ER at County?"

"It took him way too long to determine Angela was pregnant. When he finally figured that out, he should have had her on the way immediately to another facility."

"Is that your major criticism?" Dunbar asked.

"Hardly," Barnes answered shaking his head in mock disgust. "The doctor's decision to set up for and perform a Cesarean section on Angela in the ER was one of the most deplorable acts I've come across in all my years in medicine. I have no doubt that if he would have behaved in a more responsible manner Angela and her baby would both be alive today."

"So it's your opinion that Mike Ganson's behavior that night fell well below the standard of care."

"The delay in diagnosis and transport is enough in itself. His performing a surgery for which he'd received no formal training is in my opinion unforgivable."

"Anything else, Doctor?" Dunbar asked with a look of satisfaction on his face.

Barnes nodded as he turned and faced the jury. "It amazes me that the authorities haven't filed criminal charges against this man. Maybe they will in light of the new testimony I've provided."

Duane exploded out of his chair. "Objection. Objection. Objection."

"Sustained," Judge Martinez said glaring at Barnes. "The jury will disregard that last remark."

Neither Duane nor Ganson felt like going anywhere over the lunch break. The two of them hung around the courthouse and traded off going into the bathroom to throw up. It wasn't as though either one of them hadn't been prepared for what Barnes was going to say but there was a sickening reality to having to hear it so confidently and powerfully presented. The deadline for a deal with Dunbar had passed and they both knew their only option was to hang in and make whatever points they could with a jury that had seemed quite taken with Barnes' testimony.

"Dr. Barnes," Duane started in after the break, "you certainly do have an impressive list of credentials. Would you mind telling me how long it has been since you last delivered a baby?"

"Let me think about that," Barnes said as he scratched at a patch of sun-damaged skin on his temple. "It was a little over five years ago. I spent the night doing three vaginal births and a Cesarean delivery before finishing out my obstetrical career repairing a blown out ectopic pregnancy. That's a tubal pregnancy," he said smiling at the jury.

"When was the last time you pulled a shift in an emergency room?" Duane asked.

"Oh, my," Barnes answered. "That would have had to have been at least twenty years ago."

"Let me get this straight. You are here criticizing Dr. Ganson's care of a pregnant woman in an emergency room setting, yet you haven't delivered a baby in five years and haven't worked in an emergency room in twenty."

"What's your point?"

"My point is that you're holding yourself up to this jury as an expert in patient care but you haven't cared for a patient in years."

"Practicing good medicine is just like riding a bicycle. Once you've mastered it you never forget how it's done."

"Oh really," Duane replied as he approached Barnes and handed him a folder containing several bound pages. "That being the case, I don't guess you'd mind reading to the jury the final paragraph at the bottom of page three. I've even highlighted it for you."

"Objection Your Honor," Dunbar yelled out as he jumped up. "I have no idea what is in that folder. I will not permit my witness to read from anything that hasn't been admitted as evidence in this case."

"Mr. Jamison?" the judge asked with a questioning look on her face.

"Your Honor, this folder contains the Pima County Medical Examiner's autopsy report on Angela Miller. It is part of the medical record and Mr. Dunbar has had access to it since the beginning."

"Let me see that," Dunbar said as he walked over and snatched it out of his witness's hand. "Your Honor, I'd like to request a short break while I go back through my records to make sure this document is valid."

"It's valid, Your Honor," Duane responded, "but I have no objection to Mr. Dunbar taking as much time as he needs."

Everyone in the courtroom watched Dunbar return to his table and open up the attaché case he'd stored underneath his seat. They continued to watch as he shuffled through file after file before coming upon one he opened up and spread out in front of him. After locating his copy of the document in question he walked over and handed Duane's copy back to Barnes. "You may go ahead and answer his question."

-366-

"Now, Mr. Barnes," Duane said as he stepped back over to the podium, "would you please look at this document and tell me what's in the highlighted area."

Barnes took his glasses out of his coat pocket and studied the document. "This looks like—"

"I'm sorry doctor. Could you first read the name on the top of the report? It's in the upper left hand corner."

"Sure thing, counselor. It's Angela Miller."

"Very good. Now please continue."

Barnes nodded. "These are the results of a drug screen."

"Which shows what?"

"It shows the presence or absence of different drugs in the patient's circulatory system."

"And in this case the patient is Angela Miller, correct?"

"I believe you've already established that."

"Very good, doctor. Now could you tell me what if any drugs were present in Angela Miller at the time of her death?"

"The report is positive for cocaine and heroin."

"Cocaine and heroin," Duane repeated, as if he were speaking to himself. "That must mean that she used both of these drugs shortly before her death. Do you agree with that?"

"Who knows? Maybe those drugs had been in her for a few days."

"You think that's a possibility?"

"Why not?"

"What if I told you that depending on how those drugs were taken, their onset would be in a matter of seconds, with their peak activity being in a matter of minutes? The duration of their effect would be in the thirty to ninety-minute range and they could be all but undetectable within twenty-four hours."

"So what?"

"So doesn't it seem logical to conclude that Angela used those drugs just prior to her collapse in the park restroom and that was what really caused her death?"

"Objection," Dunbar roared. "That calls for—"

Barnes stopped his own lawyer by raising his hand. "Let me answer this, David," he said as he stared at Duane with a stony look on his face. "I appreciate your lesson in pharmacology but the timing of Angela's use of those drugs had nothing to do with her death."

"How can you say that for sure?" Duane asked.

"I can say that because she was in an emergency room, alive and stable at the time your client took hold of that scalpel and cut her open."

"I agree she was alive," Duane conceded, "but I think you'd be hard pressed to find a single one of your colleagues who'd call a comatose patient with a pulse over 100, a blood pressure of 90 over 60 and a temperature of 102 stable."

"Call it what you want," Barnes countered. "If this patient were stable she should have been transferred. If she weren't she should never have been operated on in that setting."

"What about her unborn baby?"

"What about her?"

"You don't think her condition should have been taken into consideration?"

"With no fetal heart tracings available to review I have no idea what her condition was. I only know what it became after Mike Ganson so recklessly intervened."

"Doctor, I take it you're familiar with the Good Samaritan Law?" Duane asked.

"I certainly am," Barnes answered.

"Couldn't you apply that to this case?" Duane asked.

"Heavens no," Barnes exclaimed with a mocking chuckle. "I'm sure there are several laws you could apply to this case but the Good Samaritan isn't one of them."

"Is it your belief that Angela's baby wasn't in imminent danger of dying if she remained undelivered?"

"I've neither seen nor heard one shred of evidence that would support the notion she was in any kind of danger."

"Dr. Ganson stated in his deposition and will testify next week that Angela's membranes had ruptured and that her baby was in such deep distress that it would have died if he hadn't operated when he did."

"It hardly comes as a surprise to me that he would say that but I've seen nothing to support that statement."

"You don't believe Dr. Ganson when he says that he was monitoring the baby with a Doppler stethoscope and that her heart rate had dropped to a life threatening level?"

"I've gone through the depositions of every person involved in this case. There are no fetal heart tracings and there is no mention of anyone other than your client having heard and identified an abnormal fetal heart rate in the baby."

"So you think Dr. Ganson made it all up?"

"I think he either made it up or didn't know what he was hearing through the earpieces of the Doppler. Whatever the case, he had neither the training nor the experience to do what he did."

Duane finished up extracting a few minor concessions concerning unborn babies in distress but was able to do little to undermine Barnes' testimony. As court was adjourning for the day he grabbed Ganson by the arm and the two of them remained seated until everyone else filed out of the room. When Dunbar walked past them he was wearing the same sickening smile Ganson had seen on him before.

"What a hairball," Duane said as he watched Dunbar exit the courtroom.

Ganson spent the evening in his room munching on Wheat Thins and Trail Mix. At three o'clock he woke up wishing he'd taken Dunbar's deal. He couldn't get back to sleep because he kept thinking about all the things Barnes had said about him in court. The only thing Ganson wanted to do with his life was to set up a simple little practice in some out of the way place where he could attend to the needs of the community. It wasn't important for him to make a lot of money but it was important for him to feel he was somewhere he belonged. At five o'clock he fell into a deep sleep from which he awoke with barely enough time to shower and get dressed before rushing to the courthouse.

Friday morning's first witness was Dr. Frederick Nix. After Dunbar went over the psychiatrist's credentials he questioned him about the two encounters he'd had with Ganson.

"Dr. Nix, could you please tell the jury of your opinion of Mike Ganson following the medical school admissions interview the two of you had."

"It was obvious to me he didn't have what it took to become a physician."

"Can you explain?"

"I found him lacking in self-confidence, defiant of authority and prone to impulsivity. That combination of traits has always been a prescription for disaster. I did everything I could to keep him from getting into our medical school."

"How did you find him following the death of Angela Miller?"

"Angry and remorseless."

After Dunbar finished with Nix, Duane took his time making his way to the podium. "Doctor, you stated that during the course of your interviewing Dr. Ganson for admission to medical school you were able to determine that he was 'lacking of self-confidence, defiant of authority and prone to impulsivity.' Have I quoted you correctly on that, sir?"

"I believe you have."

"Weren't you the head of the Admissions Committee back then?"

"Yes, I was."

"Did you personally interview all the candidates?"

"The majority of them."

"Would it be accurate to say that those interviews were a critical part of the admission process and that you had a great deal to say as to who did or did not get accepted into medical school?"

"That would be accurate," Nix answered.

"How long did those interviews typically last?" Duane asked.

"An hour," Nix answered.

"An hour," Duane repeated. "Doctor, would you consider yourself to have some kind of psychic powers?"

"Objection, Your Honor," Dunbar barked. "I don't know where that question came from but Mr. Jamison is obviously trying to discredit the veracity of my witness."

"Sustained," snapped Judge Martinez.

"Let me rephrase the question," Duane said. "When you interview someone for an hour are you always able to figure out as much about them as you say you were able to figure out about my client?"

"As a psychiatrist that's what I'm trained to do. It's what I do in my practice every day. It's also what I did for the years I devoted to helping select the qualified applicants who entered our medical school."

"Did you ever make a mistake during the selection process?"

"Objection," Dunbar called out. "I fail to see what any of this has to do with my witness's evaluation of the defendant."

"Mr. Jamison?" the judge asked.

"If you'll bear with me another minute, I'll show you."

"Very well," she said over the protesting look of Dunbar, "but please get to the point. The witness may now answer the question."

"Nobody is perfect," Nix said. "I'm sure I've missed a few quality candidates over the years."

"Do you remember Vegas Farnsworth?"

"I vaguely recall that name."

"Mr. Farnsworth was a black applicant from Casa Grande who interviewed the same year Dr. Ganson did. Arizona was his first choice but for some reason your committee turned him down and he had to catch on at another school."

"We have very strict guidelines for those we admit."

"How about a Navajo fellow named Nathan Begay?" Duane asked. "Does that name ring a bell?"

"Your Honor," Dunbar interrupted. "I can't see where –"

"Calm down, Mr. Dunbar," the judge interrupted right back. "Let the witness answer the question."

"I remember Nathan," Nix said. "He was one of the applicants who just didn't quite have enough going for him to get into our school."

"Would it surprise you if I told you those two minority applicants, both Arizona residents, attended two of the more prestigious medical schools in the country? Farnsworth went to Harvard and Begay went to Stanford. Am I to take from this that your admission standards are higher than the standards of those two schools?"

"I told you that every selection committee misses a worthy candidate from time to time."

"How about the unworthy ones? Have you ever mistakenly picked one of those for admission?" Duane asked.

"I'm sure I have," Nix answered.

"Just a few, right?"

"Not many."

"Doctor, would it surprise you if I told you that the class you selected the first year Dr. Ganson applied had more than its share of unworthy candidates?"

"I have no idea what you're talking about," Nix responded.

"Let me see if I can refresh your memory," Duane said. "Of the eighty who entered that class, one died of a drug overdose, another ended up a long term resident in the psych ward, a third turned out to be a pedophile and six others dropped out for personal reasons. That's nine entering students who didn't make it through the first year. That's over ten percent. In a class that by your own admission you all but handpicked that sounds like an awfully high failure rate to me."

"I told you the process wasn't foolproof," Nix uttered as he turned away from the jury.

"How could you have been so certain about Dr. Ganson?"

"I was quite confident of my evaluation of Mike Ganson. Judging from where we are today I'd have to say my evaluation was right on."

"Tell me this, Dr. Nix. Have you ever had any personal feelings about Dr. Ganson that might interfere with your ability to give him a fair evaluation?"

"That would not be very professional of me, now would it."

"I take it that's a no."

"That's correct."

"I have no further questions of this witness, Your Honor."

Ganson skipped lunch in favor of a walk in the park. It was a breezy winter day but he was comfortably warm in his corduroy jacket. Luther Shock had referred to the jacket as a modern day ghost shirt. Even though Ganson was well aware of the role his jacket had played in saving his life at the Second Cibecue Massacre he'd been tempted to point out to Shock how the ghost shirts the Sioux had worn a century earlier had proven to be disappointingly ineffective in warding off the .45 caliber slugs the army's trapdoor carbines sent ripping through them. Nevertheless, Ganson had decided to wear the jacket for the duration of the trial for whatever additional karma it might bestow upon him.

David Dunbar's final witness was Dr. Helen Cassidy, who appeared ill at ease in the courtroom. Her once blonde hair was now a shade of brown that matched the dark circles under her eyes. Although her breasts were as big as ever she appeared much thinner than when Ganson had seen her at his apartment the night before his meeting at BOMEX. At the end of the lunch break Ganson had come upon her sitting on a park bench smoking a cigarette. When she saw him she looked the other way. He'd wanted to say something to her about what had happened to them back in college but realized this was neither the time nor the place.

On the witness stand she fidgeted back and forth in her chair and stared straight ahead, making little effort to establish eye contact with anyone. The story she related to the jury was the same one she'd given under oath at her deposition. She claimed that Ganson had given her little information concerning the condition of his patient in the ER but that what he had told her was enough for her to direct him to transfer the patient to the Medical Center. She added that she had no clue what he was up to until she entered the ER and saw what he'd done. When asked about the physical confrontation between Ganson and her she stated that when she approached him he'd threatened to use the defibrillator paddles on her. She also said she'd had every intention of trying to save Angela herself but after Ganson knocked her to the floor she had to leave the room because she feared for her life.

On further questioning from Dunbar she explained that she and Ganson had been involved in several disagreements since he'd come to work in the ER and that for weeks she'd been considering filing a formal complaint against him. She finished up her testimony proclaiming her deep sympathy for the Millers. She stated she wished she'd been better informed so she could have done something to avert the senseless tragedy that took place.

"Dr. Cassidy," Duane asked after a short recess "is it true you and Dr. Ganson once knew each other on an intimate basis?"

"Objection," Dunbar blurted out. "Whatever relationship his client and my witness may have had has nothing to do with this case."

"Mr. Jamison?" Judge Martinez asked with her eyes peering at him over the rims of her glasses.

"Your Honor, I intend to show that it has everything to do with this case."

"That's absurd," Dunbar howled. "There is absolutely no—" he wasn't able to finish his sentence because the judge shut him up by raising her hand and throwing him a penetrating stare.

"Overruled," she said. "Please answer the question."

"Dr. Ganson and I were classmates in college but we never had what I'd call an intimate relationship," she stated.

"Were the two of you lovers?"

"Objection."

"Overruled."

Cassidy flashed a look of disdain at Ganson before answering the question. "We spent a few nights together."

"According to Dr. Ganson's deposition," Duane continued, "you would often drop by and let yourself in with the key he kept hidden under the flower pot on his front porch. Is that true?"

"I already admitted we spent a few nights together."

"Is it true that those nights together ended before you started your freshman year in medical school?"

"Yes."

"Do you recall why those nights ended?"

"They ended because I stopped going over there."

"And why did you stop?" Duane asked

"Your Honor," Dunbar interrupted again, "I can't see how any of this has any relevance to this case. Mr. Jamison is wasting all of our time trying to discredit my witness by bringing up some inconsequential event from her past."

"Events, Your Honor," Duane spoke out, "a series of events that started with the sexual relationship this witness and my client had while they were undergraduates at the university. Events that forever affected Dr. Cassidy's ability to deal with Dr. Ganson in a civil and rational manner."

"That's a bunch of fucking bullshit," Cassidy screamed as she jumped up from the witness chair.

"Doctor," Judge Martinez shouted, "you will sit down and stop cursing in my courtroom."

"I'm sorry," Cassidy said still standing, "but I can't sit here listening to someone spreading twisted half truths about me in front of all these people."

"Doctor Cassidy," the judge admonished, "you need to sit down in that chair before I find you in contempt. You may continue Mr. Jamison."

"Thank you, Your Honor. Doctor, could you please tell me what it was I said that you took such an exception to?"

Seated back in her chair, Cassidy accepted a fresh glass of water from the bailiff and drew several deep breaths before answering. "Several years ago your client and I had an arrangement that lasted for a few months. It ended amicably and we went our different ways. I have never been emotionally involved with Michael Ganson. Even if I were it would have had no effect whatsoever on the decisions I made the night Angela Miller died."

"Now Doctor," Duane continued, "you stated that your involvement with Dr. Ganson ended before you entered medical school. Is that correct?"

"You're the one who stated that. I just agreed with it."

"Is that a yes, Doctor?"

"Yes, it is."

"After the two of you had gone your separate ways did you ever again go over to his apartment?" Duane asked.

"Just once," Cassidy answered.

"And when was that?"

"About two and a half years ago."

"Was that before or after what had happened that night in the ER?"

"After."

"According to Dr. Ganson, I believe it was the night before he was scheduled to go in front of the Board of Medical Examiners."

"That could be," Cassidy said.

"Doctor," Duane persisted, "you can't recall for sure?"

"I can't remember."

"Did you stay the night?"

"I fell asleep on his couch."

"Were the two of you intimate that night?"

"Absolutely not."

"Why did you go there in the first place?"

"To tell you the truth, I don't remember."

"Do you recall the conversation the two of you had?"

"Not really."

"Why is that?"

"I already told you I don't remember."

"Was that because you'd had a few cocktails earlier?"

"I may have had a couple of drinks."

"According to Dr. Ganson's deposition you came over and accused him of purposely trying to derail your career."

"That's a bunch of bullshit."

"Doctor," the judge snapped, "this is your last warning."

"Sorry, Your Honor," Cassidy apologized. "Mr. Jamison, I can assure you that I would never have had such a conversation with your client or with any other resident under me."

"Doctor, do you know Dr. Aaron Silver?"

"Is he still a doctor?"

"Wasn't he one of your residents?"

"At one time he was."

"Did you and he get into it in the OR one night?"

"I don't know what you mean by 'get into it.' We had a minor disagreement."

Duane paused to thumb through some of his notes. "I'd like to move on to that night at the County Hospital. In your deposition you stated that when Dr. Ganson called up to the OR you told him he needed to put the patient in an ambulance and send her to another hospital. Didn't he tell you at that time that he feared for the life of the unborn child?"

"What he told me was that he wanted to have the mother delivered by Cesarean section right there in the ER."

"And I take it you didn't agree with that."

"I gave him specific instructions on what to do."

"When you gave him those instructions, is it true you referred to the patient as, pardon me Your Honor, a fucking druggie?"

"Absolutely not."

"How many times did Dr. Ganson call up to the OR that night?"

"Twice, I believe."

"The second time he called didn't he ask for you to come down and help him?"

"I was in the middle of a case."

"Didn't you have a third year resident with you at the time?"

"He was in the middle of the same case."

"But you showed up in the ER less than five minutes later."

"One of the interns came running up to the OR to tell me what was going on. I immediately broke scrub and rushed downstairs."

"When you got there Cassie was delivered and Dr. Ganson was preparing to defibrillate Angela."

"To say I was shocked at what I saw would be a gross understatement."

"So you weren't in any way impressed at how Dr. Ganson had taken charge of the situation?"

"Are you kidding? We're talking about a first year surgery resident who'd never been out of the ER. He had no training, no experience and no business making the decisions he tried to make that night."

"Even if a life were at stake?"

"There was a life at stake, but it was the mother's, not the baby's. If Dr. Ganson would have just done what I told him to do there would have been no lives lost and none of us would be here today."

"With all due respect, Dr. Cassidy," Duane said as he turned around and smiled at Cassie, who had been brought back for the afternoon session, "if Dr. Ganson had followed your orders I know one of us who I'm quite certain wouldn't be here today."

Twenty-Four

The Santa Cruz River cut a gouge in the earth across the west end of Tucson. The Arizona state maps labeled it a river but it had long ago relinquished its right to be referred to as one. Its bed was deep and wide but the only time it ever flowed was when it was flooded from the runoff of the seasonal desert storms. On the Sunday morning following Helen Cassidy's stormy Friday afternoon in court Ganson was walking along the asphalt path bordering the east bank of the riverbed when he encountered a coyote jogging toward him. The city coyote skidded to a stop and stared at him for a moment before turning and scampering away.

He'd once read a newspaper article claiming the coyote was the only North American mammal that had increased its domain over the past century. Judging from the increasing number he'd seen in Tucson over the years he had no reason to believe the story wasn't true. The coyote had become an expert at adapting to the changing conditions in its life. It was a skill Ganson wished he had better mastered.

That evening he and Duane met to discuss the witnesses Duane would be calling in his defense. Karen Hannigan, the nurse who assisted Ganson that fateful night in the ER, had given a compelling deposition but had little to add to what Ganson had said in his pretrial testimony. Luther Shock was far enough out there that the jury could well end up not believing a word he said. That left Bert.

For Ganson's case Duane had gone through the entire list of obstetricians he'd used as expert witnesses in the past. Every one of them turned him down. They all cited the fact that as specialty trained obstetricians they weren't comfortable commenting on the actions of someone not specifically trained in their field.

Ganson hadn't known a single physician who'd ever served as a defense witness. The only OB-GYN he knew on a first name basis was Bert, a mild mannered black man from Pascagoula, Mississippi. Bert's full name was Albert Arthur Wheeler. He'd spent his entire career working in the Indian Health Service. One of his duties was to provide continuing education to the outlying reservations, including Fort Apache. Bert had never considered testifying in a malpractice case but after a lengthy meeting with Duane he'd agreed "to give it a try."

"How do think Bert will do?" Ganson asked Duane as they sat across the table from each other in the lawyer's hotel room.

"He'll be fine," Duane answered as he looked up from the deposition they'd been going over.

"Do you really feel that way or are you just saying it for my benefit?"

Duane laid the deposition down on the table. "I say that for both of our benefit. If we don't have the utmost confidence in him it will show. Juries might struggle to come to grasp with the technicalities of a case but they have an uncanny ability to sense when a lawyer and his client don't believe in their own witness."

"It's not that I don't believe in Bert, but you yourself said his performance at his deposition was uneven at best."

"I admit I have some concerns about him, but it won't do either one of us any good to be questioning his abilities the night before he takes the stand for us."

"I'm afraid he's far too gentle a man to stand up to Dunbar."

"Bert could turn out to be as effective a witness as anyone we could have found. Juries respond favorably to witnesses who came across as genuine and of the heart."

Dressed in dark blue slacks, a white shirt and a bow tie, Bert took the stand on the Monday morning of the second week of the trial. He appeared nervous at first but settled down as Duane took him through a discussion of the training and experience qualifying him to be there as an expert witness. After going through the pertinent details of the case Duane paused while he sifted through the papers he'd brought with him to the podium.

"Dr. Wheeler. Do you have an opinion about Dr. Ganson's actions that night in the ER?"

"Dr. Ganson did a remarkable job in dealing with a disaster that could have easily resulted in the loss of two lives instead of one. Cassie was in such severe distress she had little chance of surviving a trip upstairs to the OR and no chance of surviving an ambulance ride to the Medical Center."

"On what do you base that?"

"The fetal heart tones had dropped to a rate that would no longer sustain an adequate circulation of blood to her brain and other vital organs."

"What about her mother, Angela? Do you think Dr. Ganson did anything that contributed to her death?"

"Angela was in pretty sorry shape the second time she showed up in the ER. She had a positive drug screen and there was nothing in the autopsy to support the plaintiffs' claim that it was Dr. Ganson's surgery that killed her. A Cesarean section is technically not that difficult to perform and Dr. Ganson did an exemplary job getting Cassie out alive."

"In your deposition the plaintiff's attorney made a big deal about Dr. Ganson operating on Angela without anesthesia and how she seemed to wake up during the procedure. Do you have an opinion about that?"

"Objection," Dunbar interrupted. "I believe it has been established without a doubt that Angela did indeed wake up during surgery."

"Sustained," the judge said.

Duane didn't pursue the point. Instead he picked up a sheet of paper from the podium and presented it to his witness. "Dr. Wheeler, what I have here is a newborn resuscitation report. Are you familiar with this report?"

"Excuse me, Your Honor," Dunbar interrupted, "but I don't recall reviewing this document."

"Your Honor," Duane said, "this was introduced into evidence at the time of deposition. I'm sure Mr. Dunbar has a copy of it somewhere." There was a brief delay while Dunbar sorted through two different briefcases before coming up with his copy. "Dr. Wheeler," Duane continued, "Have you seen this report before?"

"Yes, I have."

"Do you mind telling me what it is?"

"It's the report the pediatrician filled out after he'd resuscitated and stabilized Cassie Miller."

"I know there's a lot of technical jargon here but could you help clarify a couple of things for the court? The first one is the APGAR score. Do you see that?"

"Yes, I do?"

"It looks to me to be a one slash three slash seven. Could you tell me what those numbers mean?"

"The APGAR consists of five different physical findings that reflect the well being of the newborn. Each finding is scored from zero to two. The scores are taken at one, five and ten minutes. The higher the score, the better off the baby."

"What would be an average score for a healthy newborn?"

"Eight to nine at one minute and nine to ten at five minutes. The scores are only recorded out past five minutes if the baby isn't doing well."

"Judging from the scores on Cassie it doesn't look like she was faring so well at one or at five minutes, does it."

"Objection," Dunbar said. "Dr. Wheeler cannot give his opinion on that question because his specialty is obstetrics, not pediatrics."

"Your Honor," Duane argued, "those two specialties are interwoven at childbirth. It would be absurd to assume that an obstetrician wouldn't be familiar with the scoring system used to evaluate the newborn he'd just delivered."

"Objection overruled," the judge stated. "You may answer the question."

"Cassie was in serious trouble," Bert answered.

"To what do you attribute that?" Duane asked.

"Her scores at one and five minutes were not good. It took a full ten minutes to get her up to a seven, which still isn't that great a score. The rule of thumb is that the amount of time a newborn's organ systems have been down without adequate blood flow in the womb is mirrored by the amount of time it takes to get those systems up and running after delivery. If it takes five minutes to resuscitate a baby after its birth it means the baby has spent close to twice that amount of time under duress."

"So what do you think would have happened to Cassie if she hadn't have been delivered for say another five minutes?"

"Objection, Your Honor."

"Overruled. You may answer the question."

"She would have at a minimum suffered severe brain damage and would have in all likelihood died."

"You have no doubt about that?" Duane asked.

"No doubt at all," Bert answered.

"Dr. Wheeler, I take it that from all that you've told me, your opinion of the actions of Dr. Ganson in this case is that he in no way fell below the standard of care. Is that correct?"

"Yes sir, that is absolutely correct."

"I have no further questions, Your Honor."

Bert appeared to have found a new look of confidence but the look began to disappear as soon as a David Dunbar got a hold of him.

"Doctor Wheeler," Dunbar started in, "I intend to get to all that APGAR nonsense a little later. First I'd like to ask you a couple of things about your career. Isn't it true that the work you do with the Indian Health Service is mainly administrative in nature?"

"That is right."

"Do you still deliver babies?"

"Yes, I do."

"How many would you say you deliver a year?"

"Several."

"Is that five or ten or twenty?"

"Maybe twenty."

"And that's about how many you've delivered a year for the past several years?"

"Yes, it is."

"That's not very many now is it?"

"Not really."

"But I imagine your skills are as sharp as ever."

"I imagine they are."

"Would it be reasonable to say that once you've obtained that degree of expertise, it's not likely you'd lose it, no matter how few babies you deliver from year to year?"

"It stays with you."

"That being the case," Dunbar said in a raised voice as he

looked from Bert to the jury, "would you question the credibility of an obstetrician who has delivered thousands of babies during his career, even if he hasn't delivered one in the past few years?"

"Objection," Duane said. "Dr. Wheeler did not take the stand to confirm the credibility or for that matter the lack of credibility of Mr. Dunbar's expert witness."

"Overruled, "the judge said as she looked up from what she was writing on a legal pad. "The witness will answer the question."

Bert took a glance at Duane before responding with a shrug. "No, I wouldn't."

Dunbar nodded as he turned to the next page of his notes. "How many years did you spend in training before becoming an obstetrician?"

"I did a four year residency in obstetrics and gynecology."

"Do you know how much formal training Mike Ganson had before he operated on Angela Miller?"

"I believe he'd completed a year's internship and served four months in the emergency room."

"The four months he served in the emergency room were to be the beginning of a residency in general surgery. Is that correct?"

"I believe so."

"During his internship year and his stint in the ER how many times do you think he had the opportunity to be the primary surgeon on a case?"

"I doubt he ever had that opportunity."

"According to his own testimony, about the only procedures he'd been permitted to do were the lancing of boils and the excising of skin cysts. Does that sound like adequate preparation for the performing of a major surgery?"

"But this was an emergency."

"Doctor, you're not answering my question. Would you like me to ask it again?"

"No," Bert answered as his shoulders began to slump.

"No, you wouldn't like me to ask it again, or no, his training was inadequate for the procedure he attempted to perform."

"He did a remarkable job at—"

"Please," Dunbar interrupted, "just answer the question."

"Doctor Wheeler," the judge spoke out, "you must answer Mr. Dunbar's questions as asked."

"I'm sorry your honor," Bert said as he straightened up. "No, Mr. Dunbar, Dr. Ganson's training was lacking."

"Thank you. Now, I believe you just tried to say that what Mike Ganson did was remarkable. I think the words you used were 'a remarkable job.' Well tell me this. Is it common practice to cut into the bladder when doing a Cesarean section?"

"It happens."

"Often?"

"Every now and then."

"Were you aware that the deceased suffered a laceration to her bladder when the defendant operated on her?"

"It's a known complication of doing a C-section."

"Doctor Wheeler, approximately how many C-sections have you performed in your career?"

"Over five hundred."

"And how many bladders have you lacerated?"

"One or two."

"Let me get this straight," Dunbar said as he tapped his finger against the side of the podium. "In over five hundred of these procedures you've accidentally cut into one or two bladders. Mike Ganson managed to do it on his first attempt. Would you call that bad luck or poor technique?"

"Sir," Bert answered with a tone of exasperation, "what you're referring to has absolutely nothing to do with the outcome of this life and death situation."

"Speaking of life and death, I'd like you to tell me on what you base your opinion that Angela Miller's baby would have died if she hadn't been delivered immediately."

"Angela's membranes had ruptured and her baby's heart rate had dropped to a dangerously low rate."

"I'd like to talk about both of those supposed findings. First of all can you tell me on what the defendant based his opinion that Angela's membranes had ruptured?"

Bert hesitated before answering. "I believe he first determined that from the fact that her clothes were soaked."

"According to the testimony of the ER nurse Karen Hannigan, both she and the defendant thought the patient had urinated on herself. Not until later was it suggested that it was not urine but amniotic fluid that had soaked Angela Miller's jeans. Ms. Hannigan stated that the doctor changed his mind after he picked Angela Miller's undergarments out of the trashcan and smelled them. Is that your understanding of how things went?"

"I believe so."

"Aren't there some tests to determine whether or not one's membranes have ruptured?"

"If you can obtain free fluid you can look at it under the microscope for what we call 'ferning.' There is also a litmus tape that will turn from yellow to blue in the presence of amniotic fluid."

"Are these both dependable tests?"

"The microscope test is more reliable than the tape but either can be used in certain situations."

"Would you say the defendant's sense of smell would be superior to either of these in detecting the presence of amniotic fluid?"

"I wouldn't say that but I would say he could smell the difference between amniotic fluid and urine."

"Assuming that is so, why do you think it took him so long to smell the difference between the two, an amount of time, according to you, that was critical to the survival of this baby?"

After a lengthy silence, Bert answered. "That is not what this case hinges on."

"So what do you think this case does hinge on," Dunbar asked, "an allegedly slow heart rate in the baby?"

"That's correct."

"Could you tell me how the defendant determined that rate?"

"He listened to it with a Doppler."

"Is that what this is?" Dunbar asked as he walked back to his table and pulled one out of his briefcase?"

"Yes, that's one," Bert answered.

"Let me see if I can demonstrate how this works," Dunbar said as he placed the stethoscope piece in his ears and placed the probe against his chest. "Correct me if I'm wrong, Doctor, but I believe this part down here picks up the beats and transmits the sound up through the earpiece. Without getting too technical is that how it works?"

"Yes."

"Good. Well let me ask you this. When someone is listening through these earpieces can anyone else in the room hear the heartbeat coming through them?"

"No, not unless they put the earpieces in their own ears."

"Are you aware that, according to Nurse Hannigan's testimony, the only person who listened for those heart tones through the Doppler was Mike Ganson?"

"So?"

"Not another person heard the allegedly dangerously low heart rate and there is not a single strip of tracing to confirm what he claims he heard."

Bert threw up his hands. "Are you suggesting Dr. Ganson made it all up?"

"Like everyone else who's studied this case I don't know what he thought he heard. I do know he didn't have nearly enough experience to interpret and act on what he wants us to believe he heard."

"Fifty beats a minute is fifty beats a minute," Bert said. "It's always a sign of fetal distress."

"We don't know if there were fifty beats a minute or a hundred and fifty beats a minute, and we don't know if what he thought he heard could have been the mother's pulse, the baby's pulse, his own pulse or some internal thing going on with the Doppler. What we do know is that we have one dead mother, one neurologically challenged child and one poorly trained physician trying to wiggle his way out of being responsible for what happened."

"Objection," screamed Duane.

"Sustained," the judge said as she stared at Dunbar. "The jurors will disregard Mr. Dunbar's last remark."

"Now to all that nonsense about the APGAR score," Dunbar continued, seemingly unaffected by the judge's reprimand. "Doctor, you testified earlier that the score the pediatrician gave to Cassie's condition at one and five minutes after her birth indicated extreme distress. Is that correct?"

"Yes it is."

"And you took those numbers from the neonatal resuscitation sheet. Right?"

"Right."

"Earlier you made the point that if a baby were under stress its organ systems would begin to shut down. The longer they were down, the longer it would take to resuscitate the newborn after delivery. You did say that, didn't you?"

"Yes, I did."

"Didn't you also say that it appeared that the newborn had been under some sort of stress for at least five minutes prior to delivery?"

"Yes."

"Let me ask you this. There is nothing in the record to tell us what time Mike Ganson first cut into Angela or what time he finally got Cassie out. In deposition he himself admitted it seemed like 'an eternity.' Taking into account that he was doing his very first surgical procedure and that the patient woke up and took a swing at him in the middle of it, would it be unreasonable to assume it took him a little extra time to get the baby delivered?"

"I suppose."

"With the mother dying during the case, couldn't Cassie's distress have come from what was going on while he was trying to get her delivered?"

Bert fiddled with the document he was holding. "Are you trying to suggest the baby was in no distress prior to Dr. Ganson doing the C-section?"

"I'm not trying to suggest anything," Dunbar answered. "I just want you to tell me if what I asked you is plausible explanation for the condition of the baby at birth."

"Plausible, but not prob—"

"Dr. Wheeler," Dunbar interrupted, "I believe you still have a copy of the neonatal resuscitation record in front of you. Could you please go about half way down on the right side where the letters GA appear?" Do you see where I'm talking about?"

"Yes."

"Could you tell me what those letters stand for?"

"They stand for gestational age."

"What is the gestational age?"

"It's the estimated age of the baby."

"What are the numbers that appear right after that?"

"Twenty four slash twenty five."

"What does that mean to you?"

"It means the baby's estimated age at delivery was twenty four to twenty five weeks."

"How is that determined?"

"By the physical appearance and the neurological behavior of the newborn."

What is the number of weeks of a normal pregnancy considered to be?"

"Forty."

"Cassie came awfully early, didn't she?"

"Yes, she did."

"What is the earliest a baby can come and have a realistic chance of surviving?"

"Around twenty-four weeks."

"So Cassie just made it, now didn't she."

"Yes."

"And if she would have been, say twenty-three weeks, she probably wouldn't have made it. Am I correct?"

"Correct."

"Tell me, Dr. Wheeler, is there any way the defendant could

have known the gestational age of Angela's baby prior to his delivering her?"

"I believe he had a feeling for the gestational age of the baby by the size of the mother's uterus."

"That's not that accurate a measure, is it?" Dunbar asked.

"It's the only measure he had," Bert answered.

"Wouldn't it have been far more accurate to have an ultrasound?"

"Yes."

"Why wouldn't the defendant do one of those?"

"I don't believe there was a machine available."

"So what you're telling me is that the defendant took a wild guess at the gestational age of the baby and decided it was worth risking the life of the mother to deliver her."

"Objection Your Honor," Duane said as he stood up. "If Mr. Dunbar really wants to know what Dr. Ganson was thinking, he'll need to ask Dr. Ganson."

"I plan to do just that," Dunbar replied after the judge had sustained the objection. "Now Dr. Wheeler," he continued, "I know you've stated you believe Mike Ganson's actions did not fall below the standard of care for this case but for the life of me I can't understand how you can sit up there on the stand and support the actions of this man."

"Sir," Bert responded, "I can in good conscience condone

what Dr. Ganson did because in my mind it was a very courageous decision."

"Dr. Wheeler," Dunbar said shaking his head, "there are no courageous decisions in medicine, only responsible ones and irresponsible ones. The responsible ones save lives. The irresponsible ones result in tragedies, tragedies brought on by the actions of reckless physicians like Mike Ganson. Your Honor, I have no further questions of this witness."

Twenty-Five

D uane poured himself a third cup of coffee and went over the questions he'd be asking his client on the stand that morning. His hotel room wasn't much. At least it had a table and a desk, both of which were covered with notebooks full of documents and depositions. The growing pile of dirty clothes in the corner of the closet sent a stale scent throughout the room. It was a smell he'd become accustomed to and no longer noticed.

The second week of the trial hadn't gone much better than the first. Nurses Hannigan and Estrada had both done a credible job on the stand, as had the pediatrician who resuscitated Cassie. They came across as compassionate and concerned but none of their testimony was strong enough to challenge the claims of Hudson Barnes, or even those of Helen Cassidy.

Luther Shock was a compelling witness in his defense of Ganson's mental and emotional stability but his credibility took a major hit during David Dunbar's cross-examination. After pointing out that Shock was neither board certified nor tenured at the Medical Center, Dunbar delved into the psychiatrist's Native American beliefs and his unconventional approaches to patient care. The members of the jury had at times appeared to struggle with the validity of Shock's methods. It was Duane's opinion that they would have a problem putting much stock in his testimony.

In every malpractice suit Duane had successfully defended there had been a defining moment when the momentum of the case shifted from the plaintiff's to the defendant's side. There had yet to be such a defining moment in this one and he was down to his last witness.

Later that morning in court Duane gave Ganson a last minute pep talk before putting him on the stand. "Remember. Just be yourself and tell the truth."

"Sure thing, boss," Ganson said with a firm look on his face.

"Relax," Duane said as he patted Ganson on the back.

Ganson drew a deep breath and let it out slowly before approaching the bench to be sworn in.

Duane followed, carrying an arm full of papers with him to the podium. "For the court will you please state your name."

"Dr. Michael Ganson."

"You are a medical doctor. Is that correct?"

"Yes, sir."

"Do you have an Arizona medical license?"

"I do."

"Are you currently in practice?"

"I'm serving as a General Medical Officer on the Fort Apache Indian Reservation."

Duane shuffled through the papers he'd placed in front of him. "Mr. Dunbar is going to try to make a big deal out of the status of your license later. I just wanted to establish that yours is active at this time."

After going over Ganson's education and training, Duane got to Ganson's history with Dr. Nix. "I believe you and Dr. Frederick Nix met on two different occasions. Is that right?"

Ganson nodded.

"Dr. Ganson," Duane said smiling, "you need to express all your answers verbally."

"Sorry sir. The answer is yes."

"Judging from the testimony of Dr. Nix, would it be safe to say he doesn't have a very high opinion of your abilities to perform your duties as a doctor?"

"I'd say so."

"Why do you think he feels that way about you?"

"Objection," Dunbar said half standing up. "Dr. Nix is the psychiatrist here. How could your witness have a clue of how to answer that?"

"Mr. Jamison?" Judge Martinez asked.

"Your Honor," Duane responded, "I have a reason to this line of questioning."

"Let's hear it," she said.

"Dr. Ganson, I'll ask you again. Do you have any idea why Dr. Nix would say what he did about your medical abilities?"

"No, I don't."

"Of course you don't. No one but Dr. Nix knows that. What I'm going to ask you to help me do is establish what he doesn't know?"

"Your Honor," Dunbar blurted out, "this is utterly ridiculous and a total waste of the court's time."

"Is that another objection, counselor?" the judge asked.

"Yes, it is," Dunbar answered.

"I'm going to overrule that one, too, but Mr. Jamison, you're going to have to show me something here in a hurry."

"Thank you, Your Honor," Duane said. "Dr. Ganson, you stated in your deposition that for four straight months you worked twelve to fourteen hour days in the ER at County. Is that correct?"

"Yes, sir."

"Did you have any days off during that four month stretch?"

"I believe I had two."

"How would you characterize the work load at County?"

"I'm sorry. I don't understand your question."

"Let me rephrase it. Did you have a lot of high risk patients at County?"

"Yes, sir."

"Lots of motor vehicle accidents, stabbings, gunshot wounds and other life threatening situations?"

"Nightly."

"During that period of time, other than this case in front of us, was the care you rendered ever called into question?"

"No, sir."

Duane took a moment to look down at his notes. "Dr. Nix stated that the first time he interviewed you he found you to be lacking in self confidence, defiant of authority and prone to impulsivity. He went on to say that the second time the two of you met he came to the same conclusions. Would it be fair to say that even though Dr. Nix sees a challenging spectrum of psychiatric patients, there is no way the demands of his practice could come close to matching the life and death issues you dealt with on a nightly basis at County?"

"Your Honor," Dunbar howled as he came out of his chair, "this is absurd. If Mr. Jamison wanted to contest the opinions of Dr. Nix he had every opportunity to do so when he cross-examined him. To be bringing all this up now is nothing more than a desperate ploy to muddy the waters of a crystal clear case."

"Mr. Jamison," the judge asked, "if this is such an important point, why didn't you bring it up during your cross examination of Dr. Nix?"

Duane didn't have a good answer for the judge because the first time he'd thought about it was when he was driving to court that morning. "Your Honor, I didn't pursue this line of questioning with Dr. Nix because I felt the jury should have the opportunity of hearing it directly from Dr. Ganson's perspective."

"I hope you're about done with this," Judge Martinez said as she gave Duane a skeptical look. "Your witness can answer."

"If you don't mind, Your Honor," Duane said, "I'd like to ask my client the question in a more direct manner."

"Please do."

"Dr. Ganson, do you think there is any reasonable way Dr. Nix could be aware of the incredible degree of focus and integrity required to do the job you were doing at County."

Dunbar rose up like he was going to object again but then sat back down without saying a word.

Ganson hesitated. "Sir, I'm not sure how to answer that question."

"Why don't you give it a try," Duane suggested.

"I think if Dr. Nix had been with me night in and night out he might well have a different opinion of my capabilities as a doctor."

Duane took a break to pour a glass of water. "Doctor Ganson, would it be accurate to say that most life and death situations in the ER are chaotic?"

"I'd have to say they're all that way."

"I'd imagine when confronted with one of these situations you'd be under immense pressure to collect your thoughts and act in a responsible manner."

"Yes, sir."

"How did you stay on top of things night after night for four straight months?"

Ganson paused for a moment before answering. "I guess I'd have to answer that question by saying I've always tried to do the right thing."

"Thank you, doctor," Duane said as he tapped his knuckles twice on the podium and smiled at Ganson. "Your witness."

Dunbar brushed by Duane on his rush to the podium. "Doctor, did you do the right thing when you let Angela Miller slip away from you the first time she came into the ER that night?"

"It's not like I showed her the door," Ganson answered.

"Since you were, for lack of a better term, in charge that night, did you feel responsible for her condition when the policemen brought her back?"

"That thought never crossed my mind. I was intent on doing whatever I could to save her life."

"Did you do the right thing when it took you almost an hour to figure out Angela was pregnant?"

"I'm not so sure anyone could have diagnosed her any quicker."

"Dr. Barnes has rendered the opinion that it took you far too long."

"It's not an opinion I happen to agree with."

"That's an awfully bold statement for someone who has had virtually no formal training in the field of obstetrics. Or in any other field for that matter."

"He wasn't there."

"I hate to state the obvious," Dunbar said as he turned and pointed toward the jury, "but none of these fine people were there either. That's why in a court of law we rely on experienced expert witnesses like Dr. Barnes to help get us closer to the truth."

Ganson nodded but didn't answer.

"Even though Dr. Barnes wasn't there that night," Dunbar said with a smirk, "it is his opinion that your Cesarean section not only killed Angela but also endangered the life of Cassie. I suppose you disagree with that, too."

"I did the best I could."

"Your best didn't seem to impress the Board of Medical Examiners. Isn't it true that based on this case they took your license?"

"They suspended it for a year."

"Mr. Jamison earlier brought up that your license is now active.

What he didn't bring up is that it is still under restriction and you are still under probation. Is that correct?"

"Yes," Ganson answered.

Dunbar spent a full minute looking at the notes he'd scribbled out earlier that morning. "Doctor, I'd like to spend a little time going over the testimony Mr. Jamison led you through this morning, specifically the part regarding Dr. Frederick Nix. Do you realize Dr. Nix has published over a hundred journal articles and written seven different books in the field of psychiatry?"

"He might be accomplished in his field but I don't happen to agree with his opinion of me."

"It stuns me to think that you or your lawyer would call this brilliant man's credibility into question. His words have been studied and quoted all over the world."

"Do you mind if I say something?" Ganson asked.

"Please do," Dunbar said smiling.

Duane felt a sickening feeling bubbling out of the bottom of his stomach. From the beginning of the trial he'd been behind and on the defensive. He'd made up some ground but not nearly enough. All it would take were a few ill-advised unsolicited comments from his client to destroy what little chance they had." Your Honor, could I have few words with my client?"

"It's okay, Duane." Ganson said.

"No, it's not okay, Michael," Duane responded.

Ganson ignored him and looked over at Dunbar. "You can paint this picture any way you want but I gave everything I had that night."

"How'd that work out for you?" Dunbar asked.

"To save an unborn baby and her mother was my only intention."

Dunbar looked over at the jury. "You know what they say about good intention. The road to hell is paved with it." He turned his attention back to Ganson. "A well respected man of words penned that simple truth." He started to collect up his papers but stopped to grin at Ganson. "I don't guess you'd know which brilliant American scholar is credited with that saying?"

Ganson stared back with a straight face. "It wasn't Frederick Nix, was it?"

For a moment the only sound was that of the stenographer banging away on her machine. Then the courtroom erupted into laughter. Even the judge couldn't suppress hers. Dunbar wasn't smiling.

Neither was Duane. Ganson's heartfelt words wouldn't hurt their cause but his humor at Dr. Nix's expense could. Juries were funny about such things.

The court took its noon break. Ganson left to go outside with Shock while Duane remained to rework his closing argument. Whenever there was a death involving a mother or a baby in childbirth the prevailing perception of the jury was that the doctor must have done something wrong. Showing Ganson to be of good heart and worthy intent might gain a few sympathy points but it wouldn't get the jury to buy into the belief that Ganson knew what he was doing or that someone else couldn't have done it better.

What bothered Duane just as much was the man he'd noticed sitting in the back of the courtroom every day. At first he thought he was just another reporter but then he remembered he'd seen him before. The man was one of the prosecutors from the Attorney General's Office, probably hanging around to see if there was enough new information to file criminal charges against Ganson.

Duane was still alone in the courtroom when his client came striding down the center aisle.

"Shock thinks the man's a pervert," Ganson exclaimed.

"Dunbar?" Duane asked with an incredulous look on his face.

"No, William Miller."

"Why would Shock think that?"

"Shock's been watching Miller all week."

"Why?"

"It's his opinion that the correlation between women who overdose on drugs and sexual abuse in childhood approaches one hundred per cent."

"Who's to say that didn't happen while Angela was still on the reservation?"

Kenneth D. Jackson

"I asked him the same thing," Ganson answered. "He said you couldn't but he is still convinced the Miller clan isn't the Christian family it claims to be."

"On what does Shock base this conclusion of his?" Duane asked.

"On Miller's self righteousness, how checked out Lucille is and how there seems to be something going on between him and the nanny."

"Even if all that were so it won't help us."

"Maybe someone in the jury picked up on some of that," Ganson suggested.

"Don't count on it," Duane responded.

Twenty-Six

The courtroom was crowded to capacity. Ganson was one of the last ones back. He'd stepped out to take another trip to the bathroom. He'd eaten way too many of Duane's Tums and his mouth tasted like chalk. On his way down the aisle Cassie came running past him. She was headed for the lobby when William Miller caught up with her and grabbed her by the collar of her red dress.

For the first week and a half of the trial the nanny had held Cassie in check. The two had been in the courtroom for much of each morning and on most days had left before noon. However, the nanny had taken a cold earlier in the week. For the past two days she hadn't even been in court. The task of taking care of Cassie had fallen on Lucille, who appeared to have spent the greater part of the trial in a Valium haze. Day after day she'd sat stooped forward in her chair, staring into space, disconnected from everything around her. She'd not done well accepting the responsibility of watching over her granddaughter. On several occasions she'd received stern looks from both the judge and her husband after Cassie had taken to wandering around unattended.

The air in the courtroom had a heavy feeling to it but Ganson was still wearing his corduroy jacket. "I hesitate to tell this to you, Duane, but I think I'm more nervous now than I was the night I operated on Angela."

"You're not going to tell me you're as nervous as you were when that crazy Apache tried to shoot you, are you?"

"That was a different kind of nervous."

"I have no idea how that one feels but this court nervousness comes from knowing how little control you have over the situation at hand."

"How much control do you feel you have over this situation?" Ganson asked.

"Not nearly as much as they do," Duane answered as he glanced over at the jury.

"You don't have any more Tums, do you?"

Duane reached inside his jacket pockets and pulled them inside out. "You've taken every last one of them."

After everyone rose for the arrival of Judge Martinez, David Dunbar took the podium for his closing argument. "I would like to compliment the jury for your attention and dedication to duty. You've had to sort through a great deal of conflicting testimony. I know it's been a long two weeks but your work here is not yet done. You are probably facing the most important decision you'll make in service to our society."

Ganson was only half listening to Dunbar. At one point he leaned back in his chair to sneak a peek at the plaintiffs. William Miller was sitting with the other lawyer at the table and Lucille was behind them in the first row. William appeared as victimized as ever and Lucille was in her usual semi-vegetative state. Sitting between her and the aisle was Cassie. With the nanny no longer lording over her Cassie had pulled off both her shoes and was picking at the bow in her hair. As he was watching she pulled out the bow and offered it to Lucille, who took it and dropped it in her purse. Cassie then scooted to the edge of the aisle and stared over in Ganson's direction.

When Dunbar finally ran out of ways to portray Ganson as emotionally unstable and a threat to the general public he started in on the monetary award. He presented the data as if he were an impartial third party and made no mention of the fact that he would be collecting close to half of it for himself. "I can't tell you reasonable reimbursement for the loss of life of a woman in her early twenties. As a lawyer I don't even understand all those actuarial calculations. However, I can assure you that by the time you take into consideration the senseless nature of Angela's death and the overwhelming pain and suffering it has brought upon her family, the amount of money awarded should be well into the millions. In conclusion, I want to point out that not only will a guilty verdict help compensate the Millers for their grief, it could also go a long way toward removing a very dangerous individual from the ranks of the state's practicing physicians."

Ganson could see the stoop in Duane's shoulders and hear the strain in his voice as he addressed the jury. "Ladies and Gentlemen, this case is not about the loss of one life but about the saving of another. It's that simple. When confronted with a comatose mother and her unborn child my client could have followed the advice of his superior. All he would have had to do was to load his pregnant patient into an ambulance and ship her to a higher-level hospital. Why in the world didn't he?" Duane paused to look up and down the jury. "If you've paid attention to the facts of this case you already know the answer to that question."

Ganson had given up trying to figure out the faces in the jury. He stared straight ahead listening to Duane try to put a positive spin on things. The trial hadn't been nearly as hard on him as the aftermath of Angela's death but it had still been two of the worst weeks of his life. Although he wanted it to be over, it made him nauseous to think about having to stand up and face a guilty verdict.

He was trying to prepare himself for what he feared was the inevitable outcome when he felt a tug at the sleeve of his jacket. Standing next to him was Cassie. Unbeknownst to the Millers or their legal team she'd left her seat and crossed the aisle.

"Well hello sweetheart," he said in a soft voice as he picked her up. He closed his eyes and held her in his lap with her head tucked under his chin. She caressed the lapel of his corduroy jacket with one hand. With the other she brushed the tips of her fingers back and forth across his, like she'd done from inside her mother's womb when she'd reached out to him to save her.

He opened his eyes when he noticed Duane had stopped speaking in the middle of a sentence. Duane as well as the jury and the rest of the courtroom were all staring at him. A moment later William Miller was lording over him.

"You get your hands off my little girl you son-of-a-bitch," Miller screamed as he grabbed Cassie by her dress.

Ganson stood up to confront him with Cassie still in his arms. The bailiff and a marshal quickly converged on them and got Ganson to release her. Cassie started wailing as soon as Miller snatched her up.

"I told you to watch her," Miller yelled at Lucille as he shoved Cassie into her lap.

Duane had run across the courtroom to protect his client. "Are you okay?" he asked.

"I'm fine," Ganson answered.

Duane walked back to the podium looking a half a foot taller. When he resumed his closing argument his voice boomed out into the courtroom like it had come through an amplifier. The more he spoke the more confident he sounded. By the time he got to his closing statement he had the undivided attention of the entire jury.

"On that fateful night in the ER my client Dr. Michael Ganson summoned from within himself the courage and conviction to do what was right. All I am asking of you is to do the same."

The jury went into deliberation at three o'clock. When they hadn't returned by five Duane started pacing back and forth in the lobby. Any malpractice verdict taking more than two to three hours usually meant that the jury had already decided for the plaintiff and was hung up on deciding how large a sum they wanted to award.

It was almost six when the bailiff stuck his head out the door of the courtroom. "The jury's coming back," he announced.

Duane took Ganson by the arm and led him down the aisle to their table. They both stood at attention watching the members of the jury file back into their seats. Ganson scrutinized them for a reassuring look but only saw fatigue in their faces.

"Has the jury reached a verdict?" Judge Martinez asked.

"Yes, Your Honor," the foreman answered. "We find the defendant Dr. Michael Ganson not guilty."

As the applause began to build in the gallery Ganson put his arms around Duane and held him in a prolonged embrace. Over his shoulder he could see a stunned David Dunbar staring at him.

Twenty-Seven

The chill in the air prompted Ganson to button up his jacket and shove his hands deeper into his pockets. He could hear the horses kicking up the gravel but couldn't see them until they were halfway up the driveway. There were two of them, shadowy silhouettes in the moonless night. When they got closer he could make out the female rider atop the lead horse. She was holding the reins to the other horse, which she handed to Ganson when he met her at the gate.

"You shouldn't be doing this in your condition," he said.

"If you're coming," she answered, "you might want to tighten that cinch."

Ganson pulled it up four holes. After looping the reins over the horse's neck he grabbed hold of the mane and slipped his left foot into the stirrup. He took a stutter step with his right leg and swung it over the saddle. He tried to settle into the seat but the leather had a cold and rigid feel to it that caused him to tense up. The horse sensed this and fought him all the way down the driveway and across the road.

In the quiet of the pre-dawn the only sound other than the thumping of the horses' hooves was that of the gunnysack tied to the horn of Amanda's saddle. With every other step of her horse the sack bounced against her protruding belly, making a noise that sounded like a baby's rattle. When Ganson asked her what was in the sack she told him he'd find out soon enough.

They crossed the creek at the Buffalo brothers' camp, which appeared abandoned. Amanda led the way up the hill to the site of the First and Second Cibecue Massacres. By the time they reached the clearing there was enough light to make out the cross. She drew a fresh cutting of flowers from her saddlebag and dropped them at the base of it. She directed the horses back down the slope to Fantasy Island and turned downstream. A quarter of a mile beyond Bronco Dazen's camp they came upon the place where the body of Butch had been found. Bomar had marked the site with his own wooden cross right before he'd gone out on his coyote killing campaign but a spring flood had swept it away.

The storm that had spawned the flood had also flushed another bone out of the bowels of the reservation. A group of grade school kids on a field trip to see a rock wall full of petroglyphs had found it. It was an ulna. When the FBI pathologist got a hold of it she'd used the forensic principles of bone exfoliation and mineralization to match it to the two bones that had been deposited on Ganson's porch the year before. The ulna had reactivated Gus Martin's interest in the reservation's most famous missing persons, Harley Johnson and Major Mendoza. He'd taken to spending his spare time searching the west end of the reservation on his government mule.

"What are you looking for?" Ganson asked Amanda after she'd turned to look back over their tracks for the tenth time.

"That BIA man," she answered.

"Agent Martin?" Ganson asked.

"He's out there somewhere searching for my son."

"Isn't that a good thing?"

"I can't tell you how many times he's come back to question me about what I was doing the day Harley disappeared."

"I'd think you'd want him to be as thorough as he could."

"The first few times he was real caring. We'd sit around and talk about things we had in common. You know he's of the Mormon faith, just like me."

"You're not going to tell me he's a polygamist, are you?"

Amanda broke into a smile. "No. He grew up in Globe, married his college sweetheart and went to work for the government back east. He had five kids, all girls except the youngest.

"Did he tell you why he came back to the reservation?" Ganson asked.

"He's had his share of tragedy," Amanda answered. "His young son was abducted and never found. He spent a year looking for him. Two years to the day his son disappeared, his wife died of a heart attack."

"No wonder he has such a serious nature about him," Ganson remarked.

"He told me he eventually came to terms with the death of his wife but never got over the loss of his son. He raised his daughters by himself. When the last one graduated from high school he moved back home to Arizona to finish up his career."

"He sounds like a pretty solid guy to me."

"I know he's had some rough times in his life but he keeps messing with mine."

"It sounds to me like he's just doing his job," Ganson commented, making no mention of what Martin had told him earlier.

"It's more than that," Amanda responded. "He's obsessed with finding Harley."

Ganson and his horse finally settled down to the point they were able to enjoy each other. He let his reins dangle from the saddle horn and his legs dangle from his hips as he rocked along to the rhythm of the horse's gait. The thumping of its hooves resonated through the quiet of the early morning as the sweet scent of sweat drifted up from its lathered underbelly. He hadn't been on a horse in years and had all but forgotten the magic of being at one with one of nature's other beings.

They followed the creek for an hour before fording it and turning to the west. They rode through the forest for another hour before coming out on a ledge that led down into a rock amphitheater. Ganson had been there before. The lightning struck tree was completely dead and its limbs were sagging in a way that reminded him of an old man reaching down with outstretched arms to embrace a child.

When they reached the other end of the amphitheater Amanda took off up the spring-fed canyon. By the time he caught up with her at the ruins she'd already dismounted and disappeared into the trees to take a pee.

"I'd forgotten how long it takes to ride out here," she said when she reappeared.

"I wish you would have waited until after you'd had your baby," Ganson said.

"I can't put this off any longer," she said as she walked over to the spring at the base of the canyon wall and doused her hands and face in the water.

"I don't know what 'this' is," Ganson said, "but I can't see it being worth the risk of going into premature labor out in the middle of nowhere."

"That's the reason I asked you to come along," Amanda laughed as she returned to her horse and untied the gunnysack from the horn of the saddle. She motioned for Ganson to follow her to the kiva. "I also brought you to help me move some of these rocks."

"Not a lot of them, I hope."

"I need to dig a hole."

"How deep?"

"A few feet."

"Why here?" Ganson asked as he leaned over and picked up one of the larger rocks.

"This is where Harley's buried," she said.

Ganson dropped the rock and stared in disbelief at Amanda. "How long have you known he was here?"

"A long time."

"All those times you were supposedly riding out in search of your son, you were actually riding out here?"

"That's correct."

"And you never told anyone?"

"I didn't want anyone digging Harley up."

"What if they already had?"

"What are you talking about?"

"I'm talking about those bones on my porch railing."

"Those weren't Harley's."

"How can you be sure?"

"I rode out here the next morning. His grave hadn't been disturbed."

"What about the bone those school kids found?"

"That one wasn't Harley's, either. Neither was the other bone.

"What other bone?"

"The one on the hood of Dr. Roper's station wagon. It showed up the year before you came."

"I never heard about that one," Ganson said.

"Not many people have," Amanda said. "Trudy told me."

"Trudy?"

"Trudy Roper, Dr. Roper's wife. She came to my house the night they were moving off the reservation. The bone had showed up a few days before and her husband was convinced it was some kind of a threat."

"Did she tell you what kind of bone it was?"

"It was from a human hand. I think she called it a meta something."

"Do you think Gus Martin knew about that one?" Ganson asked as he thought back to when the agent hadn't said a thing to him about another bone.

"Of course he did," Amanda said. "I think there is very little on this reservation Gus Martin doesn't know about."

"That might be so but every time I've spoken with him he's led me to believe he has no idea what happened to Harley."

"Every time I've spoken with him he's led me to believe he thinks I had something to do with it."

"Before I become a further accessory to what must surely be some kind of a crime, I'd like to know what happened to Harley and how he came to be buried here."

Amanda nodded. "After Dazen Confused's apprentice Major Mendoza ran off, Harley petitioned for the job. Dazen Confused told him he wasn't interested so Harley hooked up with Fannie. She wasn't in possession of any power but she knew a lot of different songs and chants she taught Harley. I don't believe Fannie knew a single snake chant but that didn't deter Harley from catching rattlesnakes and using them with the other chants she'd taught him."

Ganson thought he heard something in the bushes. He held up his hand for Amanda to stop speaking. When he heard nothing, he motioned for her to continue.

"I was working that morning when I got this gut busting feeling. Right after that, one of the Buffalo brothers showed up at the back door of the café and told me I needed to come with him. When we got to the shrine I found Dazen Confused standing over the body of my dead son. Harley's clothes were all torn up and he was holding a dead snake in his hand. The first question that raced through my mind was not how Harley died but how could I keep him from being buried back in Colorado City."

The question that raced through Ganson's mind was how any sane woman could respond in such a manner. "Did Bronco Dazen tell you what happened?"

"He told me he was responsible for Harley's death."

"Why would he want to kill your son?" Ganson asked.

"He didn't kill him," she said.

"Why did he say he did?" Ganson asked.

Before Amanda could answer there was a thrashing in the bushes, followed by the emergence of Gus Martin on his mule. Martin was wearing a ridiculous looking straw hat and he had a revolver strapped to his hip. "Well fancy me running into the two of you out here," he said as he dismounted.

"Hello, Gus," Ganson said as he tried not to seem too surprised.

"Hello, Doctor. Congratulations on winning your court case."

"How did you hear about that?"

"It was in last week's Apache Scout."

"It was very considerate of you to ride all the way out here to tell me," Ganson said.

"I'm always happy to see you," Martin said with no sign of emotion on his face, "but my business today is with Mrs. Johnson."

"It's Ms.," Amanda said.

"I stand corrected," Martin said as he glanced at Amanda's pregnant belly. "What would possess a person in your condition to ride a horse all the way out here?"

"I was just getting ready to ask you the same question," Amanda said looking over at Martin's own bulging belly.

"I've tried tracking you in the past," he said, "but I must admit my outdoor skills aren't that good. I could never figure out at what point you left the creek. Fortunately for me, two horses are easier to track than one."

"Why would you be following me?" she asked.

"I was hoping to find something that would help solve the mystery of your son," Martin said, looking first down at the kiva and then over at the gunnysack. "Do you mind telling me what you have in the sack?"

"Bones," Amanda answered.

"Really?"

"Really."

"Do you mind if I have a look?" Martin asked.

"Not at all," Amanda said as she untied the sack and tossed it in his direction.

"Wait a minute," Ganson yelled, fearing the lethal looking head of a rattlesnake might come leaping out of the open end of the sack. Before he could get to where the sack had landed Martin had already picked it up. The agent turned the sack upside down and shook it. A collection of bones rattled out of it and tumbled to the ground.

"I told you it was just a few bones," Amanda said.

"They look like dog's bones," Martin said as he leaned over and picked through them.

"They're Garfield's," Amanda said.

"That crazy coyote that used to follow Dazen Confused all over the place?" Martin asked.

"That's the one," Amanda confirmed.

"What are you doing with them out here?"

"I dug them out of Fannie Hoffman's garden."

"Why would you do a thing like that?" Martin asked.

"I wanted to have my dead son's dog buried in a sacred place," Amanda answered.

"What about your son?"

"What about him?"

"Did you want to have him buried in a sacred place too?"

"I have no idea what you're talking about," Amanda said as she flipped her head sideways to get a strand of hair out of her face.

"I think you do," Martin insisted.

"I really don't."

"How many times have you ridden out here?"

"This is my first."

"Really."

"My first and my last."

Martin took his hat off and placed it over the horn of his saddle. "You mean to tell me you've been riding around this reservation all these years and you've never ridden up this canyon?"

"That's correct," Amanda answered, still fussing with her hair.

"How did you find this place?" Martin asked.

"The med..." Amanda paused. "Someone gave me a map."

"Who?"

"I can't recall off hand."

"Would you mind if I took a look at the map?"

"I wouldn't mind at all, but I don't have it."

"What did you do with it?"

"I destroyed it."

"Why would you do that?"

"I didn't want anyone else to get a hold of it."

"I'm sure you didn't," Martin said. He walked over to the ruins. After poking his head through some of the still standing doorways he returned to the kiva. "What do you think I might find if I came back out here with a metal detector?"

"I have no idea," Amanda answered, "maybe a horseshoe or two."

"You're probably right," Martin said, "but I'm advising the two of you to be on your way. I can't force you to ride back to town with me, but if I find a single stone disturbed before I get back, I'm going to hold you both accountable."

"Accountable for what," Amanda asked.

"Accountable for tampering with the scene of a crime," Martin answered.

"You heartless bastard," Amanda cried out as she dropped to her knees.

"Now Ms. Johnson," Martin said in a softer voice, "you needn't—"

Before he could finish, Amanda had stood back up with a baseball-sized rock in her hand. The rock wasn't much of a match for Martin's revolver but she threw it at him anyway. It landed a good three feet in front of him. Ganson yelled at her to stop. By the time he could get to her she'd picked up another. He blocked her arm and the second rock fell harmlessly to the ground. He put both his arms around her and held her face against his chest as she broke into a series of racking sobs. It wasn't until she stopped that he looked back to where Martin had been standing. He half expected to see the agent holding his gun on them but Martin wasn't there. He'd already climbed aboard his mule and disappeared down the canyon.

"He left," Ganson said as he let go of Amanda.

"He'll be back," she said as she wiped her nose with the sleeve of her shirt.

"You don't know that," Ganson said. "Maybe he'll choose to leave all this alone."

"There's about as much a chance of him leaving this alone as there is of him filing an official report claiming God was responsible for what happened to Harley. He's going to race back to town and put in a call to Whiteriver for the helicopter. In a matter of hours he'll be back out here with a pick, a shovel, a metal detector and a body bag for all the bones he's planning to dig up."

"You're not thinking about digging Harley up, are you?" Ganson asked.

"A part of me wants to, but I can't," Amanda answered.

"Why did you come out here today?"

"To say my final goodbye. I didn't plan on coming back"

Ganson walked her over to a shaded area. "What do you want to do with Garfield?"

"Bury him next to Harley. That way the two of them can be together, even if it's only until that BIA bozo digs them up."

After Ganson cleared enough rocks for a shallow grave he collected Garfield's bones and placed them in it. He was in the midst of covering them up when he glanced over at Amanda and noticed the grimace on her face.

"You're not going into labor, are you?" he asked.

"I believe I am," she answered.

"When did it start?"

"About the time Gus Martin showed up."

"How far apart are the contractions?"

"The one before this one was about fifteen minutes ago."

"We need to get you to the hospital."

"I first want to tell you what happened to Harley."

"You can tell me on the way."

Ganson positioned Amanda's horse next to a stump so she could step into the stirrup and swing up into the saddle without having to drag her pregnant belly across the saddle horn. The two of them took off for Cibecue. They didn't say a word as they crossed the amphitheater, climbed the slope, passed through the forest and forded the creek. Amanda never called attention to her labor pains but Ganson could tell every time she was having a contraction by the way she tensed her back and drew up her shoulders.

"How are you doing?" he asked as they followed creek north.

"I'm okay," she answered as she tried to smile.

"I've been thinking about this," he said. "You don't need to tell me a thing about what went on between Harley and Bronco Dazen. As a matter of fact I'd just as soon not know."

"You might not want to know but I'm going to tell you anyway," Amanda said as she pulled her horse to a stop. "Dazen Confused wasn't even at the shrine when Harley died."

Before she could continue, a helicopter rose up over the hills and passed directly above them, heading in the direction from which they'd come. Neither one of them bothered to comment on it.

"One of the reasons I never told anyone about Harley was that I wanted his spirit to live on, much like Major Mendoza's," Amanda said after her next contraction had passed.

"So how did Harley die?" Ganson asked having changed his mind about not wanting to know what had happened.

"He was struck down."

"By a rattlesnake?"

"By a bolt of lightning. With all that metal in him he must have been a walking lightning rod. Garfield and the Buffalo brothers were far enough away from him that they didn't get hurt. Fannie wasn't so fortunate. The lightning grabbed hold of her and flung her into an oak thicket."

"How do you know all this?" Ganson asked.

"The Buffalo brothers told me," Amanda answered.

"Why didn't they tell Martin?"

"Dazen Confused asked them not to. He didn't want Martin or anyone else on the reservation to know what had happened."

"Why not?"

"It was all because of the lightning. The Tribal Council had already taken away Dazen Confused's snakes and the lightning was the only reliable power he had left. He was afraid the word would get out that it had turned against him and killed Harley. If that happened he'd lose whatever was left of his credibility and respect."

"Is that why you didn't say anything at the time?"

"Right over Harley's dead body Dazen Confused and I cut a deal. In exchange for me not telling anyone what had happened he agreed to bury my son in the most sacred place on the reservation."

"Where we were today?" Ganson asked.

"The Apaches call it Prophesy Canyon. It's where Dazen Confused's grandfather went to receive the visions that drove him to rise up and fight the U.S. Army."

"Didn't Martin question everyone who was there at the shrine that day?"

"The Buffalo brothers told the police they'd been drinking all night and happened to find Fannie on their way home."

"What about Fannie?"

"When she got thrown into the thicket it must have scrambled her brain. The only thing she remembered was the lightning flash. To this day she believes God took Harley away."

Amanda stopped to breathe through another contraction, this one noticeably longer and stronger than the last. After it was over Ganson suggested they pick up the pace. They kicked their horses into a lope and pushed them the rest of the way. Amanda's pains were five minutes apart by the time they reached his trailer. Ganson helped her off her horse and into his truck. After he tied the horses he ran inside and called ahead to the hospital.

As they were racing down the road Amanda asked Ganson if he would be the one delivering her baby. He told her there'd be a doctor waiting to take care of her. He assured her it wouldn't be Bryce Peterson, who was no longer working in Whiteriver. Peterson had completed his tour of duty on the reservation and returned to Utah before he'd fulfilled his pledge to get rid of Ganson.

The on-call physician was Jim Mackenzie. He was standing at the ER door when they arrived at the new hospital. Ganson and Mackenzie helped Amanda on the gurney and the two of them wheeled her directly to the delivery room. Waiting for them was Olivia, who was now an RN. She was wearing a set of tight green scrubs and Ganson's thoughts raced back to the New Year's Eve they'd spent together. He wanted to say something to her but didn't have the opportunity. He was helping Amanda onto the table when Mackenzie asked him if he'd like to do the delivery.

"Your hospital hasn't yet granted me that privilege," Ganson answered.

"Didn't BOMEX lift the restrictions on your license?"

"One of the members called me and told me the board was going to permit me to do vaginal births but I've yet to see it in writing."

"I'll take full responsibility for this one," Mackenzie said.

Ganson gloved and gowned as Olivia got Amanda to slide down the table and grab hold of the handles. With the next contraction Amanda took a deep breath and gave a prolonged push. The crown of the baby's head appeared and Ganson held his hand against it to keep it from coming too fast. When the baby's chin cleared Amanda's perineum he told her to stop pushing. He suctioned the baby's mouth and nose and loosened the umbilical cord, which was wrapped twice around its neck. He placed the palms of his hands alongside the sides of the baby's face and applied enough traction to free up first the anterior shoulder and then the posterior one. The rest of the body followed.

It was a baby boy with thick black hair. After Ganson clamped and cut the cord he placed the newborn on his mother's chest. The baby looked to be about six weeks early but was breathing on his own and in no distress. The placenta came out in a gush of blood and Ganson pressed his hand against Amanda's belly and massaged her uterus until the bleeding slowed.

Amanda didn't complain about the pain. She was too busy loving the baby she'd been told she could never conceive. She finally gave him to Olivia to be cleaned up and dried off. After thanking everyone for their help she reached out for Ganson and they held each other in silence.

Twenty-Eight

G anson left the new hospital through the ER entrance and climbed the steps that led to a field filled with solar panels. Bordering the field was a chain link fence. Beyond the fence was another field, this one full of sunflowers. The inhabitants of both fields were worshipers of the sun. They spent their days tracking its rays from one horizon to the other. The sunflowers used the light to photosynthesize carbohydrates. The solar panels used it to produce electricity. The fields had shut down for the night but as he wandered from one to the other he could sense the energy emanating from each. His thoughts were engrossed in the wonders of childbirth when he looked up and saw Olivia walking toward him.

"What are you doing up here?" she asked.

"I was about to ask you the same thing," he answered.

"The women working in the ER told me they saw you climbing the steps."

"I was just getting myself ready to go back to Cibecue."

"Did you know your court case made our local paper?"

"You're the second person who's told me that today."

"The Scout gave it a full two pages."

"I can't imagine why."

"The Tribe is on a campaign to reclaim its lost children."

"Its lost children?"

"The ones adopted off reservation. The paper used your story to demonstrate the difference between what happened to my sister and me. It claimed Apache children growing up completely cut off from their culture are destined for disaster."

"Was the article the first you'd heard of what I had to do with the death of your sister?"

"I overheard Dr. Peterson talking about you one night in the hospital. He was telling the nurses how you'd killed this Apache woman in Tucson. He had no idea the woman he was talking about was my sister."

"I'm sorry you had to hear that from him."

"I didn't believe him."

"I wanted to say something to you when I first saw you in the room with the Chairman. I just didn't have the guts."

Olivia drew a deep breath. "Do you remember the night we spent together?" she asked.

"Neither my truck nor I will ever forget it," Ganson answered.

"Why didn't you make any effort to see me after that?"

"I wish I'd had the guts to do that too. The only excuse I can offer is that one of your police officer friends advised me against it."

"That was Rocky, my ex-boyfriend."

"Was he already an 'ex' that night?" Ganson asked.

"That night pretty much ended the relationship."

"When I saw you after that at the hospital you didn't look like you were at all interested in me."

"I'm ashamed to admit this," Olivia said, "but when you didn't call I was afraid you had no feelings for me. I didn't want you to know about the ones I had for you."

"I've always had this fear you'd blame me for what happened to your sister," Ganson said.

"I could have blamed my sister's death on everything from my mother's abandoning her to the drugs some dealer dealt her but I chose to hold no one at fault."

"What about your niece?"

"What about her?"

"Don't you worry that the same sort of things might happen to her when she gets older?"

"I think about her every day," Olivia said.

"So do I," Ganson said as he reflected on how Cassie had come to his rescue in court.

Duane's defense had given him a fighting chance but Ganson was convinced he wouldn't have won if it hadn't been for Cassie. It later struck him that she had come across the aisle and climbed up into his lap because she'd been drawn to his voice, the voice she'd remembered from the hours he'd spent talking to her in the Neonatal ICU.

"Have you ever thought about trying to get her away from the Millers?" Ganson asked.

"I asked Legal Aid that question," Olivia said. "They told me the only chance Cassie has of returning to the reservation is if her real father were to come forward and claim her."

"Does anyone know who her real father is?" Ganson asked.

"I doubt even he knows who he is," Olivia answered. "I'm sure Cassie is all Apache. I have no idea how many different men my sister slept with while she was here staying with my grandparents but one of those men fathered my niece."

"You're sure there's nothing the Tribe can do to get her back?"

"A hundred or so years ago they would have sent a raiding party after her."

"Maybe they should do that now."

Olivia nodded as she glanced down at her watch. "It's nice to get a chance to talk with you, Michael, but I've got to get back to work before the hospital sends someone out after me."

"Olivia," Ganson spoke out as she was turning to leave, "maybe we could go on a real date some time."

"I'd like that," she replied before hurrying down the steps.

Ganson sat down with his back against the fence and watched as the evening stars were making their nightly appearance in their private skyboxes.

At the other end of the reservation Gus Martin stared up at the same set of stars. His search had brought him many nights camped out like this one. He was confident this would be his last. It was hard for him to admit that his obsession with Harley was fueled by his failure to find his own missing son but he knew it was.

The helicopter had dropped him off at the amphitheater and he'd made his way up the canyon on foot. The state-of-the-art metal detector he was carrying led him to a rusted out horseshoe before he even reached the ruins. The signal hadn't been that strong but when he held the metal detector over the kiva it went off like it had located the mother lode. Martin was anxious to confirm what he already knew was buried under all those rocks but he had decided to delay the exhumation of Harley until dawn.

Too tired to eat, he lay half-awake on top of his sleeping bag. The moonlight streaming over the canyon wall illuminated the abandoned dwellings of a people long gone. It was as if he could still sense their presence hovering above him.

He was well aware of his own religion's claim that all the

American Indians were the descendants of the Lost Tribes of Israel. Since his undergraduate days he'd questioned the validity of that belief. The great diversity of language amongst the different Indian tribes made it highly improbable they evolved from a common source in such a short period of time.

He struggled with that and other suspect beliefs for years before finally coming to terms with the essence of his faith. The fact that there was not a single shred of scientific evidence to support those beliefs became inconsequential to him. He was grateful for having grown up in an atmosphere that promoted personal sacrifice and service as well as commitment to family and community. He was comfortable with who he was and what he'd done because he believed that the true measure of a religion was not the doctrine and the dogma it promoted but the people it produced.

His thoughts drifted back to how he was going to feel by the end of the following day. By mid afternoon he'd have dug up the boy's bones and had them on their way to the FBI lab. The pathologist would determine the cause of death and Martin would crack the case. The responsible parties would be punished and he could let go of his guilt.

Even though that's how he envisioned it, he knew it wouldn't work out that way. He was confident that the bones he believed to be buried in the kiva belonged to Harley. He wasn't so sure forensics would be able to tell him how the boy died. For sure they wouldn't be able to tell him how the body ended up at the kiva. He suspected more than a few of the reservation's residents were aware of Harley's fate, yet he'd gotten little information from them.

One of the residents not on the agent's short list of suspects was Major Mendoza. Martin was certain the bone that had appeared on the hood of Dr. Roper's station wagon was one of Major Mendoza's metacarpals. He'd first thought Dazen Confused had put it there because of the issues the medicine man had with the Apache MD.

When the two bones from the wrist and the two from the leg of the horse appeared on Ganson's porch Martin altered his theory. He believed the wrist bones also belonged to Major Mendoza, but knew of no problems between Dazen Confused and Ganson. The casts of the prints Martin had taken from Ganson's front yard were from the feet of a horse much smaller than the one ridden by Dazen Confused. When the forearm bone was discovered by the school kids Martin had become even more certain that the other bones had been happened upon by one or more persons who had taken them to a doctor because they hadn't known what else to do with them.

Martin had hoped the bones in his possession would have been enough to convince the citizens of Cibecue that the Major and his stolen horse had long since ridden to their death. What happened instead was that the surfacing of the bones had revitalized the people's interest in an Apache renegade, a renegade who'd become a folk hero. For Martin to put the myth completely to rest he was convinced he'd have to collect the Major's entire skeleton.

He dozed off to the whistling of the wind whipping through the ruins. In the middle of the night he awoke wondering if someone had called out his name. The wind had moved on, leaving the canyon in a dead calm. The only thing he could hear was the water from the spring trickling over the rocks. It sounded like a whispered voice. The longer he listened, the more convinced he became the voice was speaking to him, repeating the same four words over and over again. "Let the dead live."

He arose in a cold sweat and walked over to the kiva. The moon had risen over the rim. As he passed from its light into the shadows he was overcome by the feeling he wasn't alone. He was well aware of the Apache tale of how Dazen Confused's grandfather had come there to communicate with the spirits of the dead but the only ghost Martin had ever believed in was the Holy One. Standing at the edge of the kiva he could swear he was in the presence of another supernatural being. This one was the ghost of Major Mendoza. Missing his right arm, the Major was riding along the far ridge on a three-legged horse.

Epilogue

On the second anniversary of the Second Cibecue Massacre, Bronco Dazen saddled his newly broke mare and rode out to the site of his grandfather Noch-ay-del-klinne's original camp. The Buffalo brothers were waiting for him. Reggie and Rickie were there also. Reggie was riding Chico and Rickie was riding a mustang Ganson had purchased for him at a Bureau of Land Management auction. The boys' second horse was a source of great joy to the Buffalo brothers, who could now pack twice as many beers for their trek through town.

They broke camp by midmorning and reached the north end of Cibecue before noon. Numerous onlookers were lined up along the road. Among them were Ganson and Olivia, who were standing in the front yard of the rock house they were renting. The house was across the street from the new medical clinic the Tribe had built. The two of them had moved in after Ganson had stopped marking the weeks off his calendar and signed up to work in Cibecue for an additional two years.

Fannie was in her backyard trying to keep the chipmunks out

of her vegetable garden. She had on her green camp dress but was no longer wearing her guns, which she'd agreed to hang up in exchange for having the trading post armed robbery charges against her dropped. Gwen was sitting under an apple tree with several of her grandchildren gathered around her.

Across the street Amanda was waiting on the porch of the trading post. Bouncing up and down on her knee was her sixteen-month old boy Jacob. The Tribal Council had taken over the trading post. On the recommendation of Tiswin Richards they'd placed Amanda in charge of the day-to-day operations. She and Jacob lived in the adjoining apartment. Her homely looking horse Caesar stayed out back where Bomar had once kept Butch. Amanda had ridden out on the reservation from time to time but had stayed clear of the canyon where Harley had been buried.

Watching the procession from the front seat of his Lincoln was Gus Martin. It was an off day for the BIA agent and he'd driven out from Whiteriver to take in the event. It had been over a year since he'd officially called off the search for both Harley and the Major. Neither of their bodies had been found. When asked of their whereabouts, Martin's standard response was that he'd exhausted all resources available and that as far as he knew they could both still be roaming around the west end of the reservation.

Ganson caught up with Dazen in front of the parking lot of the trading post. Folded across his arm was the blanket the medicine man had once given to Cassie's grandparents for her protection. Ganson didn't say a word as he handed it to him.

Bronco's eyes lit up as he unfolded the blanket and draped it across his shoulders. He guided his horse across the parking lot to where Amanda was sitting. He reached out his arms and she handed him the child. The medicine man had a buckskin carrier stuffed inside his saddlebag but instead of making use of it he wrapped the blanket around the boy and sat him between his thighs and the horn of the saddle. He squeezed his young mare into a trot and the boy giggled with joy as they left the rest of the group behind and rode on to the site of the Cibecue Massacres. It was an overcast day but by the time they pulled up at the shrine the sun had broken through. With the rays of light dancing about him Bronco broke into a smile as he dropped the reins across his horse's neck and drew his son tight against his body.

~END~

About the Author

Kenneth Jackson has the true spirit of the Southwest running through his veins.

Born in the late 1940s and raised in Grand Junction, Colorado, Jackson's father was in the Uranium business and often allowed young Ken to tag along with him to the mines.

Ken was all too happy to help. Helping people, he found, was his true passion in life.

A talented, albeit sometimes wild teen, Ken attended the University of Colorado on a full academic scholarship, and later earned his medical degree from Baylor College of Medicine in Houston, Texas. After interning at a hospital in New Orleans, and still burning with a passion to help others, Ken had become "Dr. Jackson." But it wasn't until a chance visit to an Apache reservation in the mid-1970s that Ken Jackson found his true calling.

Once on the reservation, where he initially came to visit an old friend, Dr. Jackson became fascinated with the Native American culture; the people had a depth and edginess he had never seen. They were also in great need of trained medical professionals. Ken's short trip to the reservation, which started as a few days, spanned five years. During those five years, while practicing medicine on the reservation, Dr. Jackson began drafting his first western novel, aptly titled Manifest West. But he was too busy saving lives, delivering babies and stitching up wounds to actually put pen to paper just yet.

After five years with the Apaches, Dr. Jackson had the opportunity in 1981 to start a practice in Pinetop, just off the reservation, where he practiced for ten years, and then to Kingman, also in northern Arizona, in 1991. All that time, Ken Jackson never stopped reaching out to the tribes in the area. To this day, he still assists the Hualapai in Peach Springs, Arizona, and on the last Friday of each month he descends the Grand Canyon on

horseback to offer prenatal care to the Supai tribe who live within the canyon walls.

Colorful characters and vibrant Southwestern settings continue to fascinate Ken Jackson. He's twice crossed the state of Arizona on horseback, treks documented by PBS Channel 8 and Arizona Highways Magazine, as well as television and print. These adventures unleashed steady waves of creativity, and Dr. Jackson finished his first novel, Manifest West, in 2008.

Published by Treble Heart Books in 2009, from "Bitch Cassidy" to "Dazen Confused," all of the people, places and storylines that Ken Jackson brought to life in Manifest West are fictional, but based on real people and real events that happened on and off the reservations and within the medical field over the years.

Ken Jackson has a deep respect for the survivability and

resiliency of the Native American people, and a passion for their lifestyle and history. His goal is to weave stories that bring the Southwestern and Native cultures to life for all his readers.